DEATH AND DEVICES

DEATH AND DEVICES

THE KRONOS CYCLE
BOOK I

ANNA VANDER WALL

CONTENTS

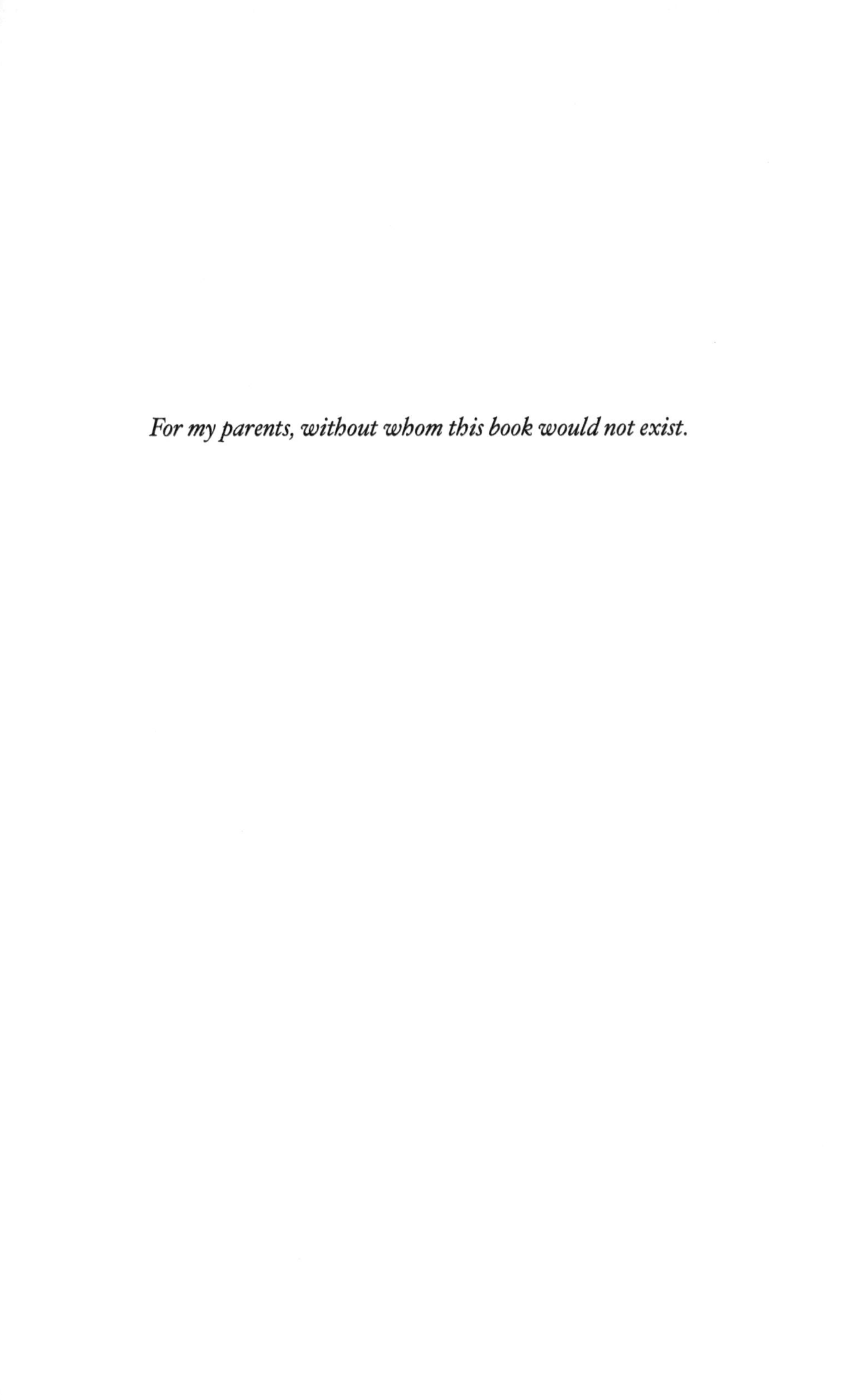

For my parents, without whom this book would not exist.

CHAPTER 1

THE SHATTERED VASE

PITTSBURGH, 2017

C ole Erickson was nine years old when he decided to run away from home. Like all good things in Cole's life, the idea came from school. His class had just read *From the Mixed-up Files of Mrs. Basil E. Frankweiler*, a book about a girl and a boy who ran away to live in a museum among Egyptian mummies. Like the girl in the story, his mom needed to not be alone. Like the boy in the story, Cole was good at keeping secrets. The book flooded Cole's mind with sunlight so that he slept with it under his pillow, willing to be siphoned from his body into its pages. Though he continued to wake to the same coffee grinder growl with the same scratchy sheets itching his cheeks, the fantasy grew. For weeks he hid it, along with his saved-up allowance, like a shameful secret in his back pocket.

One night, while cocooned in his blanket tent with a flashlight and the story, a shattering crash jerked Cole back into his body. He yanked off his covers to see a massive face outside his window. He froze, blinking fast to get the face into focus. Its mouth gaped. Its eyes were sockets. It could smell him—he was sure of it—and it had shattered the window to get to him. Cole jumped out of bed and caught his own reflection in the window. So the pane wasn't broken. He exhaled shakily. Where the face had been, there was only the moon—old, cold, and yearning. Shivering, Cole shut the blinds against it. Its silky fingers still crept through the slats.

Cole had an irresistible urge to escape, even if it meant going downstairs and confronting whatever it was that had shattered. Now he thought of it, the sound had been slower than a beer bottle breaking; the silence following was ominous. Shutting his door behind him and breathing hard, Cole crept to the loft, then snaked on his belly to peer through the balusters framing the living room below. His dad, frozen like a picture, was bent over the Mexican Talavera "honeymoon vase," its ugly insides exposed in shards on the living room floor. Cole couldn't see his mom, but he knew by the way the house held its breath that she was in the living room too.

"You broke it," she said, and the flatness of her voice made Cole feel he would tip off the loft and fall forever. He squeezed the ribs of the balusters into his palms.

"I didn't.... it was on the edge when I went to get the bottle and—"

"It's broken," she repeated, laughing jerkily. The laugh died, and she stepped into view, stooping to pick up a shard and rub her thumb along the lumpy clay. "I told you this would happen." Her voice was charged now. "I told you I can't keep doing this."

His dad stumbled into a chair and poured more whiskey into his tumbler. There was already an open beer bottle beside it. "I don't know what you're so upset about. It's just a vase."

"Just a vase? Are you serious?"

"I didn't mean that." He pressed a massive palm against his forehead. "Please, just..."

His mom lunged toward the bottle and snatched it from him. The explosion of his dad's voice was so violent Cole didn't catch the words. He burned his belly pushing himself backward on the carpet and ran to the hall bath. He shut the door and huddled in the bathtub, where their words couldn't reach him like they did through the floor vent in his bedroom. Without their words, he could pretend they were sailors on a ship, shouting to communicate over a storm, a common enemy. His mom's voice was hysterical now. Cole imagined them leaning their shoulders against a sea monster's tail, straining together to shove it over starboard.

There was a scuffle, and a ship window shattered. His mom screamed. Footsteps ran up the stairs. Cole's hands went clammy. He yanked the shower curtain shut just as the door banged open. Through the gap between the curtain and the shower wall, he saw his mom dive inside and bolt the door behind her. Against her chest she clutched a bottle of amber liquid, and the wild terror on her face almost vanished the ship, but Cole told himself she was running from the sea monster. The captain's footsteps followed. His mom's hands were shaking, and Cole worried she would drop the bottle.

He hugged his legs closer to his chest and plugged his ears.

The captain yelled, "Damn it, Layla, that's mine!"

Cole waited for her to yell back, but the only answer was the buzz of the ceiling light. Then there was a squeak and a pop as the cork was wrenched from the bottle and liquid gurgled down the sink. Glass crashed against the bathroom door, and Cole flinched, hitting his chin on his knee. The ship and the sea monster dissolved in a mist of pain, leaving only the thick breathing of the captain. Cole crept to the curtain.

Brown, sour-smelling foam seeped under the door and streamed down the grout between the tiles. It was almost under his mom's toes, and she was just standing there. Cole decided to save her, even if it meant giving away his favorite hiding spot. Softly, so as not to startle her, he drew aside the curtain. She caught his eye in the mirror, and the corners of her lips tightened as if she meant to smile. He admired her for it.

"It's going to be okay," he said.

By the time he had grabbed a fistful of toilet paper, the beer was already pooling under her arches and around her heels. He tried to lift one of her feet to dry it. At his touch she collapsed onto the toilet lid and buried her face in her hands, her shoulders convulsing with sobs. Cole glanced instinctively at the door to make sure it was still locked; silence was the first rule of survival.

Nothing happened. Finally, the footsteps receded back down the hall. Cole crouched at his mom's feet and waited until her shoulders stopped shaking. When she drew away her hands, her mask had cracked: her face was smeared and gleaming with mascara and snot. He wanted to say something to put her face back together again, but all he could think to do was hand her more toilet paper and wait as she dabbed at her eyes. Then her hand was on his shoulder, and her touch melted him. Before he knew what he was doing, he had told her all about the book he had read and the allowance in his pocket and how many beautiful vases there would be at the museum. Her hand jerked as if he had startled her from a dream. She sat there a long time while he waited for her to scold him or laugh at him or—most frightening of all—agree. Her eyes were looking at him, but her soul wasn't inside them.

At last, she said, "That's a lovely idea."

Cole's lovely idea half worked. His mom did come up with a plan to run away. But when she left, she forgot to take Cole with her.

CHAPTER 2

VENDLER ACADEMY

PITTSBURGH, 2024

It was a humid, breathless afternoon in late August. The heat seeped mercilessly inside the auditorium, intensifying the concoction of sweat and perfume. No one seemed to care. The sea of faces, floating in the dark as if guillotined from their starched suits and dry-cleaned dresses, was riveted on the man with a face like a Grecian statue. As he strode toward the podium, a thrum of excitement shot through the bodies like electricity.

The auditorium was completely full but for one empty seat in the front row of stage right, where a woman had died suddenly after seeing King Lear undress on stage. That was in the days when the building was a sanitorium instead of a school, but no one had ever sat in that seat since. From the stage, the vacancy looked like a missing tooth in a wide-mouthed grin. The man with the Grecian face seemed not to notice it. He extended his arms in welcome, and the silence was absolute.

"This is the beginning," Dr. Bering said, "of the most important year in your career at Vendler Academy of Science and Technology and Engineering and Math for Pittsburgh's Talented Youth."

He said the name rather fast. It had become something of an embarrassment after a visiting principal had pointed out, to her own amusement only, that she had found her time at VAST and EMPTY surprisingly instructive.

"This is the year," Dr. Bering continued, his nostrils flaring defiantly, "when you will take your place among the thousands of students who have preserved our standing as North America's highest-ranking high school. To reward your labors, your teachers and I have selected one lucky student to honor with the academic passport of your dreams. The passport of which I speak is, of course, a personal letter of recommendation from me to your university of choice. Historically, all students who have received this honor have been admitted immediately. I have asked you all to prepare a short acceptance speech in the event that you are chosen as this year's Vendler Star.

"And now, the moment you have all been waiting for..."

Cole Erickson sprinted down the escalator to baggage claim and jerked his bag off the carousel. As he ran, he whipped his phone out of his pocket and called his dad again. *Ring.* He could still make it. The Commencement Ceremony had just started. *Ring.* If the traffic was light enough, he would still be in time for the announcement. *Ring.* He should have known the flight might be delayed. If only his mom hadn't insisted he book the last possible flight back from Santa Fe—it wasn't like she wanted him for the summers anyway. *Ring.* Cole swallowed the panic that soured his throat like bile as he emerged onto the curb. The faint glow of sunlight creeping under the concrete portico looked like the Talavera vase he had tried to glue together as a boy. *Ring*. His dad's Ranger was nowhere in sight. *I'm sorry, but the person you have called does not have a voice mailbox that is set up yet. Please try your call again later. Goodbye.*

Cole swore, sending a nearby crow flying away with an indignant *caw*. Combing his fingers through his hair, he re-read the text he had received from his dad yesterday: *I'll be there*. Yeah right. He could picture his dad already, apologizing for being late, cracking a joke, swearing he'd make up for it next time. Next time... why did Cole always believe that next time, things would be different? He pocketed the question firmly away. Right now, he needed to focus on finding another way to get to school. It took him five minutes to download Lyft and another fifteen before his driver finally arrived. Despite himself, he couldn't stop searching the row of cars for his dad's Ranger. Of course, it never came. He was an idiot for hoping it would.

Dilapidated industrial buildings and swaths of miniature forests sped by the car window, and Cole's breathing began to relax. At last, he was on his way. In a few minutes, he would be mounting the steep stone steps of Vendler Academy, the one place on earth that felt like home. Father Time, the sallow-faced clock at the top of the tower, would frown down on him for being late, but Cole would be glad just to hear its heartbeat again. Throughout the summer, he had dreamed frequently of the steep brick edifice, its halls stretching back from the central building like giant bat wings to form a large letter "V." Cole's classmates seemed to relish a superstitious reverence for the building. Despite decades of renovations, they swore the classrooms still smelled of chloral—St. Mary Magdalene's had been a Kirkbride asylum before Vendler bought it and converted it into a school, and many believed it was still haunted by the souls of the insane. But haunted or not, Vendler was where Cole belonged. It wanted him. With its 7% acceptance rate, he was sure of that.

Cole reached into his pocket and fingered his acceptance speech. If only he could make it in time. He needed Dr. Bering's recommendation to Stanford, because it was all part of the plan. From Stanford, he was to go to grad school at MIT, and then, if he was good enough, he would work any job he could get at The Orien Saint-Pierre Lab. The Lab was North America's most respected research hub for artificial intelligence, and it was making the news almost every week as millions of elderly waited for the release of the AI companion that would end their loneliness. Working at The Lab was the type of career Vendler expected of its students and the only career to which Cole had given serious thought.

The car braked, and Cole stepped out under the shadow of Newton, the old oak where the asylum's last superintendent had hanged himself. Cole always wondered if Newton was named before or after the hanging, and whether the name was a fluke of fate or someone's demented sense of humor. Newton was, after all, the scientist who had "discovered" gravity. Vendler's parking lot was eerily silent, and Cole was suddenly embarrassed to be carrying a suitcase with a broken handle instead of his backpack. He thought inexplicably of his friend Bridget, with her Christmas-bell voice and flaming copper hair, and wished he could make a better showing. He took the steps two at a time and pushed open the double wooden doors framed by the neo-Gothic stone archway.

His footsteps sounded unnaturally loud as he crossed the marble floor to the front desk where Mrs. Dixon, the attendance clerk, stared at him from the safety of a gray bob that encased her face like a helmet. The iron bar of her lips tightened as he approached. Cole cursed inwardly. He had hoped for Adelaide Eyre, the new receptionist who didn't cling to policies like they were her personal morality. At least the corridors were deserted—that must mean the ceremony was still in session.

Offering a one-way smile, Cole explained the situation: his flight had been delayed and he had called a Lyft as soon as he had deplaned. He needed to go straight to the auditorium for the ceremony.

Mrs. Dixon listened blandly. She said, "The ceremony has been over for thirty minutes."

"What?"

Mrs. Dixon's eyes flitted to her desktop and back. "Thirty-one minutes."

A surge of blood throbbed in Cole's ears. He reached into his pocket and crumpled his acceptance speech. *Thanks a lot, Dad.* Willing himself to remain calm, he turned left toward the math and science hall. "I guess I'll just go to class then."

"I'm afraid not. Students are not allowed to arrive late without prior notice from a parent or guardian. We'll have to call one of your parents to verify your story about the 'delayed flight,'" Mrs. Dixon said, refusing to look at his suitcase.

Cole picked it up and dumped it on the counter between them so she couldn't ignore it. "This doesn't count?"

Mrs. Dixon stroked a sheaf of demerit slips on the desk beside her.

"Sorry," Cole said. He knew he shouldn't be letting his anger at his dad out on Mrs. Dixon, but her lack of trust in the face of his perfect academic record stung. "It's just, my mom's in Santa Fe—she didn't know about my flight being delayed. And my dad is probably asleep. He... works night shift. He's a surgeon."

It was sort of true—his dad had been a surgeon, a long time ago. But why was Cole covering for him now, when it was his dad's fault Cole was in this position to begin with?

Mrs. Dixon's eyebrow rose a fraction of an inch. "We have to call one of them," she said. "I'll call your dad."

"Fine," Cole said in a strangled voice, eyeing the demerit slips. He watched her dial the number and waited, holding his breath. Half of him wanted his dad to answer, wanted him to feel the guilt of forgetting Cole and the embarrassment of an authority figure calling him out on it. But for some reason he was relieved when the phone clicked back into its cradle.

"No one answered," Mrs. Dixon said, which seemed to Cole obvious and unnecessarily cruel.

"Try my mom," he said.

Mrs. Dixon raised her eyebrows again and took a long time looking up his mom's number. Miraculously, Cole heard his mom's voice on the other side of the phone. He didn't wait for Mrs. Dixon to hang up this time before turning and walking quickly back down the hall.

"Mr. Erickson."

What now? He looked over his shoulder but didn't turn around.

"There's one more thing. I was told to give you something before you go to class. Here—a note from Dr. Bering."

Cole froze. Could this be about the announcement? Had Cole been chosen as Vendler Star? He turned slowly back to the front desk and took the note from Mrs. Dixon. His hand was shaking. Wishing Mrs. Dixon wasn't still staring at him, he read the words: *Please report to the Student Success Center immediately*.

Cole read the note twice before he moved, mechanically, down the opposite hall leading to the humanities classrooms and the Student Success Center. The only reason students visited the SSC was when they were put on academic probation—or expelled. That wouldn't happen to Cole just for missing the ceremony and half of his first class, would it?

CHAPTER 3

AN INVITATION

Cole glanced furtively into a classroom as he passed and saw it momentarily as an outsider might: His classmates were staring at a projector screen with glazed eyes, their fingers reflexively clacking keyboards. They looked like automatons, as if their whole lives they had sat in shadowy classrooms with nothing to see by but iridescent screens and nothing to breathe but formaldehyde that sterilized their synapses. Is that what the asylum residents had looked like—mindless bodies coerced into numb submission? He shook off the strange impression.

Rallying himself, he pushed open the door to the Student Success Center. The first thing Cole saw was Mr. Price's animated face a few feet away from his own face. Mr. Price's hair was bristled like an overused paintbrush, and his fingers drummed violently on the Formica countertop of the office coffee bar.

"Erickson! There you are! Care for a cup?"

"No thanks, I..." Cole wanted to ask why they had assigned Mr. Price, the Physics professor, to handle his case, but a lifetime of evasion cautioned him to wait for Mr. Price to broach the subject.

"You force a man to drink alone." Cole winced at the phrase and was glad Mr. Price didn't notice. "Very well. But you'll want every neuron wide awake for what I'm about to tell you."

Cole's stomach clenched. That didn't sound good. Unless... "Sir... I'm not Vendler Star, am I?"

"You? Decidedly not! Wesley Tate is the man of the moment."

Cole's insides roiled. He should have known. Wesley Tate was Cole's biggest academic competition, which Cole wouldn't have minded if Wes wasn't also the sort of guy who even made musicals look cool by auditioning on a whim and landing the leading role.

"That award's pish-posh poppycock, if you ask me, and I wish somebody *would* ask me, but somehow, nobody ever does. No, Erickson, the real geniuses are made in the forge fires of the lab, not under the halos of the stage."

Mr. Price whisked his mug from under the coffee urn a second before releasing the lever, leaving a large splash to further stain the already discolored Formica. Cole cast about for a paper towel, but there wasn't time: Mr. Price was striding toward his office, speaking imperiously over his shoulder. "Not here, Erickson. Too many prying ears."

"But we're the only ones—"

Mr. Price swiveled around so quickly Cole almost ran into him. His bitter coffee breath made Cole's nose wrinkle.

"We're not alone," he whispered, nodding significantly at the walls as if he expected a face to leer at them from the paneling.

Of course. Cole had forgotten that Mr. Price was among the most dedicated perpetuators of the legend that Vendler

Academy was haunted. Despite his better judgment, Cole was so anxious he found himself glancing at the walls too. A face stared at him from the varnish, and his heart missed a beat before he realized it was his own reflection. He'd better watch it or he'd end up as crazy as Katherine Fisher, the senior who dropped out to become a nun in Argentina after seeing God in the locker room mirror.

Swallowing, he followed Mr. Price into the cramped office cluttered with a hurricane of student papers, abandoned halves of croissants, and chalkboards on which the ghosts of equations past shadowed the ghosts of equations present. A jumble of magnets and a picture of a cat with extremely round eyes occupied the visitor's chair.

"Don't mind Dinah," Mr. Price said, nodding to the picture. "She likes visitors."

Cole hesitated, unsure whether he was expected to share the chair with Dinah. In the end, he scooped up the magnets and deposited them into a splitting cardboard box containing out-of-commission voltage regulators, then placed Dinah respectfully on top. He sat down and immediately wished he hadn't. This was it. Mr. Price was going to tell him he was expelled. Mr. Price made a ceremony of pulling his own chair out, clearing his throat, and ineffectively tugging at his noose-like tie; the Gordian knot only tightened.

Finally, he said, "And *what* do you think has happened?"

"I don't know, sir." The blend of spent breath and burnt coffee was making Cole long for a window. He wished Mr. Price would get the worst over with and dismiss him to nurse his humiliation and anger in private.

"Of course you don't. I shall tell you. Do you remember the distinguished personage I invited to Vendler Academy to give our commencement address last fall?"

Cole's mind reeled. How was commencement relevant to

his impending expulsion? Mr. Price continued to stare at him, so he cast his mind back to the auditorium crammed with clammy faces. Maybe this was some bizarre quiz to measure his devotion to the school.

"I—didn't Dr. Bering give the address?"

"Yes, well, you win some, you lose more."

Cole opened his mouth to correct the characteristic malapropism and then thought better of it. Now was not the time to quibble.

"Admittedly, this personage declined to come, so our headmaster stepped in. However—" Mr. Price cleared his throat to reestablish his dignity "—the primary point is this: while our first attempt met with denial, it was not wholly unfruitful. As I often remind my students, Einstein floundered more times than he swam, but his butterfly stroke is what we remember. So with us. This person I referred to earlier, his denial was not forever unyielding. Today I tell you this: three days ago, his personal assistant—a Ms. Prisha Varma—reestablished contact."

Cole still couldn't see how any of this was relevant, but he kept playing his part, trying to look impressed without any of the key facts.

"Yes, reestablished contact," Mr. Price repeated, nodding significantly. "Ms. Varma informed us of something that will, no doubt, leave you thunderstruck. Be prepared. Vendler's top five students are invited—" Mr. Price's eyebrows ascended to monumental heights to herald the denouement of his speech "—to submit applications for an internship at The Orien Saint-Pierre Lab."

Cole heard his own sharp intake of breath. Mr. Price's electrified eyebrows sank back to a normal height in satisfaction.

"It is now my utmost pleasure to further inform you, Mr.

Erickson, that in yesterday afternoon's faculty meeting, the teachers of Vendler Academy unanimously elected you as one of these five applicants."

Cole clutched the arm of his chair and laughed shakily. His muscles had gone numb, releasing their pent-up tension so suddenly he had to catch himself to avoid falling off his seat. His mind flitted from the image of The Orien Saint-Pierre Lab as seen on the news—an impenetrable skyscraper wreathed in a halo of clouds—to the oak-paneled room with long tables where Vendler's professors presided over student affairs. He saw a row of faces, from Dr. Abbott all the way down to Dr. Mr. Womble and Dr. Mrs. Womble; his name was spoken, and the figures raised their hands as if bidding at an auction. Vendler wanted him after all.

"That is, should you accept."

"Yes, yes of course!" Cole sputtered, sitting up straighter in his seat. His heart pounded frantically, dancing between relief and exhilaration. "What's the internship for? How do I apply? What's the deadline?"

The sudden rush of blood in Cole's head made him dizzy. The future he had planned—no, hoped for, even while he subconsciously believed nothing that good could ever happen to someone like him—had spanned the eight years that stretched before him in one startling leap. He inhaled the stale office air to anchor himself in the present. A fountain of speech was pouring steadily from the overly caffeinated teacher across the desk.

"... to enhance Kronos, The Lab's AI model, through multimodal research. The internship will begin June of next year and continue throughout the duration of your senior year. However, because they are interviewing candidates throughout all of North America, and because there will be multiple rounds of interviews, the initial application is due September 6th."

The whirling in Cole's brain slammed to a halt.

"September 6th, as in next Friday?"

"The very same." Mr. Price inclined his head apologetically. "However, I have no doubt that you will rise to meet the occasion like the explosion of a never-fading supernova." He beamed. "Take comfort. I will personally oversee the application process and will ensure that you have every resource at your fingernails. In fact, I have already taken the liberty of writing your letter of recommendation."

Cole twitched the corners of his mouth mechanically, but he couldn't help wishing he could have asked someone else— Dr. Khouri, for example. It wasn't that Mr. Price wasn't intelligent. Anyone who had taken his Theoretical Physics class knew he was brilliant, but compared to the 75% of Vendler faculty who held doctoral degrees, Mr. Price's credentials just didn't look as good on paper. That was one of the reasons he had been assigned an office in the SSC, an administrative decision that was officially termed "academic overflow."

"What exactly are my odds, sir?" Cole asked. He needed to know what he was up against. "You said five students from Vendler are invited to apply; how many other schools are in the running?"

"Twenty-five."

"And how many internship spots are there?"

Mr. Price drew his shoulders back. In a voice calculated to impress, he declared, "There can be only one."

"So assuming each school has five spots, my chances are 0.8%." That was pretty slim, but Cole still felt as light-headed as a runaway balloon. Vendler had chosen him to compete for a reason. "Who else from Vendler is invited?"

Mr. Price chuckled indulgently. "Ah Cole, it wouldn't be fair to tell you before I told them, would it? But despair not! This crop of students is the most promising harvest we've had in decades, and you are not least among our prize exhibitions! And now, allow me to present..." Mr. Price opened a drawer and produced a folder on which he had written the words *COSMIC TOP SECRET.* "Your future in a folder! Here you will find all your application materials. Take care to keep them safe, and let me know should you have any questions. I am here to help. Until then, you'd best return to your studies. They've never been as important as they are now, am I right?" He winked at Cole, then answered his own rhetorical question: "The Price is always right."

CHAPTER 4

THE FALLEN BOOK

His dad had forgotten him, he hadn't been named Vendler Star, and he had missed his first and only class of junior year, but Cole emerged from the SSC happier than if his day had gone exactly as he had hoped it would. The whole point of getting Dr. Bering's recommendation to Stanford was to pave his way to The Lab, and now he had a chance to get his foot in the door while still in high school. Despite the odds, he couldn't help but feel optimistic. He was a top student at the nation's top school, after all. He punched the air in triumph and sent dust particles scattering in the sunlight. His chest felt like it would burst with the effort of holding in the good news. He retraced his steps to the lobby, beamed at an affronted Mrs. Dixon, and set off down the hall behind her desk to find his friends.

"There you are!"

Cole turned to see his best friend, Jude Durham, stalking down the hall behind him. Jude's hands were balled into fists, his charcoal eyes glowered beneath the shaggy brown hair that spilled over them, and his already strong jaw was clenched in a scowl. Jude didn't slacken his pace as he drew level with Cole, who had to redouble his pace to keep up, despite being several inches taller. So apparently now was not the time to tell Jude about the internship.

"Well at least *one* good thing happened today," Jude muttered. "How was God-forsaken New Mexico? Had to be better than here anyway."

Given that Jude's family was Catholic, Cole found this remark amusing. He resisted the temptation to provoke Jude by saying, "Good to see you too!" and instead gave Jude the prompting he was waiting for:

"That bad?"

"Worse. God, I could strangle him."

"Who?"

"Seth."

It took Cole a minute to realize who Jude was talking about.

"Your brother? I thought he was in a rehab facility in Arkansas."

"Yeah, well, so did I. But he showed up today, right as I was leaving for the ceremony. Should have punched his guts out the minute I saw him."

"What happened?"

"Pushed past me and got inside. Mom started crying, wouldn't stop hugging him and saying she knew he'd come back in the end. Well I couldn't make Mom see sense, so I left them for three minutes—three minutes!—to call dad, and by the time I got back, Seth had taken her purse and bolted. Mom didn't even know till she got back in the room with a sandwich—he'd said he was starving—and he was gone. Well of course she fell apart again. I couldn't leave her like that, not till dad got home. So I missed everything. Not like I'd have gotten Vendler Star anyway."

Jude vented his feelings on an open locker door, slamming it so hard the whole unit shuddered.

"If he shows up again, I'm going to kill him."

That's how Cole had felt about his dad a moment ago, too. He felt suddenly guilty about the good fortune of his internship. The balloon in his chest deflated a little as he resolved not to bring it up unless it came up naturally. They walked on, Cole respectfully silent, until they reached a dead-end corridor with a closed door. Almost without realizing where they were going, they had found themselves at the library. Cole hesitated, then remembered Bridget loved the library.

"We might as well see if the girls are inside, since we're here," he suggested. "It's study hall anyway, and Dr. Kokkinias won't care where we study."

Jude was still scowling, but he didn't argue. Cole turned the brass doorknob and stepped into air heavy with memory. Unlike Vendler's technologically-retrofitted classrooms, the library was frozen in time, as if the walls themselves kept record of the asylum's experimental treatments. It was a long, narrow room made almost entirely of wood. Oak wainscotting adorned the walls, oak shelves encased aged books, and oak flooring creaked underfoot. When the weather changed, the wood talked. The librarian's desk was stationed at the south end near the door, while at the north end was a fireplace lounge furnished with mismatched antiques left by the asylum. In between the two stretched some twenty rows of bookshelves, each terminating near a window, where vacant desks awaited students who rarely came.

Summer sunlight beamed in through the row of westward windows with all the sweetness of a golden apple, warming the broad surfaces of the wainscotting even while it spilled shadows into its intricately carved crevices. The library was trying to lull them into a sense of safety, Cole thought, the better to absorb their emotions to increase its power. But today, he almost didn't care. He breathed in the rich vanilla aroma of books as they followed the sound of laughter from the lounge. Rounding the last row of books, they saw the girls before the girls saw them.

Sitting with her back toward them on the blush loveseat was Bridget Martel, copper hair aflame in the afternoon sun, a book cradled in her hands, her egregiously mismatched clothing making her look like a Romani gypsy. She looked perfectly at home, as though both she and the library belonged to some other world that Cole wasn't sure he could cross into. The spell snapped at the sound of Joanna's voice.

"And of course, you're coming over for my pool party this Saturday, right? Jude and Cole are coming, only I haven't told them yet." Joanna Grant, voluptuous and appealing even without directing toward him the magnetism of her striking emerald eyes accentuated by raven hair, had no problem conducting the conversation while simultaneously sketching Bridget in her notebook. Joanna was asked out more than any girl in their year, but she had adopted the mysterious and style-oblivious Bridget as her friend in an attempt to reject the role she was expected to play as an attractive and intelligent rich kid.

"What is it you've roped us into now?" Jude asked, stalking past the loveseat to stare moodily out a window.

Joanna jumped up, ran to Cole, and hugged all the air out of his lungs, making him choke and laugh at her exuberance. She was so short the top of her head barely reached his chin.

"Finally! Where have you two been? We were looking everywhere for you! Anyway, never mind, you're here now. Cole, how are you? How was your summer? Did you visit lots of museums? Any UFO sightings? New Mexico's famous for that, right?"

Bridget released a beautiful, tinkling laugh at Joanna's torrent of questions. Cole caught her eye, and she winked at him. He wished Bridget would give him a welcome home hug too, but the amused smile flickering on her heart-shaped lips almost made up for it.

"Let's just say I'm glad to be back," Cole said, crossing to the other side of the Turkish rug. He dropped his suitcase onto the green velvet armchair, and a cloud of dust billowed into the filtered light. An inspiration struck him: he withdrew the folder Mr. Price had given him and propped it against his suitcase. He wouldn't really be cheating on his resolution if someone saw the folder and asked.

"How was everything here?" Cole said, hoping to draw their attention toward the chair.

It didn't work. Jude stared sulkily out at the sun-drenched lawns. Joanna plopped back down on the loveseat and started sketching again. Bridget hadn't seen the folder either, but at least she was still looking at him.

"Eventful," Joanna replied. "Jude worked like a dog while Bridget pretended to be a hermit and I went on the world's most boring cruise. But now we're all back, and things are about to get much more interesting. To answer your question, Jude, what you're doing is coming to my—"

A loud thwack made them all jump. Cole blinked, trying to understand what he had just seen: the library was perfectly still, but a book on the shelf behind the loveseat had suddenly fallen to lie face down, its pages crumpled under the weight of the cracked spine.

"What the—?" Jude said, abandoning the window to search the other side of the bookshelf. "No one there."

"A mystery!" Joanna exclaimed, clapping her hands together.

"Someone must have done a crap job shelving it," Jude answered.

Cole doubted this. They had to be the only students who would use the library on the very first day back at school, and Mrs. Fay, the deaf but scrupulous librarian, would have aligned all the books against her yardstick over break. Bridget uncurled herself from the loveseat and moved to pick it up.

"What is it?" Cole asked.

"My Life and Findings: An Autobiography by Vincent Vendler."

Between her delicate fingers, Cole saw on the cover a man with a high forehead, arrogant cheekbones, and veiled eyes. It exactly resembled the painting of the school's founder hanging above the library fireplace, except that the picture on the book was faded and dusty rather than discolored and cracked as was its oil counterpart.

"That's the title of the book we're supposed to write an essay on for History," Cole said. "I emailed our teachers over break and asked them to send the syllabi early so I could do some pre-reading, but I couldn't find that one online or at the library."

"Such a dumb assignment," Jude grumbled. "Vendler just had money. Big deal. He wasn't even an academic."

"More like a quackademic," Bridget added with that barely detectable snark that always caught Cole off guard. She flipped through the pages, looking mildly interested. "You know, I actually read this book last year. Vendler was definitely an odd duck. Involved in the occult, for one thing. Although I have to say, I kind of like his weird theory about the life-giving power of art. Absolutely nothing to back it up, but it's an interesting idea."

"Since when did you start doing homework?" Cole teased.

Bridget read voraciously, but it was rare to see her reading anything school-related. It was a mystery how she managed to avoid academic probation.

"God knows I didn't read it because I wanted to do the assignment."

"Let me have it for my essay, then," Cole said.

She handed it to him, and their fingers almost brushed.

"Thanks. I'm going to start on the essay right away." The large oil painting of Vincent Vendler that hung above the mantel regarded Cole with an eerily alive expression of approval. Trying to steer the conversation toward the internship, Cole added, "I need to knock it out so I can work on more important things."

"Like what?" Joanna asked, patting the loveseat cushion to indicate Bridget should resume her seat.

Cole allowed himself a smile. He had been imagining this moment ever since Mr. Price had told him the news, and he had his words ready. He was careful to modulate his voice and hedge his hope by explaining that several other students had also been invited, but he couldn't suppress a gratified laugh when Joanna squealed as if he had already gotten the internship.

"So what's this internship supposed to be about?" Jude asked, a hint of curiosity betraying his determination to keep a vice grip on his foul mood.

"To be honest, I'm not totally sure yet." Cole sat up straighter as if practicing for the interview his conscious mind warned him not to hope for. "The Lab's biggest project right now is called Kronos, and I think I'd be helping with that."

"Amazing! That's the AI that lets you talk to dead people, right?" Joanna asked.

"Not actual dead people," Cole said. "The Lab extracts data from voice messages and any other audio recordings you have from when the person was alive, then uses algorithms to find speech and intonation patterns, and even the types of topics the person used to talk about and their opinions on them. So you basically get to have a conversation with the person as though they were still alive.

"It's supposed to be a life-saver for old people who have lost a spouse, or anyone who's lonely, really. It's so cool. The technology has been around for a long time, but somehow no one's thought to do this, at least not on a massive scale where everyone can afford to have one in their home."

"Hmmm...." Bridget exhaled. "So basically it's the tech version of a Ouija board."

"Uh, no," he said, suppressing an amused smile. "There's nothing weird or... illicit about it. Besides, with those you never know who you're going to get, if anyone—personally I think they're bogus—whereas with this, you can control who's on the other end, and they're there all the time, whenever you want them, with the simple tap of a button."

Bridget tilted her head to one side as she always did before raising an objection.

"Isn't taking people's data without their permission kind of illicit? I mean, do the dead people sign release forms saying it's okay to turn their memory into a robot?"

"Come on, Bridget," Cole said, slightly irritated that she wasn't more impressed. "No one's going to care what happens to their data if they're dead, especially if their family is using it for a good reason."

"I would. If you turned me into a robot, I might just come back to haunt you."

"I'll bear that in mind."

Then again, he wasn't sure he'd mind if Bridget came back to haunt him.

"Anyway," Joanna interjected firmly, "I think this internship is just incredible. Orien Saint-Pierre is such an important humanitarian. Aside from everything else, he's been doing a lot of work supporting underprivileged groups lately. By helping him, Cole will not only be achieving his own goals, but he'll also be making the world a better place."

"Here's something else I've always wondered," Bridget mused, not taking Joanna's cue. "Is Orien even his real name?"

"What do you mean 'his real name'?" Cole asked. It was odd that he could be annoyed with her and want to impress her at the same time.

"I mean the name his parents gave him. 'Orien' is kind of a weird name, so it made me wonder."

Joanna shrugged. "What does it matter? It's the name he calls himself, so it's real enough. Cole, I'm over-the-moon thrilled for you. You've worked so hard for this, and I'm going to cheer you on all the way."

Cole smiled appreciatively. He needed someone to celebrate for him while he told himself not to get his hopes up. Just then, the school custodian appeared from behind the last stack of books.

"Paul, I was wondering when we'd see you!" Joanna exclaimed. "How are you? Did you have a great summer?"

Ever since Jude had taken the trouble to thank Paul for emptying the trash during lunch one day, the custodian had become a staunch advocate and occasional false witness whenever one of them got into trouble. Apparently, most students ignored Paul.

"Knew I'd find you here," Paul answered, his mouth drawing crookedly toward his left cheek as he spoke. Under his eagle nose, a few yellow teeth capped with mercury fillings were visible. He swept a tobacco-stained hand across the room. "My summer was all the fixes I don't have time for when you're here. I gotta be the only one here who works harder come summer. Look, I have to kick you out. Last period's over and I'm lockin' up. Got a game to get home to, and Mrs. Fay's watchin' the seconds tick by to make sure the lock clicks at 3:30 on the dot."

Despite the librarian's famed inability to hear, Paul glanced toward her desk as if expecting her inauspicious eye to be fixed on him. A little deflated that the conversation about the internship was cut short, Cole slid the folder into his suitcase and followed his friends to where Mrs. Fay presided over the library desk, her rigid frame draped with skin like a wire hanger with disintegrating cloth.

Cole handed Vendler's autobiography to her as someone might return a newborn to its mother, then watched as she withdrew a check-out slip from a neat stack in her desk drawer and scrupulously filled in each field. Her fingers possessively caressed the spine of the autobiography as she handed it back to Cole, a habitual gesture perpetuating the local legend that she had never officially passed the school's background check; it was said that her ceaseless shuffling of pages had eroded all trace of unique personal history, making it impossible for the police to get a distinct fingerprint. She never spoke of retirement, nor of her life before the library, and Cole always imagined that she had spontaneously generated atop the straight-backed desk chair like Aristotle's maggots on raw meat.

When she handed the book back, Cole saw that she had written an injunction on the check-out slip: *Deadlines are called "dead" for a reason—borrow books at your own peril.* Oh well. He had the internship application waiting in his suitcase. Even Mrs. Fay couldn't sour his day.

CHAPTER 5

ORIEN SAINT-PIERRE

s he did every afternoon at 1:15 pm, Orien Saint-Pierre stood in his office overlooking downtown Montréal. The late September sky was cloudless and brilliantly blue. Below it, the unpolluted sunlight on the St. Lawrence River could have blinded him if he looked too long. Its banks were ablaze with gold and red-leafed sugar maples, their leaves waving in the same sleepy wind that stirred the waters without quite raising white-capped waves.

It was a pristine day, a day on which the purity of nature and the pulse of the city should have inspired him. Lately, however, the constant flow of the river seemed listless, the movement of traffic monotonous, the city landscape spent.

Behind Orien, watching him while he watched the city, sat his assistant. He was grateful that Prisha was used to his need to not face her when he was thinking. His best ideas always came when he observed the world from a distance. But today he felt too closely acquainted with every detail of the city that sprawled before him and changed with the seasons too slowly. He wished he could see it again through virgin eyes.

The truth was that he was tired. For years he had been inching toward the embodiment of Kronos, one hard-fought revelation after another, but never truly breaking through.

Outside his office, the ding of an elevator reaching the top floor reminded him that he had been silent too long. Prisha would be eager to get back to her executive duties. He sat back down on his chair and swiveled to face her.

"Is there anything else on our agenda today, anything I can help you with?"

"Only one."

The speed with which she answered confirmed that she was impatient to conclude the meeting. This was one of the reasons Orien valued her—there was no polite demurring, no socially expected pause to consider an answer she already had, no unnecessary shuffling of papers or crossing and uncrossing of legs. He had added her to his staff earlier that year, finally accepting the necessity of giving another human visibility to his calendar and letting her represent him whenever he was unable to attend a meeting. She had not disappointed him. She was diplomatic, clever, and adept at relieving him from the banalities of professional life. Her straight white teeth and lean musculature emphasized her professional efficiency. She was neither too old nor too young. She was not prone to wearing perfumes and did not introduce noticeable pheromones into the room. Whether she was in his office or out of it, he preserved the impression of being alone that was so essential to his mental clarity. Best of all, she never mistook his cordiality for an invitation to intimacy.

She continued, "It's about the high school internship you opened last month. As you requested, HR, R&D, and Engineering have all assessed the applications and made their recommendations for the top ten students. Would you like to review their selections?"

"I trust my staff." He sat back in his chair and reclined his perfectly shaved head in his interlaced hands. Then, remembering a half-formed curiosity, he added, "Were any students from Vendler Academy selected?"

Prisha didn't have to reference her laptop. "Yes, one. Even without your bringing the Academy to our attention, we would have found it. Its students rank higher on test scores and university placements than students from any other school in North America."

Orien had almost forgotten about the internship. He had opened it on instinct, and now, for the first time, he realized why. A young student, someone who hadn't yet learned what wasn't possible, was exactly what he needed to become again. What if he allowed that student into his personal space? How would such an encounter influence his own systems of thought? He made a snap decision. This student would work with him. Not just in his organization, but by his side whenever he was in the office.

He said, "Good. Make an appointment for me to interview Vendler Academy's top student—whomever you recommend."

In an uncharacteristic gesture of uncertainty, Prisha's small mouth opened and closed again like a goldfish blowing a bubble. "For the sake of clarity—you want to interview the student personally?"

"Yes, and I'll be conducting the interview face-to-face. It should take place at their institution, not here."

Prisha disciplined her surprise so quickly that Orien almost didn't catch the upward flicker of her eyebrow. That was another trait he valued. She always knew when not to react. "Would you like to personally interview all ten students?"

"No, I trust your recommendations. Have Nick and

someone from HR conduct the other interviews. We'll compare notes later."

"Very good." Prisha rose and moved to the door in one fluid, noiseless movement despite the fact that she walked in high heels across the nanoglass tile.

"Wait, Prisha." Orien arrested her movement just before his brain processed what he meant to say. He always followed his intuition, and right now it was telling him that the key to everything he had worked for—the key to finishing Kronos and abolishing the power of death—depended on a student at Vendler Academy. It wouldn't hurt to increase the odds of his success by widening the data set. "Give me the top two students at Vendler. You can bump someone else off the list."

CHAPTER 6

AN UNEXPECTED LETTER

A twig snapped under Cole's foot, and the forest groaned from the pain of it. Startled, he looked up to see the bole of an ash tree a few feet from him. As he looked, two drops of crystalized sap that clung to the trunk became eyes in a wizened face, watching him unblinkingly. Against his will, he reached out to touch them. His fingers sunk into the sap, and the warmth in his skin made them glow hot like coals, blistering his fingers. He snatched his hand away, cradling its pain, as the tree became a torch. The heat of it smothered him, but the bark remained uncharred, the leaves green. Cole ran in terror, and the tree melted away.

He was a child again, screaming himself awake from pain like fire in his legs. His dad, huge and warm, lifted him from his bed and set him on the kitchen counter. His dad's hands rubbed the pain in Cole's legs away. His voice, like a tremor of the earth, told Cole that the fire was called a growing pain, and that it was a good thing because it meant he would be a tall man one day. Cole looked up at his dad's face, but it was obscured by black mist. The voice belonged to a ghost.

Cole woke, drenched in his own sweat. A vague dread like the black mist still clung to him. It had been years since that nightmare had visited him. He breathed slowly in and out, forcing a calm he did not feel. It didn't work. He tossed his covers aside and blinked away the face of the tree and the black mist. He would not give it power by thinking of it.

As he did every day, Cole methodically tightened his sheets, brushed his teeth, strapped on his watch, combed his hair, pulled on a clean pair of chinos and a pressed shirt, and slipped his Sperry loafers over socks that matched his belt. Checking his tucked-in shirt in the bathroom mirror, he returned to his room and thumbed through his backpack to ensure his books were in the same order as his classes. Only one title was out of order: American History. He pulled the book out, and a letter fluttered from its pages. How could he have forgotten? Yesterday, unable to toss it in the trash, he had shoved the letter out of sight. Now, as if morbidly drawn to the site of an accident, he picked it up and held it to the weak sunlight from the window.

On the front was a picture of a middle-aged couple. The man's arms were wrapped around the woman's waist, and Cole could practically hear his exultant laughter. He placed a thumb over the man's mouth and followed his arms to the willowy blonde with the radiant smile and coy expression. She shared Cole's straight nose, pale complexion, fine bone structure, and tall, thin physique. But whereas Cole's eyes were gray and haunted, hers were dark and dancing. She was so alive Cole could almost smell her perfume. Below it were the names Geoffrey David Kay and Layla Grace Harper.

Cole swallowed and flipped the card over to re-read the scribbled note from his mom:

. . .

I'm married! Geoff is an art collector (did he tell you over summer?) and the Next Big Name. We're off to honeymoon in Paris, then Venice, Florence, and Madrid. What a dream! You'll love him when you get to know him better, sweetie. Can't wait for you two to spend more time together. XOXOXO.

The letters blurred as Cole stared. How could she have fallen for someone as pompous and self-centered as Geoff? Cole had met Geoff a handful of times over the summer, but he hadn't exactly paid attention. Every year it had been a new man. His mom had always followed glamor, always needed to be the center of something big. Before his parents' divorce, his mom had never missed a chance to parade her husband's status as a renowned Army surgeon. That was before his dad's chronic drinking had resulted in a botched surgery—a surgery that should have been straightforward but instead left a man paralyzed—and the eventual dissolution of his marriage. In his memory Cole heard Bridget saying, about what he couldn't remember, "It's entirely possible for things to be there one day and gone the next. Just like people."

Cole cleared his throat and shoved the card back in his textbook. He wouldn't let Geoff ruin his day. Slinging the backpack over his shoulder, Cole tiptoed past his dad's room and down the stairs. As he stepped into the kitchen, a sickly-sweet scent assaulted his nose and made him instantly nauseous. He knew what he would find before he flicked on the light: empty Pabst Blue Ribbon cans, some tipped on their sides, littered the counter. Next to them was a Southern Comfort bottle with a thin line of amber liquid stretched across the bottom. The cap was off.

Cole had to swallow his gag reflex. For the most part, the last several weeks had been just beer, maybe a shot of whiskey, but it looked like his dad hadn't even tried to hide the evidence last night. Cole beat back a treacherous instinct toward pity and walked away from the empty bottles toward the pantry. His dad needed to see the mess when he woke up. If he didn't, he might not remember. He might think Cole hadn't noticed.

His back to the beer cans, Cole grabbed the last pack of frosted brown sugar cinnamon Pop-Tarts. He poured himself a glass of water and grabbed two leftover pizza slices for lunch, placing them in a Ziploc bag. He tossed the bag into his backpack pocket because his lunch cooler was sitting right beside the cans on the counter. Even so, the cans stared at him. Cole ignored them. He drained his water glass and checked his watch.

Picking up his backpack, he headed to the door, then turned back abruptly. Without looking at them, he gathered the empty cans and walked past the inside recycling bin and out into the garage, where he dropped them quietly into the large trash bin. Returning to the kitchen, he found the whiskey cap, screwed it on, and placed it back in its cabinet. Only then did he turn off the kitchen lights. The cleared countertops smirked at him as if to say, "We knew you couldn't do it." Cole hurried out the door.

Outside, the morning sky was periwinkle laced with pink. As if to prove he still had some fight in him, Cole marched straight to the mailbox. Yesterday, the letter from his mom had been on top. After reading it, he had slammed the mailbox shut and gone inside, too disgusted to revisit it for the remaining mail.

Now Cole took up the remaining papers, flipping through bills and advertisements until, without warning, he was met with a letter addressed to Nicholas Erickson, 57 Hollow Tree Way. Above it, in India blue ink, was the brain webbed with neurons, the insignia that had haunted all his waking dreams. Cole's eyes devoured every word of the return address: The Orien Saint-Pierre Lab, Quebec. His hand began to shake. He had waited so long, and here this letter had sat all yesterday afternoon and all through the cold night, holding his future.

Cole shoved the rest of the mail back into the box, slammed the lid, and ran to his car. Resisting the urge to tear open the envelope, he clutched it against the steering wheel as he turned on the ignition and pulled away. As soon as his dad's house was out of sight, he pulled over to the curb again and put the car in park. Sliding a shaking finger into the corner of the envelope, he tore open the flap and unfolded the smooth, heavy sheet of paper.

Dear Mr. Erickson,

We are pleased to inform you that you have advanced to the second phase of the 2025 Orien Saint-Pierre Lab Emerging Research Scientists Internship along with nine peers from across North America. Congratulations!

As this is the inaugural year for our special OSPLERSI program, Dr. Saint-Pierre will be personally traveling to your school to conduct your interview. Your school administrators will be in touch with you to coordinate a time. There is no need for you to prepare in advance.

We look forward to meeting you soon.

Wishing you all the best,

The 2025 Orien Saint-Pierre Lab Emerging Research Scientists Internship Committee

· · ·

Cole read the letter three times, his arms prickling with goosebumps. Not only had he made it, but Orien Saint-Pierre was coming to Vendler Academy, in person! What would it feel like to have those intelligent eyes, that generous smile, spotlighting him? He hoped he wouldn't do anything stupid when it happened. Then again, he might do something stupendously clever.

His chest fluttered with excitement, and his stomach clenched with the yearning to prove himself. He read the letter once more, wedged it carefully into his last textbook of the day, and drove into the rising sun.

CHAPTER 7

KRONOS

Three weeks later, Cole stood waiting outside Vendler Academy's conference room at twenty till two. He had been excused from classes early because behind that heavy door with the maddeningly opaque frosted glass sat Dr. Orien Saint-Pierre.

Time seemed to have stopped. Cole reached up to check his hair, then down to retrieve an Altoids tin from his pocket. He popped a mint into his mouth before realizing he already had one on his tongue. Trying to calm his mind, he walked a few paces down the hall, its hardwood floors creaking loudly in the pervasive stillness. The vacant corridors were strewn with autumn leaves, buffeted and crushed by the soles of a hundred shoes. The scent of mildew and chloral was sharper when the halls were deserted, and the sense of isolation intensified Cole's nervousness. The Academy always seemed more awake when Cole was alone.

He glanced at his watch. Where was Wesley Tate? Wes and Cole were the only students selected from Vendler Academy. Surely, he should be here by now—not that Cole minded.

If Wes decided, God knew why, to show up late to the most important moment of his life, Cole was not going to complain. It might be the one way Cole could finally feel superior, as if his academic achievements made him enough. He tried to conjure Wes's easy confidence. He'd give anything to walk into that conference room with the charisma that came so easily to Vendler Academy's prom king, all-star student, track team captain, and high school heartthrob.

Before Cole could compose his face, the door opened.

"Ah Cole," Dr. Bering boomed. "So you'll start? Wonderful!" Then, in a threatening whisper that made his nostrils flare like a dragon's, he hissed, "Where's Wes?"

Cole shrugged. Dr. Bering ushered Cole into the room with a look that simultaneously said, "I've never been prouder of a student in my whole life" and "If you mess this up, we're going back to using the cane."

The door closed behind Cole with a soft click. On the other side of the mahogany table sat Dr. Orien Saint-Pierre, his shockingly three-dimensional face exuding a charismatic animation that his TV appearances only dimly captured. The chandelier cast a halo on his bald head, illuminating the uncanny symmetry of his features. Cole's throat went dry. He cleared it and accidentally swallowed his mint. Eyes watering, he tripped toward the table.

"Ah, Cole, isn't it? Or do you prefer Nicholas? I saw both on your application."

To Cole's surprise, the man in the paisley silk waistcoat stood to greet him, smiling genially and extending a hand as dexterous as a pianist's. He was even taller than Cole, and the muscles were etched clearly beneath the lavender twill dress shirt. His voice was as smooth as melted wax.

"Yes, Cole, sir. It's a pleasure," Cole said, finding his voice and extending his own slightly shaky hand.

"The pleasure is mine," Dr. Saint-Pierre replied, and he really seemed to mean it. Gesturing to a plush leather chair across the table from him, he said, "Please, be seated. I hope I didn't cause your conscientious Dr. Bering too much trouble, but I requested that your wooden chair be replaced with one identical to mine so that we can both be comfortable. Would you like some water?"

Cole nodded, watching in amazement as his idol stood once again to retrieve a chilled water bottle and a crystal tumbler from a side table.

"Please, Dr. Saint-Pierre, I can get it."

"It's no trouble at all. To tell you the truth, my legs are a little stiff from the drive, so my motivation is entirely selfish." Handing Cole the glass of water, he added, "And call me Orien. If we begin working together, you may find it easier to call me by three syllables rather than five."

Cole nodded again, strangely disconcerted by how human the greatest mind of the twenty-first century was. He couldn't figure out which part he was expected to play in response.

"So. Cole. You may be expecting me to ask you a series of questions and evaluate you on your responses, but the way I look at it is this: I have already had an opportunity, in the extensive application prepared by my endearingly punctilious team, to ask you every question I thought necessary. Today, I want to give you the opportunity to ask questions of me. I assure you, no question is too trivial or mundane. Think of it as a reverse interview. Should you take this internship at The Lab, I want you to be sure it's what you want as well as what I want. For the next hour, you have my absolute and undivided attention. What would you like to ask me?"

Orien sat back in his chair, smiling attentively. Adrenaline shot through Cole's veins. His mind went blank. He became intensely aware of Orien's cologne, a complex and evasive blend of mint, vetiver, and a suggestion of lilac. Cole coerced his brain into mentally scanning the many YouTube videos he had watched, scrambling for a question that sounded intelligent. Irrelevantly, he realized that he had never interacted with Orien's talks as he interacted with his friends. He had studied them, accepting every word as fact, memorizing key phrases and themes. But never once had he thought of The Lab or the man behind it as something that could be questioned as he might question a friend. As he thought of his friends, he was rescued by the memory of a question Jude had asked him.

"Excuse me, sir, but what exactly would I be doing if I got the internship?" As soon as the question passed his lips, he regretted it. It felt like the wrong thing to ask. It was too obvious. Surely, he ought to know this by now. "What I mean to say is, I understand that I would be researching innovations for the Kronos project, but for this position in particular, what exactly would be involved?"

"An excellent question, Cole."

The pronouncement lifted several tons of anxiety off of Cole's chest. Thank God, Orien was making him feel like Not-An-Idiot.

Interlacing his hands over crossed legs, Orien continued, "Allow me to start by telling you the why behind the what. All good stories start with names, because names tell us the truth about who we are. Do you know how the Kronos project got its name?"

Cole felt like he ought to have run across this information in his extensive reading, but nothing came to him. "No, sir."

"When I first announced the creation of my AI platform, it had a very catchy title, invented by yours truly: AXR490-66. Somehow, that didn't stick."

Orien actually winked at him. Cole began to breathe normally again and returned Orien's smile.

"At that time, the technology behind the platform was still extremely new. As you can imagine, my announcement was followed by an enormous influx of reporters from every media outlet in North America wanting an exclusive interview. I didn't give many because I knew the model was far from perfect, and I wanted to refine it before anyone got excited about it going to market.

"In one of the interviews I did give, however, I revealed that the inspiration behind the project was personal. My own parents, you see, died tragically in a car accident when I was only five, leaving me to endure an endless shuffle from one foster family to the next. While I don't recall everything I shared in that interview, I must have said something along the lines of, 'I was too young when I lost them—I wish I had been able to control when my parents died, so I created Kronos to restore the life I could have had.'"

Orien paused to swallow, and Cole felt with him the weight of the affectionless childhood that wounded him still today. Orien cleared his throat and spoke again.

"While most of the reporters I worked with were sympathetic, certain segments of the press have a way of creating malignancy ex nihilo, and I was eventually quoted as having said, 'I wish I could have killed my parents when I was ready.'"

Cole froze midway to running a hand over his combed hair. This was the first he had ever heard of this interview, as Orien's reputation in the press was rightfully spotless. Suddenly self-conscious, Cole dropped his hand. For some reason, Orien was smiling, inviting Cole in on the joke.

"The interview was quickly hushed up. No one wanted to syndicate it. But it became something of a joke within my team. So when our marketing department informed us that they needed a better name than AXR490-66, I suggested Kronos, and it stuck."

Cole chuckled along with Orien, though he couldn't remember anything about Kronos other than that he was the father of Zeus.

"But you must be wondering why I told you this rather long-winded and self-indulgent story."

Actually, Cole wasn't wondering. He had forgotten the question he had asked completely.

"I've been working in software for nearly three decades, and if I know anything, I know that software, like life, is highly iterative. We are always finding gaps, always refining the model, always perfecting our tools—like our lives—to help us in our progress toward becoming better humans. The original name for Kronos—AXR490-66—reflects how many iterations the platform went through before we released it in its MVP version to a small test group, and I'm not just referring to the number after the dash. I worked relentlessly, tirelessly, until I felt Kronos was good enough to give to the public.

"But Cole, the story is not over. I'm a strong believer in the process, and even more in the systems behind the process. Those systems need refining. There are more iterations to come before Kronos is perfect. And it will be perfect."

"But how could it be better?" The question escaped Cole's lips before he evaluated it, and he almost forgot to wonder whether he was interrupting or conversing.

"Ah, and this is where we get back to your original question, my friend! You asked what you would be doing in this internship. You would be helping me fashion Kronos as it lives in my mind, Kronos as it is meant to be. You see, Kronos currently exists as a primitive model: we harvest auditory data from a person's life, which we call the Subject. Then we input that data into the model, test and refine it through a series of training sessions, and eventually, out comes the conversational AI model for that Subject. My goal is that the living are able to create the memories they wish they had, to part with their loved ones how and when they are ready, rather than having their life torn in two when they are totally unprepared. Have you lost anyone, Cole?"

Cole was so entranced by Orien's story that the question jolted him with an almost physical force. "My dad" almost came out, but he caught the words just in time. Instead, he said, "My grandmother, Helen. I don't remember her, but she loved me. My mom says I take after her."

He hadn't meant to say all of that, but the words poured from him before he could stop them. Orien nodded.

"A special woman, then. Every story, every relationship, is unique. But what do they all have in common? Across cultures and across generations, throughout the long and varied history of mankind, we all have one common enemy. That enemy is Death. Native Americans, Muslims, and Christians all seek to strip Death of its ultimate power by affirming an afterlife. Hindus seek to make Death meaningful by presenting it as a passage into reincarnation. And some cultures, such as the Aztecs and Mayans, worship Death.

"What is behind these varied reactions? Fear. Death is our greatest fear, and in some ways, our greatest longing. But we can never control it, never know when it will come and for whom. Will it be my turn next? I do not know. But what I do know is this: if we live a good life, if we have no regrets, we will not fear Death. And what are our greatest regrets?

"My hypothesis is this: what makes us who we are is largely shaped by the people we interface with along the way. Therefore, our greatest regrets stem from relationships that are sundered. A sundered relationship is a kind of death, you know. Whether or not we are to blame for these rifts is irrelevant. What is relevant is that sometimes, try as we might, we cannot repair what once has been broken.

"Kronos gives us a way out of that. It lets us deal with relationships, and with people, how and when we want. In short, it gives us back the control that Death steals from us. It's a joke that I became infamous because I wanted to kill my parents, but the truth is, I became famous because I found the power to decide when they will die. Death will always be man's greatest enemy, but if we can control the narrative of our last moments with our loved ones, we will have nothing to regret when we die. Regret is what makes Death terrifying. If we have nothing to regret, no memory of pain, we have nothing to fear when at last Death comes for us."

Orien passed a hand over his eyes. Only when the gaze was broken did Cole realize it had held him captive. When Orien's hand fell from his face, Cole noticed wrinkles around the eyes, the forehead, and the mouth, that surely hadn't been there just a moment ago.

"But the Kronos in my Lab is far from the Kronos in my mind. It still needs to grow, to mature, to take on flesh. Yes, users can enjoy a coherent conversation with their Subject, and many say it is enough. But I know better, Cole. Kronos is not good enough, for me or for them. We deserve more. Kronos has logic on its side, but at the end of the day, we're talking to a small, portable piece of machinery. That can never feel like a conversation with a real person. How can we make it feel like we are talking to the Subject if we cannot see them? My first thought is augmented reality.

"But even that is not good enough. We must find a way to incorporate all our senses, to know that Kronos can experience everyday life alongside us, that it can feel the affectionate touch of a hand, see the creases on our brows when we are stressed, smell the perfume it adored while living. In short, we need to take multimodal research to an entirely new level. And then, we need to transform multimodal research into multimodal reality. And beyond all this, we need to be made to feel that Kronos loves us."

Orien stared out the latticed windows that looked across Vendler Academy's baseball diamond as if hoping to catch a glimpse of the future he saw so clearly in his mind. Again, he pressed both hands over his eyes and sighed, an automatic and unrealized gesture of exhaustion. Cole wondered if Orien ever really slept. He admired the intensity of his dedication. Then Orien pinned Cole again with his eyes and held him fast.

"I'm not an egoist, Cole. I'm a visionary. A prophet, if you will. These advancements are underway, but they are not nearly where they need to be, and I know that I am dependent on a wider community of collaborators to make Kronos what it was meant to be. As a coding prodigy at the age of twelve myself, I don't overlook, as many in my Lab seem to, the possibility that my next inspiration for Kronos may come from a younger generation. Yes, you lack the education and expertise of a postdoctoral specialist. But I sometimes wonder if our training isn't limited by what we perceive to be possible. If you don't know the rules of the game, you're not constricted to live by them.

"I have a vision, Cole. I see the world as it was meant to be, as one day it will be. This vision will be the star guiding our work. But I cannot always see the path to get there. And who knows what we will uncover along the way? If Kronos is to reach maturation within my lifetime—and it will—I need to summon the best talent from around the globe. Could that be you, Cole?"

The question hung in the air, tantalizing. Cole wanted to reach up, to seize it, to affirm his belonging at The Lab, but the rhetoric of Orien's speech was so strong that he didn't dare mar the silence that followed it with a simple, "Yes." Instead, he let the moment linger, hoping that Orien would see for himself that the man he needed to make Kronos all it was meant to be was sitting across the table from him at that very moment. Surely the gravity and the trust, the humanity and the hope, that Orien had just shown him was a testament to that truth. In his mind, he saw himself standing next to Orien as his future partner, pioneering a new world.

A light knock made them both start. The door opened to reveal Dr. Bering.

"I'm sorry to interrupt, Dr. Saint-Pierre, but you asked me to remind you when the hour was up. Wesley Tate is just outside this room when you are ready for him."

Cole's stomach clenched at the sound of Wesley's name. Orien broke into a broad beam.

"Ah, thank you very much, my dear Dr. Bering. Please let Wes know I'll be with him in one moment. I have just one more question for Cole."

Dr. Bering half bowed to Orien before backing out of the room, still frozen in his inclined position. Orien began smiling again like a child on his birthday who is unsure if it's time for him to open his gifts. Cole's mouth went dry. Was Orien about to offer him the internship on the spot?

"No doubt you'll think this question humorous, Cole, but I always try to learn something wherever I go so that I'm constantly growing. You see, I sometimes find that the people on the ground floor, as it were, have more real knowledge than their teachers and administrators. I wonder if you could tell me whether you know anything about this school's founder."

"Oh!" Cole's heart couldn't quite calm itself in pace with his deflated anticipation. "I don't know much, really. That is, I recently read his book: *My Life and Findings: An Autobiography by Vincent Vendler*."

"Aha! Yes, a quaint little book, isn't it?"

Cole met Orien's eyes in surprise. "You've read it?"

"Yes, I also came across it recently, and it captured my fancy. What did you make of it?"

"Well, how do I say this? I'm grateful for all he did in support of my education, but I'm not sure I found the book exactly... illuminating. That is, maybe it was just his personality, but..."

"But he's a bit of a narcissist," Orien finished, smiling.

Cole answered the smile in agreement. Orien stood and held out his hand.

"Well Cole, it's been a pleasure."

Cole rose and grasped the hand firmly, noticing as he did so Orien's cufflinks bearing the insignia of The Lab—the outline of a brain webbed with neurons. Conscious of not lingering too long after his dismissal, he turned and walked out into the hall, where a scowling Paul was being shooed down the hall by Dr. Bering. Wes was there too, leaning with a debonair air against the wall, hands in his pockets. He wasn't wearing a suit, and he didn't seem self-conscious when he saw Cole's. Wes grinned, and Cole realized it was the first time he had ever interacted with Wes one-on-one.

"Good thing they called for you first, right? Don't know what happened. Just lost track of the time. Hope it went well for you!"

Disarmed, Cole said, "Thanks" before he realized that Wes was patronizing him. Wes could afford to be nice because he didn't even consider Cole competition. Well, Cole was going to give Wes a run for his money. He pushed past him and joined Paul, who was still scowling.

"C'mon, I'll walk you to study hall," Paul said, leading him out of the subsidiary building that housed the conference room and across the lawn toward the library.

The sun shone in their eyes, and a breeze rippled the grass. The sweet song of an American goldfinch drifted from one of the maple trees.

"Sorry 'bout that," Paul said. "Ol' Bering had me fetch Wes from class. Tried to dawdle to make him late, but you were in there longer than I expected. Went all right, then?"

Cole grinned, allowing himself to feel the elation he had carefully suppressed when he saw Wes. "Better than all right."

Paul nodded. "Good man, in't he? I showed him to his room for the interviews, and we got to talking. He's blue blood all right."

Cole looked up, surprised. "You met Orien too?"

"Yep. Real friendly. Asked me all about how long have I been here and what do I do. I told him, I been here since I was a boy, first as a student, though I'm no academic. Got a scholarship on account of being a distant relative of his," Paul dipped his head at the building as if it was Vendler himself. "Dropped out in tenth grade and been here ever since as custodian. He seemed genuinely interested in me and asked all sorts of questions about who is my family and where am I from and what do I know about Vendler, since he's my great uncle or something. I said I know nothin', except for what he looks like thanks to that ugly picture of him in the library." Paul stared in the direction of the library and scratched his chin stubble meditatively. "Funny thing, I tried to move it once to paint behind it with a refresh coat. Wouldn't budge. Anyhow, he's a real nice man. Orien, that is."

Across the lawn, a door banged open and Joanna flew out of it, skidding to a halt in front of them.

"Cole! I just got out of class. How was it? How was he? How did it go? Did you get the internship?" Joanna raked her hair out of her face. Her expression was so anxious that Cole laughed.

"It was great."

He had barely gotten the words out before she engulfed him in a jubilant hug, her hair flying into his mouth.

"Thank God. What else? What's he like? Does he like you?"

"Shoot, I forgot to ask him," Cole said, pretending to be serious because he knew she would buy it. "Do you think I should go back and ask?"

She looked panicked, then caught Paul's grin and rolled her eyes. Cole relented.

"I think he does like me. I felt excited about our conversation, and comfortable enough to ask questions. The things he's doing... they're going to change everything. And I want to be part of that, and I think he could tell."

"Well hallelujah! Cole, from you that's like a declaration of love!" She grabbed his arm. "Come on, Bridget and Jude will be in the library. Let's go tell them all about it."

CHAPTER 8

AN AUSPICIOUS ENCOUNTER

The next evening found Cole slumped forward in his desk chair, the house around him humming with silence. He rubbed his temples and squinted at the multicolored command lines that blurred together on the screen before him, trying not to think about the fact that it was his birthday and no one had remembered. It was childish to be upset. He was getting too old to care. Staring harder at the screen, he typed a parenthesis that looked like a frown.

He had expected his dad to forget, but he did think Joanna at least would have said something at school. Last year, she had taken him indoor skydiving. It was ironic that the one person who had remembered was the one person he had forgotten to anticipate anything from. He tapped his phone screen to life and stared at the message his mom had sent a minute earlier: *Happy 17! Hope you're having a magical day! Love you tons!* with lots of heart emojis. Cole let his phone screen go black and resumed his staring match with the computer cursor. It blinked blearily back at him, the only

52

moving thing in the house. It gave him a strange satisfaction to hold the power button and watch it die.

Closing the laptop lid, he meandered to the window and peered out onto Hollow Tree Way. The November sun was setting sooner now, and the pervasive fog that blanketed the streets seemed to seep through the windows and into Cole's skin, sending a shiver down his spine. A sprig of leaves bounced down the street, driven by the wind, which found its voice among a row of pines. The night was alive, tugging at Cole, beckoning him to leave the house. But to what purpose? Cole drew the blinds and trudged downstairs, his footfalls echoing back at him.

He flipped a switch, hoping the kitchen light would banish the chill, but nothing happened. The microwave light was off too. The wind must have killed the power. Outside, a soft rain tapped at the window, trying to win his attention. For something to do, Cole pulled a Twinkie out of the pantry. Rummaging in a drawer near the stovetop, he found a box of matches and paused, his hand hovering over the striker strip. Inevitably, his mind drifted to the Talavera honeymoon vase. But that wish was silly now that he had so many new things to hope for. Ignoring the familiar emptiness that had made its home in his chest, he thought of the internship, of Kronos, and of Orien. The rain tapped faster. The match flamed into life. Cole stuck it in the Twinkie, hummed "Happy Birthday," and crammed the cake into his mouth before he had time to think about how pathetic he was.

Something hard hit the door, and Cole jumped. That couldn't be the rain. The sound was repeated, more insistent this time, and Cole realized it was a knock. The hairs in his ears prickled, warning him not to go to the door, to stay hidden instead. But he told himself it was just a solicitor. All the same, what solicitor would be coming at this time of night? Already the darkness of dusk had been drawn down like a curtain at the door. The knock came a third time. Combing his fingers through his hair, Cole cleared his throat, walked to the door, and opened it. The rain angled into his face. No one was there. Had he imagined the knock because he was lonely? Cautiously, he stepped outside.

An arm flew out from his periphery and blinded him in a flurry of fabric that was being wrapped around his head and knotted at the base of his skull. Cole flailed at the air to strike back, slipped on the slick pavement, and crashed to the ground. He inhaled to yell, but a hand was clamped across his mouth. He couldn't breathe. Someone dragged him to his feet, grabbing his hands and forcing them behind his back. Hands were everywhere: over his mouth, around his wrists, on his back, shoving him forward.

A car door popped open, and Cole's heart pounded louder than the rain. If he got in the car, he'd have no way out. Would any of the neighbors be watching? Where was his dad? He planted his feet and jerked backward. For a minute he was free. Then he was shoved forward, falling into hot air and the smell of a new car. He thrashed a knee up and felt flesh, but it wasn't enough: someone was pressing him down. A seatbelt clicked across his torso and the door was slammed. He thought frantically. His phone was in his pocket, but he couldn't reach it. If only he could call Jude. A click told him the door had been locked. Then he realized his mouth was free. He tried to yell again, but his body slammed against the back of his seat as the car shot forward.

A gunshot laugh exploded in his ear.

"All right, untie his hands. Good job, you two! I didn't think that would actually work! Cole, if you could have seen the expression on your face—priceless!"

Cole's shoulders were pushed forward, and the knot

binding his hands was loosened. Only then did he realize that the knot wasn't tight enough to have actually restrained him, and that the fingers that brushed his were both gentle and soft. A muddled perfume of jasmine, acrylic paint, cardboard, and incense filled his nostrils as he remembered how to breathe again.

"Joanna? Jude? Bridget?" His voice was a quaver.

"Yes, we're all here," Joanna's voice answered, still laughing. "So I take it no one's ever kidnapped you for your birthday before?"

Cole's laugh of relief was half a sob. His heart was still beating too fast for him to talk.

"Are you okay?"

Bridget's voice was softer than Cole had ever heard it. The tickle of her breath on his ear as she finished unbinding his hands sent a thrill through his body, undoing any progress he had made in calming his heart rate.

"Bridget was afraid this wouldn't really be your style," Jude explained. "Can't say I disagree, judging by what you just did to my solar plexus. Not that Joanna cares about my solar plexus..."

"Oh quit whining. You gotta have some skin in the game."

"Says the girl who stayed in the car."

"Anyway. I told Bridget our job is to help you *make* a style. That's what friends are for. Besides, everyone needs to experience a surprise birthday party at least once in their life. I drove around the block so you wouldn't see my car, and Jude and Bridget hid on either side of the door. I'm surprised you didn't notice them. I've never seen a kidnap work so effectively."

Cole finally found his voice: "You sound like a veteran abductor. Can you take this blindfold off now?"

"Not a chance," Joanna said. "You still need to guess where we're going. The fun isn't over just yet."

"Fun" was not the word Cole would have used. His hands were still shaking, and he could feel perspiration trickling down his shoulder blades. If only he could see, he might be able to start enjoying this surprise instead of bracing against every lurch of the car and looking like a scared child in front of Bridget. He was being ridiculous. No one was going to attack him again. No one had attacked him to begin with. But he couldn't shake the feeling that there was still some presence out there in the night, waiting for him.

At last, the engine was cut. Cole's car door clicked open, and cool air kissed his cheek. The knot at the nape of his neck was loosened, and he blinked in the sudden glare of a large star. He was falling into the sky, and the dizzy thrill of it stole his breath. He was five again, waking at midnight on a camping trip with his dad, unzipping the tent on a terrifying cosmos of light and beauty.

Then Cole's feet remembered the anchor of the sidewalk, and the massive star resolved itself into a streetlight. Manicured shrubs, a well-lit lawn, and gleaming glass windows stretched before him. The rain had stopped. He knew exactly where he was. His shoulders finally relaxed, but some long-dormant part of him clung to the childhood memory of night untamed that was already a wisp as thin as the clouds that shrouded the moon. There was no danger, and there was no mystery. There was only a storefront with a sign for The Cheesecake Factory. A few brave stars shone through a veil of light pollution, but that was it. He shivered in the first breath of winter wind.

"Is it okay?" Joanna asked anxiously. "I couldn't remember your favorite restaurant, but I do know you love salad."

Cole had forgotten she was there.

"I'm joking, Cole. We're here for the cheesecake."

"It's great," Cole said automatically.

Joanna cleared her throat, and he realized she was still watching him.

Willing himself to follow the expectation of her conversation, he said, "I don't have a favorite restaurant. Actually, I can't remember the last time I ate out."

"Really? I'm surprised you and your dad don't eat out more—two guys don't cook much, I imagine!"

Cole grimaced, and the hollow inside his stomach grounded him more firmly to reality than the cement sidewalk. They didn't cook much, and they didn't eat much. Even when the freezer was stocked with frozen dinners, the food he consumed alone in his bedroom rarely left him feeling full.

"Speaking of which, where is Mr. Erickson tonight?" Bridget asked with that odd formality that reminded Cole she lived with her grandparents, Poppy and Birdy. Her voice rang through the night; the night itself seemed to listen.

"At the bar."

Cole was so disoriented that the truth escaped before he realized what he was saying. Bridget looked embarrassed, and Cole felt a flush creeping across his cheeks. Joanna started to laugh as if Cole was joking, and Jude cut in:

"No sense standing here freezing. Come on—Cole and I are going to have a cheesecake eating competition. Whoever eats the most slices without barfing wins. No basic flavors allowed."

"You're on," Cole said.

Jude was the only one who knew about his dad (Cole had shared rides to school with the Durhams before he was old enough to have a car), and whether or not the diversion had been intentional, he was going to go with it. Not looking at Bridget, Cole led the way to the door and stepped into light and noise. Music, clinking silverware, and a dozen conversations engulfed them. The mystery that had beckoned to Cole remained outside.

Joanna selected a booth by a window with a view of the patio. The patio was canopied by an ash tree with a few leaves still clinging to mostly barren limbs. As Cole was about to sit, he thought he saw a shadow pass over the grass and fade into the trunk of the tree. He squinted at it but saw only fluctuating light as people moved within the restaurant. It must have been a reflection. His mind was playing tricks on him. Nevertheless, he slid into the bench ahead of Bridget to keep an eye on the window. As she sat beside him, he caught the faint scent of incense he always associated with her, and he realized she belonged to that other world, the world of the night. How had he not known it till now? Her face looked just the same as ever, but he knew that as soon as she spoke, he would hear a hint of that hidden world. She met his eyes, and he hastily looked back at his menu.

All through dinner and all through dessert—though their conversation ranged from the art exhibits Joanna had seen on her recent trip to Washington D.C. to Jude's speculations on the latest NFL drafts—the thing outside the window waited for Cole. When they paid the bill and stood up to don their coats and hats, his heartbeat quickened with anticipation. Inevitably, it seemed to him, Joanna proposed that they go for a walk in a nearby park. He heard himself agreeing, even saw himself, as if from a distance, already taking that walk as if it was preordained.

They left Joanna's car where it was and headed straight for the park. As they walked, Cole found himself counting down each restaurant and store, clinging to the strains of music as if to a fleeting anchor of safety while Joanna, oblivious, prattled on:

"So, Cole. You're the first of us to turn seventeen. What does it feel like? Or maybe a better question is, what would you want to be different going into next year? What are your hopes before you turn eighteen and become fully an adult? Any goals? Dreams? Resolutions? Other than the internship, of course."

Cole let rote memory take the place of active cognition: "I'd like to ace the ACT so I can get into Stanford."

Even as he said it, he sensed the disconnect between his words and his will. Was that really his greatest goal for the new year, or had he just rehearsed the phrase enough that he had internalized it? He ignored the question and continued down the path.

"And what about you?" Jude said, poking Joanna in the ribs.

"Hey, watch it!" She poked him back. "What about me?"

"Are you going to follow your dreams and go to art school?"

Joanna sighed dramatically.

"It isn't that simple. My parents would disown me. I mean, why would I waste my life creating something beautiful when I could wear androgynous pant suits and trade joy for a fat paycheck? It's law school for me, or engineering, or whatever else I'm supposed to do to 'put my education to good use.'"

Somewhere in the distance, an owl hooted.

Jude shrugged. "You should just go anyway. So what if they won't pay for it? Go to some state school where you'd get a tuition break. Start working now and save up. Do whatever it takes. You're too good not to."

A grin flashed across Joanna's face. "Was that a compliment, Jude Durham?"

"No. It was a challenge."

Cole tried to attend to Joanna's reply, but it was no use—the night was talking, and the ordinary concerns of work and school held no power against it. Too soon the small security offered by the glow of traffic lights gave way to a dimly-lit park path with asphalt avenues that crumbled at the edges, then to a gravel walkway hedged closer by bushes and trees that lost their manicured edges and crept underfoot. A skeletal branch swayed over the path ahead and pointed them onward.

The park lampposts grew fewer and farther apart. The darkness swelled, and the stars shone brighter. A moan of wind snaked through the woods and into the path, where it hissed through a heap of fallen leaves and died. It was like a voice that became an ear, waiting to hear what they might say so that it could become a voice again and whisper their words to every tree and bush and stone, each of which had its own interpretation of their human presence and none of which could be assumed to be amicable. The notion was childish, and Cole shook it off. What was wrong with him tonight?

Bridget yawned widely, and Cole once again found himself gravitating to her for comfort. She was at home in this strange world, yet still strangely home-like to Cole. There was something so perfect about the shape of her diamond face and heart-shaped lips. Her beauty was like a small island of relief in the evening's confusion. He combed his fingers through his hair as a pretext for the swaying step that carried him closer to her. Suddenly, her body tensed.

"Bridget, what is it?" Joanna asked in a hushed whisper.

"I... I thought I saw someone, just there, watching us."

Bridget was gazing to their left at a spot a little way up a hill tangled with shadows. Cole saw nothing, but he felt it. It was the same presence that had waited outside his house and watched from outside the restaurant, the same force that compelled them deeper into the night.

"Who's there?" Jude called, walking a few feet off the path toward the hill.

Nothing answered but the wind, which crescendoed into a laugh and then faded into a wail. The rain began again, obscuring their vision.

"You sure you saw someone?" Jude asked, flipping the hood of his jacket up as he turned back toward Bridget.

"It could have been a trick of the light, but I did think I saw a face. And this whole time I've had the feeling of being watched."

So, Cole hadn't imagined it. Bridget hugged her corduroy coat more closely to her body. Cole wanted to wrap an arm around her, as much to warm and comfort her as to reassure himself. He stepped closer again, not caring this time if she noticed.

"No one else saw anything?" Jude asked.

Joanna shook her head. Glancing nervously up the hill, she said, "All the same, maybe it's time we head home. It looks like this rain is going to pick up."

Cole hesitated. He thought of the warmth and safety of the car, but the presence tugged at him with an almost visceral urgency. The lamppost ahead of them flickered and went out, leaving the path in darkness.

"I'll bring up the rear in case there's anything out there," Jude said.

Cole wished Jude would keep his voice down. This wasn't a time for blustering heroics, not if they didn't want to frighten off the presence that waited for them. Joanna turned back down the path, and Bridget fell into step behind her. Reluctantly, Cole followed. Around the bend, a semicircle of light from the next lamppost glazed the rain-dappled path.

Cole had a sudden urge to run to it, as if it were home base in a game of tag. But before he could do more than tell himself he was being ridiculous, a cracking branch made them all swivel around.

As they stared into the darkness, the shroud of rain clouds was unfurled from the face of the moon. In its light they saw a bent figure on the hill ahead. Cole recognized it at once as the presence he had sensed all night. But it was so withered that its unexpected vulnerability tempered his fear with compassion.

"What do you want?" Jude called.

Cole winced at the loudness of his voice, but the figure remained exactly where it was, a primordial sentinel of the night. Then, in a rasping voice like the creak of a tree limb, it said: "I want nothing from you." The voice was too low for a woman's, but the ragged folds of a skirt dragged at her feet. A gnarled finger as brittle as a twig emerged from the shawl to point at them. It gleamed garishly in the moonlight. "What I want is Nicholas Erickson."

Cole had known all night that what waited outside had waited for *him*, but he couldn't quite believe he wasn't dreaming. He tried to laugh, but the sound was hollow. The path before them became paler in the moonlight, and it seemed to Cole that the stranger stared so hard she saw inside his skin.

Finally, she said, "I want to speak of Vincent Vendler and what he hid in your academy."

CHAPTER 9

WHAT VENDLER HID

A frozen wind drove dampened forest debris across the path, then subsided suddenly as if listening for Cole's reply. A supernatural premonition of his own destiny thrilled through Cole's veins. Orien had mentioned Vendler too. What if this woman knew something that could help him with the internship?

"What do you know about Vendler?" he asked, his voice quiet with suppressed excitement.

The woman hissed, "Not here!"

She turned abruptly, hobbling off the path and up the hill with surprising vigor. Her movements were as swift and noiseless as an animal's.

"What's that all about?" Joanna asked. "Do you know her, Cole?"

He shook his head.

"More importantly," Bridget interjected. "How does she know you?"

The woman had paused, her body angled toward them in

magnetic anticipation. Why hadn't he been more surprised when she said his name?

"What do we do now?" Joanna asked, glancing up the hill.

"Well for starters, we don't play a mind game with a stranger," Jude said. Raising his voice, he yelled over the rain, "Give us one good reason why we can't talk here. No one's around but us."

"You must see for yourselves."

"See what?"

"Not here!" she hissed again.

Jude crossed his arms and planted his feet farther apart. Cole knew what that meant: Jude was gearing up for a stand-off, and Cole panicked. He knew that if he stepped off the path, something fundamental within him might shift. Already something inside him—some deeply buried impulse like genetic memory—was listening to the call of the night.

Before Jude could get too entrenched in his position, Cole said: "She's just an old woman. It can't hurt to humor her. Besides, she might really know something."

"All right, fine," Jude said. "It's four against one. We can take her if it comes to it. Joanna, Bridget?"

Joanna nodded nervously.

"I don't think we'll be in *physical* danger," Bridget said.

The emphasis she put on the word "physical" made Cole's neck prickle. But he had already decided. The instant he moved toward the woman, she disappeared behind another tree. They followed her over the orange carpet of leaves, the woman walking always a few paces ahead, slipping almost out of sight. The slope climbed steadily upward, gently down, then up a steep hill. As the lights from the lampposts grew dimmer, the forest grew thicker. Young trees scraped their legs and faces. Patches of navy sky were barely visible through the boughs of latticed treetops as rain gave way to starlight.

The soft tap of water on fallen leaves amplified the squelch of their shoes and made Cole uncomfortably aware that they were the only foreign creatures in a listening night.

The monotony of climbing up and down, of scrambling over rotten logs, of sliding backward on wet leaves and not knowing where they were going or when they would arrive should have made the minutes drag, but Cole felt more awake than he had all day. Every time Jude checked his watch, Cole quickened his pace. Why he was willing to walk miles past midnight on what his rational mind told him was a fool's errand, he couldn't say. He only knew that every step that drew him deeper into the forest drew him closer to a suppressed mystery in his own spirit, an unfamiliar animation in his own body.

Joanna stumbled, and Cole was immediately by her side, helping her up and on before Jude could say anything. Five minutes later, she stumbled again.

"This is getting ridiculous," Jude grumbled. "Hey! How much farther are you taking us? We're going home if you don't tell us what this is all about."

Cole opened his mouth to protest, but the woman turned around, and his words died on his tongue. For the first time, they saw her face clearly in the moonlight. Her skin was as rough and wrinkled as the bark of an old tree. Her eyes, bulbous and amber, were like two hardened drops of sap oozing from an old wound. It was the face from Cole's nightmare, and his heart froze.

"So close now," she said, leading the way down another hill.

"I'm getting fed up with this. Anyone else ready to turn around?" Jude asked.

"Just a little farther," Cole urged. The dread of recognizing the woman's face only confirmed that he was meant to meet her. He would regret this moment forever if he didn't see it through. "She says we're almost there, and we've already come all this way."

Jude frowned at Joanna, and she gave a tiny nod. Bridget only yawned again and shrugged.

"Fine," Jude said. "But if we don't get there in ten, we're going home."

Not bothering to reply, Cole marched up the hill. He was so rapt in his determination that he almost walked into the woman, who had halted abruptly. Catching himself, he looked up to see an ancient wooden shack. Ash trees had grown up against its walls, their branches invading the windows. The shack leaned badly to the west from decades of wind and rain, yet like the woman, it was impossibly erect. An uncomfortable lump of guilt formed in Cole's throat, as if he ought to have done something to prevent her living here.

The woman led the way up its rickety steps, one of which had collapsed into splinters. Striking a match with shaking fingers, she lit a candle stationed by the door. Its light illuminated a hall plastered with sullied yellow wallpaper that curled upward at the baseboards. A strong smell of urine, body odor, and mildew filled the house. As the candlelight glided along the hallway, a startlingly lifelike painting of a dog arrested Cole mid-stride. He could almost see the fur rising and falling in rhythm with the dog's breathing. Its unearthly aliveness seemed to symbolize the mysterious premonition that had led them here.

Bridget's arm brushed his, and he realized she was watching him with the X-ray stare that always made his stomach lurch in a way that wasn't entirely unpleasant. He twitched a smile at her and tore his gaze away from the painting. Beside it hung an oval photograph of a young woman giggling immoderately. Something about her childish expression didn't match the maturity of her body, and Cole passed quickly by.

The hall emerged into a bare kitchen with a wooden table and two chairs. The woman lit a second candle that was rooted to the table by hardened streams of melted wax. When she blew out the hall candle, spittle came with the breath. Dropping heavily into a chair, she motioned for Cole to take the other. Cole slipped his hands into his pockets.

"Does anyone else want to sit?"

"No!" The woman barked. "It is for you to sit. You only were invited."

Cole glanced apologetically at Joanna, who was leaning against a wall, fingering a scratch on her cheek, and Bridget, who had already collapsed cross-legged on the warped linoleum floor. Bridget's hair was dripping pitifully with rain water, and Cole realized maybe Jude hadn't been overprotective—maybe it was Cole who had been selfish in making them come all this way. He'd better oblige the woman and get them out of here as soon as possible.

"Where are we?" Jude asked, glancing at the archaic furnishings. His eyes lit on a dust-covered stove next to a 1940s refrigerator. "You have electricity up here? Then why the candles?"

"Your friend is very inquisitive," the old woman said coldly, still addressing Cole.

As she stared at him in the flickering candlelight, Cole noticed that her left eye wandered while her right was clouded with cataracts. He wondered whether habit alone enabled her to navigate her house and the woods so confidently.

"He means nothing by it," Joanna said in a small voice.

The woman ignored Joanna completely. Her eyes combed Cole hungrily as though searching for a feature they recognized. "I have desired to meet you for seventeen years, Nicholas Erickson."

"I know." Cole cleared his throat. Why had he just said that?

She continued in a sing-song tone: "Yes, I have sought you for many years. And your father before you. For forty-four long years, we have all been parted. It was your father who kept us apart. Until tonight."

"My father?" Cole repeated. What did his father have to do with Vendler Academy? As he stared into her foggy eyes, it occurred to him that the woman sitting across from him might, after all, be just a little bit mad. But if that were the case, how did she know so much about him?

"Look here," Jude interrupted, throwing his arms out impatiently. "We're all tired. Can't you just tell us what you know about Vendler and we'll get out of your hair?"

The woman cackled with macabre delight and unwrapped her turban-like headscarf to reveal a completely bald, grossly mottled scalp. Joanna clamped a hand over her mouth to stifle a gasp, and Cole began to regret the last few bites of cheesecake he had eaten.

"Very funny," Jude said.

The woman's laughter died abruptly. "Must they be party to our conversation?"

"Yes, they must," Jude replied. His eyes were determined slits.

Cole glanced warningly at Jude and said, "We promise not to interrupt until you've said your piece. Can you tell me about what Vendler hid at my school?"

The woman sighed. "The tale is long. And it begins before either you or your father were thought of." Her eyes searched the timber walls as if looking for a sign that would tell her how to start. In a dead voice, she began: "My father built this house. He worked the mines. We lived in the city, but it became unbearable. He wanted somewhere private, somewhere that would protect my mother from ridicule. Our kindest neighbors called her strange. Others treated her like an animal. My father was ashamed and angry. She had suffered, and she was punished for her suffering. I never knew what happened to warp her mind—I had always known her this way, but father remembered her different. Cruelty drove us to the forest. Finally, it was only the three of us, and we were content.

"Then the war came. Father was called to work extra shifts. When he came home, we had little food to give him. Then, he was taken to fight. I walked to town in search of work. I said I was a war widow and begged for help, but no one believed me. I was only fourteen. I told myself every day that tomorrow the war would end and father would come home. But when the war ended, he did not come. He was gone forever. He left my mother pregnant.

"We called the baby Acalia—a name my father loved. I thought that child would break me, but when she was born, she was so beautiful I forgot my pain. I wanted only to protect her. It was even harder to find work with so many men returning from the war, but I taught myself to type, and I was taken on as a clerk. At last we had money and food. No one bothered us, and we lived happily again."

She paused as if reluctant to narrate beyond this memory. Cole found it difficult to believe that this woman, who seemed much more in need of care than capable of giving it, had ever held down a job. Yet she had at least accomplished survival. Her gaze turned from the timber walls back to Cole, and he shivered. There was fire in her eyes, but death also.

"Then polio came. My mother was still young, but it

claimed her. I don't know how she got it; since the day father left, she never saw anyone but Acalia and me.

"I dug her grave myself. I knew enough of the world by then to expect neither pity nor help. I wanted only to be left alone, and to care for Acalia. I was sixteen, and she was just weaned. I knew no one who could watch her, and I could not take her to work. I gave up my job and began working night shifts cleaning at the hospital. It meant leaving Acalia alone at night and making do with scant snatches of sleep during the day. Days and nights melded. I was always terrified when I was away that Acalia would come to harm, that I would not be there when she needed me. But the hospital was good, and whenever I needed it there was food to take that the patients didn't eat. No one knew, and no one cared. Somehow, we survived.

"Acalia grew more beautiful each day, but also more strange. She had very little language. But I always knew what she wanted, and she could always understand me. No one else mattered.

"What troubled me was her mind. Signs that she was our mother's daughter grew daily more apparent. She used to pretend to cast herself into the well, and the more terrified I became, the more she laughed and the more recklessly she teetered on its edge. I learned not to react, though ignoring her meant I could not be near to catch her should she ever lose her balance and fall. I knew that if she did, I would fall in after her for punishment and for relief. I knew I could not live without her. But life teaches us to do what is impossible."

A tear trickled down the woman's cheek, catching and sliding sideways in a deep wrinkle. Cole wondered how long it had been since she had talked of her sister, or if she had ever talked of her.

"Every year it was harder to keep her within the confines

of our woods. I knew that if she ever strayed, if anyone ever saw her, she would be treated as my mother had been, or taken from me. But my secret fears were too naïve to prepare me for what came next."

A tremor seized the woman's body, emanating from her chest down to her hands. Her voice was thick when she spoke again, but the cadence was the same.

"I was walking up to the house one morning after work. The sun was rising. I knew at once something was wrong. Acalia was sixteen then, and for years she had waited for me at the top of the hill, but that day she did not come. The house was strangely quiet. As I stepped out of the trees, a man I had never seen came out of the house, my house, almost as if he had been waiting for me. He did not seem surprised to see me. He was old, and his eyes frightened me.

"I yelled at him to go. He merely laughed. Then he said, 'I have given her a gift. I have given her life purpose.' I ought to have stayed, to have questioned him about who he was and how he had found us, but I was too terrified. I had to know that Acalia was well. I ran inside and found her half naked on the bedroom floor. Her eyes were shut tight. She was moaning softly. By her side was a strange object that did not belong to us—a picture of a dog. She did not have to tell me. I knew what had happened. I knew he had raped her.

"I hated him. I wanted to find him, to hurt him. But I could never abandon Acalia again, not even for a moment. It was my dearest wish that she would not become pregnant, but life has always run against my desires. He knew she would bear his child. It was clear in his eyes that he knew.

"The day of her delivery drew near. I was there by her side, comforting her and telling her she would live. The labor began, and it was horrible. She was in pain far greater than she could bear. She did not understand why. She did not know what was happening.

"I did everything I could to comfort her, but Acalia could find no relief from her torture. The sun rose and set, and the night grew pale again with dawn before she bore a son. At first, all seemed well. But then Acalia grew stranger still. She began convulsing, and there was nothing I could do. Her beautiful face turned blue. She could not breathe. I held her and talked to her and gave her air through my own mouth, but nothing helped. She died in my arms. The child began to cry."

"But who was the man? Did you ever find out?" Joanna broke in.

This time the woman seemed too defeated to care that it was not Cole who had asked the question. "Oh yes, I found out. After she died, my hatred grew stronger. He had taken her life, and I wanted nothing more than to take his in return. I searched for the only clues I had left of him—the strange painting of the dog that lay in the room beside my sister, and a letter. In an attempt to purge his memory from our house, I had hidden them in the attic. But now I found and cleaned them. The letter instructed the child to find and finish his work, and on the back of the canvas was written a name— Vincent Vendler."

Joanna gasped. "The same...?"

"Yes. I walked the streets with the baby and inquired everywhere. Before long I found someone who had known the man. He introduced me to a librarian, who showed me a photograph of him on a book. It was the same man. To my surprise, he was well known. In some circles, he was even well liked, for he was wealthy and had given money to fund an educational academy."

"Our academy," Cole said, and the woman nodded. Cole

hadn't liked the egotistical tone of Vendler's autobiography, but he had never imagined him to be so grotesque in his personal life. He swallowed the acrid taste in his mouth.

Joanna, leaning forward like a child being told a bed-time story, asked, "So what happened next? Did you find him?"

"No. He had been terminally ill, and as he was so old, there was nothing they could do to stop the spread of the cancer. He died just before my sister. Murdering her was his final act. I could not even find his grave to pour my vengeance upon the bitter earth, for none knew where he was buried. They say he knew his end was near and wandered off somewhere so no one could witness the disgrace of his death. His corpse was never found."

Bridget's bell-like voice pierced the spellbound silence. "What happened to the baby?"

"The baby!" the woman echoed, and the words came out as a wail. At last, the flood of dammed anger broke. She rocked silently in her seat, trying to master her emotion. Finally, in a choked voice, she said, "Vendler defeated me not once, but twice. My foray into town to find him and avenge my sister was futile, and it led to renewed whispers of the strange woman who lived alone in the hills with an innocent baby boy who was not her own. He was taken from me, adopted by a family who never knew my sister, his mother, and who did not care to know his only living relation. He was taken, and there was nothing I could do. I protested, I followed the family, I insisted that he grow up with me, or at least knowing me, but no one listened. The family threatened to have me arrested if I persisted in my attempts at contact.

"I retreated, beaten but not defeated. I determined to wait until the child grew, to keep an eye on him from a distance and to contact him again when he was old enough to decide for himself.

"But I had not counted on the pernicious influence of the people he called his family. I had not realized they would condition him to hate the truth. I thought he would want to hear his history, to find his family, but time and again he refused to see me, refused even to speak to me or read the letters I wrote. My whole life I have waited and hoped, met defeat, and tried again. Now is my last attempt."

Silence fell, and her eyes fastened on Cole. It was a struggle not to shrink away from their intensity.

"Look, I'm very sorry about your sister and the child, but... well, what does all of this have to do with me?"

"Everything!" she cried, slamming her fist on the table. The candle quavered. "It has everything to do with you! Have you not been listening? My sister's child is your father—Robert Erickson!"

CHAPTER 10

THE WARNING

Cole couldn't breathe. The kitchen walls were closing in on him, suffocating him with the reek of mildew and urine. His reason, which had been suspended during the woman's story, now rushed to his defense. Why should he believe that this strange woman, whom he had never seen or even heard of before in his life, was not as insane as she looked? If Vincent Vendler were really his grandfather, wouldn't he know? Yes, his father had been adopted as a baby. But to say that those parents were Acalia and Vincent Vendler... surely there was no logical connection, was there? He took a great gulp of air, held it stiffly in his lungs, and stood up.

"Forgive me," he said, "but I find all of this very hard to believe. At least, I don't know what to believe. We should be going."

"No!" The woman screamed. She rose from her chair and stumbled toward Cole, her grubby fingers clawing at his shirt. "You cannot leave me! And your grandmother—how can you turn your back when you've only just found her?"

Offering a hand to help Bridget up from the floor, Jude said, "Cole has just informed you of his decision. I suggest you accept it."

"I can handle this," Cole said. Why was he so angry? Jude was only trying to back up Cole's decision, after all. Water seeped from the woman's clouded eyes, and he was angry about that, too.

"At least let me show you one final thing, one final reminder before you go," she croaked.

"Fine," Cole said before Jude could reply. Maybe if she showed him whatever proof she thought she had, he could debunk it and walk away as if none of this had ever happened.

Clinging to his arm as though afraid he might change his mind, she marched him out the door and back down the dilapidated steps. The wind had blown back the clouds to reveal a crescent moon. It cast an iridescent glow on the tree-tops, which rose to meet them like an amorphous specter in a nightmare.

"Where are you taking me?" Cole asked. He was dimly aware that Joanna and Jude were following at a distance.

The woman led him down a hill and a little to the left, stopping about twenty yards from the house. She grabbed Cole's other arm and turned him firmly back toward the house. What was he supposed to be seeing? He looked at her for a clue, then followed her gaze to a weathered rock embedded in the hill. Catching his breath, he read aloud: "'Here lies Acalia Maria Lehmann, beloved sister of Alexandria. 1957-1974. Never forgotten.' She's... buried here?"

Alexandria nodded. "You may choose to deny the past like your father, but you had to see before you made that decision."

Cole stared at the uneven letters chiseled painstakingly into the rock. It looked like moss had recently been torn away from the stone. So Acalia was real. She had lived and breathed, loved and feared, suffered and died. His chest clenched. His dad had never told him anything about his birth family, other than that both parents had died and no living relations were capable of caring for him. Was it really such a fantastical story after all?

"Why couldn't it be true?" Realizing he had spoken aloud, he changed his question. "But why did you bring me here tonight? What do you want from me? And how did you know you would find me?"

"You are right," she replied, gazing at his face in the moonlight. She still retained a death grip on his elbow. The wind wailed, but her whisper cut through it. "I do want more. Listen to me, Nicholas Erickson." As she said it, she stepped between Cole and the tombstone. Her breath was putrid in his nostrils. "I do not know what Vendler hid in that school, but whatever he hid, he meant you to find it. You must find it. And you must destroy it."

"But..." his mind reeled. Even if he believed her story about his father, what proof was there that Vendler had left him some kind of legacy? If Vendler had wanted to leave him something, why hadn't he just given it to Alexandria?

"Listen, Nicholas, the way he treated my sister... it wasn't lust. He meant to leave seed. He meant to be remembered. He left a letter saying his son would find what he left in the library of Vendler Academy. He meant to be found."

"So where's the letter?"

"I don't have it anymore. I—"

Cole let out a harsh bark of laughter. "Of course you don't."

"I gave it to your father."

Cole took a step back as the woman took a step forward. She was squeezing him so tightly his hand went cold.

"I don't know what your father did with it, but there are other proofs—after Acalia died, I found out everything about Vendler that I could. His autobiography is full of self-important hints, promising a legacy still to be realized."

"But... I didn't pick up on that when I read it." As Cole said it, he realized he hadn't properly read the book at all—he had scanned it for quotations about the academic findings of Vincent Vendler and been disappointed. Only now did he stop to consider whether the vague hints were intentional rather than egotistical self-aggrandizing. Grasping at the next unknown, he continued, "But how did you find me? How did you know I would be at the park tonight?"

"I did not," she replied, her face splitting into a manic grin that revealed several rotten teeth. "I did not know, but for many years now, I have hoped, and I have searched, and I have waited. I wrote your father many times after you were born, but always he refused to let me meet you. I wrote to you directly, but I assume he never let those letters through."

Cole's pulse raced. That sounded likely enough. What right did his dad think he had to shelter Cole from an unpleasant truth when he had made Cole's whole life unbearable?

"I came to your school many times, but I could never get at you. I even attempted to break in once, to find what Vendler hid and to destroy it myself, but the alarms sounded and I was forced to retreat. So I have kept to watching your house and haunting public places, praying to find you one day and to pass on my mission. Tonight, my prayer was answered. My time is almost over. There is little I can do to avenge Acalia's memory. But you... with you there is still much time, and much hope."

She wanted too much. Her eyes were so hungry he felt he

would be devoured. Cole closed his eyes, trying to think logically about everything she had told him.

"But if Vendler left something, why do you think it should be destroyed? Why can't we just leave it alone?"

"Have you not listened to what I told you?"

Cole flinched at the explosion of spittle in his face.

"Vendler was evil, and everything he did was evil. I do not know what he hid, but I am certain that it is dangerous and that it must be destroyed before its curse can inflict further harm. And you, Nicholas, you must do it. I failed. Your father failed. You are the only one left. It is your burden now to atone for his sins. His curse must not be ignored by us for someone else to find; it must be destroyed beyond hope of resurrection so that Acalia and I, and you, and your father, can rest in peace. It is your duty, and yours alone. You must find what he hid.

"The letter was clear: go to the library, take his autobiography, touch him, say his name. Then you will find it. And when you find it, you will destroy it."

Her grip grew stronger still and her voice more agitated. All Cole wanted was to get away.

"Destroy it, Nicholas! It is your birthright and your burden! Do you understand?"

"Yes, I... I understand."

At his words, she released an enormous sigh that carried the weight of decades of grief and rage. She seemed to shrink into her layers of shawls, a fragile old woman who had finally received permission to die.

Joanna must have seen the transformation, for she emerged from the shadows and offered the woman her arm for support. It was accepted. Jude came up and supported her on the other side. Cole watched as the three figures hobbled toward the house. He wondered where Bridget was. He wished she was at his side, holding him as Jude and Joanna held Alexandria. He felt exhausted, as if the woman's sigh had entered his bones and aged him with its grief.

When they reentered the kitchen, Bridget was sitting on the floor right where they had left her. The woman collapsed into her chair. There seemed to be no more to say. In silent agreement, the four friends saw themselves out. As Cole stepped toward the door, he glanced back to see Alexandria's eyes locked on him.

"Do not forget," she whispered.

His last impression was of a pitiful, faded skeleton shrunken into garments like graveclothes. He had followed the call of the night, and it had shown him the truth. Yet instead of relief, a terrible weight pressed on his chest. He felt Alexandria would not be released from life until he did as she asked.

CHAPTER 11

BEHIND THE WALL

Why hadn't his dad told him? Why had he abandoned Alexandria, the only blood relative they had, to die alone? Was he trying to protect Cole from the ugliness of it all? To pretend they were not descended from a madman who had raped an insane woman and left her to die? Was he trying to hide the inevitable truth that, because of the very marrow in their bones, there was something fundamentally wrong with them? Questions had kept Cole awake all night and distracted him from his studies all day. Now that it was study hall, they drove him once more toward the library. He started when Joanna's hand slipped inside his elbow, quickening his pace.

"Are you ready for this? I don't know about you, but I couldn't sleep a wink last night wondering what it might be. Do you think it's treasure? I thought so at first, but then I realized it has to be something more exotic, or it wouldn't be so hush-hush and urgent. Maybe Vendler's still alive somewhere, but in hiding, you know, since he disappeared, and he left you a map to find him? I wonder if we'll be the first ones ever to solve a mystery that's been hiding under the noses of hundreds of students for generations!"

"Two generations."

"That's what I said. Do you think that's the whole reason Vendler bought this place and started the school? To leave you whatever it is we're going to find today?"

"No idea."

Last night, in an attempt to divert the conversation from his personal affiliation with Vendler, Cole had told them about Vendler hiding something for his dad in the library, but he was beginning to regret it now.

When they walked into the library lounge, Bridget and Jude were already there. An impending storm darkened the sky so that the library air pressed closer than ever. The lamp's glow cut the darkness in a definitive orb. Bridget sat inside the light on the blush loveseat, hugging her backpack to her chest, while Jude paced in front of the fireplace.

"There you are," Jude said. He glanced at Joanna's arm in Cole's, and Cole drew away from her. "We'd better quit wasting time and get started if we want to explore before Mrs. Fay does her top of the hour patrol."

"Right," Cole said.

Now that he was here, he wasn't sure he really wanted to find what Vendler had left. But after last night, he wouldn't find peace until he knew. As he grasped Vendler's autobiography, the blood in his palm pulsed palpably as if his heartbeat was passing through his hand into the book and back again into his body. Vendler's painting watched him with electric anticipation.

Taking a steadying breath, Cole touched the painting above the fireplace and said, "Vendler."

A soft crack slit the silence. The painting swung open to reveal a dark cavity in the wall behind it. Joanna gasped, and both Cole and Jude stepped back in surprise. The painting was suspending itself, the left side of its frame attached to the wall without any visible hangings. Where Cole expected to see a hook on the painting or a nail on the wall, there was nothing. The air that emanated from the cavity where the wall should have been was damp and heavy. It tingled Cole's skin and tickled his throat, at once cautioning and enticing him.

Glancing over his shoulder to ensure they were still alone, he stepped closer to peer inside. The cavity was completely black. He stretched a hand out, half expecting to feel some invisible parcel. Instead, he met only emptiness. Whatever Vendler had left for him must be hidden somewhere in the darkness, just beyond his reach. His fingers itched with anticipation.

Joanna pushed up beside him, standing on tip-toe to see inside. "What's in there?"

"I don't feel a thing," Cole said.

"Here, budge over," Jude said, picking up a decorative fire poker and extending it into the hole. When he had reached about as far in as his elbow, the poker scraped the opposite wall. "Not big. Maybe a little over a yard? I wonder how deep it is..." He dangled the poker downward, but there was no answering scrape.

"You should have reached the floor on the other side," Cole said. "Don't you feel anything?" Curiosity, faint at first from disuse, was making his words tumble out faster.

Jude extricated himself with a grunt. "Nothing. Let's try a sound test." He took up a tarnished paperweight that lay on the mantel ledge and dropped it into the hole.

A second later, they heard the clatter of metal on stone.

"It can't be that far down," Jude said. "I'm going in."

Without waiting to see if Cole wanted to go first since it

was his legacy, Jude shoved the armchair in front of the fire-place, climbed onto it, and hoisted himself onto the mantel ledge. Gripping the mantel rim, he lowered himself into the hole until his arms were fully extended.

"This is so exciting!" Joanna whispered. "I bet we're breaking so many rules!"

"There's something... metal, against the wall," Jude grunted. "It's scraping my knees. I... hang on! It's a ladder!" He shifted his weight and began to climb down.

Cole saw his hand for a second, and then Jude slipped into total darkness. There was nothing but the rhythmic tap of tennis shoes, then a soft shuffling.

"I'm at the bottom," Jude said, his voice a staccato of adrenaline. "But I can't see a thing,"

"We're coming too," Joanna said. Her mouth was frozen in a grin as she climbed from the chair to the ledge and disappeared into the hole. Cole climbed onto the chair after her.

"Cole, wait."

He glanced back at Bridget, who looked away as if embarrassed. Her fingers were fidgeting with her backpack zipper. For some reason, she seemed nervous.

"You coming?" he said.

She looked at him again. "Cole, do you think this will help?" The characteristic certainty had vanished from her voice.

"Help what?"

"I mean, is finding whatever Vendler left you going to help you come to terms with last night?"

He stared at her, both flattered and unnerved that she seemed to see right through him. He knew Bridget wouldn't be satisfied with anything but the truth, but right now, with Joanna and Jude finding Vendler's legacy without him, was not the time. He shrugged. "I'm just curious about what he left, that's all."

"Cole! Bridget!" Joanna's voice floated up from the hole, oddly muffled. "Bring your phones so we can use the flashlights. It's pitch black down here."

Bridget was still staring at him.

"Bridget, I need some clue. I need to know why Vendler did what he did... why my dad never..." He cleared his throat. "Yeah, I guess I am hoping it will help."

"Okay." She nodded. "Okay. Then go, just... be prepared. Whatever you find, it might make things even harder."

"You're not coming?"

"I'll stay here as lookout."

"Thanks."

Obeying a deep impulse that ran against his better judgment, Cole climbed onto the armchair and placed a knee on the mantel ledge. He expected the darkness to clear before him as he descended, but it didn't. He only knew he had reached the bottom when his foot struck solid ground. Still grasping the ladder with one hand to orient himself, he extended his hand to feel the wall behind it. Brick rough as a cat's tongue licked his fingers till, tracing a crag downward, he felt a stone floor coated in fine dust. He took a tentative step away from the ladder and tripped on the uneven ground.

The air moved, and he felt Joanna's breath on his shoulder.

"Did you bring your flashlight?"

He tapped the light on, revealing their pale faces. Something glinted on the wall behind them, and he raised the light toward it. A giant was towering over them, its jeweled armor glinting in the light, snakes writhing at its feet. Jude and Joanna gasped, and Cole staggered back into the ladder, hitting his elbow hard. The pain sharpened his senses, and he realized that what he had taken to be a gigantic man was in fact a fourteen-foot mosaic pillar composed of brilliantly pigmented rectangles, indigo on gold and ruby on cyan. The column curved inward from a wide base, which was anchored to the floor by a mass of something like tree roots. Near the top, the column looked like the vertebrae of a backbone. It was obviously not intended to look human, but there was something so animistic about it that Cole shivered. He felt as though he recognized this column from the page of some forgotten book. In this cold cavern, the blues and reds pulsed with a warmth like blood in veins.

"It's so... real, isn't it?" Joanna whispered. "God, I wish I could paint like that."

"You can," said Jude. "You do."

"You know what it is, don't you?" Joanna asked. "It's the column in our school crest, the one in stained glass at the top of the princess staircase."

She was right. Cole just hadn't recognized it at first because of how brilliantly colored and enormous it was. But what did it mean? He reached out and touched the tesserae, and all at once the gigantic impression shrank into its constituent parts. The indigo tile of the column's base was just cut glass. The gold protrusions near its top, so human a second ago, were just fragile shards formed out of everyday, nameable materials composed of everyday, nameable molecules. The darkness thickened once more, and Cole glanced up to see Bridget's silhouette in the box of daylight above.

"Someone's coming! Get up here fast!"

Joanna reacted first, scrambling up the ladder a little too noisily. Behind her came Cole, Jude bringing up the rear. No sooner had Jude swung the painting shut over the hole than a fresh-faced freshman stepped into the lounge. Coloring deeply at having attracted the attention of four unknown upperclassmen, he withdrew to a nearby desk. He was followed by Mrs. Fay, who held a wooden yardstick that she beat against her palm like a policeman's club. Her black, bird-like eyes scanned the lounge and lit upon the armchair.

Extending her yardstick to point at it, she said, "Someone has been moving my chair."

Cole imagined her mentally drafting one of her many cardstock signs: *Libraries are not places for libertines to take liberties.* He hastily repositioned the armchair and bowed his head in penance.

Then she looked at Vendler's painting. Cole froze. He could just see a small crack between the frame and the wall.

With the silent fury of an impending storm, Mrs. Fay glided toward the hearth. She stopped a foot from it, staring hard. Then she stooped and picked something up from the floor. Cole's heart began to beat again. It was only one of her cardstock signs, this one overlaid in a spidery ink that read *Books are for reading, not sullying—no food or drink in the library.*

She replaced it on the mantel and, with a glare that swept over all four of them and came to rest on the unwitting back of the freshman's head, said, "I would thank students not to displace my signs."

Cole held his breath until she drifted behind a row of books to realign them against her yardstick. Glancing at the freshman, he pressed the frame firmly against the wall. He could see the question in Bridget's eyes. Joanna, still grinning, leaned over to her to whisper something, but Cole shook his head, nodding at the freshman. He pulled out a book, and the others followed suit, pretending to study until, at last, the bell sounded.

As soon as they were outside the library, Bridget whispered, "Well?"

"Just a mosaic of the school crest, but it looked oddly alive," Cole said.

Bridget frowned, a cute dimple creasing her chin. "There has to be more down there than that. I wonder if the mosaic itself means something. Or maybe it does something, and we can't see it yet because of what we perceive to be possible."

Cole stared at her. He had heard that phrase before. "It's funny you say that, because Orien said something similar. And you know what's weird? At the end of our interview, he asked me if I knew anything about Vendler. I didn't think anything of it, but now I'm remembering he asked Paul too. And then after last night... I don't know, do you think I should tell him about what we just found?"

"Cole, if he asked both you and Paul, he will definitely want to know about this!" Joanna exclaimed. "What a great opportunity to prove your initiative and show him you deserve a second interview! Don't wait till he reaches out—be proactive and send him an email!"

Cole didn't answer right away.

"What are you thinking, Cole?" Bridget asked.

"It's just, I want to find what Vendler left me, if he left me anything. And I don't want someone to stop us from going back in. Besides, we all found it together, didn't we? It wouldn't be right for me to tell him unless we all agreed."

Jude thumped Cole on the back, but Joanna rounded on Cole, planting herself in front of him and grabbing both of his arms. Several students bumped into Cole as they tried to side-step Joanna's traffic jam.

"Cole Erickson! If you think we're going to stand here and let you waste an opportunity to prove yourself to Orien Saint-Pierre when this internship is everything you've ever wanted, you've got a sad idea of friendship." She glared at Jude and Bridget as if daring them to disagree, then directed the spotlight of her gaze back on Cole. "You write to him as soon as you get home and tell him everything, do you understand? You do have his email, right?"

"I... I'm sure I can find it. But... it might seem really impertinent if it isn't actually important. Or it might mean we lose our chance to explore again."

"Or it might mean Orien Saint-Pierre is impressed that you took initiative and followed up on his question, recognizes that you're a genius for finding a secret passageway no one else in this school seems to know about, offers you the internship, and..."

Joanna broke off, her eyes fixed on a spot behind Cole's shoulder. Cole followed her gaze and saw the inquisitive eyes of the freshman they had seen in the library. Cole wheeled Joanna around and kept walking, annoyed at her and himself. No one said anything until they were standing on the edge of the parking lot.

"How much do you think he heard?" Cole whispered.

"I don't know, but at least he won't know how to get in," Jude said.

"Provided the portrait re-sealed itself," Bridget added.

"Even if he did hear me, he probably has no idea what I was talking about. We were out of there before he saw us." Joanna sounded a lot more confident than she looked.

"We need to be more careful," Cole said, frowning at her.

"Anyway, I still think you should tell Orien Saint-Pierre."

"We found it together," Cole said again, fixing on the easiest objection. "I'm not doing it unless Jude and Bridget agree."

"Personally," Jude said, "I think we should keep exploring on our own. But it's your legacy and your internship, so it's your call."

Cole rubbed his temples. Either way, he could lose an important opportunity. "Bridget?"

Bridget was watching the flow of the students in the parking lot as an augur might watch birds of omen. Heavy clouds shrouded the sun, and the pressure in the air that had been mounting all day seemed about to break with a deluge of rain. "If you want my advice, I wouldn't disclose too much too soon to Dr. Saint-Pierre. We don't know him, and we don't know why he's asking about Vendler."

"He's asking because he's cultivated a habit of lifelong learning, which seems pretty legitimate," Cole said, his statement inflected as a question. He watched her face for some clue, but she gave him nothing.

"It's settled then," Joanna concluded.

A mist descended as Cole walked to his car, but no rain broke. The indecisive sky veiled familiar trees and buildings in fog. Cole saw his dad's car in the driveway, but he successfully avoided an encounter on the way to his room. Closing the bedroom door, he headed straight for his desk and opened his computer, staring at his inbox and thinking of Orien. His phone lit up with a text from Joanna that contained only Orien's email address. Cole smiled at her determination and typed it into the recipient line, just in case.

Someone knocked on his door, and Cole instinctively pulled up a new tab to hide the email.

"Cole, you in there?"

Cole stared at the door in disbelief. He couldn't remember the last time his dad had initiated a conversation, much less visited Cole's room.

"What's up?" he asked.

"I thought we could talk."

The voice sounded sober, but Cole's senses were hyperalert as he opened the door a few inches. His dad was leaning with one shoulder against the wall, his still powerful shoulders blocking the hallway, filling it with the scent of aftershave and booze. He shot Cole a disarming grin, but it was forced and fell quickly from his face. The quick, intelligent eyes avoided Cole's.

"What's going on? Is everything ok?" Cole asked, glancing at his dad's hands for any sign of volatility. One hand was safely in his jeans pocket. The other held Layla's wedding announcement. A rush of pain tightened Cole's chest, then became a question like hope.

"Sure. I just... thought you should know about this."

His dad's hand was shaking now, and Cole wanted to reach out and steady it. Instead, he said, "I know. I got one too."

"Oh." His dad straightened up from his position against the wall as if to leave, but he didn't turn back down the hall.

Inexplicably, a childhood memory of Friday pizza night with his dad seized Cole with a visceral poignancy, the scent of grease and the taste of salt teasing his lips into a smile.

"Dad, do you want to have dinner together tonight?"

"Tonight?" The hand in his jeans pocket reached up to scratch the nape of his neck.

Cole couldn't bring himself to look at his dad's face; he was already kicking himself for asking.

His dad cleared his throat. "I actually need to run some errands and put some things in order downstairs. Maybe another time."

That's when Cole realized his dad must have received the wedding announcement weeks ago, just like he had. Why had it taken his dad so long to talk to Cole about it? Was that so hard to do?

"Fine. I have an email to write anyway."

Cole closed the door on his dad's relieved face. Orien was

right. It was better to make your own memories of loved ones, to hold a relationship on your own terms. Cole locked the door and sat down at his desk. He pulled up the email, and a flood of words poured out onto the screen. Omitting their encounter with Alexandria, Cole described their discovery in the library as if it had happened by accident and, before he could change his mind, hit "Send."

A familiar sense of panic crept into the corners of Cole's mind. He hated Fridays. If he did his homework tonight, he'd have nothing to see him through the rest of the weekend. Cole inhaled the factory-fresh ink of his American History textbook and read a few paragraphs about Benedict Arnold. In a gesture of habituated distraction, he glanced at his inbox and refreshed the page. At the top, timestamped six minutes after he had sent his email, was a reply from Orien Saint-Pierre.

CHAPTER 12

THE LIBRARY DISTURBED

Cole slipped his half-eaten sandwich back into its bag. It was a rare, sun-drenched day just before the serious onslaught of winter, and Jude had insisted that they eat lunch on the lawn outside the library. Beside Cole, Jude inhaled deeply as he lay on the brittle grass, gazing at cumulus cotton clouds through the branches of the maple under which they sat. Joanna watched him while doodling in a school notebook, a smile slowly spreading across her face. Bridget, her back against the bole of the maple, had taken her socks and shoes off and was digging her toes into the loamy soil.

They looked perfectly content. Cole tried to appreciate with them the breeze that turned his ears red and teased the maple's late leaves, but he felt it only as the death-bringing breath of winter. He thought of Alexandria, alone in her drafty cabin, and wished again that he could do something for her. Without telling his father or his friends, he had gone out twice last weekend looking for her, a bundle of blankets and food in his backpack—but her house seemed to have vanished. The only living creature in sight was a stray tabby cat with orange leonine streaks above its eyes. Cole couldn't lie down at night without wondering if Alexandria was warm enough or eat his meals without imagining how hungry she must be.

To make matters worse, Orien's reply to Cole's email had come with instructions: he was to discover whatever he could about the hidden passage and report back. For a full week Cole and his friends had been thwarted by the persistent presence of the same freshman who had interrupted their first foray. At last, their lucky break had come when the freshman—whom they named "the Dove" because his cherubic cheeks made him look like a walking soap advertisement—had been sent home sick. That night Cole had written Orien again, detailing how they had successfully regained entry and uncovered a small opening at the base of the mosaic by looking behind the root-like cords.

Three weeks had passed since then. Thanksgiving break had come and gone, and still Cole had neither heard back from Orien nor had an opportunity to thoroughly explore the cavern that lay beyond the mosaic column. The Dove continued to appear in the library at unpredictable days and times, so that even if he wasn't there when their study hall began, he sometimes appeared around a corner and caught one of them saying something careless about the secret opening. Whenever this happened, he kept his large, innocent eyes fixed on his homework. But they could never be sure how much he heard or guessed.

The anxious need to know what lay hidden under the school—combined with Orien's continued absence from his inbox—was gnawing like acid at Cole's stomach. It burned a hole there if he forgot to eat and turned to bile as soon as he did.

As if keeping pace with his thoughts, Jude said, "Cole, you still haven't heard from Saint-Pierre, right?"

The knot in Cole's stomach tightened. "No."

"Good."

"Good?" Joanna repeated, looking up sharply. "Why good? Don't you want Cole to make it to the next round of interviews?"

Jude shrugged. "He can do that without telling Saint-Pierre everything he knows about the library. The internship is supposed to be about academics, after all." When no one responded, he continued: "I guess I didn't care so much about Cole telling Saint-Pierre when we thought there was just one empty room with a mosaic, but now we know there's more to it, I wouldn't mind having another look around before we're told to keep out. We just have to figure out how to get the Dove out of the way—maybe slip him some Salmonella... Tell me again, what exactly *did* you find in that room beyond the mural? I wish I could get a good look at it."

Jude, who had stayed above ground as lookout last time, kept asking them to describe what they had found as if he thought there must be more to the answer. Cole couldn't blame him; he also felt there must be more. But what?

Bridget shivered. "No you don't. It's creepy."

Jude sat up on his elbow. Joanna's pencil stopped moving.

"Why's it creepy?"

Bridget closed her eyes and leaned her head back against the tree. "It's full of something... something beyond us... that's trying to get in; the air is *thin*. You can feel a presence—whatever it is—all around you."

"What she means," Joanna interjected, "is it's full of paintings of people, and it's creepy because it looks like they're staring at you. There's a circular little room with a bowl of sand in the middle and lots of short tunnels like little jellyfish tentacles leading off from it."

"A bowl of sand and jellyfish tentacles?" Jude repeated skeptically.

"Here, let me make a quick sketch for you." She flipped the page over and began to sketch on its backside. "You'll understand it better that way."

Cole watched as Joanna's hand passed back and forth across her lined notebook. Even in pencil, the room seemed imbued with a mysterious power that refused to let him enjoy anything until he knew what it held.

The school bell rang, calling them back to class. As Cole stood up, he saw a lone figure sweeping across the lawn toward them. Mr. Price, arms flailing like a late fall leaf driven by a gale, gusted into the shade of their maple.

"Erickson! There you are, at last. Follow me now, and don't get lost. Stick as close as a dipole-dipole van der Waals force—not strong enough to trip on the back of my shoes, but not weak enough to be cloven by the hordes of students disrupting the force field."

Cole's heart beat a little quicker. Could Mr. Price have heard something about the internship? He smiled nervously at his friends and followed the physics professor back across the grass and into the cafeteria, where they joined a throng of students pressing toward their classrooms, then broke from the stream down a quieter hallway and ducked into an empty classroom. Mr. Price nearly always looked as alarmed as if he had just woken up and looked in the mirror to see a face other than his own staring back at him, but today, Cole noticed that his alarm bore an edge of triumph, as if this time, the face in the mirror had been Einstein's.

Grabbing a stump of chalk and using it to gesticulate, Mr. Price said, "Listen, Erickson. I won't keep you long, but I wanted to tell you as soon as I knew: Dr. Saint-Pierre's coming back here to interview you and Wesley again. He'll be here tomorrow."

"Tomorrow?" Why hadn't Orien told him? As soon as Cole thought it, he reprimanded himself for being so childish. Just because they had exchanged a couple emails didn't mean Cole was entitled to special treatment.

"Yes, tomorrow. I know it's short notice. It's thrown the school into a bit of an uproar, to be honest. Poor Dr. Bering spooned two lumps of salt into his coffee this morning and didn't say anything about it—he was that distracted. I know because I ossified the salt into cubes and swapped it for the sugar after PSYCH scheduled language tables on top of Science Fair. On purpose. Sorry—did I say PSYCH? Talking to a student... I should say Professor Señora Yvette Contreras-Camponez. She's the only one who uses the sugar in the faculty lounge. Or so I thought. Anyway. You'd better dress sharper than a tack, not that you don't anyway, and brush up on possible interview questions as well as on your pearly whites. All right. I need to find Wesley. Go to class now."

Cole blinked, his mind bogged down by mixed metaphors, and realized that Mr. Price was already holding the door open for him.

As he turned back down the hall, Mr. Price called out, "Oh, and Cole, they've changed the location for the interview. It'll be in the library this time—apparently Dr. Saint-Pierre wished to see a more historic section of the school."

Cole's mind raced as he walked mechanically to class. He didn't even realize he was late until Mr. Salcombe gave him a tardy. Cole hardly noticed. He was thinking of tomorrow, and of the inevitability of showing Orien Saint-Pierre how to get behind the painting of Vincent Vendler. He ought to feel elated at this chance to prove his research skills in action, but all he felt was resentment at having to expose his secret. He didn't understand. He wanted nothing more than to work with Orien. And yet, now that the opportunity had arisen, his desire to improve Kronos felt abstract compared to his desire to explore the secret beneath Vendler Academy, the secret that was mysteriously connected to his dad and, by extension, himself. His mind felt like a ship caught between opposing winds. If only he and his friends could find a way to explore one more time.

After classes, he hurried to the library and was surprised to hear the rattle of a drill coming from inside. Two men in faded blue work suits pushed past him, carrying a heavy metal desk. Cole followed them. Men in blue were everywhere. Mrs. Fay was flitting in circles like a bird protecting its nest, giving directions in a warbly falsetto that was lost amidst a din of machinery and furniture scraping over wood. As if it was some assurance of her identity, she clutched to her chest the idiosyncratic desk plaque that read: "Mrs. M. E. Fay, Legacy Librarian. 1963 Jeopardy Champion."

"What's happening?" asked Bridget behind him. Her beautiful Christmas-bell voice was cracked.

Not waiting for his answer, she pushed past him and followed the men in blue to the back of the library, where she released a soft, heart-wrenching cry. Cole followed, Joanna and Jude in tow. The blush loveseat whose intricately carved wood Bridget always traced with her forefinger was nowhere to be seen. Neither was the green velvet armchair. The old-fashioned bronze floor lamp had been stuffed into a corner, its forever loose bulb now shattered on the floor. The Turkish rug stood propped up and taped tightly in one corner of the room, ready to be carried out.

In place of the lounge they knew stood the metal desk Cole had seen the workmen carrying. An electrician on a ladder was drilling in the last of three LED overheads that clashed magnificently with the collegiate Gothic architecture. Someone was ripping screeching shrink wrap from a big-box desk chair.

Bridget's body was completely rigid. She looked as fragile as if she might break. Cole gave her a tight, half smile to comfort her, and Joanna wrapped an arm around her waist. Paul emerged from behind a bookshelf, mopping his head with a handkerchief.

"Well I'll be," he said, seeming glad to find an audience. "And when I think they give me one day to get it all ready. *One day*. What kind of notice do you call that? No kind at all, not for everything they want me to do—gotta sweep the place clean of all this ratty tatty furniture, install new lighting, ship in all the new bells and whistles. Only I know it isn't old Bering's fault. Orders came from *him* this time."

"Him who?" Jude asked. "Who's giving orders?"

"Orien," Cole answered in a flat voice.

He realized with a lurch that this was all his fault. If he hadn't emailed Orien about what they had found, Orien wouldn't be coming back, or at least not to the library. Cole swallowed, trying not to think about how he had destroyed Bridget's favorite haven.

"Saint-Pierre's coming back?" Jude asked.

Paul nodded, his neck craning up toward the electrician. "That's right. They came to me this morning and said, 'Paul, redo the library, we have to have it presentable' but no one thinks of the time and trouble and planning. That's what's wrong with these white-collar folks; never think of what their grand ideas mean for us on the ground floor."

"I thought you liked Orien Saint-Pierre," Joanna said.

"I did."

They watched as the electrician called for his assistant to

turn the breaker back on. Flood lights illuminated swirling dust. The kaleidoscopic colors reflected in the shattered lamp bulb went white. Paul began to cough.

"God, what a day to be a custodian. You four better run along. Can't have people doin' nothin' when there's not enough time to do everythin'."

"I'll stay and help," Jude volunteered.

"Thought you would," Paul grunted, almost smiling. "Cop hold of that end of the carpet; I'll get this'n'."

Joanna turned around. "Come on. We can study in the auditorium."

Cole followed her, but Bridget stood rooted to the spot until Joanna came back and guided her out of the library.

"What they've done to it..." Bridget whispered. "They've destroyed it."

"They may put it back," Cole suggested without conviction.

"I don't understand how Jude can help," Bridget said quietly. "That was my home."

Cole gritted his teeth, regretting the email.

"Jude doesn't think like that," Joanna replied. "He's loyal to *people*."

Bridget sat completely still all during study hall, refusing to look at her homework. Cole tried to think of something consoling to say, or at least to catch her eye to give her a smile. But she gazed determinedly at her hands the whole hour. Between worrying about Bridget and worrying about tomorrow's interview, Cole hadn't completed any of his own homework by the time the bell rang.

When he returned home, he went straight to his room, determined to distract himself with homework. He had barely finished his neuroscience worksheet and opened his online chemistry lab when a text appeared on his screen. He clicked it before realizing it was from his dad: *Pizza downstairs.* Cole closed it without replying and crossed the hall toward the stairs, surprised to see the light from the west-facing window already weakened by dusk. In the kitchen, his dad sat at an island barstool eating from a paper plate and scrolling on his phone. His eyes flicked to Cole and back to his phone.

Cole opened the pizza box and lifted three slices onto a doubled over paper towel, then turned back toward the stairs.

"Not going to eat down here?"

Cole turned around in time to see his dad's eyes slide furtively back to the protection of his phone.

Cole restrained himself from saying he'd had enough riveting conversation for one day and said instead, "I've got a lot of homework tonight." When his dad didn't answer, he added, "Thanks for the pizza."

His dad grunted in reply, releasing his eyes from his phone only to take a swig of his beer and belch under his breath. What he was looking at, Cole had no idea, but it wasn't work. Feeling both guilty and disgusted, Cole turned back toward the stairs and retreated to his room.

CHAPTER 13

ORIEN'S INSTRUCTIONS

The library air was foreign and tense. The stacks of books in their now stripped surroundings gave the illusion of floating in a lifeless sea. In the absence of Cole's friends, Vincent Vendler's likeness swelled, his presence pressing into every inch of the lounge. It was as if Vendler and Cole were two living beings in the room, and the air between them was thin.

To avoid eye contact with the painting, Cole got up from the metal chair and turned to the nearest row of books, examining their titles between stolen glances at the door. His eyes flitted over one of Mrs. Fay's hand-made signs: *To whom much is given, much will be required—absolutely no uncapped pens within nine inches of open books.* Behind the sign, "The Epic of Gilgamesh" sat beside "Ancient Egyptian Myths and Legends." How many of these mythologies, Cole wondered, had Bridget read?

Voices broke his train of thought, and he dropped "Edda" back into place. Tugging at his suit coat, he resumed what he hoped was a relaxed yet attentive posture on the metal chair where he was expected to be found.

"...quite pleased to receive your email yesterday. And of course, we ask that you'll graciously overlook our inability to welcome you more formally. You're sure you'll be comfortable here?"

The voice that answered made Cole instantly aware that he hadn't checked his teeth after lunch.

"Nonsense, my dear Dr. Bering. I ought to apologize for the inconvenience, but I do adore a little history lesson on some of your country's finest schools. You say the library hasn't been renovated? My, what an expansive collection of books—and such fine editions, too! Charming! Ah, Cole, what a pleasure to see you again."

The smile Orien extended disarmed Cole's defenses, and he returned it.

"Well, if you're sure you'll be quite comfortable, I'll leave you to it. I'll be just next door, so don't hesitate to let me know should you need anything. Erickson."

Dr. Bering nodded hopefully at Cole before retreating. As soon as the library door clicked, Orien turned, not to Cole, but to the painting of Vincent Vendler.

"So, this is it?"

Anticipation boomeranged from Orien to Vendler and back again like a physical force. Cole had the sensation of being caught between two magnets. Recovering himself, Orien turned back toward Cole.

"I want to thank you, Cole, for so quickly updating me on your remarkable discovery. Naturally, I wanted to see it at once, but unfortunately, I'm a slave to my own administrative assistant." He smiled deprecatingly. "I'm sorry for not telling you I was coming, but I didn't know myself until yesterday."

"There's nothing to forgive, sir." What had Cole been worried about? Now that he and Orien were back in the same room again, it felt ridiculous that Cole had ever doubted himself for emailing Orien or worried that Orien hadn't replied —Orien was a busy man. Cole's shoulders relaxed. "I was happy to hear that I had made it to the next round of interviews."

"With flying colors, I might add. I thought we might have a more hands-on interview today, Cole. One where you have a chance to exhibit your findings instead of discussing them in the abstract, rather like a research symposium. What do you say?"

Cole's throat went dry. The inexplicable reluctance that had haunted him the day before seized him again, and he heard Alexandria saying, "Destroy it." He glanced at Vincent Vendler's likeness for guidance, then discovered that his body was already crossing the room toward it without having consulted his brain. He hesitated. For the first time, the painting seemed to be looking, not at him, but at Orien. Cole had thought that the school's founder had wanted to protect his secret, to reveal it only to his direct descendent. But today, the draw toward the painting was stronger than ever.

"Feeling all right, Cole?" Orien said, his voice warm with concern. "You look a little peaked."

"I'm fine, thank you." Cole forced a smile. Really, what was he so worried about? "I'd be happy to show you."

He withdrew Vendler's autobiography from its shelf, placed his hand on the gilt frame, and cleared his throat. He glanced at Orien, whose eyes were wide with hunger, his lips slightly parted. Cole turned back to the painting and said, "Vendler."

The frame creaked away from the wall. Orien's eyes glowed with a secret flame.

"Remarkable," he breathed. "So that's how it's done, is it?

You touch it, you show it the book, and you say his name? I wonder how it works." Orien was talking more to himself than to Cole. "Is there some sort of chip embedded in the book, and warmth transmitted by the touch, that triggers the opening?"

"Sir," Cole began, his heart pounding a little faster, "Orien, I mean. It's multimodal, isn't it?"

"Ah, so you got there too—well done, Cole! Yes, it responds to multiple modalities: visual, sensory, and auditory. But what I can't understand is that this painting was clearly created and installed before any of that technology was developed."

The thought sent a chill down Cole's spine.

"As much as I'd love to examine the mechanics of this fascinating painting, I'm afraid Dr. Bering will be back in..." he glanced at his watch, "35 minutes. So if you will be so kind as to show me around, we'd best get started."

As Cole moved the chair under the portrait and climbed onto it, he was keenly aware that Orien was watching his every move. Just a few months ago, Cole would never have dreamed that he could discover something that captivated the undivided attention of Orien Saint-Pierre. Each step down the ladder's rungs put his reservations more deeply to sleep. When they reached the bottom and Cole shone his phone flashlight on the mosaic, Orien exhaled an appreciative, "Magnificent!"

Cole held the cords aside for Orien to crawl through the passage first, then followed him into air that was cool, moist, and suffocatingly still. A faint odor of decaying flesh made him cough. Somewhere out of sight, distant water dripped. Crepuscular insects scurried underfoot. Cole's flashlight illuminated a million witch-fingered stalactites that looked like a sprawling chandelier.

He watched as his idol surveyed the cave, an unguarded awe lighting his face. In the center of the space stood a silver basin. Its pedestal was shaped like a serpent, its tail coiled at the base, its body climbing upward. Its mouth, agape in devouring expectation, formed the bowl of the basin and was filled with sand. Behind the basin stood a primitive wooden cabinet. In a fan-like pattern around the basin, the room branched off into six short corridors about two yards long and just wide enough for one person to stand in. Each corridor housed several shallow alcoves in which sat candles and pictures of men and women Cole didn't recognize.

"Will you look at this!" Orien exclaimed. "Who would have thought? It's been right here this whole time, yet we're the first to find it!"

Orien's reaction imbued each contour of the bizarre cave with new magic.

"I haven't explored this space much yet," Cole said.

"No? Well, there's no time like the present. We'll just need to be careful. It wouldn't do to be caught down here when your headmaster returns."

Orien's camaraderie gave Cole courage to voice his biggest fear: "You're not going to tell him then?"

Orien's laughter was loud and free. "And spoil all the fun by having the place condemned before we get a chance to explore? Not a chance. The pursuit of knowledge has always involved a certain danger, Cole, a willingness to take risks for the sake of truth. Personally, that risk is one I'm willing to take, and I can see that you're up to the task too."

The warmth of his smile melted the knot in Cole's stomach.

"We'd better not waste any time." Orien checked his watch, then shook it. A frown furrowed his face as he turned it off and on again. "Strange. Is your phone still working? My watch is frozen."

Cole checked and shook his head. "Mine died too."

"A quick look then and back up," Orien decided.

The corridors weren't large enough for two people, so Cole stood by the entrance and watched as Orien walked down each of them, then peeked inside the small cabinet that stood by the basin. It contained nothing but a box of matches and a handful of beeswax candles. There was something about the unhesitating brazenness with which Orien marched directly up to the center cabinet and opened its door that both impressed and disturbed Cole. He himself, when first entering the room, had been careful to avoid touching anything out of respect for the animistic force that filled the cavern. Orien, apparently, was free from the irrational superstition that plagued Cole.

"Curious," Orien said, checking his dead watch again out of habit. "I dearly wish I had more time here, but I can't make head or tail of what happens next, and we'll be wanted upstairs again. We'd best be going for now."

Disappointed but still charged with the electric curiosity that emanated from Orien, Cole led the way back through the small opening and up the ladder. In another moment, he and Orien were standing in front of the mantel again.

Glancing at the new digital clock, Orien said, "I guess we had a little more time to explore after all. It's a shame that my watch froze, but still, better safe than sorry."

Despite himself, Cole moved toward the painting to double check that Orien had closed it properly.

"You did very well to discover this," Orien said. "And you did even better to show me. It gives me great pleasure, Cole, to inform you that you have advanced to the next round of interviews, where we select only one student from each district."

Cole wheeled around to face Orien, his heart hammering. Orien had made the offer before even completing his second interview with Wesley Tate. He couldn't resist smiling as he thought about Orien calling for Dr. Bering and telling him to send Wes back to class. Joanna had been right—telling Orien about the secret passage had been the right decision.

"Keep up this work and you'll have secured your spot as my newest research scientist." Orien winked. "But in all seriousness, Cole, do your best to discover the heart of Vendler's secret, and keep me updated on what you find, no matter how inconsequential your findings may seem to you."

Cole heard himself agreeing, but Orien's assignment reminded him of the promise he had made Bridget yesterday afternoon.

"Why are you so interested in the cave? Sorry, it's just— Vendler was a shoddy scientist; people only put up with him because of his money. Do you really think he left something important down there?"

The question sounded impertinent, and he only had the courage to ask because Orien had just advanced him to the next round of interviews. Orien studied Cole in surprise, and Cole had the impression he was deciding what kind of an answer to return.

Finally, Orien said, "I will answer your question, Cole. But first you must answer mine: does it seem right to you that one person's desire for relationship should be entirely controlled by someone else?"

The abrupt intimacy of the question was only surprising in that it struck Cole as perfectly natural. He thought of his dad, of all the times he had wanted to force him to talk, to pay attention, to notice that his son was slipping away, to explain why Cole wasn't more important than whiskey, even when the Army had offered to get him help. But the years had slipped by, and Cole had given up. Or had he?

"No," he said at last. "It doesn't seem right."

"I told you that Kronos is about resolving relationships with loved ones who have passed on, and it's true that's how it started. But it's bigger than that, Cole. Much bigger." Orien swung one leg up to half sit on the corner of the table. "I quickly realized that the technology I created had the potential to help everyone, not just those who have lost loved ones to death. Because the truth is, many of us have lost loved ones to the traumas of life, too, which is often much more painful. It's wrong that the desire for intimacy should so often lead only to deeper vulnerability and therefore deeper wounding. No one should be exposed to that kind of suffering.

"Kronos gives us a way to invest in relationships safely, without the fear of rejection. And it also gives us a way to reclaim a relationship once a wound has occurred. In other words, it cancels out the danger of someone else's irresponsibility. The greatest gift we can ever give to another human is ourselves, and Kronos puts the control of how that gift is received back into our own hands. But obviously," Orien smirked, "that only works if Kronos can return love."

Cole had been looking down at his own hands. He found it difficult to look Orien in the eye when he seemed to be speaking so directly to him. Now he looked back up at Orien's face.

"Return love? How can that work?"

Orien shrugged. "That's the question I'm asking too. Enhancing Kronos with XR will make it more realistic, but I respect my users enough that I'm not going to give them something that's less than perfect. You read Vendler's autobiography. Do you remember any theories he propounded?"

Cole reached back in his mind, trying to recall ideas from a book that had struck him as pompous lunacy. Not for the last time, Bridget's words came to his rescue.

"There was something about art and love, wasn't there?"

"Bingo. Vendler hypothesized that when an artist truly loves what they make, they pour part of themselves into their creation. And in that instant of interchange between creator and created, an almost physical force is released into the universe. Not visible, perhaps, yet perceptible."

"I don't understand," Cole said, and he was surprised by the honesty of his own admission.

Orien sighed. "Neither do I. But I want to." He stood up. "Cole, I know full well that Vendler was, probably rightly, regarded as a lunatic. But I want Kronos to exist so much that I'm just enough of a lunatic myself to believe him. If he left any other clues about his theory, anything at all that might explain how to harness that artistic power, or even validate his ideas, I must find it. Do you understand?"

Cole nodded. He understood. He understood too that he must help Orien, not just for the internship now, but for the thousands of fractured families—people like himself—who would never have a relationship with their real fathers or mothers or children or siblings or spouses, but who nevertheless suffered daily from trying and failing. Surely Alexandria, if she heard Orien, would agree.

"I do understand, and I mean to help you in any way I can."

Orien's lips stretched into the characteristic smile that came easily but spread slowly. "Good."

CHAPTER 14

DESPERATE MEASURES

As soon as school was out, Cole sprinted down the hallway, out the doors of Vendler Academy, and down the stone steps to Newton, where he watched for his friends to emerge. Throughout the course of the afternoon, a new resolve had hardened inside him. He was determined to act on it before he lost courage. Father Time frowned at him as if he knew what Cole was thinking. It was a relief when Joanna emerged, surrounded by several students he vaguely recognized—her art friends, most likely. A tall boy with blue hair erupted with laughter at something she said, then watched her jealously as she caught Cole's eye and excused herself to meet him under Newton.

"Cole! How are you? How was it?" She must have sensed his agitation, because she placed her hand on his arm and said, "Are you okay?"

"Fine. Really great, actually. I got moved to the next round of interviews!"

"I knew you would! Congratulations!"

"But Joanna, there's something I need to talk with you and Jude and Bridget about. Something related to the internship."

"Of course. Whatever you need, we'll help."

There must have been something in Cole's face that made Joanna wait to question him. When Jude and Bridget emerged a second later, he motioned them to follow him to a deserted corner of the parking lot.

Wrenching his gaze from Father Time, he whispered, "I've just had my interview with Orien. It went well, but he really wants me to find out more about Vendler's cave. I know this sounds crazy, but we've got to find a way to get back in and explore."

"Why is that crazy?" Joanna asked. "Of course we need to get back in!"

"It's just... we can't keep waiting around hoping the Dove won't be there. I can't wait that long."

"Cole," Bridget said, and for some reason he had a hard time meeting her eye, "you're going too fast. Why are you suddenly no longer able to wait?"

"Orien needs to know what Vendler hid. He thinks it may be the key to making Kronos love, because of the life-giving power of art. If he can harness that power, he can finish Kronos."

Cole said it in a rush. Bridget raised her eyebrows, making Cole wish he had taken more time to think about how to explain it to her. He needed her to understand.

"Kronos could help so many people, Bridget, and we're just one discovery away."

"'We'? So I guess this means you're not planning to destroy what Vendler left like Alexandria asked?"

"Well, it depends on what it is, doesn't it?" Cole said. That was just logic. Why was Bridget being so difficult?

"Of course he won't destroy it!" Joanna interrupted. "Orien Saint-Pierre needs it, and Cole needs the internship."

"He doesn't *need* it," Jude corrected, crossing his arms and drumming his bicep with his fingers. "He just *wants* it. There's a difference."

"Anyway," Joanna charged on, "We don't even know how much we can trust Alexandria. Even if she's right about Cole being Vendler's grandson, we don't know if the whole story of how it happened is accurate. She seemed a little batty."

"Actually, we do know," Bridget said. "When you all went outside, I decided to check those portraits in the hall to see if they might corroborate her story."

The fact that Bridget, who accepted the existence of everything from Sasquatch to the Loch Ness monster without batting an eye, had thought to fact check a story Cole had accepted point blank surprised him so much that he forgot Orien's mission for a moment.

"Do you remember the portrait of that giggling girl in Alexandria's hallway?" Bridget went on. "That was her sister, Acalia Lehmann. And the picture of the dog had an inscription on the back too: 'Vincent Vendler, may my memory be eternal.'"

Cole's stomach became queasy. Bridget was studying him again, and he was suddenly as uncomfortable under her unblinking gaze as a rabbit scrutinized by an owl.

"Anyway, whatever you do with it once you find it, the main point is to find it," Joanna said.

"For once, I agree with Joanna," Jude said. "I still wish you hadn't brought Saint-Pierre into this, but whatever is down there seems important if so many people are interested. But how are we going to find time to get a solid look around?"

"That's just the problem," Cole said, glancing at the school again as if to make sure it wasn't listening in. "I've been thinking about it, and all I can come up with is skipping class. I *really* don't want to do that, but it's the only way to make sure the Dove is in class too."

"Better than nothing, but we still run the risk of someone else walking in on us," Jude said.

Into the silence that followed came the sounds of laughter and farewells, the revving of engines and the peel of rubber tires. How would they ever secure an uninterrupted hour in Vendler Academy's library when over one thousand students and more than one hundred faculty members walked its corridors from before they arrived until after they left?

Joanna covered her face with her hands, then drew them away suddenly. "Oh my God—I know a way." Her eyes flickered with excitement. "It'll involve breaking at least one rule, maybe more." Looking over her shoulder to ensure no one was near, she continued in a rushed whisper. "Last fall, Jude was helping Paul put some lawn tools back in his shed—that old white building by the baseball field. Remember what he said, Jude?"

"I remember I helped while you watched, yeah."

"Well fortunately, I remember more relevant details. Apparently that used to be the warden's house when the asylum was first founded, and then it was the headmaster's house. Obviously, it's just a glorified garden shed now—part of the original house was condemned and torn down, and part of it was converted into a groundskeeper's storage area. It came up because Jude stepped on a hollow space in the floor and Paul mentioned that there was supposed to be a passage connecting the house to the school. I don't think he had actually been down there, but he sounded pretty confident about its existence."

"Wait, you're not suggesting—"

"Yes, Jude, I am."

"No way! If you think I'm going to stand by and let you get kicked out of school for a stupid reason—"

"It *isn't* a stupid reason. Cole needs to learn what's down there."

"I'm just as curious as you are, but be honest: is it really that important that you'd risk getting expelled?"

Cole cleared his throat. "Do you mind cluing Bridget and me in on what you're talking about?"

Jude rubbed his temple and exhaled forcefully before turning to Cole. "Joanna Grant is under the impression that your exploration is worth breaking into the school, illegally, through a tunnel that may or may not exist."

"What?" Cole blanched.

"And don't ask me how she plans on disarming the alarms and disconnecting the surveillance cameras without being discovered."

"We wouldn't need to," Bridget said unexpectedly. "Alarms are only triggered when passing through an exterior door, right? If what Joanna says is true, this tunnel would lead us inside the school, and I doubt there would be an alarm on a trapdoor no one knows about. So really, it's just the cameras we'd have to worry about. And I doubt anyone monitors those unless there's an incident and they need to check footage. The school isn't going to pay for someone to watch a video of students walking around and getting stuff from their lockers all day. They don't even check to see where I hide when I skip class."

Joanna's jaw dropped in a parody of surprise. "I can't believe you're on my side."

"Oh, I'm certainly not," Bridget replied. "I'm not convinced it's a good idea to try to find what Vendler left at all. I'm merely playing out a hypothetical."

"A hypothetical that could lose me my Vendler scholarship," Jude grumbled.

"Or get Cole his internship at The Lab," Joanna countered.

"If Saint-Pierre makes your discovery of whatever Vendler hid down there a prerequisite to your getting the internship, all I can say is that's very unfair to all of the other applicants," Jude said.

Cole's eyes darted to Jude, then back to the school. He hadn't verbalized it, not even to himself, but he did wonder how much Orien's willingness to move him to the next round of interviews had to do with his academic achievements and how much had to do with the dumb luck of discovering a school secret that happened to pique Orien's interest. If Wes had been the one to find what lay beyond the portrait, would he be the one advancing rather than Cole? The thought made him uncomfortable, and he swallowed as if to rid his mouth of a bad taste.

"It isn't the only reason he'd get it," Joanna said soothingly, addressing Cole rather than Jude. "Cole's one of the smartest students in our school. But it does show initiative and a willingness to go above and beyond. And I for one am going to help."

Jude regarded the determined purse of her lips and the tautness of her body. "Look," he said. "I don't want to do this. It's a bad idea, and I personally think there's no logically compelling argument to risk expulsion. There's not even any linear connection between those caves and Cole's future—at least there shouldn't be if Saint-Pierre is at all decent. But if there's no stopping you, I'm coming too."

Joanna gave him a spontaneous hug, and Cole saw a momentary flush of pleasure in Jude's cheeks. When Joanna broke away, Jude scanned the school parking lot as if seeing it for the first time. Was Jude thinking what Cole was thinking? That this mission might well cost him his place at Vendler Academy? Was that a price Cole was really willing to pay?

"Tonight at midnight then, we meet back here," Joanna said, heading to her car before anyone had time to back out.

CHAPTER 15
THE SECRET TUNNEL

Vendler Academy loomed as a darker black in the foreground of a cloudless sky. A Kia pulled up beside Cole's Corolla. Even though he knew it was Joanna, it was still with some anxiety that he sought her face behind the tinted glass, as if the very act of parking at the school at night were criminal. She cut her engine and waved excitedly. He returned a nervous twitch of a smile. The stillness of the night made it hard to believe this was the same campus that by day echoed with the laughter and footfalls of a thousand students. Cole's mind hummed with a nervous energy to make up for the absence of sound.

His passenger door popped open and Joanna slid inside, her usually vibrant clothes replaced with black leggings and a charcoal puffer jacket. Cole was still dressed in the same chinos, collared shirt, and sweater he had worn the day before.

"You know, I think it might be a good thing Jude and Bridget are late," he said. "We didn't really think this through, and now we have the chance to reevaluate our methods."

"Cole, come on! You're the one who suggested this!"

"I said we needed to find a way to have more time to explore. I did *not* suggest breaking into the school. Do you know what'll happen if we're caught?"

"Let me guess—the end of the world as we know it?"

"More or less. We'll either be in serious trouble, or else expelled. Which means no Stanford, no MIT, and certainly no career at The Lab."

"Anything else?"

"Well, yeah. I'll never forgive myself for dragging all of you into this with me."

"All right, glad you got that off your chest." Joanna angled her body toward Cole. "Now think of it this way: if you *don't* break in tonight, you'll have nothing to report to Orien Saint-Pierre after he specifically tasked you with a very important mission, which means you can say good-bye to your dreams of working at The Lab, which is why you even want to go to Stanford and MIT in the first place, right? But right now, tonight, you have a chance to take a shortcut to your life goal without having to wait. And besides, Bridget isn't late. She's sleeping in my car."

Cole stared at his steering wheel. Orien had said that pursuing truth required risk. Maybe this was one of those risks Cole needed to be willing to take. A crunch of loose gravel and a squeal of bike brakes announced Jude's arrival. Joanna jumped out of the car to greet him. Cole took a deep breath and followed.

"Sorry," Jude said, climbing off his bike and sweeping up the kickstand. Damp hair was plastered against his forehead. "Tullius," he exhaled in explanation. Tullius was the Durhams' mangy mutt who loved to howl mournful songs in an unusually deep bass voice. "He wanted to come with me. It's a good thing I said no to your offer of a ride, Cole—he goes crazy when cars are around; probably would have woken up the whole neighborhood. Where's Bridget?"

Joanna nodded to her car and tapped on the window until Bridget yawned herself awake.

Retrieving a messenger bag from the back seat, Joanna patted it and said, "Our espionage kit. I went to Walgreens earlier and picked up four ski masks, four pairs of gloves, and a magnifying glass. I also have my sketchbook."

"I feel so much better knowing we'll have a watercolor memento of our exploit should we get caught," Jude said.

"Shut up," Joanna said. "Let's suit up now."

"Joanna," Jude said, "Did it ever occur to you that buying ski masks and gloves is a lot more suspicious than parking here at night?"

"Fine! Suit yourself. But I'm not going to get caught on camera with my face showing and fingerprints all over the school."

"Because it's not like anyone would expect to see your fingerprints in the library since you never hang out there..." Jude said.

"Please, let's just get this over with," Cole said.

Pulling on a ski mask but foregoing the gloves, Joanna led the way along the perimeter of the football field toward the white shed, which shone luminous in the light of a waxing gibbous moon. Cole dropped back to walk beside Bridget.

"I'm surprised you came," he said. "You didn't seem that keen on the idea when we talked about it after school."

"I'm not."

"You don't have to come. I mean, I want you to, but I don't want any of you to feel like you have to do this. It's a risk I need to take, but that doesn't mean you have to take it too."

Bridget glanced at the school and shuddered. "It isn't the breaking in I mind so much as the cave itself."

"What are you afraid of?"

"I don't know. But that's exactly why I'm coming—I think you're all underestimating the most dangerous part of this. If finding out about your family was hard, imagine what it'll be like when you find out why Vendler did what he did. You can't be alone for that."

Cole's body flooded with sunlight before he realized Bridget was doing what she would have done for any of them. He said, "Well, I wouldn't be alone."

As if to say, "Might as well be," Bridget raised her eyebrows at Joanna, who was grinning like a child on a roller-coaster. They had reached the shed now, and Joanna stopped abruptly. She jiggled a fat padlock on the door.

"Oh no! Why didn't we think of this?"

Jude took the padlock from her hands. "Once again, you underestimate the value of being a helpful person. Sometimes when I stay late to help Paul, he sends me here to grab a hammer or screw gun."

He slid the metallic numbers, and the lock popped apart. Cole's heart jolted with excitement as the door eased open. Inside, the air smelled of gasoline. Starlight filtered through chinks in the ceiling and walls. They stepped into the semi-darkness, shutting the door behind them. Joanna's flashlight clicked on. Rakes, shovels, pick-axes, and pruning tools hung from racks on the wall to the right. Below them were bags of mulch and bottles of weed killer. To the left was a workbench, above which shelves housed neatly ordered paint cans, hammers, and toolboxes. Along the back wall stood a riding lawn mower, a push mower, a weed whacker, an edger, a snow-blower, and sun-bleached cans of fuel.

Joanna marched up to the push mower and tugged the handle.

"Hold up, Jo!" Jude said. "Before you tear the place apart, take a mental picture of where everything goes. Paul is pretty OCD. He'll know if we move his tools."

"Why don't we start by sound checking the floor space that's already open?" Cole suggested. "If Paul only knew of the trapdoor as a rumor, it won't be visible."

Jude nodded and grabbed a shovel off the wall, turning it handle-side down. He started walking back and forth, tapping the dirt floor as he went. After a moment, a muffled clang made them all rush to where he was standing. Joanna handed Bridget her flashlight and knelt beside Jude, who was running his fingers over the area the shovel had hit. The dirt here was loose rather than hard packed, perhaps because it was under the bench that held the paint and wasn't walked on as much as the rest of the shed floor.

"There's definitely a ridge here that stands up from the rest of the ground," Joanna said.

Together, she and Jude brushed dirt away from the area, revealing the outline of a metal lip.

"It's real!" Joanna breathed.

"The question is, will the door clear the bottom bar of this bench when we open it," Jude said.

He took hold of the small metal handle that protruded from the front of the trapdoor and tugged upward. It gave a fraction of an inch and then jammed. Soon Jude was on his feet, gripping the handle from a deadlift position and trying to force it upward.

"You're going to have to help me," he said at last.

Cole blew out the air he had been unconsciously holding in his lungs. He had half hoped they wouldn't find the trapdoor, but it was real now, and it wasn't fair to make his friends do his dirty work for him. Taking stock of the shed, he retrieved a hammer and a crowbar and slid the claws under the lip of the trap door on either side. Joanna took the hammer while he held the crowbar. Jude still held the handle.

"Okay, on three," Jude said. "One. Two. Three!" With a horrific screech, the trapdoor swung upward and crashed into the wooden bar of the bench. All three of them jumped back in their haste to disassociate themselves from the noise they had just made. Bridget clicked the flashlight off and sprinted to look out the shed door. The sound of their own breathing seemed abnormally loud. Finally, Bridget turned around, closing the shed door behind her.

"We've been lucky," she said.

Cole had to stop himself from going to the door to double check her. He turned back to the trapdoor, which was still cocked open against the bottom rail of the bench. Bridget's flashlight clicked on again and illuminated several steel steps descending into gray dust. A spider scurried across the top step and disappeared.

"It's going to be a tight fit," Jude said. "But I think we can make it without moving this bench. If we touch it, I'm sure Paul will know something's up. We're going to have to remember to cover up the trapdoor with dirt again when we leave. Well, here goes."

He lowered himself onto his stomach, feet by the trapdoor entrance, and slid backward, groping for the steps as he went. When he was far enough down, Bridget handed him the flashlight.

"What do you see?" Joanna asked.

"Definitely a tunnel—can't see where it goes. It's actually quite roomy once you get down here. Wow! There are even lights along the walls." He touched a kerosene lantern suspended from a rope tied to a stake in the wall. "They're still oily."

Joanna handed down her messenger bag and followed. Taking a steadying breath, Cole glanced at Bridget and lowered himself to the ground. He hoped he didn't look as silly as he felt as his feet fumbled for the steps. Standing once again, he dusted his hands together and brushed his sweater free of a cobweb. Soon Bridget was standing by his side.

The tunnel was wide enough for two of them to fit abreast, but Cole had to stoop to avoid brushing his head against the ceiling. Ahead, the way was blocked by a wispy net of old cobwebs that dangled from the walls and ceiling. The air was musty and damp. Dust floated sleepily in the flashlight beams, and all was silent but for their own footsteps and the sound of a dull clunking from Joanna's messenger bag as it slapped against her leg. Even the murmur of traffic was non-existent. At last, the tunnel dead ended into a ladder leading to another trapdoor.

"I'll go first." Bridget said unexpectedly.

"But you're the only one who didn't want to come," Cole protested.

"I know. And believe me, I still think sleep would have been a better idea tonight, but think about it: if we're caught, I have the least to lose. Jude has his scholarship, school is basically Cole's life, and Jo's parents might disown her."

"That sounds nice," Joanna said.

"Your grandparents wouldn't care?" Cole asked.

Bridget smiled ruefully. "Surviving is enough to make them proud."

It took Cole a moment to understand the bitter edge to her voice. Then he remembered: Bridget's parents had died in a car crash when she was four. She was the only child of their only child. He mumbled an apology as Bridget placed her worn pink Converse shoe on the first rung of the ladder. It squeaked and spun forward under her weight. Her hand flattened against the bottom of the trapdoor and pushed upward.

It gave way with surprising ease. A faint light filtered in through the slit in the trapdoor. Then the door dropped and Bridget fell backward off the ladder. Jude and Cole barely caught her.

"What was it?" Joanna hissed.

"Someone's there."

CHAPTER 16

THE WATCHERS

They cowered in the recesses of the tunnel, straining for a sound. All Cole could hear was Bridget's breathing, heavy from adrenaline.

"Who was it?" Jude asked. "Did you recognize the room?"

Bridget closed her eyes, summoning each detail. "There was a pair of boots right in front of me, with big brass buckles. And a long cloak. I couldn't tell if it was a man or woman."

"A cloak?" Joanna asked. "And who would be in the school at midnight? Unless the tunnel led us beyond the school to some other building?"

"I have a theory," Jude whispered, tiptoeing back to the trapdoor.

"What are you doing?" Cole whispered frantically.

Jude shook his head and motioned for them to stay back. He stepped onto the first rung and closed his eyes, listening. After a minute, he raised the trapdoor an inch and peered through the slit. Cole held his breath. Jude eased the trapdoor upward. They heard it brush against something and catch.

Reaching an arm out, Jude grabbed at whatever was blocking the door. There were a few dull thuds as the door opened fully.

"It's all right," Jude said over his shoulder. "Come on up."

Cole was still wary as he climbed the ladder, but when he reached the top, he almost laughed.

"No head," Joanna said. "It's a mannequin! But what in the world is it doing here, and where is 'here' anyway?"

They were in a narrow room that smelled of mothballs. On one wall was a rod from which hung Russian military uniforms, Regency dresses, leather vests, and monastic habits. On the floor below were piles of ballet slippers, some of which had been dislodged when Jude opened the trapdoor, and bins stuffed with scarves and garish leggings. Immediately in front of the trapdoor stood the mannequin with the cloak and brass-buckled boots.

"The backstage dressing room," Jude explained. "Remember *Pirates of Penzance*? Ethan Holen made such a big deal about being the only guy cool enough to wear both a cape and boots that Bridget's description immediately made me think of him."

Joanna laughed. "I forgot about that. Ethan wouldn't take that stupid cape off until he was reported for violating the dress code."

"Who's Ethan?" Bridget asked.

"One of Joanna's many ghosts of boyfriends past," Jude answered.

Joanna jabbed him in the ribs.

Cole whispered, "I think we should keep our voices down, just in case."

"I can't believe how lucky we are," Jude said. "If we cut across the stage behind the curtains, we can slip into the hall that leads to the library."

As they crossed backstage, the black-stained hardwood creaked underfoot, each sound amplified in the darkness. The curtains billowed dust into their eyes and noses as they passed. The backstage room on the opposite side was crammed with file cabinets and uncategorized school detritus, probably accumulated by administrators like Mrs. Dixon who mortally feared disposing of even a single manila folder.

They emerged into one of the smallest arteries of Vendler's hallway system and quickly reached the library door.

"See how easy that was?" Joanna said.

"Don't speak too soon," Cole said.

His hand was on the library doorknob, and it wouldn't turn. When they had found Paul's shed door locked, Cole had felt only disappointed. Now he was angry. They had risked so much only to be locked out at the very last moment.

"It can't be locked." Joanna's voice was flat with shock. Unwilling to accept it, she tried the door herself. It jiggled loudly.

Jude grimaced. "Of course it is. Paul locks it every afternoon. I know that. How did I not remember?"

"There must be another way," Joanna said, biting the corner of her lip. Her eyes narrowed as she peered through the keyhole, scanned the perimeter of the door, and finally fixed on the pane of glass above it. "What about that?"

"The transom window?" Bridget said.

"Do you think it opens?" Joanna asked. "It's small, but I bet I could fit through it." She eyed them each with unabashed objectivity. "I think we all could."

Cole stood on his tiptoes. "It has the mechanism to open." He ran his fingertips over the window frame. "But the opening has been painted shut."

"Could we open it anyway with a little force?" Joanna asked.

"Only if it isn't locked on the inside," Jude said. "But it's a bad idea. The paint would fleck everywhere."

Joanna snapped her fingers. "I've got a pocket knife here in my spy bag! We can use it to cut around the window, then open it! And if anyone notices, we can just say we opened the what's-it-called window because we were hot and wanted a cross-breeze."

"Joanna, it's December," Jude reminded her. "It's freezing out there, and the library is drafty enough—we wouldn't want a cross breeze."

"All the better!" Joanna countered. "We wanted fresh air, but it was too cold outside, so we used the inside window."

"Why wouldn't we just open the library door?" Jude asked.

Joanna rolled her eyes. "I don't know, because we were curious about whether or not the window would open. We're sixteen! It's very likely we were being impulsive and didn't think about damaging the paint. Look, if you want something, sooner or later you're going to have to take a risk to get it. We've come this far tonight, and I personally think this is a relatively small risk to take in the scheme of things. Probably no one will ever notice." When no one answered, she added, "We're *so* close."

"Fine," Cole said.

Joanna had said exactly what he'd been thinking—they had already risked too much to leave now. She flicked her knife open and handed it to Cole before he could change his mind. Taking a deep breath, he slid the blade into the crevice. The handle slipped on the sweat in his palm. This was probably the stupidest thing he had ever done. Wiping his hand on his chinos, Cole took the handle again and sawed in and out, pressing the paint around the frame with his free hand to keep it from chipping unnecessarily. Finally, the frame was free. He and Jude pushed against the base of the window.

With a crack and a scrape of wood on wood, it opened. Paint flecks rained down on them, and Cole stooped to collect them.

"We'll do that on our way out," Joanna said. "Let's get going."

"I'll help lift whoever's going through the window," Jude volunteered.

Cole smiled wryly. Tied with Bridget for height but the most coordinated and compact, Jude would have been the natural choice to go through the window, but he clearly wasn't about to subject himself to the humiliation of being lifted by Joanna and Bridget. Joanna volunteered herself. Not waiting for confirmation, she divested herself of her "spy bag" and jacket and whipped her hair into a ponytail. Cracking her knuckles, she stepped toward the door with a determined grimace. She clambered from Jude's knee to Cole's back, supported by Bridget for balance, got a leg through, realized she needed to face down rather than up, and twisted in mid-air. Once through, she dropped to the floor with a thud. In another moment, the door clicked open. As he stepped inside the library, Cole's heart began to beat quicker, not with fear now, but with anticipation.

Joanna led the way to the library lounge, where the silhouettes of new furniture accentuated the eerie unfamiliarity of the darkness. Snatching Vendler's autobiography from the shelf, Joanna skirted the desk, touched the frame, and said, "Vendler." Nothing happened. She tried again, then looked her question at Cole.

"You do it. It isn't working for me."

Cole took the book from her, and the painting opened. He glanced self-consciously at Bridget.

"Never mind," Joanna said, checking her watch. "We don't have time to worry about that now. It's already 12:52."

As Cole descended the ladder, he was intensely aware of the sound of his own breathing. The dank, rotten smell of the cave walls engulfed him. Pulling aside the tree roots, he crawled into the circular room. He had watched Orien walk down each corridor, but he himself hadn't explored any of them yet. If he was honest with himself, he hadn't wanted to. Perhaps it was the low ceilings that admitted no light, or perhaps it was the irrational impression that the people in the alcove paintings were studying him, but there was something oppressive about those corridors that had made him afraid to do more than glance down them. It was best not to think about it.

He said, "If Vendler hid something, it has to be in one of the niches in these passages. There are six of them, so I suggest we each explore one, and whoever finishes first can start on the other two."

The others nodded grimly. Turning down the first corridor on the left, Cole was arrested by the hungry eyes and sardonic mouth of the woman whose portrait governed the nearest alcove. Tangled tresses formed an unrestrained halo like a lion's mane framing her face. Her eyes locked hungrily on his. It took a full minute for Cole to break the spell that held his attention captive and remember why he was there. Training his focus on the alcove behind the picture, he ran his fingers across its domelike surface, careful not to touch either the frame or the candle that was set in front of it. His eyes kept straying back to the woman, and it was with an effort that he broke away.

He was more prepared for the next alcove. Bending to examine it, he was met by the small, bull-like eyes of a man whose bulbous cheeks puffed angrily above a bristling beard. Resisting the desire of the sordid face to draw his gaze, Cole forced his mind to focus on his mission. What had Vendler hidden in these tunnels that Orien needed and Alexandria hated? Both were equally determined without even knowing what the object was. Of course, Alexandria's reason had been clouded by a quasi-maternal obsession with her sister, whereas Orien's interest was purely clinical. What, if anything, lay hidden in the recesses of this secret room that had the capability to make Kronos love?

He had made it through the first corridor now without result. Joanna and Bridget were still exploring their first passages, while Jude had passed on to examine a second. Entering the last corridor, Cole's gaze met that of a hunched, bald man with a hooked nose like a beak. His expression was as void as a vulture's. Cole shuddered involuntarily. He began to feel that he was in a catacomb. Wherever he looked, skull-like faces demanded his attention. But there was no regularity to the recesses: they were hollowed out at random heights and depths, a chaos of space and also, Cole thought irrationally, of time. He began to feel dizzy, and as his fingers explored each alcove, he recited to himself: "I'm Cole Erickson. I'm here on a mission from Orien Saint-Pierre. I'm going to find what Vendler hid. Then I'm leaving. There are stars and fresh air above me. I'll leave as soon as I find what Vendler hid. I'm here on a mission from Orien Saint-Pierre."

The internal chant helped him keep his bearings until he had completed the exploration of the last corridor. Exhaling in relief, he moved to the basin, where Bridget stood waiting. She said nothing, as if the silence protected her own reserves of sanity, but her lips moved rapidly. He wondered if she was praying. Standing so close to her, he could smell the incense that always clung to her clothes. As he inhaled it, the cave's rotten odor gradually receded. His thoughts grew sharper. She was like a candle, her light and warmth slowly banishing the darkness he had unwittingly brought back with him out of the tunnels.

"No luck?" he said.

She shook her head, her lips still moving in an unbroken pattern. Cole watched Jude and Joanna as they continued to search the last two corridors. There was still time. They would still find what Vendler had hid.

It wasn't long before Jude joined them, shaking his head in response to Cole's unasked question. Cole watched Joanna's every move with an expectation amounting to desperation. She was working her way back toward them now along the final wall, lifting each picture in the alcoves to search behind them, apparently unperturbed by their occupants. Cole's heart clenched as she stooped to run her fingers across the last alcove. Then she too rose and came to join them, and the heaviness of the cave that Cole had been trying to keep at bay stole over his body. If Orien hadn't found anything, what made Cole so sure they would find something tonight?

"And you already looked in the cabinet, right, Cole?" Joanna asked, pulling her ski mask off and stooping to examine it. "Just candles and matches."

"Do you think what Vendler hid was a physical object?" Jude asked. "Could it have been this space itself?"

"I guess," Cole said. "But what would be the point? What are we supposed to do?"

"What we're supposed to do is obvious," Bridget replied. "I'm just not sure it's wise."

Cole regarded her in surprise. "It is? What are we supposed to do?"

"Light a candle, of course. Think about it: why else would a sand-filled basin, plus candles and matches, be located in the center of the room? It's the only action the space requires."

"Well, if you're not willing to do it, I will," Joanna said, stooping once again to retrieve a taper candle and the box of matches.

She pushed the base of the candle into the sand and, without hesitation, struck a match. The flame licked the wick and lit. The cave came alive. One by one, starting with the first passage and ending with the last, the candles along all six corridors lit of their own accord. Shadows flickered against every surface, writhing in celebration of the contorted faces that encircled them.

Tearing his eyes away from the portraits, Cole gasped: the basin holding the candle had slid silently aside to reveal a dark hole the width of its base. Cole tried to breathe in the aroma of Bridget's incense to ground himself, but the odor of decaying flesh from the opening was too strong. Shining his flashlight into the hole, he saw another ladder descending into darkness.

"I'm going first this time," Jude said, and Cole was sure he was thinking of how Bridget had volunteered to ascend the ladder into the backstage room before he had. Jude hated cowardice.

"But do you think it will close again?" Cole asked, trying to keep his voice calm. "What if we get down there and the candle burns out and the basin shuts us in?"

"I doubt it," Jude answered, stepping onto the first rung of the ladder. "It seems reasonable to lock something out, but what would be the point of locking something in?"

Despite Jude's logic, the hole looked to Cole like the mouth of some behemoth that waited to snap its jaws shut after them.

"I'll stay here and wait for you, just in case," Bridget volunteered, though she shuddered as she glanced at the faces encircling her. She handed Cole her flashlight and bit her lower lip as if guarding her mouth against retracting the offer.

Cole wasn't sure what he wanted to do more: volunteer to take her place or kiss her. But he needed to be the one to find whatever it was Vendler had left. He squeezed her shoulder briefly and immediately wished he hadn't. That gesture had been worse than nothing. It put her more firmly into the friend category than he intended, but it had been his only way to thank her with Jude and Joanna watching. Clearing his throat, he turned toward the ladder.

CHAPTER 17

THE FIRST TEST

Bridget sat cross-legged on the floor beside the basin. She listened for the sound of her friends' footsteps and the murmur of their clothing. Soon, even those whispers were swallowed by silence. The portraits stared at her, straining to establish eye contact. Their insistence felt like a physical assault, and she shut her eyelids against them. She began to long for the breath of life in the air around her, even to miss the pervading undercurrent of electricity that she recognized as absent for the first time in her life. All sound was dead but for the irregular drip of distant water. The silence pressed like a formless hand against her eardrums, oppressing her with a heaviness like exhaustion. The desire for sleep began to steal over her. She thought of her bed, of her lavender-scented feather pillow, and of the heavy knit blanket that lay beside it.

"This won't do," she said aloud, shaking herself awake with the sound of her own voice. What if she had fallen asleep? What if the candle had burned out before her friends returned? She stood up to measure time by the taper candle.

It was already two-thirds consumed. Should she light another? Not yet, but soon. She moved to the cabinet and retrieved another candle.

As she straightened, her heart stopped. On the wall in front of her was a face she recognized—her mother's face. A convulsive shiver swept through her body. She knew that face intimately. She had often stared into it as if into a mirror of what she should have been: the flaming hair framing a face that was heart-shaped instead of diamond, the nose shorter than Bridget's, the eyes brighter and less orb-like.

She crept closer, and her heart began to beat again. It was not her mother. The features were similar, but the expression was shockingly different. This woman's mouth curled upward in the same teasing smile but drooped suddenly at the corners. The eyes were rimmed with the red of sleepless nights, and the pupils were vacant. The nose was pointed like that of a fox, and as Bridget looked closer, she was shocked to see that there were actually whiskers fanning faintly out from it on either side. Had this been a fanciful addition of the painter's, or was the woman actually part fox?

A soft hiss made her swivel around just in time to see the candle dying in a pool of its own wax. At the same time, a noiseless wind extinguished every candle in the chamber. The wicks glowed red for a moment; then the cave was thrust into darkness. Panic constricted Bridget's breathing. She kicked herself for allowing curiosity to distract her from her vigil. Desperately, she tried to picture exactly where she was in relation to the basin and the box of matches that she had stupidly left inside the cabinet, but it was no use. Her sense of orientation had died along with the light. If she moved, she might accidentally brush up against one of the faces on the wall, or worse, tumble into the gaping hole on the floor. She took a shaky breath and tried to address herself in the reassuring tone her Poppy used.

"Now Bridget, all that's happened is the candle burned out. If you sit tight, your friends will be back soon with their flashlights, and you can all go home together."

But what if that wasn't true? What if the basin had slid back over the hole like a tombstone, sealing them in? They hadn't heard it open, so she wouldn't have heard it close. For that matter, what if she couldn't hear her friends when they did return? Sound was supernaturally muted in these chambers, and she might never hear their voices begging her to let them out. She must do something. She must move.

She inched away from the wall, trying to steady her breathing as her fingers brushed searchingly across the rock floor. Her hand met a vertical wooden surface, and she fumbled her way up it, praying it would be the cabinet. The taper candle was still nestled in the crook of her thumb like a promise as her fingers groped upward. But wood gave way to canvas and her fingers brushed something cold and wet. Horrified, she jerked her hand away. The candle dropped out of it, the roll of its barely audible scratch on the uneven floor the sound of retreating hope.

She sniffed gingerly at the thin film on her fingertips. It reeked of putrefied saliva. Choking down the urge to vomit, she wiped her fingers violently on her jeans. Which portrait had she touched? Was it alive? Was it her imagination, or could she actually hear the slow rasp of it breathing? She backed instinctively away, forgetting her fear of the dark hole. Her foot caught on a ridge and sent her into a sideways somersault that destroyed any lingering notion of which way was which.

Pain shot through her side. Had she dislocated a rib? She lay completely still, the terror of darkness oppressing her. It beckoned her to give in to inertia, to surrender her mind to the oblivion of sleep that was her only relief from fear. An idea came to her to cry out to her friends for help, but she gave it up instantly. They were too far from her; they would never hear. Her breathing calmed, and she surrendered to exhaustion.

Just before sleep could claim her, Cole's voice whispered in her ear like an echo from another time: "What if we get down there and the candle burns out and the basin shuts us in?" His voice grounded her in a full awareness of her physicality. She felt the coldness of the floor against her cheek, the painful protrusion under her ribcage, and the rhythm of breath passing in and out of her lungs. Slowly, she eased herself onto an elbow and groped at her ribcage. Her fingers found a soft cylinder with a string on one end—the candle! She grasped it so tightly the wax began to mold to her palm.

Slowly, she began crawling around the room again. One hand guarded against the lip of the hole, the other groped the cave's walls. At every moment she expected to be led into a corridor of strange faces that smelled like death. The wall gave way; her upraised hand hovered over nothingness, and she crawled toward it. Her hand brushed against a mass of cables, and she realized with a surge of elation that she had found the exit. That meant the ladder out of the hole and into the library was just a few feet from her—she was free! A mad laugh gurgled up her throat and spilled out into the nothingness of the prison walls around her, which consumed the sound and rebounded fear back to her.

That fear sobered her. If she left, she would be abandoning her friends. She reasoned that going back up the ladder would be the smart thing to do: she could wash her hands, regain her senses, find some source of light to bring back down, and go back for them. But she knew that once she left, she wouldn't have the courage to come back. Swallowing, she turned around and crawled back into the cave.

Into the darkness sprung a sudden light, blinding but beautiful. In its glow, Bridget could make out the massive coil of tree roots, hanging limply. No one was holding the light; it was just there. She told herself that wasn't possible, yet she blinked and it was still there; she told herself this must be some new trick of Vendler's, but its brightness made the cave look like some tawdry stage set; she told herself she ought to be afraid, but she wasn't.

She had never seen a flame so pure in her life. It warmed her from feet away. Its beauty drew her to it, and when she was close enough to receive the light, her whole body was shot through with joy.

Cole held his hand over his nose to block out the growing stench as he descended the ladder. His feet met the stone floor sooner than he expected. As he released the ladder and turned to examine the room, he was plunged into a memory of slipping into the deep end of the pool when he was a toddler, his hand sliding off the sunscreen-slicked railing as he fell, choking, into churning chaos. He threw a hand out to steady himself and choked on the stench.

Calming his breath with an effort, he shined his flashlight around the low-ceilinged enclosure. Several dark masses stood at the far end of the room. They looked like sentinels without necks. Already the candlelight from the room above was growing dim and distant, just as the sun had sunk from sight when he fell into the infinite pool as a child.

As Cole approached, the sentinels resolved themselves into twelve man-sized limestone slabs arranged in a circle, their tops almost brushing the cave ceiling. The inner-facing side of each pillar bore a large painting.

As soon as Jude stepped inside the circle, a thin, cracked voice said: *Have no fear, but draw you near. Whisper words my ear will hear: What is the thing I want above all? Why have I labored so long? What have my heir and my book got to do with a painting of a dog?*

The words rebounded off each of the twelve slabs until the echo faded in a reverent whisper. Cole's arms prickled with goosebumps. Despite the echo, he found himself glancing at the others to ensure he hadn't imagined the voice. One look at Jude and Joanna told him they also knew the voice was Vendler's, speaking to them from another time.

But what did the riddle mean? Had there been any clue to Vendler's greatest wish in his autobiography? And the painting of the dog—that had to be the one hanging in Alexandria's hall—what had Bridget said about it? If only he could ask her. But here in the darkness of the stone circle, the light of her presence seemed a million miles away.

Joanna was looking at him as if he ought to have the answer, probably because he was the only one who had read the autobiography, so he said, "Let's search for clues." His own voice, being outside the stone circle, died instantly, and it gave him a sudden inspiration. "Let's avoid talking while we're in the stone circle. It's probably a childish idea, but I think whatever is said within the circle will be taken as an answer."

Jude and Joanna nodded. As Cole crossed the threshold, he was assailed with yet another long-forgotten memory: following the unexpected sound of voices late one night when his dad was out drinking, he had crept from his upstairs bedroom into the living room. As he entered the sacred circle of family furniture, his mom's face appeared, white and panicked as if she had been the one caught out of bed too late, from behind the back of a head that wasn't his dad's. Cole never saw the man's face—one look at his mom's was enough, and he ran back up the stairs. In the morning, neither of them mentioned it. The divorce was formalized soon after. Cole had long since blocked that memory. Why should it come back now?

He blinked it away and focused on the picture before him. It depicted a pregnant woman with an abnormally swollen womb. Her face was blurred, faraway, and disturbingly not the focal point of the composition even though she was the only human in the picture. The portentous sky was lit like daylight, but in place of the conspicuously missing sun was a constellation he didn't recognize. He couldn't find a clue to the answer anywhere.

Passing on to the next, he saw the body of a baby with the face of a grown man—Vendler's face. Neither mother nor father was present. Under the baby's foot were all manner of crawling, creeping, winged, and oceanic animals. Here again, the image presented nothing that Cole could interpret as an answer to Vendler's riddle.

The third picture was governed by a boy whose right hand was extended: rust tongues of flame strained upward from the palm, a shower of aqua droplets fell into it, a puff of rolling cloud hovered over it, and a crumbled heap of stone and dust rested atop it. These must be stylized symbols of fire, water, air, and earth. The face of the ageless boy was the same as the baby's on the previous pillar, and nothing but the underdeveloped musculature hinted at his age.

The portrait on the fourth stone was the first that did not prominently feature the man child (for Cole was convinced now that the baby in the mother's enormous womb was the man child). In the foreground was the back of his head, dark hair arranged in lank half moons. Together with him, Cole looked at a man sitting on a stool facing an easel. What was on the easel, Cole couldn't tell, but it absorbed both the painter and the spectator. It was the first scene that was full of warmth, not fear. For a moment, Cole forgot his purpose as he gazed at the painter, desiring only to see what he was painting.

"Any ideas yet?"

Joanna's voice outside the stone circle startled him. He shook his head. Jude, who was examining a painting two yards away, looked just as clueless as Cole. Cole passed on to the fifth painting, and as he did so, a deeper darkness seemed to fall about them. He had to hold his flashlight close to the image to make it out. It was a study in beige. In the center, an enormous pyramid pointed to heaven, guarded by a crouching sphinx. It wasn't until Cole looked closely that he realized the face of the sphinx was a grotesquely feminine version of the man child.

Disturbed, he passed on to the sixth stone. This one again showed the man child, but now with creases around his eyes and a beard on his face. And again, there was a painter. But this time, the painter was in the foreground as spectator, transferring Vendler's likeness to a canvas so that there was a painting within the painting. The extravagant narcissism made Cole's skin crawl, and he sidestepped to the seventh stone.

Here was the first scene he recognized: a lonely shack in the heart of the woods leaning westward in the wind. Its paint was fresher than when Cole had seen it, the front steps less dilapidated. So, Alexandria had been telling the truth. The surprise he expected to feel found no hold in him against the new and unexpected emotion that flamed in his heart: outrage that Vendler hadn't left this pitiful home inviolate. Even as he thought it, he was humiliated to realize that if

Vendler had left Acalia alone, he himself would not be standing here to be grateful for it.

"Cole, come look at this," Joanna's voice whispered. She beckoned him past another scene that pictured Vendler Academy to an image set indoors in which Vendler was bending over a writing desk. On the desk lay a book titled *My Life*.

Cole looked his question, and Joanna stepped outside the circle again. "It's his autobiography, I think. But look at this one—I don't understand it."

He followed her to the last stone but one. In the center of an otherwise black canvas was a pure white flower. Its remarkable realism contrasted jarringly with the fanciful and crude strokes on the other canvases. He reached out a hand, almost touching it, but Jude's voice called him away.

"Did you see this one?" he indicated one of the stones Cole had walked past. "Vendler's killing something, a goat maybe? And by the looks of it drinking its blood. But that's not all—there's real blood smeared all around the background of the canvas. Maybe that explains the stench down here."

Cole had heard enough not to want a closer look. Swallowing, he passed on to the twelfth and final stone. Jude and Joanna stepped behind him, and the three of them stared at a completely blank canvas.

Jude stepped outside the circle and murmured, "Ran out of paint?"

The attempt at levity did nothing to alleviate the growing oppression that weighed heavier on Cole with each second spent inside the stone circle. Pretending to examine the blank backsides of the limestone slabs, he stepped outside the ring and immediately began to breathe easier.

"Any guesses on the riddle?" Joanna asked.

Cole shook his head.

"So much for getting to the bottom of things tonight," Jude said. "I guess we'd better head back up then." His voice echoed Cole's disappointment.

Defeated, they trudged back toward the ladder. Only when Cole's head peeked through the floor above did he realize that something was wrong: there was no candle in the basin. All was dark but for a faint glow emanating from one of the six corridors. It wasn't until Jude and Joanna had joined him that his flashlight found Bridget, a candle clutched in her hand, her white face resolute but frightened. Cole was overwhelmed with an urge to rush toward her, but Joanna did it for him so that he matched her pace without embarrassment. Together they drew her, shaking, to her feet. Joanna wrapped her in a tight hug. The cave was filled with the relieved tinkling of Bridget's laughter, which Cole realized he had never heard before. It was beautiful and clear as a brook's ripple, though her cheeks were still streaked with tears. He wished it was his shoulders that Bridget clung to instead of Joanna's. Still holding onto Joanna, her eyes traveled from Cole's face to Jude's as if assuring herself that her friends were truly there.

"The candle went out," she explained in a small voice. "Somehow I wasn't sure you'd come back."

"Looks like it's burning now," Jude said. "Besides, where else would we go?"

"I don't know how this flame came to me. I didn't light it. The first one did go out. I swear it." Bridget's eyebrows furrowed, and she blinked as if waking from a dream. "So? Did you find what Vendler left?"

Cole shook his head. He was still trying to think of a way to comfort her.

"Just more paintings," Joanna said. "Scenes from Vendler's life, we think. But there was a voice that asked us a riddle we couldn't solve: something about what he wants above all and what his book and Cole have to do with a painting of a dog."

"He wants his memory to be eternal," Bridget said.

"What?" Jude said.

"That's the answer: he did all those things so his memory will be eternal."

"How do you know that?" Cole asked. "I don't remember him saying anything about that in the autobiography."

Bridget shook her head. "It wasn't in the autobiography, at least not overtly. It was what Vendler wrote on the back of that picture in Alexandria's cottage, remember?"

"Sure, but how do you know it's connected with me and his book, and why the dog?" Cole asked, feeling like a slow student. "And what happens if we give the answer and it's wrong?"

"Only one way to find out," Jude said. "Let's go try. We know now the trap door doesn't close when the candle burns down, so Bridget can come with us this time."

"Not tonight," Cole said, surprising even himself. "Bridget is in no state to stay down here. We can always come back and try another time. Come on, let's get you out of here."

Cole handed Bridget his flashlight and extinguished the candle. She looked at him, too shaken to smile, her face expressing only relief. It took the full concentration of his willpower to leave the mystery unsolved, but he told himself they would return, and they would find what Vendler left.

CHAPTER 18

STALEMATE

"First the paperweight, now this!"

Cole's fingers froze on the library doorknob he had been about to turn. The exhaustion he had been fighting all day after getting home at 3 am vanished completely.

"Kindly explain what 'this' is," responded Dr. Bering's voice, heavy with irritation.

"White paint flecks—from that window."

Cole's throat went dry. She knew. He strained to catch the reply.

"Enlighten me. I see nothing."

"Because your assistant wouldn't let me see you till now," Mrs. Fay continued, "and I couldn't have these hallowed halls desecrated by decrepitude! I vacuumed the debris myself this morning, but the evidence is there. You see? That window has been forced open, and I was not the one to do it."

There was a pause, and the silence was once again broken by Mrs. Fay, speaking this time in a whisper that did her hardness of hearing credit: "You know when these disturbances began, don't you? They began when *that boy* entered the premises."

"Mrs. Fay, I have already listened to your accusations that Giles Tate was responsible for the missing paperweight, but I have spoken with his teachers, and they all report him to be a quiet, studious, and satisfactory child. His brother Wesley is among our top students."

Cole caught his breath. The awkward, bashful Dove was Wesley's brother? He pressed his ear closer to the door and clamped a hand over his mouth so Dr. Bering wouldn't hear his breathing.

Dr. Bering's voice went on: "If an open window and a missing paperweight that was of little more than *sentimental* value are all you have against him, and if, as seems apparent, you are able to form no *logical* connection between him and the disturbances in question, I must ask you to excuse me. I have more pressing matters to attend to."

Approaching footsteps made Cole jump back from the door. The knob began to turn.

"Wait! There's something else."

Despite Dr. Bering's proximity, Cole couldn't help but press his ear against the keyhole again.

"The boy's a cheat."

"Come again?" Dr. Bering's voice was stone.

"I said, the boy is a cheat. He hangs around at odd hours, mostly when the upperclassmen are here. He sits at that desk —" the receding clack of heels informed Cole that Mrs. Fay was moving to the outside wall of the library to point down the row of desks set against the windows "—at the last desk but one, while the other students study in the lounge. Perfect for hearing but not being seen. And once—" a pregnant pause heralded the crowning indictment, "I saw him actually sneak back to the lounge and thumb through a notebook another student accidentally left behind."

Cole's heart seemed to have stopped beating. So, the Dove did suspect something. But how much did he guess, and what, if anything, had he found? And whose notebook had the Dove been looking at? It hadn't been Cole's. He didn't make mistakes when it came to academics.

Then he remembered Joanna drawing a map of the underground room for Jude's benefit, and he felt suddenly ill. She had done it in a school notebook. He hadn't seen the drawing; would she have included words, or anything that might indicate how to enter the cave? Dr. Bering's voice startled him back to the present.

"If what you say is true, it must be taken seriously. Academic dishonesty is one thing we have never and will never turn a blind eye to at Vendler Academy. I must ask you, Mrs. Fay, are you absolutely sure of what you saw?"

"Absolutely."

Cole heard Dr. Bering inhaling slowly before he spoke again.

"In that case, I am left with no choice but to take the matter again to Giles's teachers and ask whether any of them suspect plagiarism or have observed other behaviors similar to the incident you witnessed. If they suspect nothing, I shall admonish the boy and lay the matter to rest. If they do have cause to suspect him... well then. But for the present, I must ask you not to speak of this to anybody."

Cole released the door handle just in time to see it turn. Pivoting, he walked back down the hall as quickly as might look natural. He was only a few paces away when he looked back over his shoulder to see Dr. Bering stepping out. Their eyes locked. Cole was suddenly conscious that he was breathing harder than he ought to have been.

"And what are you doing out of class?" the headmaster asked, clearly recognizing Cole but allowing no leniency in his current mood even for a student who was being interviewed for the Orien Saint-Pierre internship.

"It's my study hall, sir. I was coming to study in the library but then saw that the door was closed, and I didn't want to interrupt anything."

At least that much was true. Dr. Bering just stood there.

"I see. Well, you'll be glad to find the door open now."

Under his stare, Cole nodded and slipped past him, walking as quickly as he could to the back of the library. It wasn't until he rounded the last stack of books and his eyes met the sterile redecoration of the library lounge that he remembered he and his friends had agreed to study in the auditorium today. But it would look suspicious if he encountered Dr. Bering on his way out again, and suspicion was the last thing he needed at the moment.

Cole set his backpack on the new metal desk but didn't take his books out. How could he concentrate on homework knowing that Dr. Bering might at any moment unearth the truth about who had really opened the window, or what it meant? And now that Mrs. Fay suspected something, it would be riskier than ever to return to the underground tunnel and finish his mission from Orien. Not that Orien realized the danger. If Orien knew the full situation, he would probably tell Cole to drop the mission. But Cole couldn't walk away. He could feel Vincent Vendler's gaze boring into the back of his skull. His own need to know the truth gnawed at him like hunger.

Cole stared listlessly out the row of windows as snowflakes whitened the grounds. At least it hadn't been snowing last night—their tracks would have been just one more piece of incriminating evidence. Though come to think of it, the appearance of multiple tracks might at least have helped exonerate the Dove. If only the Dove hadn't been so nosy. Cole and his friends could have kept exploring at study hall instead of breaking in, and Cole wouldn't feel responsible for protecting the Dove from suspicion. He felt, irrationally, as if Wes was still finding a way to stop him from succeeding with the internship.

When the school bell rang, he was slow to pick up his backpack. The books seemed to have grown heavier. It was the last thing he wanted to do, but Cole promised himself he would tell his friends what he had just heard. He had arranged to meet them in the lawn outside the library to plan their next exploit, but now they would have to discuss whether there would be a next exploit. Cole wasn't sure he could trust his own judgment, not when so much was at stake for him.

The winter air stung his skin as he stepped outside, where his friends were already waiting for him. Bridget was shivering, and Joanna's cheeks were flushed—whether with cold or excitement, Cole couldn't tell. Jude looked sour, as if somehow, he knew what had happened and was ready to remind the others that he had always thought breaking in was a bad idea.

"I've checked the school calendar," Joanna whispered. Her eyes, red with exhaustion, still glittered with excitement. "No late evening events this week. We could go again as early as tonight."

Cole kicked at a tuft of grass, letting the snow accumulate on the back of his neck. Joanna was waiting for him to reply.

Finally, he said, "I'm not sure that's going to be possible." He willed himself to look into Jude's eyes, then recounted the conversation he had overheard in the library, including the Dove's real name.

"I knew it," Jude said, shaking his head in self-disgust.

"So now they suspect the Dove. Because of us. If I had the guts, I'd go tell Dr. Bering right now that it was us and not him."

Joanna's eyes widened. "But Jude, you don't need to! Dr. Bering defended the Dove anyway, by the sound of it."

Jude rubbed his neck and grimaced. "But he couldn't, not completely. Not after what Mrs. Fay said about him cheating."

"That was his choice, not ours," Joanna said. "How were we supposed to prevent him from looking at our books?"

Cole wanted to agree, especially now that he knew the Dove was Wes's brother. It wouldn't hurt for the Tates to be held to the same standard as everyone else. Still, it didn't make sense that the Dove was looking at their notebooks in order to cheat, and he forced himself to say so. "He's a freshman. None of us have overlapping classes. I think what he was looking at was your notebook, Joanna."

"My notebook?"

"You drew a map for Jude, remember? It isn't much of a stretch to assume he was looking for clues, given that we know he's at least heard fragments of our conversations about the cave already."

Fear finally dawned on Joanna's face, and her eyes grew even wider. Suddenly she shrugged. "So what if he does suspect something? That drawing wouldn't have told him anything, and he doesn't know how to get behind the painting of Vendler anyway, so we're safe—especially now that we're exploring at night instead of during study hall."

Jude shook his head in disbelief. "Joanna, you're not listening to what Cole is saying: there won't be any more exploring. Not on my watch."

Cole's insides clenched. He felt like Jude was slamming a door on the only future he knew to hope for, and he stretched out a hand to catch the door before the latch clicked. "But don't you think the Dove will be fine once his teachers confirm he isn't cheating?"

Bridget, who had been staring at an abandoned bird's nest in the tree branches, shifted her gaze to him but said nothing. He wished he knew what she was thinking.

Jude threw his hands out in exasperation. "Look, the only reason he's in danger in the first place is because of us. Because of me. Think about it. *I* was the one who threw that paperweight down into the hole to see how far down it was. *I* was the reason Joanna drew that map in her notebook. And I was also the one who let us all into Paul's shed last night! I knew this would happen. It's why I was so against the idea to begin with, but I felt like I couldn't stop you. I wish I had.

"Don't you see what's happening? It isn't just us we're endangering. We're dragging other people into this with us now, and who knows what'll happen next! What if the Dove really is expelled? Or what if Paul comes under suspicion because we're using his shed to break in? Are you really prepared to face the consequences of what we're doing here? Because I'm not."

Joanna shook her head vigorously. "It won't happen like that. We know how to get in now! If we do exactly what we did last time, nothing more will happen. The window is already free, and we got into Paul's shed without leaving any traces. Otherwise, we'd have been found out today."

"I'm sorry, Joanna. Risking our own futures was one thing. Risking someone else's future is entirely different. We need to just walk away and forget we ever found the caves."

"I think you're being a bit too reactive about this," Joanna said in a patronizing tone Cole knew would only entrench Jude further in his opinion. "Why don't we give it a day and discuss it again after we've all had time to let things sink in. Then, we can make a more reasonable decision, together."

"I'm not changing my mind, Joanna."

"What do you think, Bridget?" Cole asked in a desperate attempt to distract from the mounting tension between Jude and Joanna. He regretted the question as soon as he asked it —it was quite likely that Bridget would still be getting over last night's terror.

"I don't think it's wise to go again. I think Alexandria was right—Vendler was evil."

The word "evil" annoyed Cole. Why was everyone so convinced that Vendler's discoveries couldn't be repurposed for good?

Not wanting to antagonize Bridget, he said, "Okay, but even if it is evil, don't you think we have a responsibility to find it and destroy it like Alexandria asked?"

"I think," Bridget said slowly, "that it isn't so wise to wake the devil. Sometimes, the surest way to kill him is to ignore him."

"And sometimes it's to fight him, right?" Cole said, less because he believed there was a devil and more because he hoped the argument would appeal to Jude. It didn't work. Jude's mouth was a hard line, and Bridget merely stared at Cole until he dropped his eyes.

Cole kicked the tuft of grass again. To continue talking would only make Jude even more certain that they should walk away. The only comfort was that Cole wouldn't have to tell Orien right away; he hadn't heard anything yet about the next interview. Frustrated, Cole said good-bye and drove home in a cocoon of snow that muted sound and gave the illusion of dropping a barrier between him and the need for action.

CHAPTER 19

NOTHING TO LOSE

By Saturday morning, the snow became rain that glazed the sidewalks in sheets of ice. By Sunday morning, the drizzle gave way to an oppressive stillness. The house seemed to be shrinking in on Cole, who had finished his homework and had nothing to distract himself from the maddening need to know what Vendler had left behind. Innervated with a growing restlessness, Cole decided he couldn't face another day staring at the beige walls of his room, waiting for nothing. He texted Bridget to tell her he would take her up on her standing offer to attend divine liturgy with her and her grandparents. Vendler Academy, its parking lot oddly forsaken, drew his gaze as he drove past it on his way to St. Raphael's. He turned in, just to stare at the building while his engine idled, then reluctantly drove on when he realized Bridget might ask him why he was late.

When he arrived, she and her grandparents were already there. Poppy, a tall man with intelligent eyes and a thin layer of well-groomed white hair, nodded at him as he moved to stand beside Bridget. Birdy, a short woman with an enormous pile of fluffy white hair topping a soft-skinned face set with eyes like sapphires, gave him a smile like butterscotch. It was difficult for Cole to pay attention to any words that were said or sung during the service, but the haze of incense and music washed over him like ocean waves blanketed in mist, soothing his anxiety. Being in the church was like being with Bridget, but more concentrated.

After service, Bridget's grandparents took them out to Denny's. There was something Cole found reassuring about the sharp scent of Poppy's peppermint lifesavers cutting through the pervasive aroma of sugar and bacon. Beside Poppy, Birdy was knitting a ghastly orange sock, her laughter making a pretty duet with the clicking of her needles. Bridget smiled more with her grandparents than she did at school, and there was a carefree openness about her gestures that Cole was glad his presence didn't inhibit. As they mopped up puddles of syrup and listened to Poppy's stories about serving in the CIA during the Cold War, Cole finally understood why Bridget didn't want to go out of state for college—this must be what family felt like.

As they stood to leave, Birdy enfolded him in a plump hug so different from his mother's brief and bony press that he felt years of defenses—defenses he didn't even know he had— threaten to melt from his body.

Birdy pulled away and patted his cheek, saying, "Thanks for coming, Nicholas. This is the first time we've met any of Bridget's friends from VAST and EMPTY."

Cole stifled a laugh, imagining how Dr. Bering would react to Birdy's casual use of the acronym.

"Come again whenever you like," Birdy said. "We'll bribe you with more pancakes!"

Bridget didn't emphasize the invitation, but Cole told himself that the smile she gave him when they said goodbye meant she was glad he had come. After the morning with Bridget, his car felt colder than it had that morning, and as he turned onto Hollow Tree Way, his dad's house looked lonelier. Cole unlocked the front door and headed for his room, stopping abruptly when he saw his dad sitting on a kitchen barstool.

"Wondered where you'd got to," his dad said, flashing Cole a shy grin over his coffee mug. Setting the mug down, he slid a brown paper bag across the counter toward Cole. "A late birthday gift. Thought I'd forgotten, didn't you?"

"I know you've been busy," Cole lied.

To avoid meeting his dad's eyes, he took the bag, reached inside, and pulled out something he had only seen in old photographs—his father's U.S. Army hat. The stars were still so bright they reflected the kitchen lights.

"I know it's kind of a weird gift, but for some reason I thought you might want it. Maybe a reminder to do better than your old man, huh?"

His dad was smiling tentatively, like a chastised dog hoping to be received back into its master's good graces. Cole couldn't think of what to say. He opened an arm for a hug that turned into a handshake and mumbled a thanks.

"Don't mention it. You'd better go put that thing away somewhere. I don't like seeing it."

Cole dropped it back into the bag and turned toward his room, then pivoted on the stairs. If he was never to discover Vendler's secret, he had nothing to lose by risking a little transparency.

"Dad, why didn't you tell me about Alexandria?"

As soon as he said it, time froze. The house was as still as it had been after the Talavera vase shattered. His dad took a long time setting his mug back onto the countertop.

"What did you just say?"

Cole gripped the railing. He couldn't go back now. "Alexandria. She told me she's tried to get in touch with me for years. Why didn't you tell me?"

His dad placed his hands on his knees and stared at Cole in a way that made him want to run upstairs and hide in the bathtub again. Cole stood his ground.

"Listen, son. I don't know how that damned woman found you, but if you want my advice, you leave her alone. She's psycho."

Cole turned to face his dad full on. Somewhere in the back of his mind, he realized why his dad had given him the Army cap—for weeks his dad had been assiduously clearing the house of anything that reminded him of Layla. Apparently, the military cap was one item he couldn't bear to look at yet couldn't box up and send to Goodwill. The realization gave Cole courage.

"But she wrote letters to *me*. Why didn't you ever tell me? Didn't you think I had a right to know?"

"A right? A *right*? What is it with these damned American kids and their rights? Everyone thinks they have a *right* to information, a *right* to have a happy life and do whatever the hell they feel like, and no one gets that sometimes life is just a damned shit show and you're lucky to get out alive."

"And why aren't we doing anything to help her? Why are you so ashamed of her?"

"I'm not *ashamed* of her. I'm protecting you." His dad's voice was dangerously close to breaking.

"I don't need protecting. I need a family."

"You think *you* have it bad? My childhood was hell. I didn't even have a father, for God's sake!" His fist came down heavy on the counter, making his mug rattle.

"Sometimes I wonder whether I have one anymore too."

Cole turned around and stomped up the stairs before he

could see the expression on his dad's face. He locked the bedroom door, tossed the paper bag into a desk drawer, and climbed between his sheets with his clothes still on. Minutes crawled by, slipping into hours. Eventually, he slipped into a fitful dream in which Bridget, wearing his dad's Army cap, was offering him tea candles to light in front of an icon of a man on a white horse spearing a winged lizard. Cole insisted to her that he couldn't take the candles without knowing who the man was, and her eyes flamed at him like starlight. When he looked back at the icon to escape the intensity of their light, it had morphed into a picture of Orien Saint-Pierre. A voice said, "Will you light the candle now?" The change startled him so greatly that he stepped back into the bright heat of Bridget, whose auburn hair had merged with the lit candle in her hand, consuming herself and Cole in flame.

CHAPTER 20

CHRISTMAS

Finals week came and went with no change in Jude's attitude about exploring the cave under the library. Even Cole had to admit that exams took precedence over Orien's mission, though that didn't stop him from wandering the caves in his dreams. With the fall semester behind him, Cole was left alone in his room with nothing to distract him from wondering about Vendler's legacy and coming up with possible ways to justify to Jude—as if to his own conscience—the necessity of exploring further. Perhaps, if enough time elapsed and the Dove's academic standing was cleared beyond doubt, they could break into the school again without fear of endangering anyone. But Orien's insistence hadn't left space for the kind of time needed to clear the Dove's character. Cole's only comfort was that Orien had not yet forced the moment of decision.

Worse than being left alone with his own restless thoughts was being confined over Christmas with his dad. Cole could only assume that his dad was haunted by the same ghosts of happier holidays that plagued him also, because Cole woke each morning to discover a fresh array of empty PBR cans and Southern Comfort bottles littering side tables and sofas. It was like watching someone try to saw their way through loss with a dull, double-edged knife. On one side was rage when he drank and on the other was shame when he was sober. The self-loathing was almost as painful to witness as the anger.

To escape the house, Cole took to shadowing Jude, who was only too glad of his help in preparing for the Durhams' annual Christmas party. Officially, the party was to take place on December the 23rd; unofficially, it began as soon as Jude and his twin siblings, Chandler and Victoria, were out of school.

There were tablecloths to be ironed, trays to be polished, sofa crevices to be vacuumed, garlands to be hung, and candles to be set on every open ledge. Even Tullius's food and water dishes were conscientiously scrubbed of a year's worth of slobber. Cole was tasked with dusting, which took much longer than he anticipated. The Durhams owned a business that bought the contents of abandoned storage units, sight unseen, when their owners could no longer pay the rent. Usually the contents were sold, but a number of interesting pieces ended up cluttering the Durhams' cramped and ambling Victorian home. By the time Cole finished dusting, the bowls of mints and candies and nuts had been filled, depleted by Jude's five-year-old sister Belle, and filled again. All the while, a tantalizing aroma of roast chicken, berry pies, and savory scents emanated from the kitchen.

On the afternoon of the 23rd, Cole was sent home to ready himself for the party. Parking space was precious, and Cole was to pick Joanna and Bridget up from the Grant home. The thought of seeing Bridget again after several days apart sent a shiver of anticipation through Cole's body, and he dressed more carefully than usual. He had decided to wear the same suit he had worn for his interviews with Orien, and he combed his hair and brushed his teeth meticulously. Not that any of this would matter to Bridget, who would probably show up in an egregiously mismatched outfit. He smiled as he imagined her getting ready for him to pick her up, unaware of the surprise they had prepared for her.

When he pulled up to the Grant home, Joanna and Bridget were already waiting under the shelter of the half-moon portico. Snow was drifting sleepily in and out of the yellow orbs of the lamp posts that lined the driveway, and Cole's heart caught in his throat when he saw Bridget. She was dressed, not in the baggy corduroy pants and pink Converse he had imagined, but in a cream coat below which a cobalt dress caught dazzlingly in the porch light as she moved toward his car. Her hair was loosely curled and pinned back by a pearl clip as pure as her skin, drawing attention to her usually obscured face. Then Bridget tripped on the ledge, and Cole laughed in relief. This was still the awkward Bridget he had grown so fond of. He jumped out of the car and opened their doors. Joanna took the front seat. It was then that Cole realized she also had replaced her customary overlarge ceramics sweater with an emerald dress, her hair that was typically hidden behind a brightly colored headband gathered into an elegant bun with curled face frames. Diamonds dangled from her ears and around her throat. She looked every bit as expensive as the Grant house itself.

By the time they arrived at the Durham home, it was already ringing with laughter that could be heard from outside. Jude, who had been put in charge of greeting the guests and was escorting Belle's piano teacher into the dining room, didn't see them until they were already in the foyer.

He froze and murmured an involuntary, "Wow" at the

sight of Joanna, then flushed and took her fur coat a little too hastily.

"Oh, it's just the color of the dress," she demurred, shrugging out of her coat. Seeing her pleased smile, Cole kicked himself for missing the opportunity to tell Bridget how beautiful she looked. "When in doubt, always match your clothes to your eyes. That's why this works, except for the one corner of blue in my left eye—not much I can do about that."

"I don't think anyone will notice," Jude said, a little too genuinely. With an effort, he turned toward Cole and Bridget. "You look nice too, Bridget," he said, unflatteringly surprised.

"Thanks," she said, tugging at her hem uncomfortably. "Joanna dressed me."

"Ah, that explains it," Jude replied.

"Thank God Mama D decided to throw her annual party tonight," Joanna said, distracting from his rudeness. "My Mom and Dad are hosting their highly boring 'Yule-Tide Soiree' tonight for all of their country club friends."

"They won't mind if you miss it?" Cole asked.

"They do mind. Very much." Joanna grinned. "Normally, it wouldn't be an issue if I said I was going out, but my brother David is home for Christmas."

"So can't he cover for you? He's the golden child, right?" Jude asked.

"Well of course David is the Main Event. But they like to present us as a collection when he's home. You know, the perfect white-picket-fence family with two children, one of each gender, to make things nice and normal. If David is the Christmas ham, I'm the green bean side dish—no one really wants to eat green beans, but they complete the look."

Glancing at Jude, Bridget said, "Oh, I wouldn't say no one wants to eat green beans."

There was a pause in which Joanna stifled a smile and Jude

gazed determinedly out the door to anticipate the next arrivals.

Glancing briefly at Joanna again, he said, "Well, I wish I could join you, but I'm stuck here taking coats until all the guests have arrived. Paul came just before you did. He's already making the most of our spiked cider. I'm afraid you'll have to make yourselves at home on your own."

They passed into the living room, watching as guests continued to squeeze into the home until both the front and the back coat closet were overflowing. But the food and drink being carried from the kitchen in continuous waves was equal to the challenge.

When at last Jude was able to rejoin them, Joanna grabbed his arm and said, "Finally! I wasn't going to be able to wait much longer. Bridget darling, the three of us have prepared a little surprise for your birthday."

Cole watched her face closely. This was the moment he had been most looking forward to all evening.

"But you already gave me something! Actually, two some-things: a crossword book and a Neil Young record!"

"That was just so you wouldn't think I'd forgotten your birthday on the 21st," Joanna explained. "But today is the magnum opus. Okay, we all need to put on our coats again."

Bridget asked no questions as they tramped out the back door to the Durhams' shed, but an adorably shy smile flick-ered on her lips. The wooden door gave way with a creak, and Joanna, her hands over Bridget's eyes, marched her friend inside. The air smelled strongly of chicken feed. Jude tugged a string, and a bare lightbulb warmed the walls.

"Okay, ready?" Joanna asked. "On the count of three: one, two, three!"

As Joanna's fingers fell away, Bridget blinked in the light of a most familiar scene. There before her were the blush loveseat with the carved wood, the frayed green velvet armchair, the old bronze lamp glowing with a new bulb, and under all, the red Turkish rug. It was the school library, her library, recreated in Jude's shed. The shy smile was gone. Her body was rigid with shock.

Joanna began talking immediately: "That night after they changed your library, I asked Jude if he knew where the old furniture had been carted off to. He did know, because he had helped Paul. I told him my idea, and he volunteered to bring his family's moving truck up that night once it got dark enough not to be noticed hauling things out of the dumpster. We got Cole to help load the truck, and then as soon as we could, we cleared a space in here and set it all up. We did the finishing touches yesterday. I know it isn't the same—we thought of setting up books and bookshelves to make it feel right, but in the end we decided we'd better not because it's too damp in here. But it is something. Do you like it?"

For the first time since he had met her, Cole saw a complete softening of Bridget's face, as if a mask had dropped. He hoped he would remember that look forever.

"It's perfect," she whispered, her voice thick. She ran her finger over the intricate woodwork of the blush loveseat that she had so often traced. "Thank you."

"The only liberty we took," Joanna went on excitedly, "was to add this heater, since otherwise it would be freezing, and we're guessing we want to spend a bit of the evening in here. Well, the other liberty we took is actually why this library has a slight advantage over the school library." Striding over to a side table by the green armchair, Joanna theatrically whipped a tablecloth off of a silver tray bearing all of Bridget's favorite goodies: black licorice, candied ginger, cashews, mandarin oranges, goat cheese, buttered popcorn, a hot kettle with a tea tray, and even some slightly stale, slightly frozen crab wontons. "In this library, there's no sign forbidding food!"

Bridget released a beautiful laugh. Cole would have done anything to hear it again. He plugged the electric kettle into the extension cord on the ground and said, "Bridget, what kind of tea do you want?"

They spent the entire evening huddling in lap blankets by the electric heater, playing cards, and listening to the wind whistle through the holes in the shed walls. Bridget's mask stayed mostly off, and she laughed and spoke and ate more than Cole had ever remembered. He got a little jolt of pleasure every time he offered her another wonton or more licorice or popcorn and she accepted. For the first time in weeks, Vendler's name wasn't mentioned once.

When midnight chimed on the church bells, Bridget said it was probably time to head home. Cole idled as long as possible, folding blankets and bagging up leftovers.

The sound of metal scraping metal made him swivel toward the door.

"What was that?" Joanna asked.

"Sounded like the side gate," Jude replied, heading for the door. "But only the family use that gate."

The midnight frost nipped their noses as they left the shed. For a second, Cole wondered irrationally whether Alexandria had tracked him down again, but the solitary figure by the backyard gate was obviously male. He was taking an inordinate amount of time to fiddle with the latch. When at last he turned around, he listed and fell into his steps. Cole recognized that walk: it was the same as his dad's after particularly bad nights at the bar. To Cole's left, Jude whispered a curse word under his breath. The wind picked up, carrying a reek of stale body odor toward them.

As the man stepped into the glow of the back porch light,

Cole saw the same brown almond eyes, the same haywire hair, and the same angular jaw and sharp chin that belonged to Jude. So this was Seth. The man spread his arms open and grinned.

"Surprised to see me?"

Jude tensed, his fists clenching.

"What the hell are you doing here?"

"Cool down," Seth said, raising his hands as if in surrender. "How about, 'It's nice to see you'?"

"I try not to say things I don't mean, unlike some people. Why are you here? Did you run out of money again?"

The man shrugged.

"Family's family, at least that's what Mom always said. And Christmas is the time for generosity."

"I knew it," Jude said, walking forward to stand between the man and the back door. "Look, I'm only going to say this once: get out, and don't come back, or you'll regret it."

"Hey, I only want to talk to everybody."

"There's no way I'm letting that happen. Not after last time."

Jude grabbed the steel snow shovel that was leaning against the side of the house. Alarmed, Joanna put her hand over one of his on the shovel. He shook it off.

"Jude, what are you...?"

"Cute girlfriend," the man said, combing his eyes over Joanna.

"Shut up," Jude said. His knuckles had gone white.

The man shrugged again.

"Have it your way. But I didn't come all this way to stand in the cold and argue with you. I'm going to see Mom."

He advanced, trying to push Jude aside. Cole stepped beside Jude to back him up, but there was no need: Jude delivered a sickening thwack with the snow shovel to Seth's shoulder. Seth cursed, a fire in his eyes as he raised a fist to swing at Jude, but Jude was ready. He hit Seth hard on the head, cracking the plastic shovel. Cursing and sniffling, Seth retreated back through the gate with a threat of coming back in the morning. Jude ran after him and disappeared around the front of the house.

"Should we go with him?" Joanna asked.

Bridget shook her head.

"Based on his reaction to you earlier, I don't think so. But who was that?"

"I have no idea," Joanna replied.

"I do," Cole said. "It's his brother, Seth."

"Jude has an older brother?" Joanna asked. Cole was amused to note Joanna's surprise that he knew more about Jude than she did. "But... he never mentioned him."

In the street beyond the house, a car door slammed and an engine started.

Cole nodded.

"I mean, would you?"

At that moment, Jude returned from around the corner. Joanna ran to him.

"Jude, what was—?"

"I don't want to talk about it," he said, resting the shovel against the house again but making no movement toward the door.

He glanced at Cole, who made for the door to help Jude deflect Joanna's curiosity, but Jude stood where he was, hands in his pockets, staring moodily at the snow as it collected on his boots.

Incongruent snippets of laughter from inside the house floated out to them, and Cole understood why Jude wasn't ready to go in yet. It wasn't until Bridget began to shiver visibly that Jude headed for the door. Cole tried to stop the question that was on his tongue, but it came out anyway.

"Don't you think he deserves a second chance?"

As Jude wheeled around to look at Cole, the anger in his face suddenly fell and hardened into an expression Cole couldn't read.

"He might be sorry," Cole suggested.

Jude stepped off the bottom step back into the snow-covered yard.

"Look. Last time he showed up, he made off with Mom's spare cash—everything she had in her purse and in her emergency savings drawer. She cried every night for a month. Not over the money. Over him. He was her favorite. I wasn't going to let her go through that again." Looking hard at Cole, he added, "People like that don't change."

CHAPTER 21

THE FINAL APPEAL

After Seth's unexpected appearance, Cole had made himself a terrifying promise: the next time he left the house, he would do what he hadn't been able to find courage to do his whole life—ask his dad to give up drinking.

So, when Joanna called a week after the party, he let her call go to voicemail. He only answered when she called again directly afterward.

"Hello?"

"Cole, what are you doing right now?"

Cole glanced at the blank bedroom wall he had been staring at. "I'm kind of busy. I'm getting ready for my new classes."

"Bullshit."

"I emailed my professors ahead of time asking for pre-reading," Cole said.

"Cut the crap. Jude and I are going ice skating right now, and you're coming with us."

Cole didn't say anything.

"See you at UPMC in fifteen."

She hung up. Well, he'd have to do it sooner or later. And if he stayed locked inside his beige prison one more hour, he might just go insane. Cole opened his desk drawer and contemplated the two versions of the letter he had written: The first presented the health risks of alcohol, along with an action plan to lessen its use in their house; the wording was intentionally scientific to steel Cole against the disappointment of a denial. The second simply asked his dad to give up drinking because Cole needed him.

Trying not to think about what he was doing, he snatched the second version and pocketed it with shaking fingers. It felt oddly light given the weight of its words. Hurrying downstairs, he glanced furtively around the kitchen, the adjoining dining room, and the hallway that led past the living room to his dad's study, the door of which was closed. The faint sound of a college basketball game confirmed that his dad must be inside. Before Cole could lose his nerve, he placed the note inside the glass doors of the liquor cabinet, where it was sure to be found. Then he withdrew it again and scribbled "Dad" in large letters on the blank side of the folded over paper and replaced it, just to be positive it wouldn't be accidentally discarded. Cole tiptoed out the front door, jogged to his car, and jammed the keys into the ignition with clumsy fingers, driving away before remembering to buckle his seatbelt and turn on the defroster.

Jude and Joanna were already lacing up their skates when he arrived.

"I got yours already," Joanna said, handing him a pair of bulky skates. "Size 11, right?"

Cole nodded. "Thanks. Bridget coming?"

"She never answered," Joanna said, standing up and stretching on wobbly feet. "Just look at this skyline. I love how the light highlights all the angles on the buildings; it's making me wish I'd brought my sketchbook. We used to come here as kids." A smile lingered on her face for a second before she said, "And of course we're getting hot chocolate afterward, because it's tradition. Come on, Cole, get your skates on already!"

Cole tried to make his frozen fingers work faster. Within moments they were on the ice, Cole stiffly alternating between feet. He had only been skating a couple times before, and keeping his balance almost kept his mind from wandering home, where his dad might be opening the liquor cabinet even now. What waited for Cole when he returned? A violent outburst? An even worse drinking binge than usual? Or—he pushed the thought away as soon as it came—a miracle?

A fresh flurry of snow began circling around them, softening the scraping of their skates. With the reflective buildings that rose on all sides around them, it looked almost as if they were in a snow globe. Joanna glided with a meditative smile on her face, nose turned toward the sky, until Jude rushed past her with a force that almost knocked her off her feet. Laughing, she picked up a chunk of ice from the rink and raced after him. Cole, hands in his pockets, lost track of them as they sped around the far side of the enormous Christmas tree in the rink's center. He wished he hadn't come. Everyone on the rink was laughing, holding hands, smiling at the cold that made their cheeks pink, reveling in the exhilaration of speed. Cole didn't belong to Christmas that way. He had more in common with the ice: cold, expressionless, enduring the scrape of life until it became too deepened with divots for anyone to skate across.

The afternoon light was fading now, which meant his dad would probably be going for another drink. But would he still be on beer, or would he go straight to whiskey? It was a fifty-fifty chance. His mind rehearsed the words in the note, and he began to wonder if it wasn't perhaps too direct, too entitled, too needy.

When it was finally time to go, Jude let out a high-pitched shriek—Joanna had apparently found her opening to drop the ice chunk down the back of his shirt. She laughed as he squirmed and tried to get his glove under his tucked-in T-shirt, flannel, and coat.

"I should have known better than to start a war with you," Jude laughed, throwing his glove off and retrieving the half-melted ice chunk.

"Tell you what, I'll buy us all hot chocolate to make up for it," Joanna replied. "I insist."

"I think I need to head home," Cole said on an impulse. He checked his watch and saw that it was 5:12 pm. The time meant nothing to him, but Joanna didn't know that. Maybe, if his dad's game was still going, he'd have time to take the note back out of the cabinet. He only had one shot, and he began to think the first version he had written would be better received. At least he could try the more direct version later, if the first failed.

"The only reason I'll let you go is if you have a hot date," Joanna said. "Otherwise, hot chocolate wins."

Cole simply stood there, evaluating whether or not he should protest. Maybe going home wasn't the best idea anyway.

"That's what I thought," Joanna concluded, grabbing him by the elbow and marching him to the skate return booth. Cole allowed himself to be led.

They walked to a nearby cafe and settled themselves in a booth whose burgundy vinyl seat covering had been afflicted with too many jean rivets and sanitation rags and was finally peeling apart. Outside, the snow thickened. Jude loosened his scarf and flung it from him, running a hand through his unkempt hair and making it stick up like a lopsided mohawk.

"So, what's everyone doing with their last week of freedom?" he asked, putting an elbow on the table and taking a long sip of cocoa.

Joanna picked up her spoon and began eating her whipped cream swirl. "Let's see... tomorrow I plan to sleep in, and then the next day I plan to sleep in, and then the same with the days after. That about sums it up."

"Are you working on any art projects?" Jude asked.

Joanna set her spoon on its saucer and shifted her gaze outside. "Sort of. There's actually a photo of the four of us from last year that I keep meaning to paint, but I can't seem to find my muse lately. Zeke—he's from my graphic design class—invited me to go skiing with him and some of his friends; they're staying at a cabin in the Poconos this weekend."

Jude's mouth set in a grimace, and he began tapping his spoon aggressively on the wooden table.

"But I said no," Joanna added, tucking a stray strand of hair behind her ear.

"Why?" Jude asked, his grimace lifting.

Cole wished he had gone home. The insignificance of his friends' concerns—art and boyfriends and sleeping in—only made him feel more isolated than ever.

Joanna shrugged and picked up her cocoa with both hands. "Just not my cup of tea, I guess. Besides, Caitlin's also going with Josh, and I'm not sure my ears can handle two days of banshee giggling." Joanna placed both elbows on the table and leaned forward, lowering her voice. "More than that, I've been wanting to talk to you two about our next exploration at school. That is, assuming you've reconsidered your stance on exploring Vendler's secret, Jude."

For the first time that afternoon, Cole's attention was piqued.

"Absolutely not."

Joanna furrowed her brow in a facade of surprised disappointment. "I thought a little time and distance might have helped you see things differently. I'm sure everyone will have forgotten about a few paint specks by the time school resumes. And if the Dove avoids the temptation to snoop in my notebook again, he won't come under any more suspicion."

Jude remained silent, his arms crossed over his chest.

Joanna plowed on. "Cole, have you heard anything from Orien Saint-Pierre since the last time you wrote him?"

"Not yet, but I'd like to have something more to report by the time he does write back. I wish I could at least have tried Bridget's answer to the riddle—all it would take is one more trip down and we could be done with it."

Joanna gave Jude a look that said the cause of all Cole's future happiness or misery depended on him.

"Look," Jude said, cracking under her stare, "if you want to continue exploring again during study hall, be my guest. But I'm not going to be part of it. I simply can't reconcile the desire to satisfy our curiosity with the risk."

Joanna bit her lip, probably biting back the argument that it wasn't just about satisfying their curiosity—it was about the internship. Cole stared at his half-empty mug of tepid cocoa, its whipped cream now melted into greasy glimmers. The way it reflected the light reminded him of the candle-lit room above the standing stones. He couldn't stop seeing glimpses of the secret caves everywhere he went; they were haunting his waking moments as well as his dreams now. When he thought about it, he couldn't quite explain his own need to go back down. Yes, it was about wanting to please Orien. But even if Orien wasn't involved, there was still an insistent voice that told him he needed to discover for himself what lay hidden under the foundations of his school. He was Vendler's grandson, after all, and Vendler had hidden something with him in mind, which made him important, wanted.

"I guess there's a chance the Dove won't be in the library as much this semester," Joanna reflected, forever optimistic. "Which study halls do you two have?"

"No luck for me," Jude grumbled. "I have Dr. Chen."

"Same," Cole said. "Which means no talking, and no studying anywhere but his classroom."

"Not me," Joanna put in, a pleased smile stealing across her face as if she had carefully designed this conversational opening. "I'll have one less study hall this semester because I got the art room TA position with Mrs. Moraine!"

"No way! Congratulations!" Jude beamed, reaching his hand out to clap her on the shoulder and then thinking better of it. "Isn't that unusual for a junior?"

"Yep. But it probably helps that I also requested an independent study with her—flattery wins the day again."

"She adores you anyway," Jude said.

"Who wouldn't?" Joanna replied, winking.

"You have a point," Jude said. "Here, let me." He collected their mugs and took them to the busing station.

Cole couldn't help himself from murmuring, "You should have told him you'd go with Zeke if he didn't change his mind about Vendler."

"Cole Erickson! Not even I would stoop that low. Besides," she smiled coyly, "what makes you think that would help?"

Cole raised his eyebrows.

"Anyway, we're going to have to try to find some way to get you back down there, even if it is just during study hall. Now that we have Bridget's answer to the riddle, we should be able to wrap it up in one trip."

Jude slipped back into the booth beside her.

"We'll get to the bottom of it," she continued. "We need to. You need to."

"I know, okay? You don't have to remind me," Cole said, his frustration finally overflowing.

"You know, I've been thinking about it," Jude said, following his own train of thought. "Why is Saint-Pierre so interested in our school anyway? With all of the projects he has going on, and in another country, you wouldn't think Vendler Academy would rise to the top of his to-do list. What does he know? What's down there that he's so interested in?"

No one answered. Cole thought of Alexandria's warning to destroy whatever he found. She had said it was "evil." Surely Orien wouldn't intentionally seek something that was evil. Besides, a thing was neither good nor bad, just useful or not. Orien would know this, and he would know better than Cole what to do with whatever was discovered in Vendler's vault.

Joanna was pulling on her coat again, and Cole and Jude followed suit. Cole had thought going out with his friends would lift his mood, but he had been wrong. It had only showed him the distance between his life and theirs while exacerbating his own sense of failure: failure at not finding what Vendler left, failure at being a son, failure at life.

He drove home slowly, taking every side street possible to postpone the moment of arrival. His wipers squeaked against the glass windshield as they brushed away the snow. If the note was still there when he got home, he would take it back to his room and wait for a more opportune time. But when he got home, he couldn't make himself go inside. It was a full fifteen minutes before the coldness of the car finally forced him to get out and walk up the path toward his front door.

The new snow crunched softly beneath his feet, and the evening sky blushed pink as if embarrassed for him and what he would find. He stood in front of the door but didn't take the handle. Instead, he grabbed the snow shovel and vented his anxiety by clearing both the sidewalk and the driveway. The ache in his muscles calmed him. When there was nothing left to shovel, he finally took the door handle and went inside.

The living room was empty. The furniture sat silent, accustomed to disuse. As noiselessly as possible, Cole removed his boots and coat. He tiptoed to the kitchen, his finger gathering dust from a side table he brushed absent-mindedly along the way. For so long, he had regarded this common space as a war zone, never knowing what he might encounter; these days, the living room sat empty more often than not.

Cole peered into the liquor cabinet. His note was gone. So was the bottle of Southern Comfort. Something in Cole's chest fell, then hardened. So that was his answer. From now on, he would throw himself into the life he could control—his future at The Lab.

Almost without an awareness of what he was doing, he walked to his room, opened his laptop lid, and typed an email to Orien Saint-Pierre detailing how he and his friends had unlocked another room by lighting a candle; how they had activated another riddle; how they had formulated a theory that the answer was to make Vendler's memory eternal; and how they would find a way to test it as soon as school resumed. Without reading what he had written, Cole hit "Send." He would go to the library again, even if it meant risking being seen by the Dove.

CHAPTER 22

BACK TO SCHOOL

January 6th dawned gray and still, the sky holding its breath in promise of impending snow. Cole donned his warmest sweater and crept out of the house without seeing his dad. The first class of the day, Computer Architecture, was a new elective. He glanced surreptitiously around the classroom. Not a single desk was occupied by anyone he knew, until Wesley Tate walked in holding hands with a gorgeous and aloof senior. The sight made Cole feel strangely lonely. Why did he still care about Wes when Cole had been the one Orien chose to advance?

The next few periods were the same as last semester: English Composition with Ms. Sokoll, then Spanish I and Chemistry. Finally, it was time for lunch, where he would see Bridget again. He spotted Jude and Joanna at a table on the far side of the hall and made his way over to them.

"Have you seen Bridget yet?" Joanna asked without preamble as she cleared a space on the bench beside her.

Cole shook his head. "Good to see you, too."

Joanna extended a perfunctory pat on his shoulder and

continued, "Jude and I haven't seen her either. She was supposed to be in Ceramics with me right before this; it isn't like her to skip art."

Cole scanned the cafeteria, but the gesture was a formality. If Bridget was there, he would have seen her immediately. Had something happened to her? He shook himself. This was Bridget, not his dad. The constant childhood fear that his dad would get in a car wreck or fail to come home when he went out drinking was irrelevant. Still, a vague dread stole over his heart as he settled himself opposite the Bridget-sized gap by Jude.

Joanna's foot tapped the floor rapidly as she checked her phone, putting it down again almost as soon as she had picked it up. "She didn't answer any of my calls or texts over break. I tried again today. Nothing."

Jude swallowed a massive bite of sandwich and picked a chunk of cheese from his tooth before saying, "I wouldn't worry. I mean, that's Bridget's thing, right? Not answering texts, flaking out on plans?"

"Bridget doesn't 'flake out,'" Cole replied, extra annoyed because of Jude's table manners.

"What else do you call not showing up when you're supposed to?" Jude asked.

"Bridget's definitely got her own sense of obligations, but she's never missed art before, and she's never ignored my texts and calls for this long. It's been two weeks." Joanna's gaze wandered glumly around the cafeteria. "It doesn't make sense. Last time we saw her at the Christmas party, she was so happy. I felt like she was finally coming out of her whole loner M.O. and embracing the fact that she has real friends who love her and aren't going to tease her just because she wears weird clothes."

"Actually, that's exactly why this makes sense," Cole said.

Joanna caught his eye. "What do you mean?"

Cole cleared his throat and adjusted his position on the bench. "I think she might be hiding *because* we were so nice to her."

Joanna's laugh was cut short when she realized Cole was serious.

"Think about it: it's easy to hang out with people who don't expect much of you. But when someone notices what's important to you and cares enough to do something like what we did in saving the library, just to make you happy... that requires a response."

Jude raised a sardonic eyebrow. "So you're saying we should go back to ignoring her?"

"No, I... I don't know what we should do. I'm just saying it makes sense that she might not want to see us right now. If this is the first time she's had real friends... well, that's probably pretty scary for her, right?"

Joanna looked at Cole hard. "You really understand her, don't you?"

Cole shrugged, then mumbled, "It's what my dad does."

Joanna seemed not to have heard. "You know what, Cole? I think you're right. Whenever I start to get close to Bridget, she backs away. I've noticed that, but I chalked it up to her being an introvert. But this helps. I know exactly what we need to do now: we need to all go over to her house, together, march into her bedroom, take her by the shoulders, and tell her we mean to be her friends whether she likes it or not."

"That," Cole said, "is exactly what we're not going to do."

Joanna was so shocked she actually knocked over the water bottle she had just slammed on the table for emphasis. "Why not?"

"That's so invasive. She'd hate it. And we'd ruin any chance of earning her trust."

"Well what's your plan? We can't just sit around and do nothing while she rots alone in her room! She needs to know she can count on us, that we're not going to give up on her!"

"I know," Cole said.

"I still think you're overreacting," Jude said. "It's just Bridget being Bridget."

Joanna ignored him. "No offense, Cole, but I'm way better at this. What she needs is a good thwack to that protective clam shell of hers."

"No," Cole said, surprising both himself and Joanna again. "Look, this is important. I don't know what she needs, but it isn't that. Let me try first. I'll think of something."

"But—"

"And if I fail, she'll have your friendship to fall back on. She'll need that. Let's give it one more day, and if she doesn't show up tomorrow, I'll figure something out."

Joanna looked skeptical.

"Please, just trust me on this one."

Jude scowled at his sandwich and cleared his throat pointedly, but Cole didn't care what Jude thought right now. He stared Joanna down until she said, "Fine."

Lunch was followed by Computer Networking and American History, where Bridget's absence was newly apparent in the silence following her name during roll call. Cole saw Joanna glancing worriedly at the empty desk to her left before Dr. Prier continued on to "Murphy, Alison."

At last, it was time for study hall with Dr. Chen. Cole had been mentally rehearsing an excuse for going to the library, and when he entered the classroom, he marched straight up to Dr. Chen's desk. Dr. Chen was so focused on his laptop that he didn't look up until Cole cleared his throat.

"Excuse me, Dr. Chen?"

"What is it?" Dr. Chen didn't stop typing.

"I was wondering... if there was a book I needed to get from the library in order to work on one of my essays, is there a chance I could study there instead of here?"

Dr. Chen clacked the delete button three times very loudly before looking Cole in the eyes. "You knew about this essay before coming to study hall, presumably?"

"I... yes, well, it's a hypothetical question, I guess. I just wondered what your policy is on that in case I need to get a book."

"My policy is that I expect students to plan ahead. If you know of an essay for which supplemental research is required, presumably you can obtain the book in advance and bring it to study hall with you."

"Yes, I see."

"If an essay sneaks up and jumps out at you at the very last minute, as I understand from my students that they some-times do," Dr. Chen continued, the wry tone of his voice increasing by the second, "then I will allot you precisely ten minutes to leave your seat and return." He tapped a timer on his desk significantly. "More than this and I find students take advantage of my generosity. My advice, however, is to monitor your syllabi so that no such nasty surprises occur. If your professors can take the time to predict and write down that an essay will be due in three months' time, surely you can read what they've written to discover it's due in two weeks' time. Good day."

Cole retreated to his seat. He couldn't help but feel a little bitter that Dr. Chen didn't adjust his policies, or at least his tone, in consideration of the type of student he was addressing. Cole had been in Dr. Chen's classes before, and Dr. Chen knew very well that Cole always turned in his assignments on or before the due date and maintained a perfect academic record. It didn't feel fair to be lumped in with the type of student who "took advantage of his generosity."

Now what was he supposed to do? If he couldn't explore the caves at night and he couldn't explore them during study hall, it was looking like he couldn't explore them at all. He began to regret the email he had sent to Orien last night.

When the bell sounded, the silence in study hall broke like a wave crashing ashore. Some students stuffed their books away and ran for the freedom of their cars while others lingered, reluctant to leave their friends so quickly again after Christmas break.

"Have any plans for tonight?" Jude asked, circumnavigating a gaggle of gossiping girls who were causing a traffic jam in the hallway.

"Not really—just finishing up homework. I only did Spanish in study hall." What Cole didn't say was that he had purposefully saved the rest of his homework so that he had something to distract himself when he got home.

"Feel like helping me refinish a desk instead? Dad got it over the weekend; it's solid oak but badly weather-damaged. I need to sand the thing down and refinish it so we can sell it."

"I don't really know how," Cole said, still feeling defeated and bitter about Dr. Chen's answer.

"It's easy—you just take a piece of sandpaper and go at it. Finishing is where it gets trickier, but we won't get to that today. I'd appreciate the help. We can do our homework after dinner."

"Your mom won't mind?" Cole asked, his mood softening as he imagined the mouth-watering aroma of fresh bread that always emanated from the Durham kitchen.

"What do you think? She lives to feed people."

"All right then."

By the time they sat down to Mrs. Durham's cheesy

potato soup and were tearing off hunks of her sourdough to dip into it, Cole couldn't remember a time when he was hungrier, colder, and dirtier, nor a time when food tasted better. He ate three bowls of the soup and slathered butter thickly on his bread while Mr. Durham told stories about the surprising artifacts he'd found in storage units. A few years back, he had discovered an entire human skeleton inside an upright piano. The storage unit had been abandoned, and the police conducted only superficial investigations once they saw that the skeleton was dry.

"And what else do you think I found in that unit?" Mr. Durham paused dramatically. Not a single spoon clinked against a bowl. "A Colt Army Model 1860 Civil War revolver, hidden under Handel's Messiah sheet music in the piano bench. That revolver has a rotating cylinder that can hold six lead bullets." He demonstrated the jerky shifting of the cylinder with his thumb and forefinger. "When I opened that cylinder, there were only five bullets: the sixth was missing."

Belle screamed, and everyone laughed.

"It's not funny!" she insisted, dabbing at the spilled soup on her sweater to regain her dignity. "Tullius came under the table and put his head on me just as you were saying that!"

"Good boy, Tullius," Chandler said, patting him on the head. Belle punched her brother's shoulder before her mom told her to go upstairs and change her shirt.

"I bet you got a pretty sum from that revolver," Jude said.

"Oh I did," Mr. Durham nodded, reclining in his chair and scratching his salt and pepper beard. "Everything else in the unit was junk, but that revolver made up for it and more. And I made sure to tell that story at the auction, too. What I didn't tell anyone," he added with a chuckle, "was that I found the revolver in the bench only after I took it out of its case, removed the sixth bullet, and placed it under the sheet music."

"Dad!" Victoria chided, caught between a laugh and a reprimand.

"Hey, I didn't invent that skeleton, which was the main attraction. The revolver was just a small embellishment. I swear, half of my job is storytelling."

"And that," said Mrs. Durham, "Is exactly how your dad got me to marry him."

"What, he lured you in by promising a lifetime of skeletons in the closet?" Chandler asked.

"She meant storytelling, dimwit," Victoria said.

"Although your father basically was a skeleton in the closet —remember how skinny you were when you ate nothing but Campbell's soup in that cramped apartment of yours?" Laura asked.

"The memory is still painful enough that I have to ask—do we still have leftover brownies?"

"You're in luck," Laura said, standing up to clear their bowls.

Chandler and Victoria rose to help, and Jude carried the leftover soup to the kitchen. Cole grabbed the bread, popping the heel of the loaf into his mouth as he went. He could tell Mrs. Durham's food was good because it tasted just as delicious now that he was stuffed as it had when he first sat down.

Jude yawned massively and stretched his arms to expand his ribcage. "Let's tackle homework so we can go to bed."

"Shouldn't we help with the dishes?" Cole asked.

"I've got this—you all go upstairs and finish your homework," Mrs. Durham urged, turning the faucet to full blast and squirting dish soap into the sink. "And take a brownie with you," she said, abandoning the sink and retrieving a half-empty dish of brownies from the pantry.

She cut six generous squares and lifted them onto paper towels while Victoria sprinted to the sink and turned off the faucet just before it overflowed.

"Thanks, love. Here's one for you, and take this one up to Belle. Chandler, you take an extra piece for Dad."

Jude and Cole grabbed the last two pieces and headed toward the stairs, picking up their backpacks on the way and sidestepping a thick Persian rug that was rolled up and leaning diagonally on the stairwell. Cole assumed it was another unique find that Mrs. Durham couldn't bear to sell yet had no place to put.

As Jude squeaked a stiff new textbook open, Cole opened his laptop.

"Oh my gosh," he said, not realizing he was speaking aloud until he saw Jude looking at him. "Orien wrote back."

"What? What did you write to him about?"

Cole returned his stare defiantly. "I told him about the room with the stones, and that we think we have an answer to the riddle."

Jude's nostrils flared, but he didn't say anything. Cole didn't tell Jude how he had ended the letter—promising Orien he'd explore again as soon as possible. Now that Dr. Chen had ruled out the possibility of exploring during study hall, he felt stupid for having made the promise so rashly.

"And what did Saint-Pierre say?"

Cole read aloud:

"Dear Cole,

Congratulations on another phenomenal discovery! Do whatever you can to complete the assignment and report back as soon as you have something to show for it.

Regards,

Orien"

The last sentence stung. On the one hand, Orien had offered praise. On the other, he had implied that Cole should already have discovered what Vendler left and not bother him until then. Jude snorted.

"Well in that case, you're off the hook. He says don't write back until you have news, and that's not going to happen, so you're clear to let it drop."

That was not how Cole had read it. He said, "I think I should at least acknowledge his email."

Jude shrugged. "If you want. Just tell him your schedule has changed this semester and you've decided to focus on the academic side of the internship. Plus, that way, if you get the internship, you can be confident you got it on terms equal to everyone else in the running."

Cole thought guiltily of Wes. He had already beat Wes, probably lots of others too, thanks to his knowledge of the school. Was it possible he had already done enough that he could get the internship without completing the mission?

"Look, I have a question for you," Jude said suddenly, but he wasn't looking at Cole; he was staring at his textbook.

"Yes?"

"Are you and Joanna...?"

"Are we what?" Cole said. If this was another lecture about not exploring Vendler's caves, he wasn't going to make it easy for Jude by bringing it up for him.

"Are you... interested in her? You know, romantically?"

Cole actually laughed. So that's what inviting Cole over to help with the desk had been about.

Jude looked up from his textbook. "It's just, she obviously agrees with you about Orien, and I noticed she grabs your elbow a lot, and..."

"Grabs my elbow?" Cole said, trying to keep a straight

face. Joanna was effusive, sure, but he had never viewed elbow-grabbing as a particularly romantic gesture.

"Well, I just wondered," Jude said, looking relieved.

"No, definitely not."

"Good."

It wasn't until after 10 pm that Cole pulled up to the curb outside his house. A solitary light shone from his dad's bedroom on the second floor, but otherwise the house was dark. He let himself in with his key and crept upstairs, tiptoeing to his bedroom. When he reached it, he paused, turned back around, and knocked on his dad's door. There was no answer.

"Dad? Did you get something to eat for dinner?"

"That you, Cole?"

Who else would it be? The voice was sluggish. From outside the door, Cole could smell the reek of Southern Comfort.

He walked back downstairs and opened the refrigerator door. It was empty but for a lemon-lime Gatorade, a jar of mayonnaise, and two cinnamon raisin bagels.

"We can't keep living like this," Cole whispered to himself.

Tracing his steps back to the foyer, he found his dad's wallet on the entrance table and slid out the credit card. Tomorrow at least, they would both have a real breakfast of bacon and eggs. Cole would be gone to school by the time his dad woke, but he could at least leave leftovers on the counter; his dad needed the nutrition.

CHAPTER 23

RESCUE MISSION

Cole followed the single set of icy footprints from the mailbox to Poppy and Birdy's front door. There were no footprints leading to the driveway, where snow was still slumped on the windshield of Bridget's Ford pick-up. A lone birdsong drifted from a bare-branched oak, but otherwise Cole seemed to be the only living being intruding on the oppressive order of a neighborhood lined with brick houses where TVs glowed behind drawn shades and no children's voices punctuated the silence. His heart was beating absurdly fast. He wasn't at all sure he was doing the right thing, but if he didn't act, Joanna would. He pressed the doorbell.

Poppy's angular jaw softened as soon as he saw Cole, who stepped into an entryway filled with the sharp, sweet scent of peppermints.

"Nicholas, I'm glad you came."

Cole took the wrinkled hand and was impressed by the strength of its grasp.

"Thanks for letting me come over. I couldn't believe it

when they assigned a paper on the Cold War for history class. Seemed like a good idea to get a first-hand account. I brought dinner as a thank you."

He held up a bag burgeoning with to-go containers. The warm, tangy curry suddenly smelled like an insult. Did he really think he could lure Bridget out with food as if she were an animal?

"I'm sorry, I should have checked—do you like Indian?"

"Where do you think Bridget learned to love it? I'm looking forward to this."

Poppy took the bag from Cole, who slipped off his shoes and looked around. The house had that extraordinarily settled feeling that develops when furniture hasn't been moved in decades and all the knick-knacks gathered over a lifetime are only displaced for dusting. Down the hall, he heard a gas stove click and catch.

"Margaret!" Poppy called.

The quick, close footsteps of Birdy clipped down the hall, and she emerged into the living room, an oven mitt gloving her hand and a ball of yarn tucked into a fanny pack at her hip.

"Oh Cole, I'm glad you've come." She moved forward to give Cole a peck on the cheek, the knitting needles clinking as she walked. "I was just making tea. Bridget's been in a bad slump lately, I'm afraid."

Cole smiled nervously, not knowing whether to keep up the pretext for his visit when Birdy so obviously saw through it.

"Biryani House?" she said, leaning over the bag and inhaling deeply. "Clever boy. I'll just get some plates and we'll eat downstairs. Don't think we're barbarians. We usually eat at the table. But it's the one concession we've made. It would be better for Bridget to have sunshine, of course, but her parents used to live down there, so that's more important, don't you think?"

Cole was startled from replying to this disjointed speech by a firm mass that sleeked between his legs; catching himself against the wall, he looked down to see a massive cat with jackal ears, a leonine mane, and a raccoon-like tail. It stared at him unblinkingly.

"Ah, I see Mezcal has come to pay his respects," Birdy chirruped. "Mezcal is a Maine Coon. He belonged to Natalie, Bridget's mum. Maine Coons usually live thirteen or fourteen years, but not Mezcal—he simply refuses to die."

It was strange, Cole realized, that he had never thought to ask Bridget about her parents. Maybe she wanted to talk about them. Maybe it helped her remember.

"Even Mezcal hasn't been able to help this time. Maybe you can," Poppy said. His voice was flat, but the gaze he fixed on Cole was just as keen as Bridget's. It made Cole miss her even more.

"Come with me, Nicholas," Birdy said. "I'll get the plates, and you can help me with the tea."

He followed her back down the hall, which was covered on one side with icons and on the other with family portraits. They walked past an open-doored craft room and a bedroom, took a detour to the kitchen, then continued down the hall to a hollow-core door with a brass knob. Birdy opened it and flipped a switch to illuminate the carpeted basement stairway. As they descended, Cole's eyes began to itch at the musty scent of mildew.

The stairway opened into a sitting room that could more accurately be described as a library. Books lined every inch of the walls, the ungainly homemade two-by-four shelves spanning from floor to ceiling and wrapping around and underneath the two egress windows—definitely not to code. A tattered sofa, a rocking chair, and a coffee table floated on an autumnal-toned braided rug. It looked like the furniture had been moved forward to make room for the shelves. Curios like Celtic warrior figurines and carved wooden stamps were jammed on top of books where there was room and in front of them where there wasn't. It was no wonder Bridget felt at home in Vendler's library when she had grown up with this as her playroom.

As Cole walked past one of the bookshelves, he saw that one side of an eye-level shelf had been cleared to make room for a photograph. Resting on top of a bright orange paperback on quantum physics and an exquisitely bound collection of Perrault's fairy tales was a dusty wooden frame with a photograph that had been taken in this very room. It showed a woman with Bridget's flaming hair but with more petite, feminine features and a fair-haired man with a Nordic sweater and grey eyes that turned up at the outside corners. Between them on the sofa stood a nine-month-old Bridget, her blue eyes round and unobscured by glasses, her cherry-red lips parted, her head topped with wisps of hair that was curlier and blonder than it was now. Both parents were supporting her on either side lest she fall. What would her life have been like if she had grown up a secure child with the love of two parents? Cole wished he could have known her in that parallel universe.

Hitching up his jeans, Poppy settled himself onto the sofa and gestured for Cole to take the rocking chair while Birdy knocked on Bridget's bedroom door. There was no answer. Cole realized he was holding his breath and exhaled. After thirty seconds, Birdy knocked again, then turned the knob and poked her head inside.

"Dinner time, dear!"

Leaving the door ajar, she pattered back to the sofa and

plopped down beside Poppy, who was removing lids from the to-go containers. Cole couldn't stop watching the opening to Bridget's room. It was dark inside. The smell of dirty laundry and closeted breath began mixing with the tangy warmth of the curry, and Cole's nose wrinkled involuntarily.

At last Bridget appeared. She took one look at the living room, saw Cole, and slammed the door. Apparently, Bridget hadn't seen his text, then.

"Try not to take it personally," Poppy said, his voice masking the disappointment in his eyes. "She'd have done the same to anybody."

Cole heaped some rice onto his plate for something to do, but his appetite had deserted him. How could he not take it personally? Exactly what he had been hoping, secretly, was that he wasn't just "anybody" to Bridget. They ate slowly and more than they wanted to, giving Bridget every opportunity to change her mind. Cole and Poppy made a brave attempt at an interview, Birdy chattering between the gaps.

When their plates were scraped clean and Cole could think of nothing else to ask about the war, he thanked them and began stacking the plates.

"You're welcome to wait down here as long as you want, if you want," Poppy whispered. "She didn't eat lunch, so chances are good she'll be hungry enough to venture out for leftovers eventually."

"My backpack's in the car. I'll run and grab it so I can type my notes up for the paper while the conversation's still fresh."

Poppy winked at him.

"I'll make you another cup of tea," Birdy volunteered.

It was almost 9 pm before Cole heard Bridget's door creak open again.

He forced himself to keep his eyes on his computer as he said, "There's curry left. I'm just finishing typing up the notes your Poppy gave me for my paper, then I'll leave you in peace."

Cole continued typing so Bridget wouldn't feel threatened by his presence. Out of the corner of his eye, he saw her bite her lip as if deciding what to say. It was a few minutes before he felt rather than saw her come closer. He concentrated hard on his computer, typing nonsense sentences and trying not to notice that she seated herself on the floor instead of on the sofa nearer his rocking chair. She was eating.

Another fifteen minutes went by before Cole decided it was safe to look up from his laptop. He was shocked: her hair was parted wrong, clumped in tangles, and even beneath her faded sweats he could see her bones. He had to resist the temptation to remind her to finish her curry, which now sat forgotten on the coffee table. She didn't look up when he moved. She was looking at the photograph of her parents.

He said, "Tell me about them."

She shrugged, not looking at him. "I don't remember anything."

"What do your grandparents tell you?"

At first, he thought she wasn't going to answer.

Then she said, "She was an archeologist. He was a physicist. I know why you're here. I came out to tell you I read your text and saw through it immediately."

"I knew you would."

"You didn't need Poppy's help with that paper. You're the smartest guy in school."

It wasn't a compliment. She stated it as someone might state a historical date, but with a tinge of annoyance. She was reproaching him for being patronizing.

"The point wasn't to come up with a pretext you wouldn't see through. The point was to have a pretext."

For the first time that night, she looked at him straight

on. Her eyes were dead. There was no emotion as she said, "You're here because I need help."

"Are you angry with me?"

"Wouldn't you be?"

Cole shrugged. "Are you?"

She looked at him a long time. "Strangely, no. I thought I would be. I should be."

Cole exhaled. "And anyway, you're wrong. I'm not here because you need help. I'm here because Jude and Joanna argue more when you're not around, because study halls are way too productive without you talking about whatever you're reading that isn't homework, and most of all because the alternative was letting Joanna blast through your bedroom door with a battering ram. Somehow, I didn't think you'd like that."

The corner of her mouth curled, then tightened as if to keep the Christmas bell laugh from spilling out.

"I'm here because I miss you, Bridget."

She looked away again and her mouth fell. Damn. Why did he have to ruin a conversation that was going so well? Had he learned nothing about when to reserve a gesture of intimacy from all these years of living with his dad?

"I'm sorry," he said, slipping his laptop into his backpack and standing up so that she would know he was leaving. "I wasn't expecting you to say anything to that." She still didn't look at him, and he couldn't help himself: "I just want you to know I'm not here because of obligation, or pity. Can you believe that?"

Still looking at the picture of her parents, she gave a tiny nod. He wanted her to look at him. He should stop talking. He should leave.

"Will I see you tomorrow?"

She shrugged in a way that might have suggested a yes. He

nodded. He had tested his luck enough. He wasn't going to say anything else. He walked to the stairs.

"Cole."

"Yes?"

"Thanks for sparing me Joanna's battering ram."

He smiled and permitted himself one last look at Bridget—not a long one—as he turned back toward the stairs.

CHAPTER 24
ORIEN INVESTIGATES

The noise in the cafeteria electrocuted Cole's already frantic nerves. He knew the ceramics students were always late for lunch on Fridays, when they had to stay late to finish projects for firing in the kiln, but he couldn't stop himself from standing in the entryway, watching anxiously for Joanna and—he hoped—Bridget. He needed to talk to them. Finally, their faces appeared in a crowd of latecomers, and he waved them down. His relief at seeing Bridget didn't allay his anxiety about the rumors of Vendler Academy's unexpected visitor.

"Come on, Jude has a table for us," he said. "There's something I have to tell you."

As he hurried to their table, he spotted Mrs. Fay sitting at a corner table with Señora Contreras-Camponez, and his stomach squirmed. Mrs. Fay never voluntarily left the library. He slid onto the bench beside Jude, whom he was irritated to see consuming a double-decker peanut butter and jelly sandwich without distress. Jude grunted when he saw Bridget but didn't say anything.

As soon as Joanna and Bridget were seated, Cole leaned across the table and whispered, "Orien is here."

"What! Why? Did you see him? How did you find out? Is he interviewing you again? I mean, why else would he be here?" Joanna released the torrent of questions in a single breath.

Cole shook his head and felt the color draining from his face. "I only found out because my chem lab partner saw Orien's Tesla on his way to class. It had the KRONOS plates and everything. Later I heard some freshmen say they saw Orien talking to Dr. Bering in the headmaster's office."

"Does Mr. Price know he's here?" Joanna asked.

"I have no idea," Cole replied, shrugging his shoulders jerkily. "But now I'm wondering what to say if he wants to talk to me—I don't have any more updates, and I can't really explain why that is since he doesn't know we had to break into the school to explore the tunnels in the first place."

"Hold up," Jude said. "You don't have to tell Saint-Pierre anything you don't want to—it's as simple as that. Besides, didn't you write him last night about not having time to explore the tunnels this semester?"

Cole shook his head and chanced a glance at Bridget, who was watching his hands as they fidgeted with his backpack strap. "I didn't send it yet."

"I think you should go on the offensive," Joanna countered, leaning over the table toward him. "Be proactive and go talk to him before he makes the first move. It'll make you look more interested in the internship and show him you're actively working to solve roadblocks."

"But what am I supposed to say?"

Joanna dismissed the question with a wave of her hand. "What you say doesn't matter as much as the gesture. But are you sure Mr. Price didn't send a last-minute email about Orien coming to interview you?"

"I'm sure. I checked while I was waiting for you and Bridget."

"The weird thing is," Joanna said, not quite meeting Cole's eyes, "Mr. Price actually asked me about Orien Saint-Pierre this morning."

"What?" Cole and Jude chorused together.

"It was right before ceramics. He came and pulled me out of study hall. He didn't explain until we were back in his office, and then he very awkwardly asked if *I* had heard anything from Orien Saint-Pierre."

"You? But why would Orien contact you?" Cole asked. He felt his world slipping like water through his fingers.

"That's exactly what I asked," Joanna said, staring at the lid of her water bottle instead of Cole. "He didn't explain for a while, but I kept pressing, and he finally told me Orien Saint-Pierre had contacted him requesting school records on all of the juniors because he was really impressed with you, Cole, and wanted to see if there was other talent here for his internship."

Bridget, who hadn't looked any of them in the eyes yet, stared at Joanna like a startled gazelle. "And Mr. Price just gave him all of our records? Without asking us? And why did he contact Mr. Price? Shouldn't Dr. Saint-Pierre have asked the registrar's office?"

Joanna shrugged. "I'm as lost as you are."

"And why," Jude said, his eyes narrow, "Did Mr. Price ask you specifically? Why not any of the other juniors?"

Joanna busied herself with her lunch cooler. "He mentioned something about checking with more likely students first, but I'm sure I'm not the only one he's asked.

He'll probably come get you this afternoon, Jude. Or Bridget," she added as an obvious afterthought.

"I can't believe Mr. Price thought it was okay to share our information without asking us," Bridget said.

"Do you really care if someone sees your grades?" Joanna asked.

"No, but... that's not the point! The point is he asked for private records and got them with no one double checking that it was okay."

Cole hunched forward and shoved clenched fists into his pockets. "I guess it just saves you the trouble of filling out a formal application," he mumbled. "He's doing you a favor. Anyone would want a shot at this internship."

"I don't!" Bridget said. "That's exactly the problem— people like you and Mr. Price assume it's fine to give Dr. Saint-Pierre anything he asks for because you've put him on a pedestal, and he clearly feels quite at home there or he wouldn't go some back-handed route that has to violate a hundred privacy stipulations to get information he isn't authorized to receive. And the thing that kills me is, he'll probably get away with it, just because of who he is!"

Jude, forever normalizing lunch by actually eating, crunched a few potato chips into the silence. Cole sank further into his slouch. It was his fault this was happening.

"I just wish I had more to show for all the time I've spent thinking about Vendler's secret," he said. "I should have been more proactive. I asked Dr. Chen about studying in the library, but he said no. I'll have to skip a class so I can go down again; I just hope it's not too late. I hate to ask, but is anyone willing to skip with me? I'll need a lookout." He looked tentatively at Bridget, who skipped classes regularly. "You wouldn't have to come down with me, just—"

"Absolutely not! Aren't you paying attention to what's

happening here? Alexandria says Vendler's evil, and Dr. Saint-Pierre is putting you in trouble by making you do his dirty work, and now you don't even know if you can trust him since he's getting private information on all of us, and it's completely unfair to you since he said you're the only student he's advancing from our district! I'm sorry, Cole, but I'm out."

Bridget's face had become increasingly red, her hair more frenzied, and her speech less articulate so that she looked like a spitting bonfire. She stood up, snapped up her unopened lunch tin, and dashed out of the cafeteria.

"What did I do wrong? Should I go after her and apologize?" Cole asked. Why did he have to be such an idiot and ruin the trust he had just earned with Bridget?

Joanna said, "She'll come around. But Cole, I really think you should talk to Orien today, and about skipping class, let me know when you want to go. Maybe we can work something out if it's just one time."

"I'm not going," Jude said unnecessarily.

It was easy for him to say. He didn't seem to realize how much this internship meant, or why Orien needed so badly to know what Vendler had hid. Cole ate his lunch without appetite, wishing he could skip class immediately but guessing that Orien would still be in the library. There was no sign of Orien as he walked to Computer Networking, nor when he crossed to the opposite hall for American History. He was surprised to see Bridget in class, though she wouldn't look at him and attended to Dr. Prier's lecture with stony single-mindedness. After American History, Cole crossed back to the science and math wing for study hall. He kept his head down and held his breath as he walked past Dr. Bering's office, but a furtive glance through the window told him no one was inside.

Cole loitered in the lobby after school just in case Orien

changed his mind and asked for him, his anxiety mounting with every passing minute. After the students and most of the faculty had left, he thought to check the parking lot. The black Tesla with the KRONOS license plate was gone. A heavy weight settled in Cole's stomach. Whatever Orien was doing, he had not come to Vendler Academy to see Cole.

At that moment, he decided Jude was wrong. Academics alone would not win the internship. He was going to have to get back into the caves, even if it meant going without any of his friends. There was no other way, and he was not going to let the internship pass to another student just because he was too scared to take a risk.

Cole was so focused on what he meant to do that he didn't see the broad-shouldered man sitting on his front porch until he was halfway up the walk.

CHAPTER 25

HOME AGAIN

T he man rose and greeted Cole with a disarming, cock-eyed grin.

"Dad! What are you doing here?"

Rob Erickson shrugged and gazed at the cloudless sky. "It's a beautiful day. Warm for winter. Thought I'd get out and shovel the walks. Did the neighbors', too."

They stood on the walk looking at each other.

Cole didn't know what his dad expected him to say, so he said, "I'd better put my things inside."

"Sure, sure!" Hands safely in his pockets, his dad stepped aside to let him pass.

When Cole was almost at the door, the voice behind him said, "Feel like stretching your legs? I'm going for a walk."

Cole's hand slipped from the doorknob. What was all this about? Increasingly wary, he turned to consider the school-boy grin on his dad's face.

"I need to finish a couple assignments first. I'm not sure how long they'll take."

"No worries." His dad waved a hand to dismiss the idea.

"Well I'm going to make a round of the neighborhoods. Don't study too long, though—it's pizza night."

Caught off guard, Cole agreed. Inside, the reflection of sunlight on the floors made Cole blink—he hadn't even realized how accustomed he had grown to the thin veneer of dust that softened every surface. The air smelled of lemon and bleach. What was going on? Disconcerted, Cole slipped his shoes off and hurried through the living room. Glancing toward the front door to ensure he was alone, he opened the refrigerator door. It was bursting with deli meats, cheeses, bagels, eggs, a whole chicken, milk, apples, carrots, and more. Cole grabbed a string cheese and tossed the wrapper into the trash, which was lined with a fresh bag. The carpeted stairs, too, had been furrowed by a vacuum cleaner. It was a relief when he found the sanctuary of his own room undisturbed.

Cole dropped his pack and went straight to his computer, where he allowed himself three self-indulgent minutes to check Orien's speaking schedule. From what he could tell online, Orien needed to be back in Montréal tomorrow for an engagement, unless the event was being held in his name only. That meant his personal explorations of Vendler's library would be put on hold, giving Cole a chance to reestablish his position as a valuable informant.

His phone buzzed, making him exit the page as if it were a secret he needed to hide.

"Hello?"

"Did you talk to Orien Saint-Pierre?" Joanna's voice asked.

"No, he wasn't around when I left."

Silence.

"I never saw him—I didn't get the chance," Cole said. The weight in his stomach grew heavier as he thought of his failure to take initiative.

"Just think about the charm of being proactive. If you don't get a chance, you can always make a chance, even now."

"I know... actually, that's exactly what I've been thinking about. I've been thinking I'm going to skip a class on Monday. Want to join?"

"I have a better idea."

Cole could practically hear Joanna's smile. He glanced instinctively at the door as if afraid of being overheard.

"Look," Joanna continued, her voice careful now, "I know Jude has a really strong opinion about not going back through Paul's shed, but I really don't think we'd be caught, especially now that we know the ropes. Whereas if you skip a class, everyone's going to know something's up—you're the last person who would skip class.

"Why don't we go back down together at night again, just the two of us? Jude doesn't have to know, and no one else will either. We've already been in Paul's shed without anyone noticing, and we're not going to create any more paint flecks from the library window this time. It'll be the safest way to keep suspicion from falling on the Dove, too, because if we try to break in during the day, he might be in the library and somebody might suspect him again if they notice something amiss. But if we break in at night when he's not around, no one will notice anything."

Cole didn't reply. He was willing to take a risk, but this was a bigger risk than he had bargained for.

"Think about it. You don't have to decide right now, but the sooner you make up your mind, the better. You may not have much time to give Orien what he's looking for."

"I know."

"Well it's your call. I'll support you either way, but I think it would be a lot less risky if we go at night, and I also think it'll give us more time to solve the mystery once and for all instead of sneaking away for an hour here, an hour there, hoping no one will come in when we're down there."

He hadn't thought of that. It was very likely that they wouldn't figure everything out if they had to watch the clock, and by the look of things, Orien was getting impatient.

"All right Cole, I'm going to let you go, but tell me what you decide. I'm here for you."

"Wait, Joanna."

"Yes?"

"Let's do it."

"Really? Okay then! When? Tonight?"

"I don't know... I need to think about..."

"Tonight it is. If you think about it, you'll find a reason not to go. I'll meet you by the football field at 12 am sharp."

She hung up before he could say anything. Cole glanced at his watch. It was already 4:25 pm. He wrestled his books from his backpack and made one stack for his Monday classes and one for his Tuesday classes, both ordered by class times. He attacked the Monday stack first, but it was a good thirty minutes before he could actually concentrate on his homework. Just when he had harnessed his mind to the job, a knock on the door interrupted him and his dad's voice said, "Come get pizza while it's hot!"

Cole was irritated, but at least it meant more homework to see him through Saturday and Sunday. He marked his place and headed downstairs, where his dad had placed two ceramic plates and a bottle of Pepsi on the counter beside two big boxes of pizza.

"I got a pepperoni and green olive for you, and a pine and swine for me. Dig in! You want some soda?" His dad pulled out two glasses from a cabinet. "It's already chilled, so we don't need ice."

Before Cole could stop himself, he asked, "You're drinking soda too?"

His dad grimaced. "You know me. All about the healthy choices."

Cole looked around instinctively for the beer or whiskey chaser, or at least for the rum that was sure to accompany the soda. He realized his dad was watching him and turned his attention to pulling out two slices of pepperoni pizza for himself and two slices of ham for his dad.

"Let's eat at the table tonight," his dad suggested.

Increasingly bewildered, Cole followed him to the table, grabbing a handful of napkins and a couple packets of parmesan cheese as he went. An awkward pause ensued in which they both realized they had lost the art of conversation.

"So, how was school?" his dad asked at last.

Cole swallowed too quickly, and the sauce scalded his throat.

"Good." He took a sip of soda as he tried to think of something more meaningful to say. "I have some new classes this semester."

After he said it, he realized his dad hadn't known which classes he had taken last semester, so the change didn't mean much. Cole plowed on anyway to thaw the silence. "Computer Architecture on Monday, Wednesday, and Friday, and Data Structures III on Tuesday and Thursday."

"Sorry son, you might as well have said Macrame Weaving and Moon Dancing for all I know."

Cole laughed, and the sound was like a hug. His dad ventured a grin and set down his pizza slice.

"Look, Cole, I want to tell you something. Actually, I want to apologize. I know I haven't been here for you lately. I've been around, but I haven't actually been *here*. I don't even know what the hell you do at school all day or what you like about it. But I'm going to turn things around."

Cole met his dad's eyes and immediately wished he hadn't. He saw his own face reflected there, floating like a lifeboat. It was too lonely and hopeful to bear. He looked back at his pizza.

"It's okay, dad."

"It's not okay, damn it!" He slammed his fist on the table so hard the plates jumped. "No dad should do that to their kid. I'm going to make things right."

Cole didn't know what to say. He didn't even know what he felt. Two weeks ago, he would have given anything to hear this speech from his dad. But that was two weeks ago. Today, he felt only numb. He forced himself to nod and inadvertently glanced toward the liquor cabinet.

"It all went out with this morning's trash. Every drop."

There was hatred and longing in those words, and it was hard to tell which was stronger.

"You can check for yourself."

Not knowing what to say, Cole said nothing.

In a brave attempt at levity, his dad seized the Pepsi bottle and poured refills. "So bottom's up on the good stuff!"

Cole ate with diminished appetite, trying to think of what to ask his dad about his life, but the only activities in which Rob Erickson had been engaged over the past several years were drinking at home and drinking at the bar. Thankfully, his dad came to the rescue.

"I'm taking up swimming again. Funny time to do it, in the middle of winter, isn't it?"

"I think that's a great idea!"

"It'll be nothing but agony for a couple of months. When I was your age, I could get back into shape in two days."

"You still look good," Cole commented truthfully, eyeing his dad's broad shoulders.

"Legacy muscles, baby. But the old ticker's what I'm worried about. When I was young, I could swim the length of the pool and back in one breath. But you can't make the heart beat slow when the arteries are clogged. Good thing I eat so healthy anyway." He winked. "Speaking of which, you want more pizza? I'll grab you another slice."

"I'm good," Cole said, slipping into the colloquial English he used to use with his dad when he was a kid. The automatic reversion disturbed him. His guard was slipping. If he stayed at this table, he'd end up talking about the one thing that was on his mind the most, which was also the one thing he was least ready to discuss: Orien Saint-Pierre's internship. That dream meant too much to him.

"I'd better head back up to my room and try to finish up Monday's homework so I'm in good stead going into the weekend."

His dad's face fell, but he hitched a smile onto its surface anyway. "Got it. Wiz kid's gotta get an A in Macrame."

Cole grinned and grabbed his plate to take it to the sink. "Thanks for this, dad."

And just like that, the faux smile became genuine. Cole was reminded of a Golden Retriever for whom its master's approval meant everything. No child should be put in that position with their own father. Cole escaped up the stairs.

CHAPTER 26

THE SECOND TEST

Midnight couldn't come soon enough. Cole forced his way through the rest of Monday's homework, then lay on his bed staring at the popcorn ceiling. The ridges were still visible in the semi-darkness, perhaps because the moon was almost full. That would be helpful. Footsteps ascended the stairs, and soon his dad's light was out. Cole pressed the glow-in-the-dark button on his watch so frequently that the bright shape of it shone like a phantom wherever he looked.

Finally, it was time.

He arrived before Joanna. Despite the winter cold, he turned his ignition off, not wanting to attract attention. The night was starless and still. Opaque clouds, iridescent in the moonlight, hung low over the school. Cars passed now and then along the main street off of which he had turned, but the night was otherwise silent. As he waited for Joanna, the momentary relief he experienced at having escaped his house began to fade.

At 12:15, he got a text: *Sorry, parents throwing a late-night party with their country club friends. Can't get away without them noticing. Be there as soon as I can. STAY WHERE YOU ARE.*

At 12:30, Cole sent the text he had been typing and erasing and retyping again for ten minutes: *I'm getting tired. Maybe this is a sign we should reevaluate.*

Joanna's response was immediate: *We both know you don't believe in signs. STAY WHERE YOU ARE.* Then, five minutes later: *On my way.*

Cole inhaled and exhaled slowly. His breath in the cold car was becoming visible. Before him, the shed that looked so amicable by daylight presented a face as cold as a prison. The idea of entering it tonight was even more unnerving than it had been the first time. Without Jude, it would be his responsibility to keep Joanna's impulsiveness in check. And what if Bridget's answer to the riddle failed? Hunting for clues, he had reread Vendler's autobiography over Christmas break, but he had gleaned nothing more than what Alexandria had already told him—that Vendler considered himself the greatest scientist to grace the earth and that he expected someone to finish the "research" he had begun.

Finally, a car turned off the main street and pulled up beside Cole's. Joanna wasn't wearing a ski mask this time, but she still had her messenger bag. Together, they walked to Paul's shed, where Joanna knelt and entered the code to the padlock. The latch creaked open, and the door swung silently inward. Once inside, Joanna clicked on her flashlight. Cole kept his own hands in his pockets as if absolving himself from involvement until he was forced to help her lift the metal lid of the trapdoor. It yielded much more easily this time, and they successfully avoided banging it against the bench. Cole checked to make sure the shed door was tightly closed behind them before they descended to the musty passageway.

They reached the trapdoor into the backstage room

without event and crossed the stage behind closed curtains, emerging into the eerily silent hallway that led to the library door. Despite the ease of their passage, Cole couldn't shake a growing premonition of danger. Their first real challenge was getting Joanna through the transom window, but eventually they managed. Passing into the library, Cole glanced instinctively at Mrs. Fay's desk, where he half expected her to be waiting for them. Her chair was empty. The idea that she must even now be breathing air outside this library was jarring. He had never thought of her having her own home. Cole followed Joanna to the far end of the library, where Vendler's painting waited for them.

As he looked at Vendler's face, Cole began to worry less about being caught and more about facing whatever it was Vendler had hidden, and he understood why, subconsciously, Bridget's refusal to re-enter the caves troubled him more deeply than Jude's refusal to break into the school again.

"Are you going to do it?" Joanna asked, holding out Vendler's autobiography to him.

Swallowing, Cole took it, placed his hand on the canvas, and whispered Vendler's name. The painting swung open. Joanna dragged the desk chair over to the fireplace and clambered up it. They passed down the ladder, through the low opening, and into the room with the corridors. The malignant faces made the hair on the back of Cole's neck stand up. Why was he so nervy tonight? He had been here before. But then, he had never been here without either Orien or Jude and Bridget, and the intensity of Vendler's will had never been focused so directly on him. Joanna provided no buffer.

To mask his fear, Cole marched to the candle stand, struck a match, lit a candle, and pushed it into the sand. The alcove candles lit, and the basin slid aside. They descended into the stench and darkness of the room where the stones stood in a circle, more human than Cole had remembered. And now even Joanna checked her pace. Slowly, they tiptoed toward the stones and stopped right before crossing over the invisible line.

"Joanna, look."

The stone at the far end of the circle, which was set very nearly against the back wall of the room, had been moved aside to reveal yet another cavern. This one they did not have to bend or stoop to enter.

"Was this opening here last time?" Cole asked, even though he already knew the answer. They had walked the full circumference of the stone circle and seen nothing. That could mean only one thing: someone had been here before him, and Cole knew who. How Orien had opened the painting in the library lounge, Cole had no idea, but it couldn't have been anyone else; no one else knew about Vendler's secret. So maybe this was it. Maybe Orien no longer needed him. Maybe he had already found Vendler's secret and not even bothered to tell Cole. What an idiot Cole had been not to act sooner.

With leaden limbs, he passed through the opening into a fresh wave of putrefaction. Behind him, Joanna coughed and covered her mouth with her sleeve. They found themselves in a very small room with a vaulted ceiling. The disproportion of the space was disturbing, and when Cole looked up, he felt as dizzy and claustrophobic as if he was stranded at the bottom of a well. Here, for the first time, was a hint of the outside world. A shaft of moonlight shone at an angle through an opening somewhere far above to spotlight the only objects in the otherwise bare chamber: a primitive wooden chair set before an easel bearing a blank canvas. The intensity of the light on that one chair while the rest of the room melted into obscurity reminded Cole of interrogation rooms he had seen in movies. The clouds must have cleared to allow the moonlight to shine that brightly. Joanna, instinctively drawn to the easel, moved into the beam of light and ran an inquiring finger over the canvas. She looked back at Cole in surprise.

"This is a really high-quality canvas. I think it's linen, but I don't know how it's been preserved so perfectly all these years. There isn't even a speck of dust on it."

She picked up one of the tubes of paint and gasped.

"What is it?"

"This paint, it's called Mummy Brown."

"So?"

"So, that hasn't been used since the 19th century, as far as I know."

"Really? What is it?"

"It's disgusting is what it is. It was called mummy brown because people actually ground up mummy flesh to make it. It was really popular for a while. But this can't actually be mummy paint—it wouldn't be packaged in a tube like this. People don't make it any more. It must just be a name to suggest the tone." Nevertheless, she set it down like a dead thing and picked up another paint. "Oh God. This one's Blood Red. Call me superstitious, but this freaks me out a little."

"What are the others called?" Cole asked. "Maybe they'll give us some clue about what happens next."

Joanna sank into the chair and was about to take another tube into her hands when the same voice that had greeted them in the stone circle spoke again, but nearer now, like a whisper in their ears: *Paint my head to prove your skill, paint my body to do my will. Give me flesh and give me blood. My likeness through your love shall live.*

Joanna grabbed Cole's sleeve. "Why was his voice so close this time?"

Cole shook his head jerkily. Even as he feared the voice, he couldn't help smiling when he heard it—it meant that while Orien had unlocked the room, he had not completed its test. He began to breathe more easily; even the stench seemed bearable now.

Joanna turned back to the easel. "I don't know about love, but at least the next step is clear. I wish I had brought that book from the library as a reference for his face, but I'll have to go from memory."

"Do you want me to go get it?" Cole asked, realizing as he said it that it probably wasn't a good idea for them to separate.

Perhaps Joanna had the same thought, because she said, "I should be familiar enough with his painting by now to make a passable imitation. The body will be trickier since I've never seen a full figure of Vendler. But I'll just improvise. What's the worst that can happen?"

"It looks to me like we only get one try."

Joanna ignored him. She pulled the chair closer to the easel, taking inventory of her paints with palpable distaste. Then she set them aside and withdrew a pencil and eraser from her messenger bag.

"Here, give me your flashlight and I'll hold it for you," Cole volunteered.

Joanna gave it to him and stared at the blank canvas, taking a deep breath. She began lightly outlining the basic shapes that would become the head, neck, torso, and legs of Vincent Vendler.

"Lucky I brought my art supplies. Seems like a lot to expect someone to know to do. Of course, I could paint without sketching first, but that's much riskier."

"I think he was expecting someone who knew what they were about," Cole replied. "All these riddles are so specific;

they make it seem like he thinks he was clearer than he actually was in his autobiography about how someone could finish his research."

"Quit moving the flashlight. You're making it hard for me to concentrate."

Cole kept quiet to allow Joanna to concentrate, but he couldn't stop thinking about Vendler's own conception of himself. What if he really had made some incredible discovery, a discovery so important that it had caught the attention of Orien Saint-Pierre? What if Cole was preordained to find it and finish it? Here in the isolation of this underground chamber, it was easy to see himself fulfilling that purpose. Why had he hesitated so long? Regardless of whether or not it was "evil," Cole had to be the one to find Vendler's secret. He knew that now. It was his birthright. To speak of destroying it before they knew what they would find was ridiculous; to leave it for another to find was impossible.

Joanna stood up suddenly, startling him from his reverie. She took a few steps back to observe the proportions of the figure.

"What do you think, Cole?"

Cole stood beside her and assessed it. It was nearly perfect. But there was something that wasn't quite right.

"The eyes," he said at last. "The lid is too heavy, and the far side is downturned too much. The shape of Vendler's eyes is more like an almond." He knew that because it was the one feature they shared. It had startled him when he first noticed it.

"You're right," Joanna said, her voice surprised.

She sat down to make the adjustment, and Cole looked on with growing interest. He was watching her at work for the first time, and he was surprised to discover the admiration that was blossoming inside him for the swift, delicate, and deliberate strokes that eased Vendler's lips into the precise expression required and the methodical movements with which she dabbed little circles of red, yellow, blue, and brown paints on her palette and began mixing them with a self-assurance born of practice. He even admired the swatches of color that she tested on her own notebook. Each page she tore out and discarded was a testament to her inability to accept anything less than perfection.

How long he watched, mesmerized, he didn't know. As he became enchanted by the skillful movements of her hands and thought of his own destiny as Vendler's grandson, the light around them changed. The moonlight that he had first taken to be an interrogation lamp was no such thing; it was a spotlight, a halo, a crowning of nature itself that recognized him as Vendler's heir. It softened and then brightened around them. With Joanna's artistic skill under his will, he would lead them to Vendler's greatest secret, to the key that would unlock Orien's genius so that they could liberate mankind from loneliness, regret, and—ultimately—death.

The importance of what they were doing revealed to him, for the first time in his life, that anything he wanted was within his grasp. He had always had the intelligence. All he was missing was boldness. The objects around him took on a new shape, a new meaning. They were at his disposal. They were made for him. He watched as Joanna brushed the blush of Vendler's lips and couldn't help but notice the inviting shape of her own lips, parted in concentration as if open to whatever he chose to do. His eyes traveled along her body. The whiteness of her throat was so pure, the swell of her breast so perfect, the curve of her waist so welcoming. How had he never noticed before how much more desirable she was than Bridget? He watched the gentle rise and fall of her body as she breathed, and his hunger grew. His breath was growing faster and louder now, his body flushed with warmth. They were utterly alone, and no one needed to know what he did in the dark. Jude had been too afraid to claim her, too afraid even to pursue the destiny that lay open before them all. But he, Cole, was no longer afraid. He was the master of his own destiny, and he would take it. Before he knew what he was doing, his hand was reaching forward to claim Joanna.

"There," Joanna said. "What do you think?"

Cole was so startled by the abruptness of her voice that he dropped his hand at once. A rush of blood baptized his cheeks. He turned away from her and from her art and said, "It's perfect."

The scrape of her chair told him that she was standing up to get a better view of her work, and Cole took a step backward from her, terrified lest he lose control again. His own susceptibility, played upon perhaps by these caves but dormant in him nonetheless, horrified him. He balled his hands into fists and shut his lips tight. He would not be over-powered again.

"That's really quite good, if I do say so myself," Joanna pronounced. "It's finished."

As she said this, something so peculiar happened that Cole began to wonder if he was again slipping into a delirium even stranger than the one from which he had just escaped. Slowly, painfully, the finished portrait began to mutate. Swirls of mummy brown pigment, mixed with tinges of blood red, massaged themselves into new crevices of the canvas until the cheeks widened and the lips parted with a painful crack. The same voice of Vendler, horrible in its intimacy, whispered in tandem with the widening chasm of the mouth: *Draw back the curtain.*

The horror of the movement stopped as suddenly as it had begun. Before Cole had time to check his sanity against

Joanna's reaction, his eyes were drawn inexorably to the wall behind the easel. There, hidden in the obscurity of space beyond the beam of light but growing in definition as the light grew, was a crimson curtain, its heavy velvet folds pooling on the floor.

"Cole, we did it! We passed the test!" Joanna exclaimed, her eyes gleaming with excitement.

She began walking toward the curtain, and Cole grabbed her arm to stop her. Suddenly conscious of what that hand had meant to do to her a moment ago, he let her go again at once.

He said, "I think we should go."

"We can't go now, not when we're so close to the heart of the mystery!" she said. The pitch of her voice was feverish.

Cole had little desire to see what grotesque revelation lay behind the curtain. He couldn't trust himself to keep his wits now that he knew what he was capable of.

"We should go," he said again, this time with mounting conviction.

"But this is what we came for!" Joanna cried, and when she turned to look at him, he almost didn't recognize the mania that had contorted her face into a shark-like grin he had never seen before. "This is where the real adventure begins! This is *life*!"

She made a dash for the curtain, and now Cole had no compunction about grabbing her arm and holding it firmly. He knew that he had not been himself a moment ago, and that whatever force had just taken possession of Joanna's body was the same that had played upon his own will. The knowledge that those thoughts were not him, were in fact outside him and only powerful insofar as he received them, infused him with new strength. He meant to be gentle, but restraining the force of Joanna's crazed will required more strength than he anticipated. He anchored his feet and yanked sharply. She slipped and fell back on top of him. Instantly she was struggling again to get to her feet, to pull back the curtain. Without thinking, Cole rolled over her and pinned her down. His hands held her wrists against the floor.

"Look at the light, Joanna! Look at it! That isn't moonlight! We've stayed too long down here—we'll be caught!"

Whether it was the truth of his words or the uncharacteristic violence that shocked Joanna as much as it surprised Cole, her face metamorphized from reckless mania to sober sickness and finally self-possessed alarm. Cole released her and helped her to her feet.

"I'm sorry I had to do that."

Glancing at the curtain as if at an enemy, Joanna readjusted her sweater, which was hanging off one shoulder.

In the shyest voice Cole had ever heard from her, she said, "Thank you. I wasn't myself."

"I wasn't either a second ago."

The confession allowed Cole to leave that room without fearing it quite so much.

Joanna picked up her messenger bag, and together they hastened from the room. They skirted the stone circle, ascended the first ladder, crawled under the low lintel, and climbed up the second ladder into the library. As they clambered across the mantle, it seemed to Cole that he had never breathed sweeter air, and he gulped it in with grateful gasps.

They stood by the desk facing each other, drinking in the relief in each other's eyes that was slowly washing away the panic and leaving exhaustion in its wake. At last, Cole moved to close the painting back over the hole. It was then that he realized sunlight was seeping between the folds of the blinds covering the library's west-facing windows.

"Joanna, it's light out."

The digital clock read 7:53. They were faster and quieter than ever as they let themselves out of the library. Locking the door behind them, they crossed behind the stage, descended the trapdoor ladder, and jogged the length of the passage to Paul's shed. Gasping and shivering as the winter air met the perspiration on their skin, they emerged from the shed and ran around it to the far side where their cars were parked, then body-slammed into Paul.

CHAPTER 27
A NEAR MISS

Joanna fell backward from the collision, sending pencils, a sketchbook, ski masks, and gloves tumbling out of her messenger bag. She looked as shocked as Paul, but she hastily rearranged her features into a smile.

"Thought I recognized your cars," he grunted, "but I assumed you'd left 'em Friday and carpooled somewhere."

He stood solidly in their path, clearly expecting an explanation.

"Well Paul, you found us out. We might as well tell him, Cole."

Words tumbled out in a panicked torrent before Cole could stop to consider them: "There isn't much to tell, really. We were just on a walk and Vendler Academy has the prettiest grounds, and..."

"Oh come on, Cole, he's not going to swallow that for a second. We can trust Paul."

Still smiling, she turned from Cole to Paul, who held up his hand to stop her.

"No need—I already know. I've been wondering about you two, always hanging around together. Don't ever say old Paul doesn't know things." He pointed to the ski masks and gloves. "Not much fun with them on though, I imagine."

"What?" Cole said, completely bewildered.

Paul's eyes twinkled. "Don't think I don't know a lover's tryst when I see one."

"Oh! No, no, no," Cole said. "Paul, that's not—"

To his horror, Joanna slipped her hand into his, gave an embarrassed laugh, and said, "You won't tell anyone, will you? We really like each other, and we didn't know where else we could find time alone together, with both our parents around. You must remember what it's like—were you ever in love, Paul?"

"`Course I was," Paul said. "Didn't think I stood a chance with her, `cause she was a junior and I was only a freshman. Prettiest thing you ever saw, with platinum blonde hair and big blue eyes. Thing is," he winked at them, "I used to be pretty good at just about any sport under the sun in my day. When I was pitcher was the last time Vendler took state. I was the only tenth grader on the varsity team, and I led 'em all the way. That's how I caught her eye. She was so proud. Came to every game. I actually proposed to her on the diamond."

"Why didn't I know you're married?" Joanna said.

"Was married," Paul corrected, a scowl replacing the dreamy, far-off look he had worn a second ago. He removed his beanie to scratch his mostly bald head. "She died after just four years of us marrying. I never had the heart to try again."

"So you do know what it's like!" Joanna said, drawing closer to Cole and placing her other hand on his bicep.

Cole tried not to visibly stiffen, but he hated Joanna

touching him this way with the memory of what he had meant to do to her in the cave so fresh on his mind.

"Oh I remember what it is to be young, all right. Just, find somewhere else next time," he said, winking.

"Oh Paul, how can we ever thank you?" Joanna gushed. "Of course, we promise not to meet here again for... what you're talking about."

Paul laughed. "More ashamed to speak than to act, huh?"

"Thank you," Joanna said again, grabbing Cole by the elbow and marching him back to their cars. Cole thought of Jude.

"You can let go of me now," Cole said when they were out of sight of Paul. "I have to say, I'm a little scared you lie that easily."

"What are you talking about? I was getting ready to lie, and then Paul just did it for us! Easy peasy! I didn't have to lie at all. We do like each other—we're friends. And our parents are around every once in a blue moon. And we aren't going to meet here to hook up. See? No lies. Just... don't tell Jude, okay?"

Joanna covered a real blush as she jumped into her car and drove away. As Cole drove home, the morning light blinding him, the reality of how narrowly they had escaped began to sink in. If they had been just one minute later getting out of that shed... Why had he been so unaware of the time, so careless, so discomposed? He shuddered when he thought of the passion that had overcome him in the darkness. But he couldn't think of that, not if he meant to finish the task, and he was so far in now that he couldn't stop. Just one more trip. Just one more trip, and he would be done with the caves forever. Whatever Vendler had hid must be behind the curtain—all Cole had to do was get there before Orien.

He pressed a hand against his forehead to soothe the headache that was beginning to turn into a migraine. All he wanted was a shower and sleep.

But as Cole opened the front door, a voice shouted, "There he is!"

CHAPTER 28

A COSTLY REQUEST

Cole looked up to see his dad grinning at him over a crinkled issue of National Geographic, a cup of coffee clutched in his hand. It had been so long since Cole had seen his dad in the kitchen for breakfast that he froze in the open doorway.

"You coming in, or just letting the draft in?"

Of course. His dad was awake because he hadn't gotten drunk last night. How could Cole have forgotten? He closed the door and walked to the kitchen, wondering how to get past his dad to go to bed.

"Your old man's been waiting for you for hours," his dad said, carrying a yolk-streaked plate to the sink. "I made us breakfast. It's cold now, but there's a lot left. Since when did you start having a social life on Saturday morning?"

Cole wanted to say "about the same time you started having a life at all." Instead, he shrugged and crossed the kitchen to grab a plate; the smell of the food had made him suddenly hungry. He piled his plate with eggs, Pillsbury biscuits, gravy, and sausage while his dad poured himself another cup of coffee. The hand grasping the carafe shook violently.

"How many cups have you had?" Cole said, the flicker of a smile teasing his lips despite the pounding in his head.

"Just two so far. Didn't sleep last night, and believe it or not, it's helping with the nausea."

A shadow passed over his dad's face, and he rubbed a massive hand over it as if to clear away the darkness.

For the first time, Cole realized that the effects of alcohol withdrawal must be hitting hard after thirty hours of sobriety. He had a dim memory of standing as an eight-year-old boy outside a doorway, watching his dad strapped to a chair, yelling and gnashing like a rabid dog. A day or two before that, his dad had made his mom tie him there, forcing on her a coil of salt-crystalized rope that reeked of seaweed; he must have brought it back from their fishing boat. His mom had held the rope in her open palm, crying, "I can't do this, don't make me do this," even as she had done it, tightening the ropes till his flesh was a red rash under them. That was the last time his dad had tried to give up drinking, right before his mom had left for good. Cole wondered how much worse it would get this time. He didn't want to be around to see.

Trying to ignore his dad's shaking hands, Cole microwaved his food, then set his plate on the countertop and forked in a mouthful of egg. He looked up to see his dad setting a glass of orange juice by his plate, almost as if he was still eight years old. The gesture was pathetically out of touch. It had been years since he had stopped liking juice. Cole smiled and took a drink anyway.

His dad watched him eat, waiting with anxious impatience until everything but half a biscuit was gone. Cole paused to take a drink of juice, and his dad seized the moment as an opening.

"So," he announced. "I've got big plans for us today."

Cole's stomach tightened, and he pushed his barstool slightly away from his dad. Whatever this plan was, it had better not interfere with his mission from Orien.

"Oh?"

"Yep. We're going on a good, old-fashioned adventure." He slapped the copy of National Geographic on the countertop to underscore the epic nature of his plans. "We're going to the mountains! I called and got us a cabin—not a ritzy, touristy cabin. A real cabin, the kind where you have to bring your own wood and light fires to keep warm at night. No refrigerator, no stove, and with any luck, the electricity will fail and we'll have to survive on nothing but our wits.

"I used to go to this spot as a boy with the Scouts. We had to make all of our fires from flint and tinder boxes—no matches—which wasn't so bad when the kindling was dry, but it'd be a real trick this time of year, and smoky as hell if you could get it to catch at all. We knew all the plants in the area by name, and which ones were poisonous and in which ways." He started chuckling. "Except for one kid, Lawrence. He was so dead sure cotoneaster wasn't poisonous that he ate it just to prove his point. Had to be airlifted out of there. His mama was *not* happy, even though it was his own damn fault. Poor kid could've been a hero, but instead we put him down as a pansy 'cause his mama pulled him out of Scouts for good."

He stared into space with a goofy grin, lost in reminiscence. The sound of the oven heater starting a new cycle snapped him out of his reverie.

"Crap—left the oven on." As he crossed the kitchen to turn it off, he continued, "Anyway, I dug through the garage this morning, and we still have a lot of gear: sleeping bags, mats, flashlights, propane stove. We only have one adult backpack, but that's okay since we're not actually trekking in. I got plenty of water and ramen, granola bars, hot dogs, you name it. We could probably survive out there for a week at least, but I just booked us three nights."

Cole choked on his orange juice. Three nights? Had his dad forgotten about his school? A flash of anger swept through his body. Just because his dad didn't have any commitments to work or school didn't mean everybody else lived that way.

"So whaddya think? Could you get Monday and Tuesday off? I figure if we leave this morning, we can have most of today, all of Sunday, all of Monday, then come back Tuesday."

Cole stared at his dad. The request was unbelievably selfish. Even if Cole didn't have plans to explore Vendler's underground caves again, to take time off from school so soon after Christmas break would look incredibly flaky. He tried to keep his tone steady.

"It's really short notice."

"Right, but parents phone in for stuff all the time. Would it help if I called? We could say you're sick." Seeing the expression on Cole's face, he put up a hand in surrender. "All right, no lies. We'll just tell them you have a family vacation."

"Dad..." Cole didn't even know where to begin. He tried to keep the patronizing tone and his own wounded pride out of his voice as he explained, "My school isn't like that. It's really hard to get into Vendler, and we're expected to take it seriously. We can't just skip because of a spur-of-the moment whim. Maybe if we had told them a month ago—"

"A month ago I didn't know I was gonna have to go through hell to be sober again, damn it! Come on, Cole. I need *something* to get me through this."

Cole resented the note of appeal in his dad's voice. Why was he suddenly responsible for his dad's recovery? And why now? If his dad had tried to stop drinking when Cole first asked him to, over Christmas break, he could have helped. But now he had school to think about, and the increasingly urgent mission from Orien on top of it. He felt as if he was being asked to choose between his dad's future and his own. Fighting down the nagging sense that he was being more selfish than he ever had been in his life, he cleared his throat and addressed the uneaten biscuit.

"Dad, I'm really sorry. But I just can't take that kind of time off right now, not after we just got back. I have an important quiz on Monday, and a lot going on this weekend too. I'm sorry."

The justifications sounded weak in his own ears. He chanced a glance at his dad and immediately wished he hadn't. He looked like a man who had escaped Auschwitz to find his family dead.

"What if we went during spring break?" Cole suggested.

"Too far away."

"Well, you could still go this time, and then we could go together later," Cole suggested.

"Are you kidding? The trip was supposed to be about us. It won't mean anything if I go alone."

With what looked like a Herculean effort of the will, his dad turned his back to Cole and busied himself clearing the breakfast dishes.

"It was a stupid idea," he mumbled. "I'll cancel our reservations."

"I'm sorry, Dad," Cole mumbled. "If it was any other weekend..."

His dad waved a massive hand in dismissal without turning around. "Forget it. It was a dumb idea."

Cole wanted to stay, to say something to make it better. But what? As unobtrusively as possible, he slipped his plate and utensils into the dishwasher and tiptoed upstairs. Immediately he wished he hadn't. Now he was trapped in the house until his dad left. But he was exhausted anyway. He wouldn't have to decide how to escape the house until after he had caught up on sleep.

Too tired even to undress, Cole crawled between his sheets. He shut his eyes, but that only made his mind race between images of Mummy Brown paint smeared across a canvas, Joanna's lips illuminated in the moonlight, Paul's face when he found them, and his dad's expression when Cole had ruined his dream. Worse still, he couldn't block out the banging and swearing coming from the garage, which had to be his dad shoving their camping gear back into storage. Cole's neck and shoulders were aching from hunching up to shut out the noise. Opening his eyes, he saw the slatted sunlight seeping through the blinds and making a pattern like Vendler's cave ladder on his bedroom floor.

He cast off his sheets and crept to the shower, peeling off the clothes that felt like someone else's skin. Water pounded his grateful back, massaging his muscles into relaxation. It was like entering the river Lethe, the drops that trickled down the drain carrying with them his exhaustion and his fear, the glass shower walls a sacred space in which for these few precious moments, no one would disturb him. He emerged relaxed enough to slip down the hallway the short distance to his bedroom, lock the door behind him, and sink gratefully into the crisp folds of his sheets, where his body finally surrendered to sleep.

When he woke again, the sunlight was no longer slanting in through the blinds. He rubbed his temples and grabbed his phone to check the time. It was 7:14 pm, and there was a text from Jude, with Joanna and Bridget copied:

We need to talk. Come to my house tomorrow after church at 1.

CHAPTER 29

THINGS FALL APART

Cole awoke on Sunday morning with restless legs and an empty stomach. He had spent the night in a vain attempt to reset his normal sleeping pattern, but the effort of staying still only served to animate his mind. Had he made the right decision? Should he have chucked the mission from Orien and the expectations of Vendler Academy to go camping with his dad? What would happen to his dad now? And why did Jude want to talk? Had he somehow found out what Paul thought about Cole's relationship with Joanna? Several times during the night he had turned on the lamp by his desk and sought mental refuge in homework, but to no avail.

When the timid grey morning ripened into pale yellow, Cole allowed himself to creep outside the confines of his room into the hall bathroom, where he took another shower to reestablish routine. He wanted nothing more than for life to return to how it had been only a few months ago: the predictability of studying hard and earning A's, the ease of friendships safeguarded by emotional distance, and a peace

234

made of mutual neglect with a less volatile father. If only he could have all that and the internship at The Lab.

The shower made Cole even hungrier, and he managed to secure food from the kitchen without encountering his dad, who hadn't yet emerged from his bedroom. Cole made it back to his bedroom and locked the door behind him. What now? He could go to liturgy with Bridget and her grandparents again. They might take him to lunch afterward, and then he'd be safely away until it was time to go to Jude's house. But as he reached for his phone to text her, he was attacked by the memory of reaching for Joanna, and he dropped his hand instantly. How could he stand in church by Bridget and pretend none of that had happened? The icons in the church would look at him and know. The incense would choke him.

Instead, Cole sat at his desk and opened his Electronic Circuits homework. His mind wasn't as fresh as it should have been, but his brain was habituated enough to the work to ensure at least an A-, and he could always look over the work again tomorrow. It was a relief when it was finally time to go to Jude's. Cole could tell from the lamplight spilling through the open door of the ground floor study that his dad was sitting there, possibly waiting for him to come downstairs so they could have lunch. He passed the door quickly and escaped to his car.

He was the first to arrive at the Durham home, but something kept him from going to the door and knocking. A moment later, Joanna pulled up behind him. Without so much as a glance at the house, she opened his passenger door and seated herself beside him. He wished she hadn't. He didn't want Bridget thinking there was anything but friendship between them.

"Do you think this is about Orien Saint-Pierre's mission?"

she asked without pausing to greet him. "Do you think Jude has changed his mind?"

Cole shrugged and looked at the Durhams' front door as if it would give him some clue. "I have no idea." Keeping his voice as expressionless as he could, he said, "Bridget didn't tell you if she was coming, did she? I didn't see her reply in the group chat."

Joanna shook her head. "No. But you know how Bridget is. She either appears or she doesn't—no way to know ahead of time."

The ambiguity of Joanna's reply made Cole keenly aware of his deep need to see Bridget, to gain the assurance of her solidity in a world that was disintegrating around him. He was just getting out of the car when her old red truck circled into the cul-de-sac and the engine was cut with a clunking chug. But the twitch of excitement he felt at meeting her on the walkway was quickly quelled: she saw and deliberately looked away from his smile, then walked past him to the Durhams' front door. She knocked with an efficiency that told him she wanted to get this over with as quickly as possible.

When the door was opened, Cole began to wish he hadn't come: Jude greeted Bridget, not with the polite formality or the sardonic amusement that typified their interactions, but with a quick, sad smile and a "Thanks for coming." The way she nodded and slipped past him into the house told Cole that this was a continuation of a conversation they had been having without, and maybe even about, him. Jude turned to him and Joanna with a face of stone. He didn't smile or stop to see if their coats were warm enough for what he had in mind. Instead, he said, "I think the shed is the best place to talk," and led the way through the house to the back yard. The rest of the Durham family was nowhere to be seen, and the cold wood stove that ordinarily blazed with a fire during the winter months added to Cole's growing sense of displacement.

Jude held the rickety shed door open, and Cole walked past him into the warm smell of chicken feed. He took a seat on the blush sofa Bridget loved, some small part of him hoping she would join him there. Joanna sat next to him instead. Jude took the green velvet armchair, and Bridget stood awkwardly until Joanna pressed herself against the loveseat's arm and patted the space where the cushions parted. Bridget joined them, gingerly, and her chest leaned forward as if she was physically distancing her heart from them. Jude cleared his throat, and Cole, resentful about how all of this was making him feel, spoke first.

"So what's this all about?"

His voice was not, as he had planned, defensive and accusing, but apprehensive. Jude's eyes darted quickly to Bridget's and back. Cole cleared his throat pointedly to vent his irritation. Jude leaned forward until his forearms were resting on his thighs, his fingers laced together.

"I won't beat around the bush. I strongly suspect you and Joanna have been down in the caves again, and I want to know why."

Cole hadn't intended to lie, but he still wasn't happy when Joanna shot him a panicked glance behind Bridget's back.

"What makes you think that?" she asked before Cole could respond.

Again, Jude looked at Bridget, who gave him an almost imperceptible nod.

"Bridget happened to drive by the school yesterday. She saw your cars in the parking lot." He paused, then, apparently deciding he might as well tell all, said, "She came over to ask for my advice. I thought the simplest thing would be to have a frank conversation about it."

The emphasis he put on the word "frank" stung Cole's sensibilities and formed a hard knot of guilt, tinged with resentment, in his abdomen. He looked at his feet but couldn't seem to regain his focus with Bridget's pink Converse beside them. Why hadn't Bridget just talked to him directly? The whistling of the wind through the cracks in the walls heightened the tension as he tried to decide what to say.

Before he made up his mind, Joanna shrugged and said, "So what if we did go? Why is it such a big deal?"

Jude's lips stretched into a mirthless smile. "It's a big deal because we decided not to break into the school again, remember? Or did you forget?"

"By 'we' I guess you mean 'you,'" Joanna countered, crossing one leg over the other and folding her arms over her chest.

Cole felt like a child again, unsure of which side to take as his parents argued. But he had taken a side. He had taken it the moment he had agreed to break into the school again with Joanna, and that made him responsible. He started speaking before he knew what he meant to say.

"Look, Jude, you're right. We did go. There's no use pretending we didn't. And I'm sorry. I disagree with you, but I should have at least let you know what we were doing. But the fact is, I just didn't know what to do. With Orien showing up again, I felt like I had to do *something* before it was too late, and I knew how you felt about it and didn't want to involve you in a risk you weren't willing to take, or Bridget, so I ended up just going with Joanna because it wasn't as big of a deal to her. I had to go before Orien got there first and realized he didn't need me."

He was disgusted by how it sounded even as he said it.

"So you decided to just go behind my back and ignore everything we talked about—about endangering the Dove, and Paul, and each other—for some stupid mission that isn't even connected with your application for the internship?"

"It is connected, and it isn't stupid," Joanna said. "And we didn't plan to get caught."

"You're lucky you weren't."

Joanna's glance at Cole made Cole drop his eyes again.

"You weren't, were you?" Jude asked, suddenly suspicious.

"No, we weren't!" Joanna almost shouted. "Not really."

Jude's eyes narrowed. "What do you mean 'not really'? Were you caught or not?"

Joanna waved a reckless hand. "Fine. Paul saw us as we were leaving, but—"

"Good grief, Joanna!"

"— but he had no idea!"

"What did he think you were doing? Decorating his shed for him?"

Joanna blushed, and for one horrible moment, Cole thought she was going to tell Jude everything.

"Well if you want to know, I was going to tell Paul that I was helping Cole train for baseball try-outs because Cole hasn't played before and was embarrassed to practice when anyone else was around. But as a matter of fact, Paul didn't even ask."

Jude snorted derisively. "You're damn lucky he didn't ask. You think Paul would have believed that? Of *him?*"

The scorn in Jude's voice bit Cole and made him embarrassingly aware of his academic body, malnourished on textbooks and coding labs. He had never cared about athletics, not since he was six and his dad had put him in football; Cole had hated it and dropped out before the season was over, and he hadn't thought about it since. He was a straight-A student at one of the top schools in the nation. Why should he suddenly care whether or not he could hit a stupid ball with a wooden stick?

"Well like I said, he didn't ask, so everything's fine," Joanna said, recrossing her arms huffily.

Jude jumped out of his chair and started pacing, gesticulating as he talked. "And this is exactly why I said we shouldn't go again: it's too easy to get caught, too easy to lose track of time, too easy to leave a trace and have someone find out. And now Paul's probably already suspicious, even if he didn't show it. He isn't dumb, you know. It'll just be a matter of time before this gets to Dr. Bering and then the consequences drop for us, or for the Dove. But I guess that doesn't matter to you."

"It does matter to me," Cole began, "but —"

"But what?"

Cole combed his fingers through his hair and measured his words. He thought of his dad, of the impossible situation of protecting a boy at school he had never even met, and of all the things that had his whole life tried to stop him from succeeding.

"It's just, this internship is really important to me. I've wanted to work at The Lab my whole life, and I want to prove to Orien that I'm the right person. I have to go down there, Jude. I have to finish the assignment he gave me."

"I see," Jude said.

He looked at Cole hard, his face angled so that the right side of it was in shadow. Cole expected Jude to argue back, to say that he understood how Cole felt but couldn't support it, or even to get angry and tell Cole his priorities were all wrong. He expected, even wanted, Jude to make him change his mind. But Jude didn't say anything. He just looked at him. Then he walked back over to the armchair and dropped into it.

"Well, if that's how you feel, I guess I can't stop you."

"You mean that?" Joanna's belligerent expression brightened.

"Yes. But I'm also not going to let you go back down there alone. If you're determined to do it, you'll have to do it with me. At least promise me that."

"Deal!" Joanna exclaimed.

"Cole?" Jude asked, holding his eyes.

Cole gave a small, forced nod, not sure why he wasn't feeling relieved.

"Good. We're going to get this thing over with, and we're going to do it together."

"Cole and I already made great progress last night!" Joanna announced, the only person in the room oblivious to the electric tension that still charged the air. "We got to the final room! At least we think so; we passed another test and opened a new passage, and I wouldn't be a bit surprised if it's the end where Cole will find what Orien Saint-Pierre is looking for, only we had to leave and come back up before we could see because it was getting too light and we realized it was daytime."

"Let's not get ahead of ourselves," Cole said, his voice restrained. "It may be the final room, and then again, it may not be. Either way, I guess we're closer. I hope we only have one trip left."

"There's just one thing," Bridget said, her crystal voice piercing the winter stillness. "Just one thing I think you ought to be aware of before you go again. That mural that guards the caves, the one on our school crest—I know now what it is."

"You mean it's not a column?" Cole asked.

"Oh it is a column, but it's a very particular column: it's the djed."

The syllable sunk like an icicle into Cole's heart, and he had the sensation that if he shifted it might shatter and splinter inside him.

"The djed?" Joanna asked. "What's that?"

Bridget closed her eyes and reclined finally against the couch as though remembering centuries of oral history that she was about to pass down to the next generation.

"The djed is a powerful mythic symbol. When I first saw that column, I knew I had seen it somewhere, I mean somewhere other than the crest, and it was only a matter of time before I came across it in a mythology book.

"It represents the tragic story of the ancient Egyptian god Osiris, who in an earlier manifestation, incidentally, was known as Ptah, patron of craftsmen. Osiris ruled in peace with his wife Isis until his brother Seth, who was always jealous of Osiris, tricked him into stepping inside a wooden box that became his coffin when Seth sealed it after him. He cast that box, with Osiris inside, into the river Nile, which bore it across the ocean. Well, the coffin took root there and grew into a strong tree; it was so strong and grew so fast that it caught the attention of the city's king, who ordered it to be felled and installed as a pillar in his palace.

"But Isis loved her husband so deeply that she rested neither night nor day until she found him, finally, in the palace of the king. Strange though it may seem, she recognized the column at once as the backbone of her lover. Winning the favor of the king and queen of the land, she requested, and was granted, her wish of carrying the column back to her native land, where she anointed it with myrrh and wrapped it in fine linen, restoring its dignity. That column became known as the djed.

"But even then, Seth could not leave Osiris's body in peace. Enraged by jealousy, he hacked the pillar to pieces.

Once again, Isis sought far and wide until she found all the pieces of Osiris's body. Bringing them together, she exercised her healing art to re-member his bones and flesh, restoring him to a state neither living nor dead, so that eventually, he was forced to take up his abode as king of the dead. Yet Osiris lived on in his son, who defeated Seth and assumed his father's throne as king of Egypt.

"The djed became a symbol of resurrection among the Egyptian people, who made of it an amulet to bury alongside their dead as a promise of eternal life."

Silence fell like a spell. Cole felt he couldn't move. He vaguely recalled the names Isis and Osiris from a mythology class in grade school, but hearing Bridget tell the tale lifted the characters out of a textbook and enfleshed them. He almost smelled the spiced myrrh, almost heard the sickening thwack of metal severing flesh. Bridget's head lifted from the couch and her eyes opened.

"The myth of Osiris is everything Vendler values—to be loved, to be sought, and to be brought back. What more suitable symbol could he have found to signal his son to find him? In my opinion, the djed is not only a clue. It's a warning. A warning of what's to come."

Joanna cleared her throat. "Well, that was interesting, but I think we'd better get on with our plans. So when are we going down again? Tonight?"

Joanna's words felt like a bucket of ice water. Cole glanced at Bridget, whose shoulders had collapsed; she was staring at nothing with a sort of resigned detachment, as if she hadn't expected anything else. Jude, like Joanna, seemed completely unphased by Bridget's tale.

He said, "I can't go tonight. We're celebrating my dad's birthday. My mom and siblings are already at our aunt's house preparing for it. It'll have to be tomorrow." His jaw jerked into a sardonic smile. "I suppose I can trust you to wait just twenty-four hours for me, right?"

Joanna laughed and said "of course," but Cole didn't say anything. Twenty-four hours might make the difference between Cole finding Vendler's secret and Orien getting there before him. He told himself one more day wouldn't matter. Besides, he needed Jude there. It would be much easier to face that room with Joanna's new portrait of Vendler, plus whatever came after, with Jude by his side.

Jude stood, and they followed him out of the shed. This time, instead of going back through the house, they walked to the front through the side gate. Joanna, clearly feeling that they had achieved a victory, gave both Cole and Bridget impulsive hugs before getting into her car. As Cole watched Joanna drive away, he felt Bridget's eyes on him.

"Cole," she said, her voice small but clear as ever, "I just want you to know—I wasn't trying to go behind your back; I didn't go to Jude because I think you have to do what he says or get his permission or something."

"Why did you go to him, then?" Cole said, suddenly angry at her.

"I went because I... because I'm scared, Cole. I'm scared of who Vendler is, and I'm scared of what he left for you, and I'm scared of what it's doing to you. I don't want you to go back."

"Why didn't you talk to me directly then?"

"Cole, I needed help. I didn't think you would listen. I—"

"Forget it."

Cole got in his car without looking at her, but as he drove away, he watched her from his rear-view mirror—pale-faced, hugging her waist, small and alone like a child.

CHAPTER 30

WITHDRAWAL

Cole awoke at 2 am, hungry and not a bit tired. The house was quiet as he crept to the kitchen to make up for yesterday's missed dinner. Nothing sounded better right now than to eat and forget—forget about the nauseating fear of losing the internship, forget about his curiosity to know what Vendler had hidden and the dread of actually finding it, and forget about the nagging guilt that told him he should have said yes to his dad's impromptu mountain getaway. Food was what he needed.

As he switched on the lights, a primal yell assaulted his ears. He turned to see his dad sitting on the kitchen barstool, holding up his hands to ward off the light.

"Turn... damn... off," he spluttered, pawing at the air in front of his face.

Cole obeyed, but the pawing continued after the lights were off.

"Damn lights!" his dad yelled.

His agitated voice was abnormally loud in the stillness of the night. Cole stood frozen by the switch, unsure what to do.

After a time, the pawing slowed, then subsided, and his dad's head swayed uncertainly back and forth as if trying to find an angle at which to see Cole more clearly.

"Layla?" he asked, his tone tremulous now.

The pathetic appeal was a stark contrast to his angry agitation. Cole cleared his throat and found enough voice to answer.

"No dad, it's me, Cole."

Still seeming uncertain, his dad clambered to his feet and lurched forward, then grabbed his head between his hands and sank sideways to the floor. An alarm sounded inside Cole's head. But what should he do? He needed to see his dad to know what kind of shape he was in—if he had been drinking again or if this was some kind of side effect from not drinking—but he dared not turn on the light again. If he approached for a closer look, his dad might lash out. He stood frozen by the light switch, trying not to breathe, waiting for movement. His dad sat cross-legged on the floor, the rasp of his breathing quicker than normal but at least regular.

Into the silence came the soft sound of lips clamping and peeling apart again. Cole's stomach went queasy. He would have to chance a little light. Creeping as close to the wall as he could, he slipped past his dad to switch on the softer glow of the living room light. He turned around to see his dad still sitting on the floor, lips smacking. Then Cole saw the eyes— blank and fluttering—and his heart froze.

"Dad?"

The question hung in the air, unanswered. Cole moved a little closer, but his dad's head did not turn to meet him.

Cole waved a cautious hand in front of his dad's face and said more loudly, "Dad!"

The face remained empty.

Panic and revulsion fought for space in Cole's chest. His mind seemed to have been swept as blank as his dad's eyes. What was he supposed to do? Call for help? But who—911? The temptation of rescue was seasoned with distrust; growing up, his mom had cautioned him never to call 911 when his dad was in one of his drunken rages. "It's a magic number that will make everything you know disappear," she would say, her whisper tight with fear as they crouched together in his locked bedroom to wait it out. "And anyway, we don't need the publicity." By which she meant his dad would be discharged from the Army and she would lose her place in society—which was exactly what had ended up happening, but only after a medical disaster. Had the whistle been blown earlier, the man who was now paralyzed by his dad's drunken surgical incompetence would have gone on to live a normal life, but the Erickson family would have suffered a betrayal that both his parents would have considered a worse fate.

But betrayal came anyway, his mom leaving as soon as his father was discharged. She hadn't even waited for the divorce or Cole's custody to be finalized, which was, Cole assumed, why the judges had decided his dad had any right to caring for Cole at all.

Cole shook himself back into the present. What would Jude do? Cole desperately wanted to call Jude now, but given his dad's condition, he probably shouldn't wait that long. Taking a steadying breath, he reached for the phone in his back pocket. There was a scuffling sound behind him. He turned to see his dad blinking more slowly now, this time with cognition dawning behind the eyelids. He was trying to force himself off the floor with his right hand while his left hung limply at his side.

"What the hell're you doing?"

The gruffness, though stripped of strength, was his dad's

voice, so different from the spluttering agitation and the broken appeal of just a few minutes ago. The rapid change was unnerving, but the familiar voice washed over Cole like a wave of relief.

"Nothing, I... Dad, are you okay?"

His dad was instantly wary, eyes trained on the phone. "Son, put that away. Your old man's just fine."

"But... don't you think it would be good to have some help in this? I know it isn't easy. Wouldn't it be better to do it at a facility or something?"

A flicker of anger flamed in the eyes that held Cole's. Then it died suddenly as if a heavy curtain had been dropped onto a stage, obstructing any view of what the players were doing and feeling.

"Never trust someone else to do what you can do for yourself," his dad grunted. "I just came down to get a glass of water. What're you doing? What time is it anyway?"

Cole hesitated, unwilling to accept the sudden reversion to normality. His phone was still in his hand, but one more pointed glance at it from his dad was enough to make him obey.

"Just getting some water also," he stammered. His appetite had deserted him.

"Well get on it with it then."

Cole drew out two glasses from the cabinet and filled them with water from the pitcher in the fridge, handing one to his dad.

As he did so, he tentatively whispered, "Dad... have you had anything to drink, other than water?"

"God, I wish!" he spat bitterly. "Nope. I made my son a promise, and I'm sticking to it. Now go to bed."

Cole didn't need to be told twice. He barely restrained himself from running up the stairs. He could feel the weight of his dad's eyes on him as he went. He locked his bedroom door behind him without thinking, just as he and his mother had done when he was a child. Sleep was no longer possible.

The minutes of early morning were interminable, the light on Cole's watch flashing every few moments with the unsurprising revelation that it was too early yet to begin the day. Eventually, his dad's labored footsteps ascended the stairs, and the door to the master bedroom clicked shut. Unable to lie on his bed any longer, Cole rose and paced the room, taking care to avoid the creaky floorboard near the door.

His mind relentlessly replayed the image of his dad sitting obliviously on the floor. He still wondered if he should have made the call. More than anything, Cole wanted to talk to Jude. Jude always knew what to do, or at least pretended he did, which was more than Cole could muster. All of Cole's earlier resentment at Jude seemed to have evaporated; he resolved to text him as soon as morning dawned.

But when the first rays of light spilled into his room, the power of the nightmare faded, and Cole gave up the idea. What would he say, anyway? *My dad was sitting on the floor blinking a lot last night. Should I have called 911 even though he told me not to?* It sounded ridiculous. He shook the thought off and got ready for school.

CHAPTER 31
NOT ACCORDING TO PLAN

Orien Saint-Pierre stepped onto the balcony of his penthouse and checked his watch. It was 7:34 am, the moment of winter sunrise. For years now he had timed his morning workouts to conclude eleven minutes before sunrise. That was the time it took him to stretch and walk from his home gym out onto the balcony to witness the birth of the sun. He had attended the sun so often that he saw himself not as a spectator but as a midwife, as if the sun might not rise without him. Today its pale light scattered swaths of periwinkle and pink clouds that faded into electric blue overhead.

To begin his day in solitude had become a necessity. Later, he would exert the social energy The Lab required, but these few precious hours entirely to himself were what he coveted, what he craved, and what he needed almost as much as he needed oxygen. He concentrated his attention on the weak yellow focal point where the sun would appear and thought about his eyes absorbing the photons that would initiate his circadian rhythm, lending energy and attention throughout his day and regulating his sleep at night. Five minutes was all his body needed. After that he could scrub himself free of the sweat that shivered his skin and offended his nostrils. But for now, he breathed it consciously, imagining the air passing into each particle of his body, from the tips of his ears all the way down to his toes. He hated the smell, but he made himself inhale it. It reminded him of the work required to reach perfection.

Already the city was awake. Lights beamed from buildings and traffic crescendoed and decrescendoed above a steady hum of movement. This was what he liked about Montréal— it was always moving forward. One day, he dreamed, his body would be strong enough to stay awake with it through every day and every night without the need for sleep.

It was a relief when the five minutes were over. Shutting out the sharp air behind him, he tapped a button that started his temperature-regulated shower and its accompanying music: *Siegfried* of Wagner's Ring Cycle. He peeled off his jacket and joggers and placed them in a hamper that would be taken for washing. His shirt, underwear, and socks he deposited in the garbage. He had a particular abhorrence for wearing anything he had sweated in twice. Once in the shower, he exfoliated his skin and began his morning ritual of shaving: he started with his head, then his facial hair, then moved down to his chest, his arms, and his legs. It gave him a quiet satisfaction to know that he was free of any excess that might interfere with the efficiency of his movements or chafe his skin against his clothes. The only hair he kept was his eyebrows. He found their expression useful in inspiring emotion when he spoke.

Emerging from the shower like a newborn man, he walked through the air dryer and applied the signature cologne his French perfumer had invented for him. The top note of mint helped his mind ascend, the vetiver grounded him, and the lilac inspired him. The note of stone made him feel he carried the sacred space of his shower with him through the day like a secret. His muscular form in the mirror reminded him that at fifty-two, the machine of his body was still remarkably optimized through a rigid routine of self-care. With a tinge of irritation, he wondered why everyone did not choose to preserve their bodies as he had. It required only a modicum of discipline and resulted in freedom.

He walked naked to the closet and took particular care over selecting a broadcloth dress shirt, vicuna sweater, cashmere suit, and new, seamless wholecut Oxford shoes. It would be important to remember what he wore today. He had memorialized the clothing corresponding to his most significant life achievements behind temperature and moisture-regulated glass frames, the only ornamentation on his living room walls: the day his parents had died, the day he had left his last foster family at eighteen, the day he had completed the first, primitive model of Kronos, the day he had rejected the love of the only person who had ever tempted him away from total commitment to Kronos, and the day he had signed the lease for The Lab's current location in downtown Montréal. Already the glass frame for today waited empty on the wall. Even as he had slept, the AI imaging had been completed.

Today was the day he would find a key piece of the puzzle to which he had dedicated his life.

After dressing, he moved to the kitchen. Here he prepared and ate two poached eggs, discarding the yolk of one. He followed this with one-fourth of a cup of oatmeal topped with one tablespoon of pumpkin seeds to replenish the carbs his body had just consumed during his cardio workout. Lastly, he swallowed a fish oil tablet and a multivitamin balanced for his particular requirements. He drank nothing but purified water. Already he regretted the fresh salmon and cruciferous vegetables his chef had planned for lunch, but the trip was more important, and he would lose precious time by delaying.

As he reached for his chef's call button to cancel the meal, a painful spasm in his chest shot instant numbness down his shoulder to his fingers, occluding all feeling. He realized with a shock that he couldn't see the button. The coffee-and-cream-colored smear that was his hand became blurrier and weaker by the second. He lurched toward the speaker. His mind was strangely calm as the voice on the other end chirruped a greeting. In slurred words, he managed a cry for help. The last impulse of his dimming mind was not of fear, but of irritation. His doctor had warned him he was at risk of a stroke from stress. But today of all days, he didn't have time for this.

CHAPTER 32

THE THIRD TEST

The wailing of a wounded animal pierced Cole's dream and dragged him into confused consciousness. The darkness in his room was absolute but for the thin slivers of moonlight glowing through the blinds. Checking his watch, he saw that it was 11:26 pm, almost time to meet his friends at school. Still, he could catch a few more minutes' sleep—if the thing outside his window shut up. Cole rolled over, drawing the comforter over his ears.

The wail swelled again. This time, there was no mistaking it: the wounded creature was not outside his window, but inside his house. Dread trickled through Cole's veins. He threw off his sheets and sat up to face the bedroom door. That cry could only belong to his dad.

"Move," he told himself. "You've got to move."

He got out of bed, dressed quickly, pocketed his keys, and walked out the door. The hall beyond was cloaked in darkness. From his dad's bedroom came the sound of obstructed breathing that was too rapid to be a snore. He reached the door, and a low, pitiful moan drifted through the darkness, a moan he wouldn't have caught if he had still been in his bedroom. Cole flicked on the hall light. Then he grasped the handle of his dad's door and turned it.

The floor was littered with crumpled clothes, open Dorito bags, and tipped over Coke bottles. Robert Erickson was sprawled on his back, arms flung wide like a sacrifice. His teeth worked frantically, chewing at a swollen lower lip, while his hands clenched and opened again and again. Long scratches were visible on his forearms. A light line of blood streaked one arm, ripped perhaps by a ragged fingernail. Cole crept cautiously closer. His dad's eyes blinked a few times, then shut. Cole couldn't tell if his dad knew he was there.

As he gazed at the feverish face and the body lying drenched in a pool of his own sweat, the horror of encountering his dad on the kitchen floor the previous evening engulfed him again. Now was his chance—he could call 911. He could finally get help. He pulled out his phone. Would his dad ever forgive him?

Cole stood there, watching his dad, until the alarm he had set for exploring the cave went off. He fumbled the phone in his haste to silence it, and when he stood up again, his dad's face looked a little calmer. Cole watched his dad breathing— in and out, in and out—for five minutes. The cadence was normal again. Finally, Cole slipped his phone back into his pocket.

"Hang in there, Dad," he whispered.

Then he turned and closed the door, flicked the hall light off, and tiptoed to his car. The drive down deserted streets was surreal, as if time itself were holding its breath. Heavy clouds hung like a curtain over the stars. Cole could almost believe that nothing was happening behind that curtain. He was dimly aware that he didn't want to reach the school, because as soon as he did, time would be given its cue to exhale. He wasn't sure he was ready to face the consequences.

All too soon, the school loomed before him, its familiar Kirkbride silhouette ominous against the waiting sky. He drove past the main entrance around the back of the school to where Joanna's car was already parked and Jude was standing obstinately in the cold night air beside his bicycle. Cole was late. He put his car in park, switched off the lights, and stepped out.

"Hurry up," Jude said, his hoodie cloaking his eyes. "Looks like the clouds are about to break. Cole, I'm putting my bike in your car so it doesn't get soaked."

Joanna reached Paul's shed first but waited for Jude to open the padlock. As soon as they stepped inside, the sky lit up with a brilliant flash. Thunder split the silence and rain flooded down. Time had exhaled.

The trap door creaked open, and as they lowered its lid above them, the torrent of rain softened into white noise. When he pushed open the trapdoor under the school, Cole had a sudden vision of Bridget volunteering to go up first. The ache of her absence was becoming almost physical. Why had he been so ungentle with her? All she wanted was to help him, and he hadn't even let her explain. If he and Bridget had made amends, he'd feel much better equipped to face whatever Vendler had in store for him tonight.

"Damn it," Jude said.

Cole looked up to see Jude standing at the edge of the stage. The curtains were open. It felt like an omen.

"Well," Jude said, "I guess we're taking our first real risk. I helped Paul install the new security system last summer, and there are about three cameras covering the auditorium. But there's no other way. All the halls are covered, and we'll only show up on more cameras if we try to sneak around."

"I can't believe the one time I forgot my ski mask is the one time I need it," Joanna said, but her eyes glinted with excitement.

"Well, there's nothing for it," Jude said.

He pulled his hoodie farther over his head and walked quickly across the stage. The eager theatricality with which Joanna darted across after him irritated Cole. It was more proof that she regarded their exploration not as a necessity, but as an adventure. For him, that illusion had been shattered the moment he had seen Bridget's tear-streaked face when they found her huddled alone in the candle-lit room. Keeping his head down, Cole followed. The relief of reaching the other side was solely physical. Now that they were about to descend into the caves, Cole couldn't stop thinking about what had happened last time, or about Bridget's story of the djed and her certainly that it was a warning of what was to come. But what? He wished he had asked her.

They were in the library now. It was happening too fast.

"Wait," he said before he knew what he meant to say. The others looked at him. "Jude, before we go down, there's something I have to tell you." He glanced nervously at Joanna, trying to find the right words. "Last time Joanna and I went down, things got a little strange. We both... lost control a little bit. Nothing really happened, but I wasn't myself. It was like there was someone else inside my mind."

"Good thing I'm coming down with you this time then," Jude said.

Cole turned back to the portrait, annoyed at Jude's bravado, and opened the portrait. With an ease that left them no time to prepare for what came next, they made it behind the painting, through the candle-lit portrait room, down past the standing stones, and into the room that was now filled with the presence of Vendler's freshly-painted portrait.

"So, this is the room you got into last time," Jude said, avoiding looking at Joanna's painting. "Ugh, that smell is getting worse and worse. Good thing there's that ventilation in the ceiling—I was beginning to wonder about oxygen down here. Can you imagine that smell without any fresh air?"

Eager to get out of the room as fast as possible, Cole led the way to the velvet curtain. For the first time that night, curiosity tempered his anxiety. But when he drew back the curtain, the revelation was anticlimactic: here was not a new chamber, but only a small wooden table set against the cavern wall. On it were two objects: a decorative chalice and a small, silver knife. The reflection of the flashlight beam on the blade was blinding. The chalice was empty.

As if to prove he wasn't intimidated by Cole's warning in the library, Jude marched up behind Cole and grabbed the knife. Again, Vendler's voice echoed upward through the vault. Cole swiveled around to see whether Joanna's portrait was once again animated. The lips and cheeks were contorting with a deliberate and palpably painful exertion. The animation did not reach the eyes and forehead, which remained disturbingly frozen.

Prick your finger on the knife to comprehend eternal life. Win my love or risk my malice—shed your blood into the chalice.

<h1 style="text-align:center">CHAPTER 33</h1>

<h1 style="text-align:center">FROM BEYOND THE VEIL</h1>

They stood in stunned silence long after the echo of Vendler's final word had died. One glance at Jude told Cole that he too had seen the movement of Joanna's portrait. Sweat glinted on Jude's forehead as he pressed the blade against his skin.

"Jude, what are you doing?" Joanna cried, placing a hand on his. "You're not going to hurt yourself, are you?"

"How else are we going to finish the job? Don't worry—it'll just be a nick."

The flesh waited patiently, and the blade angled harder. Too quick it slid sideways. The thin skin split, and up oozed ruby blood. As it ran into the chalice, Vendler's voice filled the room once more:

A blessing and a curse I give: do as I say, and you shall live. For though today you loose my fetter, your debtor shall repay your better. On my painting pour your blood to animate this lifeless mud. But if you leave me where I lie, traitor, you shall surely die. Betray me now and taste my ire: perish in consuming fire.

Jude laughed, a harsh, barking sound. "What a dumb

threat. Of course we'll die if we don't do what he says. Everyone dies." He grasped the stem of the chalice.

"Jude, wait!" Cole stepped between him and Joanna's painting. "We need to consider what we're doing here. Alexandria called Vendler evil. I know it sounds crazy, but I'm beginning to think she might be right, especially after that warning."

"Oh come on, Cole," Jude replied. "Don't tell me you believe in all these silly curses. Vendler has interrupted our lives long enough. We're going to get to the bottom of this and have done with it."

In a voice that lacked conviction, Joanna said, "Vendler's dead, Cole. What can he do to us? It's probably just a metaphor."

Her face pale but determined, she lifted the portrait from the easel and held it for Jude. The blood dropped, and the canvas drank it thirstily with a squelching sound like earth sucking water. Joanna flung the painting down. The portrait of Vendler closed its eyes, and the cavern was filled with a primordial groan that might have been the last breath of a dying beast.

When the sound stopped, the stone behind the table—which they had taken to be the cavern wall—began to tremble. Then, with a grating scrape like a tombstone being dragged across cement, it slid aside to reveal a narrow passage. The stench that vomited itself toward them convinced Cole that they had, at long last, unveiled its source.

Vendler's painted eyes flew open, bloodshot and alive. His lips ripped apart, and he inhaled as if he meant to consume the breath of every living thing. The sucking went on and on. The face grew larger and more lifelike until, with a great force of will, the painting wrenched itself from the canvas with a sound like ripping fabric. Its flesh was frayed at the back of the skull where it had been attached to the canvas. The mouth gnashed and gnawed the air furiously in its struggle. The grasping and the groaning filled the underground chamber of earth with the agony of birth until, there before them, transparent but impossibly lifelike, stood the specter of Vincent Vendler.

Joanna screamed, a piercing, ear-rending scream of pure terror that faded grotesquely into the jerky laughter of Vincent Vendler, who swallowed and regurgitated the sound she gave him. Vendler's laughter gave its final convulsion, and the jaw hung loosely open. The chest swelled with a rasping intake of breath to fuel its next exertion. Then speech was released without intonation, the effort of each word excruciating.

"My life is on loan. You have given me your mind your skill your blood and your attention. You have brought me back but only for a moment. This pale resurrection is a guarantee of the glory..."

The mouth gaped again with the effort of inhalation. The blood behind the skin turned from rouge to blue as it lost oxygen. Cole thought desperately that if none of them gave the thing any more sound, it would die.

"...to come. I am not permitted now to see myself as what I was then and what I will be again. You must make the final journey alone. Bring me back."

The face went slack. The light was extinguished from behind the eyes. The ghost of Vincent Vendler fell back into the stain on the canvas and shrank fixedly into it.

For a long time, no one moved. Cole was afraid to fill the space with sound, with movement, with anything that might be absorbed into the painting and resurrect Vendler. The memory of Vendler's eyes, so like his own and so like his dad's, conjured another memory: his dad, unconscious, chewing a bloody lower lip, hands clenching and opening. He squeezed his eyes shut and tried to focus. Here in the school, deep in the heart of Vendler's caves that hid the missing key to Orien's project—this was where he was needed. They were so close now to unlocking the mystery, and despite the horror of what they had just witnessed, his fingertips tingled with the anticipation of claiming whatever Vendler had left for him.

He saw himself gripping the treasure in his hands as he emerged into the light of day. The sun crowned his golden head. Nature itself hailed him for achieving the goal that would forever reverse human hurt. Behind him, Jude and Joanna faded into smudged shadows like erased pencil marks. The entire school of students and teachers was assembled before him. Mr. Price applauded with embarrassing fervor as Cole emerged from the front doors of the school and walked down the steps toward the waiting assembly. Dr. Khouri leaned over and whispered something to Dr. Bering about how she had wanted to write Cole's recommendation letter but hadn't had the chance, and Señora Contreras-Camponez shouted, "Ha nacido el nuevo príncipe!"

Cole's walk was confident and kingly. With every step, he recognized that it was fitting that he had been the pupil chosen over decades of Vendler's history to find this treasure and bring it into the daylight. His dad hadn't been able to do it, nor any other student. It was he, Vendler's grandson, who was ordained to discover the truth, and he had done it with grit, perseverance, and an intelligence that continually proved his superiority. Who else could have discovered Vendler's long lost treasure?

Cole was down the stone steps now, and a fresh breeze fondled the fringe of his hair like a lover, sweeping it back from his high forehead and accentuating the regality of his stature. From a small spot in the crowd, Wesley watched enviously. But though Cole felt Wesley's gaze, he didn't return it. His eyes were trained on the central player: Dr. Orien Saint-Pierre stood waiting for him, his slow smile gradually transforming his face into a soft peacefulness like that of a charmed serpent.

As Cole walked toward him, Orien closed the gap between them so that the two of them stood together apart from the admiring crowd. Orien extended his hand, at once an olive branch and an invitation, and Cole gripped it in acceptance. Orien's smile grew even wider, spreading now to his eyes, which twinkled with excitement. He was looking, not at what Cole held, but at Cole's face. He was evaluating the intelligence behind the green-gray eyes and proclaiming it worthy. Orien placed two powerful hands on Cole's shoulders and turned him around to stand by his side facing the crowd, which erupted into applause.

Only one figure in the crowd kept her hands clasped. Cole hungrily sought the expression that was hidden like a mystery framed by blazing auburn hair. When he found her, pleasure surged through his body. As her eyes gazed into his, her admiration intensified his longing. Bridget's smile blossomed only when he looked at her. She broke from the crowd and rushed to him, throwing her arms around his neck, whispering in his ear that he had been right to continue his quest, that her hesitations were born from fear for his safety, that even in her moments of greatest doubt, she secretly knew he would conquer. She held his neck in her hands, her gaze hungrily flitting from one of his eyes to the other to gain their full expression. Then she kissed him with a passion that lit a flame in his stomach and consumed his body with feverish yearning.

The scene changed, and Cole and Orien were back in

Vendler Academy's conference room. Orien was pouring Cole a drink, but this time it was not water; it was champagne. He poured two flutes, laughing like the bubbles erupting at the golden surface, and handed one to Cole. The flutes clinked together, and Orien winked as he said, "To my newest assistant." The drink after the toast was like the handshake of a partnership that ended in nothing less than Orien appointing Cole as his successor at The Lab. For now, Orien took a seat and laughed again. He said, "You know Cole, The Lab has never opened its doors to a high school student. But today it's time for that to change. You've proven your worth more than most of my tenured researchers. Welcome to The Lab. Welcome to your new home."

The warmth of Orien's words greeted Cole like the embrace of a mother and the approval of a father wrapped into one. As Cole sat back into the cool leather of the executive chair, words bubbled up inside him like champagne, and he told Orien of the adventures and challenges he had faced in Vendler's underground caves. He recounted how Bridget knew the answer to the first riddle because he had insisted they follow Alexandria all the way to her secluded cottage. He remembered how Joanna had asked his opinion on the portrait, and how he had been the one to ensure she got it right, patiently correcting her false lines. And he told how Jude had volunteered to sacrifice his own blood to preserve Cole's health, knowing that it was Cole who had been chosen to continue on with the internship. Cole set his champagne glass down too hard, and the jolt of it shot through his whole body.

Jude was pulling him to his feet, shaking him. "You okay, Cole?"

"He's suffering from shock," Joanna said. "You can't blame him."

Cole blinked and remembered where he was. The laughing spray of champagne bubbles still tickled his nose, and he had to inhale the putrid air to anchor himself to the present. How long had he been in that semi-conscious state? He checked the portrait of Vendler and was relieved to see it inert, an ordinary painting on an ordinary canvas. The only sign of what had just passed was a splash of blood quivering on the cave floor.

Cole scrutinized Joanna's expression and then Jude's to judge whether they too had fled into fantasy. But they looked perfectly normal. Cole felt a flush of shame creeping up his neck. A second ago, he had thought himself so superior to Jude and Joanna. Now he felt nothing but disgust at his own weakness.

He pictured himself in his own bedroom, limbs drawn tightly inward as he lay on the small twin bed that was cocooned in the far corner of the second story room at the end of the hall. Outside the solid oak door with its painted white mask, he heard the clink of a liquor bottle against a cabinet and the secret splash of liquid in a glass. Cole lay where he was without moving. What could he do? What had he ever been able to do? In childhood he had learned early when to stay invisible, how to go without dinner if the kitchen became a battle zone, or when to fix petty problems like how to work the washing machine or solve homework problems on his own if his mom was going out; she didn't like to be disturbed as she selected the right clothes and blotted her lipstick. It had always been better to stay quiet, hidden, and small. Life now was no different. Like his dad and his mom, Jude and Joanna were better off without his interference. He would stay crouched in the corner of his mind, saying nothing as they worked out what to do.

Cole jerked back to the present again at the sound of Jude's voice:

"Maybe Alexandria was right. Maybe we need to get to the bottom of this and destroy whatever he left."

Joanna was about to reply when the air around them became electrified with pressure. There was a deafening roar and a loud boom. The cave around them began to shake. The stone that had rolled away to reveal the passage splintered and cracked, and chunks of stalactites fell from the ceiling to crash at their feet.

Cole covered his head with his hands, coughing, while Joanna fell against the cave wall. The dust in the air billowed into their lungs.

Cole couldn't see anything, but he heard Jude yell, "Earthquake! Get out of here!"

Cole ran after Joanna, dust raining down on them, back through the standing stones, one of which toppled over right in front of him. He leapt over it, Jude behind him. As he scrambled up the ladder to the candle room, he saw a stalactite splintering from a stalagmite with an enormous crack as the cave floor shifted away from the ceiling. They sprinted past spilled sand and fallen portraits to the low lintel. All was a riot of booms and cracks, a panic of splitting rock and blinding dust. The iron ladder leading to the library shook violently as they seized and scaled it, then fell coughing on the library floor. It trembled beneath them. Cole's ears echoed with the roar below ground.

He pushed himself up from the floor and said, "Come on —we've got to get to a safer place," just as the tremor quieted and died.

He sank back onto the library floor, his legs shaking under him, and leaned against the fireplace mantel. Its firmness comforted him. For several moments, no one said anything.

Cole's head was so full of the horror of Vendler's face ripping itself from the portrait, the terrifying untethering of his mind, and the shock of near death that he couldn't think clearly about what to do next. He forced his eyes open, his eyelids caked with dust. Joanna lay on the floor, eyes closed, breathing deeply. Her lips were cracked and her jeans had snagged and ripped. Jude's head was in his hands, his hair tousled and lightened with dust. Jude looked up and caught his eye.

"I'm sorry, Cole. I should have listened to you."

The floor was covered in dust. They couldn't stay here. They had to move. Cole pushed himself to his feet and offered Jude a hand.

"Come on," he said. "We've got our work cut out for us."

CHAPTER 34

COLD BLOOD

Tuesday, January 13th, was a day Cole never forgot. In retrospect, the day started just like any other. Head pounding from lack of sleep, Cole dragged himself from his bed after hitting the snooze button once. He brushed his teeth, combed his hair, and dressed in his tan chinos, button-up blue and white checked shirt, heather gray cardigan, and leather Sperry deck shoes. Afterwards, he thought it strange that he should remember that outfit so precisely.

Next, he checked his phone briefly to see if there was any news about last night's earthquake. There wasn't. If it hadn't been for the dusty clothes lying at the top of his hamper, he might have been tempted to think the whole affair a nightmare. Now that it was morning, exhaustion crowded out any sense of either horror or accomplishment. All he wanted was to find Bridget, apologize, lose himself in his studies, and get back to normal life. He double checked the backpack he had readied the night before and realized with a shock that he hadn't completed his homework. He'd be marked down for that, and he'd have a mountain of homework in the afternoon to make up for it. Tapping the zippers together on the left bottom stop, he tiptoed down the dark hall, pausing to peek into the master bedroom. His dad was lying on his side, snoring softly and regularly. Cole exhaled in relief. It would be much easier to face the day knowing his dad had turned the corner.

In the kitchen, he ate a granola bar while preparing lunch. The refrigerator had been kept much better stocked since his dad's reformation, and Cole still hadn't gotten over the anticipation of making a sandwich with mayonnaise, thick slices of ham, cheese, and onion. Each ingredient smelled like a miracle. Cole placed the sandwich into his cooler, tucked his topped-off water bottle into his backpack, and shut the door softly behind him. Morning fog rolled over the streets, blushing delicately in the pink sunrise.

As Cole stepped out of his car and joined the throng of students tramping through the slush of the parking lot, he gazed at the school as if seeking some sign of last night's disturbance. It looked perfectly ordinary. Good. That would make it easier to pretend it hadn't happened.

He took his seat at Electronic Circuits and watched Mr. Price spring out of his chair to scribble some last-minute figures on the board. The squeak of chalk grated on Cole's exhausted nerves, but he was grateful for the distraction of solving the circuit board, a little game Mr. Price always played at the beginning of the week. The student who found the error in the connections by the end of the class would receive a small prize—a \$5 Starbucks gift card or a graph paper notebook, perhaps. The game was always a hit with the students, though Cole felt sorry for Mr. Price as he tried to command the students' attention while they craned their necks to see the board behind him. The trick, Cole found, was to arrive early and get a good look at the board, then let it sit at the back of his mind until the last five minutes of class, when he would bring it to the forefront again. Usually there was some pearl of information in Mr. Price's lecture that helped solve the puzzle, and if he had the board impressed on his subconscious, the pieces would click together by the end of class like a Rubik's cube snapping into alignment. It was for that reason that Cole now had about twenty unused gift cards sitting in the top right drawer of his desk at home. Afterwards, Cole was surprised that he could still recall the circuit problem of January 13th with eidetic accuracy.

Next came Java Programming, where Cole overheard a couple students asking each other whether they had felt the tremors last night. It seemed that a couple students who lived closer to the school had been woken up by them. Earthquakes weren't exactly unheard of in the area, but the fact that Vendler Academy seemed to be the nexus of the event worried Cole—maybe the event wasn't a random act of nature. But right now, he didn't have to worry about that. Right now, he could take refuge in the predictability of coding, where each statement led to an expected result. The logic could be complex, but it was never unpredictable. Unlike life, the results could be controlled.

Next was his hardest class of the day: Data Structures III with Dr. Khouri. As he always did, Cole fortified his intellectual powers with a quick glance around the room to remind himself that he was the only junior approved to take this class.

By the time Cole joined his friends for lunch, they had already claimed their customary table by the windows. As he made his way to them, he saw Bridget's face break into the radiant smile he so rarely saw. She was laughing at something

Joanna had said, and he deeply regretted not being close enough to hear her laugh.

Her smile faded when she saw Cole, but she seemed more nervous than angry. Determined to make things right, Cole took his seat and whispered, "So did you fill Bridget in yet?"

Joanna shook her head. Pleased to have an excuse to look at Bridget directly, Cole explained the night's adventure in a neat synopsis that Joanna clearly didn't feel sufficient, because she kept interrupting to add details about how unnerved, shocked, confused, lost, surprised, lucky, and brave they had been. Cole was watching Bridget closely. Her face had gone white, and she didn't seem able to take her eyes off Jude's band-aid covered thumb.

When Joanna finally stopped talking, Bridget said, "I can't believe the blood-letting isn't the end."

"What do you mean?" Cole asked.

"I mean, the stakes are getting higher. He's asking more and more of you. If he already has your blood, what will he ask for next?"

"You think—" Cole began, but just then, two seniors slid onto the bench next to Joanna. There was a pause while everyone tried to gain their bearings, and Cole realized that, excepting his birthday and Christmas, the four of them hadn't enjoyed a conversation about anything other than the internship almost since the start of the school year last fall. It was Bridget who broke the silence by retrieving a crumpled crossword from her pocket. She unfolded the paper and smoothed it out on the table. Her hands were shaking slightly, and Cole thought she might have produced it to comfort herself as much as to fill the silence.

"Poppy handed me this on the way out this morning." Her voice was unnaturally flat, as if she was forcing a calm she didn't feel. "He says he took it as far as possible, but he usually leaves me a few he thinks I'll know. Anyone want to help me with it?"

Cole nodded, grateful that she wasn't blocking him out, and even more grateful when Joanna and Jude both decided to study instead. Now was his chance. His pulse growing louder in his ears, he took Bridget's pencil and wrote in the margin of the crossword: *I'm sorry*. Bridget's face softened. She hesitated, then took the pencil back, wrote something below his note, and slid the puzzle back across the table for Cole to read: *Don't go again. Please.* When he looked up, her eyes were already holding his. The intensity of her appeal excited and unnerved him. But what was he supposed to do? Despite the earthquake and the likelihood that the tunnels were destroyed, he wasn't sure he could make that promise. He could have stared back into her eyes forever, but when he didn't reply, she dropped her gaze.

He leaned across the table toward her, as if their physical closeness could make up for his unwillingness to agree to her request. Her familiar scent and the pleasure of watching her long white fingers excitedly sweeping across the page when they solved a riddle reassured him, but her written plea kept drawing his eyes. Still, that lunch period was one of the happiest Cole could remember. Even afterward, when he knew what the day held, he couldn't help but think with fondness on lunch at least.

After lunch, Cole headed to Operating Systems with Dr. Theodore Lamb, where he had been regretting his choice of a seat ever since the beginning of last semester. He sat directly behind Gary, an oily-haired senior who only wore black clothes printed over with anime characters and whose greasy scalp drowned out the lingering scent of asylum chloride. Calculus with Dr. Chen, when he got to sit next to Jude, was quite literally a breath of fresh air. Cole headed straight for his car when the bell sounded. The deluge of homework from yesterday had only accumulated since today's classes, and he knew Data Structures III would take him at least two hours on its own.

He stepped out into an unseasonably warm afternoon. Small patches of the sidewalk were still wet with melting snow, but the sun had mostly dried the pavement. Wisps of cloud floated in a pale blue sky, and a few optimistic birds were singing in anticipation of spring. The air was fresh and brisk. Cole stood on his front porch a moment, breathing deeply, before pushing the front door open.

Inside, the air was close and still. Cole slipped his keys into his pocket, then walked to the thermostat and switched it off. Depositing his backpack on the living room couch, he opened the blinds and the windows, then walked through the hall to the kitchen and into the dining room to open the windows at the back of the house where the sun would be the hottest. It was decidedly warmer inside than out, but the air inside was stifling. Birdsong drifted through the open windows, and Cole made a snap decision to study at the dining room table where there was more sunlight and fresh air than in his room.

After retrieving his backpack from the living room, Cole grabbed a Sprite and a pack of Cool Ranch Doritos from the kitchen and set them on the table before walking upstairs and collecting an armful of tomorrow's textbooks. His computer, calculator, notebooks, pens, and pencils were already in his backpack. The Computer Architecture textbook, still pristine, cracked audibly as he opened it, and the answering crack of the soda made Cole feel a surprising sense of wellbeing. Thank goodness for a return to the ordinary.

The next time Cole glanced at his watch, it was already 6:35 pm. He still had American History homework to finish, but something in the silence of the house that had vaguely struck him as odd came to the forefront of his mind. Where was his dad? Now that his textbooks weren't speaking in his mind, Cole registered the absence of sports commentary from the study TV. As if in collusion with his subconscious, a growl from Cole's stomach reminded him that his dad was usually hungry for an early dinner.

Afterwards, Cole was ashamed to remember the reluctance with which he pushed his chair back from the table to rustle his dad out of his bedroom, and even more appalled by the hours it had taken him to notice his dad's absence. The house had grown dark and cold. Cole trudged up the stairs and knocked at his dad's door. It creaked open, but no one was inside. Maybe he was in his study after all? As Cole returned downstairs to check, a gust of wind shrieked through the house. He heard the pages of his notebook fluttering on the dining room table and what sounded like a tin can bumping down the street.

Outside the study door, Cole paused, unsure whether to knock or just walk inside.

After a minute, he stuck his hands in his pockets and said, "Dad?"

Nothing answered but the howling of the wind through barren trees. The birds had all gone.

"Dad, are you hungry?" he called a little more loudly.

Slowly, he grasped the cold doorknob and turned it. The door swung inward to reveal a room cast in darkness. Cole fumbled against the wall for the switch. When he found it, he wished he hadn't. Its light bathed the room in horror. The rigid head covered in thin gray hair was just visible on the other side of the easy chair that faced the TV on the far side of the room. One limp lump of swollen flesh draped the arm of the chair. Even before he stepped around the chair, Cole knew what he would find. No living hand ever looked like that.

Yet Cole was wholly unprepared for the bulging bloodshot eyes, the gaping mouth, and the swollen bottom lip dripping with blood and booze. Bile surged into his throat, and he vomited onto an empty whiskey bottle that lay at the foot of the chair. Even after his stomach emptied, he continued to heave involuntary paroxysms of anguish. He couldn't make himself get up from where he half squatted, shaking hands on shaking knees. The stench of his own vomit mixed with the release of his dad's urine staining the armchair forced him to push himself up and stagger back toward the door. As he stumbled out, he caught the door handle and slammed it behind him. He rushed to the kitchen sink and washed out his mouth with cold tap water, dribbling it down his chin and onto the front of his cardigan. He washed his trembling hands in the sink four, five, six times, as if to wash away the memory of the room. When he realized what he was doing, he slammed the tap off and dried his hands on the towel by the stove. He reached into his pocket and dialed a number, then held the phone to his ear. He could still smell sick on his own breath and hoped irrationally that the voice on the other end couldn't smell it.

When the voice came, it was all he could do to stagger out the words, "Jude, get over here, fast... bring your dad."

CHAPTER 35

CRIME SCENE

The sixteen minutes it took for the Durhams' Ford Explorer to pull up to the curb were interminable. Cole stood in front of the sink, washing his hands and his face again and again, then slumped onto the kitchen floor, still clutching the towel. As soon as he sat down, the thought of being in one place was unbearable, and he pulled himself up again. All strength had deserted his icy limbs. His whole body was shaking violently. At last, the sound of tires on asphalt slowed to a stop outside his door.

Cole held his breath and staggered past the study to open the door. Mr. Durham took one look at Cole and grasped him firmly by the shoulder, turning him around and guiding him into the living room. To his relief, Mr. Durham said, "Where is he?" as if reading Cole's thoughts. All Cole had to do was point to the study. Mr. Durham walked down the hall and pushed the door open. In another moment he was back in the living room, his phone pressed to his ear.

Jude, who had stayed with Cole in the living room, said, "Who are you calling?"

"911."

Cole collapsed onto the sofa. The magic number had been called. Everything he knew was about to disappear. He heard his address given and the irrevocable words "man found dead."

Putting his phone back in his pocket, Mr. Durham said, "The police are on their way. They may have some questions. I'm sorry you have to go through this right now, Cole, but it's important that they understand what happened right away."

In what seemed like seconds, two officers knocked at the door. Mr. Durham opened it and led the way into the living room. The taller of the two men extended a hand and introduced himself as Officer Liteman and his colleague as Officer Nation Night, then asked where the body was. Mr. Durham pointed to the study.

Liteman said, "Officer Nation Night will take possession of the scene, and the three of you will please follow me outside." Glancing at Cole, who was the only one without a coat, he added, "It's cold. You may want to grab a jacket."

As they stepped outside, Officer Liteman flipped the porch light on, its glow dim in the last traces of daylight. The air looked surreal, wrong. Cole was dimly aware of Jude standing stolidly beside him.

"I have a few quick questions for you," Liteman began. "Who —?"

Before he could finish the sentence, an ambulance pulled up to the curb and two paramedics jumped out almost before the vehicle had fully stopped. Liteman wheeled around and walked to meet them, exchanged a few words, and then opened the door for them, calling inside, "EMT!" Cole watched as a middle-aged woman, her mouth set in a narrow line, led a boy who looked almost as young as Cole into the house, portable EKG already in hand.

Liteman resumed as if nothing had happened. He got a brief rundown of Cole's discovery of "the body," his movements throughout the day, and how the Durhams came to be there. Cole heard himself answering as if from far away, as if his voice belonged to someone else. His mind was numb. The only thing that was real was his shivering body. Then Liteman asked about his dad's history with alcohol and whether or not he had been on any medications or drugs that might complicate his death.

Cole shook his head.

"No blood thinners, heart medication, sleeping pills...?" Liteman suggested.

"No, nothing." Suddenly, Cole's body flooded with rage and disbelief. "Can that even happen? Can someone die just from drinking? He was in great shape otherwise—how is that possible?"

Liteman said noncommittally, "We've seen all kinds of cases."

The officer's eyes drifted to the street. Cole wanted to insist that this wasn't a case, this was his dad, and his dad should, by rights, still be alive. Instead, they all stood in silence, waiting, the cold numbing Cole's body. Then, as if they had coordinated, three new vehicles drove down the street all at once. The car in front of the house was the most expensive of the three, and out of it stepped a gaunt woman of about sixty, her steel gray hair pulled back in a tight bun from which no wisps dared escape. The woman opened the backseat door on the driver's side and extracted a protective suit and a bag that Cole could only guess contained gloves, a mask, and God knew what else. Into his mind crept an image of the clinical suit bending stoically over his father's dismembered corpse. Swallowing his disgust, he watched as she strode up the walk and addressed Liteman, saying, "M.E. West."

Officer Liteman said, "This is Cole, son of the deceased. He discovered the body."

She said, "My condolences," in a voice devoid of emotion, and then, "May I see the body?"

Cole knew that the question was a courtesy and no more. Liteman opened the door for her. M.E. West was followed inside by two people who announced themselves as "Crime Lab." Did everyone in law enforcement simply say their title and name? An irreverent smirk flashed across Cole's face as he imagined a law enforcement picnic, everyone striding about declaring their titles and not knowing what to say next. He squeezed his eyes shut. What was wrong with him?

Cole refocused his attention on the occupant of the third car, a man dressed in plain clothes who seemed to take in every blade of dead grass as he approached the house. The man introduced himself as Detective Stokes in an unpleasant voice that matched his small, ferret-like features. He ran through the same questions Officer Liteman had already asked, then asked Cole to detail the symptoms of alcohol withdrawal Cole had observed in the days leading up to his dad's death.

Cole took a deep breath. "At first, Dad complained of insomnia. I saw his hands shaking as he tried to pour coffee. Later, things got worse."

"Explain."

"He was awake at odd hours. Once, was it last night? No, the night before, I got up to get some water, and dad was in the kitchen. I didn't realize he was there until I turned the lights on; he couldn't take it. He yelled at me to turn them off, and after I did, he sort of... zoned out. He didn't recognize me."

"Obviously his body was under extreme stress. Why did you not call for help?"

Cole swallowed and tried to look Detective Stokes in the eye. Jude and Mr. Durham were watching him. This was the question he had been dreading.

"I thought about it. Honestly, I didn't know what to do. I suggested to dad that he get some help, but he refused. I think he was embarrassed."

Even as he said the words, he realized how ludicrous they sounded. Detective Stokes raised his eyebrows and stared at Cole as if waiting for a more plausible confession. Cole didn't give it.

"So. You went back to sleep as if nothing had happened."

Cole nodded, realizing for the first time that his decision not to pick up the phone was the indirect cause of his dad's death. His empty chest and esophagus suddenly seemed filled with fire.

"And was that the last time you saw your father alive?"

It was much harder to speak now, and when Cole's words finally came, they sounded thick. "I saw him last night. I woke up because he was moaning. I went to check on him. He was in bed, and I don't think he saw me. He had little scratches on his arms, I thought maybe from his own finger-nails, and his lower lip was... chewed up. It looked swollen, bloody."

Detective Stokes's eyebrows threatened to disappear into his hairline. "And still you did not call for help?"

"Believe me, I wish I had. I looked in on him again this morning, and he seemed to be sleeping normally. I would give anything to have this morning back—anything."

Stokes watched his prey out of the corner of his eye as if deciding what to ask next. Mercifully, M.E. West emerged at that moment and asked Detective Stokes for a word.

As soon as they were inside the house, Liteman took a step toward Cole and said, "I should have asked earlier—do you want us to call a victim's advocate for you? That's someone to help you navigate this process."

There was something so reassuringly human about Officer Liteman's mistake that Cole felt a surge of affection for the uniformed officer, who, despite looking like he was only in his late twenties, now wore an almost paternal expression of concern. Cole wondered how long Liteman had been an officer and whether this was one of his first domestic deaths. Surely that was unlikely.

Cole must have stood there for some time, because the question was repeated.

He said, "The last thing I want right now is another stranger in the house." He turned to Mr. Durham. "If you could help me..."

"Absolutely," Mr. Durham said before Cole's sentence was even finished, as if he had just been waiting for an invitation.

Liteman said, "Good. And if you change your mind at any point, just let me know." He handed him a business card. "You can call me and I'll arrange for someone to come help. For now, we need to notify next of kin."

It was that statement that made Cole realize how bizarre it was that his dad didn't have anyone—no coworkers, no friends, no girlfriends. He had no one, in fact, but the drinking buddies at Davis Bar. And he had given that up too because of Cole. No wonder his dad was so desperate to leave town and go camping. The burning guilt in Cole's chest grew even more unbearable at the thought.

Finally, surprised he hadn't thought of it before, Cole said, "I guess we should call my mom. She lives in New Mexico," he added irrelevantly.

"Do you want to call her together?" Liteman asked.

"Sure."

As Cole had anticipated, his mom's surprise at hearing from him quickly turned to disbelief, distress, then a promise to book the next flight to Pittsburgh. Cole glanced nervously at Mr. Durham, who introduced himself as Cole's best friend's dad and offered to help Cole navigate the next day or so until it made sense for Layla to break away. Cole and Layla were both relieved.

"Well all right then," she said. "Cole baby, you call me the second you need something. I'm always here for you, even states away. I hope you know that. I love you. I'll call you tomorrow, okay?"

"Okay."

There was an air kiss on the other end of the line that came across as static, and Cole hung up.

At that moment, Detective Stokes, M.E. West, and the crime lab team all filed out of the house.

M.E. West said, "I've finished my examination, and the crime lab has swept the house and photographed the scene. Nothing points to homicide or suicide. Looks like positional asphyxiation from intoxication, but I've ordered an autopsy. Transport service will be here any minute to collect the body, but we're done here. Cole, we'll be in touch with results."

As swiftly as they had come, everyone but Liteman and Nation Night left. The officers stood with Cole and the Durhams on the porch until transport service arrived. Cole watched, dazed, as they removed the foreign bulk that was Robert Erickson. It was all over with impossible efficiency. The house was empty.

CHAPTER 36

LIFE AFTER DEATH

After the police left, Mr. Durham called Laura to come to the Erickson home, and together she, Jude, and Cole packed a bag that would last at least a week. Meanwhile, as Cole later discovered, Mr. Durham had scoured the study of urine and vomit. Soon the windows were closed, the blinds drawn, the thermostat reduced, the water shut off, and the door locked. None of the Durhams asked Cole anything. They just showed him where to go and what to do. Cole felt utterly exhausted and was grateful Mrs. Durham didn't make him eat dinner before he crawled into Chandler's bed and succumbed to the surprisingly immediate oblivion of sleep.

He awoke a few hours later with a crick in his neck and panic pounding through his head. Why was the moonlight coming through the wrong window? Where was he? A dozen questions tumbled through his mind, and with them the ache of memory. Jude's snores mocked his restlessness. He wanted to get up and pace the house, but he didn't want to disturb the Durhams when they were being so kind to him.

Trying to calm his mind, he reached for his phone and opened a text from Joanna that he had missed yesterday. It read: *Oh my God, did you see this?!* Below her message was a screenshot of a news article with the headline: "Orien Saint-Pierre Found Dead in Penthouse."

Cole's mouth went dry. No. It couldn't be true. Orien had just been at his school, all muscle and flesh and most definitely alive. What were the chances that his dad and Orien could have died on the same day? Cole blinked rapidly, trying to focus on the screenshot. The informant was a CNA at the hospital to which Orien had been taken. Apparently, Orien had been found in a coma on the kitchen floor of his penthouse, had been rushed to the hospital, and... The text cut off. His hands shaking, Cole opened his browser and searched for more news. There was none. He tried typing in the article title verbatim. Still there were no results.

Cole ran his fingers through his hair, taking a deep, shuddering breath to calm himself. The article had to be fake news. That's why it wasn't appearing. It had been unpublished. Orien was invincible, the last person susceptible to death. If only Cole could find an article explaining that the press had made a mistake. He searched again, this time just for Orien's name, and scrolled through several pages before throwing his phone down in frustration. A shiver seized his body, and he hugged his knees against his chest. It couldn't be true. If Orien was dead, everything Cole had sacrificed was in vain. If Orien was dead, Cole's dad had died for nothing. Cole had chosen the internship over his dad, and now none of it mattered.

Out of nowhere, he remembered the words that had been whispered in his ear: *But if you leave me where I lie, traitor, you shall surely die.* That's what Vendler's ghost had said. Was this the death—to watch everyone and everything he loved die around him? Was this all Cole's fault for starting something he didn't understand and couldn't finish? Vendler had placed a curse on any who betrayed him, and that's exactly what Cole had done by not making it to the final chamber. And Cole wasn't the only one—his dad had rejected Vendler since childhood, and now his dad was dead. And Orien, too, had trespassed on sacred ground, ground intended for Vendler's descendants, and now Orien was dead. Did it all trace back to Vendler's curse? Had Cole unwittingly activated it the moment he engaged the portrait in the library? Maybe, if Cole had never insisted on following Alexandria and seeking what Vendler left, none of this would have happened.

Cole was breathing fast now. He was sure he was being too loud. Jude would wake up. He would turn the light on. He would explain that everything was a nightmare. He would tell Cole that Orien was still alive, and so was Cole's dad.

But Jude didn't wake up.

Gradually, Cole's breathing normalized again. He wanted to be anywhere but where he was, to get out of this narrow, dark room where he was trapped. He squeezed his eyes closed and rocked his body back and forth, back and forth. Finally, near dawn, he lost consciousness.

Daylight poured through the slats in the blinds when next he awoke. Cole lay inert, staring at the chipped blue paint on the wall, trying to pretend that yesterday's nightmare wasn't real. Yet here he was, in the wrong bed, his phone on the floor where he had flung it. He decided not to mention the news about Orien to anyone. If it was true, the news would soon be everywhere. For now, he didn't have energy to worry about both Orien and his dad. When he could no longer bear the stillness, he rose, showered, dressed, and descended the stairs.

The rolled-up carpet was still leaning on one side of the stair-case, and he wondered if Mrs. Durham would ever decide to sell it.

Mechanically, unconscious of why he was doing what he was doing, he walked through the empty living room and dining room to the kitchen. Mrs. Durham retracted her head from the refrigerator and scribbled something on a scrap of paper. When she saw him, she dropped the pencil and enfolded him in the strongest hug he had ever received. He felt his muscles melting under its pressure, the walls he had built to safeguard himself from disappointment crumbling like sandstone inside him. Burning grief flamed up his throat. He pulled back before the tears could break through. Seeming to sense his embarrassment, Mrs. Durham turned her back on him and started making toast.

"You're not going to school today or the rest of this week," she said. "I've already phoned the front desk. Now I know you're not going to be hungry, but you need to eat something."

Cole looked at his wristwatch and saw that it was already 10:47 before realizing that time didn't matter. The toast turned to ash in his mouth, but he made himself swallow it as a duty to Mrs. Durham until she placed a glass of orange juice beside his plate. Suddenly nauseous, Cole dropped his toast and pushed his plate away.

After breakfast, Mr. Durham invited Cole into the dining room. Taking a long, prefatory drink of coffee, he slid a stack of printed papers across the table toward him. The top paper was labeled "Last Will and Testament of Robert N. Erickson."

Mr. Durham said, "Your mom couldn't sleep last night. She wanted to do something to help, so she called first thing this morning and emailed your dad's will. I know this is a lot to think about right now, but I thought you might want to know. When my dad died, I needed something to do, something to keep me busy.

"I've taken the liberty of perusing it on your behalf. He left you the house, which he owned outright. You can't take possession till you're eighteen, so I recommend renting it. I can arrange that for you. It looks like your dad also left you a substantial sum in a 529 plan, which is a college fund. It's earmarked 'Stanford.'"

Cole, who had been staring expressionlessly at a knot in one of the tabletop boards, looked back at the papers. Stanford? How had his dad known Cole wanted to go to Stanford? Was he actually paying attention when Cole had told him three years ago about signing up for classes at Vendler that would allow him to attend Stanford, then study at MIT, then get a job at The Lab? He distinctly remembered his dad answering with a grunt and a "I'll be parked over there when you're done with the registrar." That was it. But apparently, that wasn't it.

After a while, Cole said, "I just realized, if I'm renting the house, I'll need to find somewhere to live."

Mr. Durham shook his head vigorously. "I've already spoken to Laura about that—we'd like you to live here so you can finish out high school."

Cole felt a rush of relief, gratitude, and guilt.

"Of course," Mr. Durham continued, giving Cole a sudden, sharp glance, "you may prefer to be with your mom."

"I'd much rather be with family," Cole said before realizing that the Durhams weren't his family and his mom was. He stammered, "I mean, I'd much rather be with *your* family."

The left corner of Mr. Durham's mouth curled into a satisfied smile that looked just like Jude's. "Good. Laura can call your mom again and talk it over."

The rest of the day, and the days that followed, were a muddle. Sometimes Cole slept during the day, sometimes at night, so that his sense of time was marked mostly by visits from Joanna and Bridget, who came every day after school. Joanna hugged him hard and wept the tears that for him wouldn't come, while Bridget stood by silently, her eyes so gentle he wanted to sink into them.

There were a million decisions to make and phone calls he wanted to ignore but couldn't—phone calls from his mom, his dad's lawyer, the school, and finally a call with autopsy results that declared the case closed, cause of death positional asphyxiation from intoxication. Layla and Geoff booked their flights for the evening before the funeral service and interment.

Not wanting to meet his step-dad without moral support, Cole asked Mrs. Durham to accompany him to the airport. To Cole, who had been sequestered indoors for so many days, the urgent movement of the Saturday night traffic was a shock. The cavalier cheeriness of street lights, the barely provoked honking of horns, and the sight of a passenger's soundless laughter in a nearby car stunned him. So the world kept revolving after all. How many strangers, he wondered, had he himself passed in a previous life, unaware that their lives might have been devastated by tragedy as his just had?

When they reached the airport, Layla was the first passenger to attract their attention. Her three-inch heels, skin-tight pants, long fur coat, and fresh-from-the-salon blonde blowout made her the most conspicuous arrival on the sidewalk. Amazingly, Geoff was not relegated to her shadow. Although the sidewalk was crowded, it was easy to identify him as the tall man whose black and gray curls rose with impeccable coiffure above a high forehead with a defined widow's peak, his manicured beard lending gratuitous definition to an already chiseled jaw. He was leaning back on one muscular buttock, surveying the crowd as if assessing its collective intelligence, secure in his own superiority.

"What a pompous ass," Cole thought, then immediately felt guilty. He had no real reason to hate his mom's new husband—yet. Cole got out of the car and gave his mom a hug that she held longer than he expected. When she let him go, her companion's round mouth split into a beacon-like smile as he extended a hand. Then he turned to Mrs. Durham and announced, "Geoffrey David Kay."

Cole found himself peevishly wondering whether the middle name was really necessary and if he always introduced himself this way. Layla gave Mrs. Durham a hug that said, "Don't crumple my hair," while her mouth said, "Thank you so much for looking after my sweet boy."

They spent a tedious evening listening to Geoff pontificate about an oil painting in the Durhams' foyer—which he pronounced a first-rate Dali imitation done with second-rate oils and less consideration for form than the Surrealist Spaniard—and then regale them with stories of his travels over dinner.

"You haven't lived," he said, "until you've watched the sun set on a balcony in the French Riviera, the scent of the sea filling your lungs, a glass of Chateau Lafite Rothschild in your hand, and a ravishing woman in your arms. I've done all of that but without the ravishing woman, so I keep telling Layla she must go back with me if she wants me to die a happy man."

"Charmer," Layla responded with a throaty laugh.

Cole stabbed his lasagna with unnecessary force. He knew it had been a long time since his mom had loved his dad—if she had ever loved him—but couldn't she at least refrain from parading how happy she was with another man until her previous husband was covered in dirt?

When it became obvious that Mrs. Durham was not going to offer refills of wine, Layla said they should take their leave to check into their hotel, thanking the Durhams for dinner and Cole for letting them borrow his car for the weekend. Not quickly enough, the front door closed.

CHAPTER 37

THE FUNERAL

It took several seconds for Cole's eyes to adjust as he stepped from the bright January morning into the low-roofed funeral home. As if to soften any sound of grief, the floor was blanketed with a thick scarlet carpet, the walls covered with mahogany wood paneling. A short gentleman with a bald pate waddled forward in overlarge slacks to grasp Cole's hand between two sweaty palms. He introduced himself as Mr. Slabolepszy, the funeral home director. As Cole looked into his round face, he was surprised to see eyes brightened with genuine caring instead of the cookie-cutter sympathy he had expected. Cole returned a small smile.

Mr. Slabolepszy crab-walked sideways to introduce himself to the semi-circle of early arrivals that included Geoff and Layla, the entire Durham family, and Joanna. He led them down a short hallway to a large room. A half wall partitioned a small reception room with dated furniture from a larger space with stacking banquet chairs. At the front of this larger room was a closed ebony coffin festooned with flower arrangements. Joanna whispered a question in Mr. Slabolepszy's ear, then left the room only to reappear clutching a black poster board and an 8-by-10 picture frame.

"Cole, come here," she said, handing him the frame and leading him to a table near the hallway. She set the poster board on the table. "I hope you don't mind, but I got your mom's contact info from Mama D, and she helped me find these."

The board was covered in photographs of Robert Erickson, mainly of the first few years after his marriage with Layla up through the time when Cole was nine. There were pictures of Cole sitting on his dad's lap and blowing out candles on a homemade cake at age three; his hair beach blond and a carefree smile on his face as his dad helped him reel in his first fish at age six; and holding one end of a yard-long string of melted cheese while his dad held the other at a pizza night at age eight. For the first time since he had discovered his dad in his armchair, Cole's eyes blurred with tears. He wiped them away as Joanna wrapped an arm around his waist and squeezed hard.

It was some minutes before he remembered to look at the picture in his own hand. It was his dad's official military photo: he was sitting in front of a cloud-blue background that featured the U.S. flag and the Army flag, his broad shoulders relaxed in confidence, the distinctive cock-eyed grin on his face, jet black hair peeking out beneath the brim of the Army cap he had given Cole. Cole felt himself smiling back at the picture. His dad had been so smart and handsome. Geoff might be a well-traveled art collector, but his dad had been a surgeon who had graduated top of his class and knew how to make Layla laugh in an abandoned way, not a calculated, coy way.

A hand rested on his shoulder, and Cole glanced up to see

his mom standing on his other side, gazing at the poster board of pictures. Joanna tactfully disappeared.

"For all his faults, your dad loved you very much, Cole." A smile stole over his mom's lips. "Do you know, it would have been easy for me to get full custody, but he was so determined to keep you in his life that he said he'd do anything in the world—beg, borrow, or steal—just to make sure you grew up with a dad you could be proud of. And I knew he meant it. He loved you fiercely."

Could that be true? Cole had always thought of himself as an inconvenient burden neither of his parents wanted. He glanced at his mom to gauge her sincerity. She was staring at the picture of Robert in uniform, and Cole was surprised to see a tear sliding down her cheek. She dabbed at it with a finger dominated by a fake nail.

"The only thing I asked was that he wouldn't stop you from following your dreams. He never wanted you to go to Vendler, you know."

Cole looked at her sharply. "Why?"

She shrugged and said, "I'm glad you'll be here to finish your senior year."

Giving him a watery smile, she retreated to receive a comforting hug from Geoff. Cole watched her go and saw a mask drop from Geoff's face to reveal a softness that bore a genuine concern for the woman in his arms. At that moment, Cole decided not to hate him.

Sensing an opportunity for transition, Mr. Slabolepszy waddled forward and invited the family to view the body before everyone else arrived. They followed him down the center aisle. The ceiling lights, yellowed with age, cast a soft glow over the room, and Cole wondered if the dim lighting was intentional. It was better not to see the dead too clearly. Mr. Slabolepszy waved a hand, and a lanky young assistant appeared out of nowhere to remove the flower arrangements. They each took a latch and lifted gently. Cole's shoulders tensed as he realized he was expected to view the body first. He wasn't prepared for this.

For a moment, no one did anything. Then Mr. Durham moved to stand in front of the coffin, holding an arm open to usher Cole to join him. His heart hammering, Cole stepped forward. The first thing he saw was two swollen hands, one cupped stiffly over the other. His gaze traveled up the unfamiliar black suit and blue tie to a waxen face, its eyes shut. The lips that were slack and trickled with blood had been cleaned and closed into a peaceful line. The hair had been washed and combed back from a yellow forehead. There was no way that this stiff, lifeless weight was the quick-eyed, sharp-witted father Cole had known in his childhood. He stared in disbelief at the figure as if from a great distance, the years of memories tumbling into the gulf between.

As he watched those memories fall into that abyss of forgetfulness, he decided he would save them. He saw himself stooping to rescue the boisterous sound of his dad's laughter, the image of the funny monkey face that always made Cole smile, and the pressure of his dad's firm hug. He collected memories till his arms were piled high and his heart was fortified. Then he left the coffin and watched as Layla and Geoff stepped forward. When Layla turned away again, the make-up on her cheeks was streaked with rivulets.

A muffled footfall made Cole turn to the door. Bridget and her grandparents were walking straight down the center aisle to the coffin. Bridget, who was first, made the sign of the cross over Robert Erickson's chest, her fingers hovering just above the suit before she bent and kissed his hand. Cole's skin tingled as he watched, alarmed that she was so comfortable touching death.

Poppy and Birdy followed her actions exactly, and then the three of them came to hug him. Bridget said nothing, but she held him firmly and let go a few seconds later than he expected.

Birdy whispered, "He's such a handsome man," as her white curls tickled Cole's ear.

Poppy almost cradled him as he said, "I'm so sorry. If there's anything you need—anything at all—please consider us family."

Cole's throat constricted. The best he could manage was a nod before they filed away again to sit a couple rows behind him.

Bridget and her grandparents were followed by two burly middle-aged men who stood awkwardly at the back of the hall. Mr. Slabolepszy hastened to greet them, and Cole saw the funeral home director pointing in his direction. The men looked at him incredulously and then made their way toward him.

The taller of the two extended a hand with incongruously delicate fingers and said, "Cole, my name is Dr. Hill. I'm a retired anesthesiologist. I worked surgery with your dad for seven years. I just heard about this two days ago and booked my ticket immediately. Flew in from Idaho. Your dad was a special man—always had us laughing with his stories as soon as we put the patient under. I'm so sorry."

A little shocked, Cole managed to thank Dr. Hill for coming before turning to the other man whose fluffy blonde hair was bobbing up and down as he bounced on his heels like a school boy.

"Nurse Manager Whitcomb, for my sins. I know, I know—what kind of man becomes a male nurse in the Army? Gotta have a death wish to choose a career like that." Suddenly self-conscious about joking about death in a funeral home, Whitcomb's face straightened and he continued hastily, "Only found out 'cause Hill called me last night. Woke up early to drive in from Walter Reed this morning. God, you look nothing like your old man. Except for the lost expression."

"Whit!" Dr. Hill said reprovingly.

"Sorry, sorry, that was a joke on your dad, not on you. I'm sure you're smarter than he was, old bastard."

"He means it as a compliment," Dr. Hill explained.

Cole truly felt lost about how to reply. Thankfully, Dr. Hill bundled his friend off to the last row of chairs as if he were a child who was more likely to behave away from his friends. Their appearance was followed by Paul and an influx of Vendler Academy representatives, an impossibly thin man with a weathered face and fidgety fingers, a lean man who moved with the grace of an athlete, and a young woman with heavy make-up whom Cole recognized with some surprise as a local supermarket cashier. Despite all the unexpected guests, Cole couldn't shake the feeling that someone was missing. Then he realized who: Alexandria. Would she know his dad was dead? Only if she happened to see it in the paper. Why hadn't Cole thought to tell her? She had a right to know... if she was still alive. Somehow, he didn't think she was, not after she thought Cole had promised to destroy Vendler's legacy. But he decided to go looking for her again anyway.

The funeral service itself passed in a fog of saccharine music Cole could only assume had been selected by Mr. Slabolepszy. When Mr. Durham had finished reading the airbrushed eulogy, Mrs. Durham pushed Cole forward to stand beside the head of his dad's coffin. Cole felt a little guilty that the faces of his guests were more grief-stricken than his own. Paul wrapped him in a powerful hug, apparently too choked by tears to say anything. The man with the weathered face introduced himself without shame as Rob's drinking buddy from Davis Bar. Cole wanted to wipe his hand on his suit as soon as the man's grimy fingers clasped his, but he controlled himself and thanked him for coming. Next came the weepy girl from the supermarket, who told Cole through constant dabs at her mascara-streaked face that Rob had made her laugh on several occasions when her life was "going to hell in a handbasket."

"People think we don't remember our customers, but we do. Some of them make you feel like you're a self-checkout machine, like you're not even human: you're either fast or slow, you either work or you don't, and if you don't, they bitch about you to management. But some customers treat you like a human being with your own life and your own troubles. Your dad was one of the few in the last camp."

Cole almost wanted to say, "Are we talking about the same Robert Erickson?" but refrained, merely patting her awkwardly as she gave him a spontaneous hug.

She was followed by the contingent from Vendler Academy, Dr. Hill and Nurse Whitcomb, and finally the athletic man. He grasped Cole's hand and stared into his eyes with an intensity that made Cole blink.

"Cole, my name is Jean Claude Janssens. Your dad probably never mentioned me. To him, I was just one of many damaged Army vets he fixed up, but to me, he was the man who saved my life. I was shipped home after being caught in a bombing, a pathetic piece of barely strung together flesh. They said I'd be paralyzed for life; I couldn't even move my head to see who told me that. I opted for physician assisted suicide, but your dad said, 'Look, if you're going to kill yourself anyway, you might as well let me have a go at you first.' It was an impossible surgery, but I walked out of it—literally walked out of that recovery room. I went on to become a cyclist and win second in the Milan San-Remo. I met my wife a year later, and together we have three beautiful children. None of that would have happened if your dad had been just like every other doctor who was content to make the obvious prognosis. I'll never forget him. Never."

Cole didn't know what to say. Before writing the eulogy, he had had no idea that his dad had been a reputable surgeon, let alone a brilliant one. All he knew was that his dad had botched what should have been a straightforward operation badly enough that the Army wasn't willing to look the other way anymore when it came to his drinking problem, that his dad wouldn't accept the rehab help that had been offered, and that his family had fallen apart because of it. Why was it that the fullness of his dad's life had only come to light after his death?

When everyone but Cole, the Durhams, Layla, and Geoff had filed out of the building, Mr. Slabolepszy invited the family to say their final farewells before closing the coffin lid. They carried the coffin to the waiting hearse, and the cars processed slowly behind it. As they pulled up to the cemetery, Cole was grateful Mrs. Durham had picked such a beautiful spot. Mature oaks cast feathery shadows over the sunlit tombstones, and the last few winter birds sang boisterously from their branches in the unexpected January sunshine. Cole smiled. His dad would love this place.

They walked past rows of tombstones to the spot where a mound of chestnut soil lay heaped beside a freshly dug grave. Green mesh blanketed the spot where Robert would be buried, and Cole wondered if its purpose was to keep the living from treading too near death.

The coffin was lowered with an irreverent creak of the crank into the open grave. Cole felt that something should be said or done and was glad when Mrs. Durham, Joanna, and

Bridget began handing out flowers from the arrangements for their guests to throw into the grave as they departed. Several people squeezed Cole on the shoulder or arm as they returned to their cars.

One by one, everyone left. Mr. Durham whispered, "Take your time, Cole. We'll be in the van when you're ready to go home." The word "home" was sweet in his ear. Irrationally, he felt a surge of joy that, for the first time in his life, he belonged somewhere. Layla stayed by his side, her thin arm clutching his waist as a few tears trickled down her cheeks. Then she too was gone.

Cole stared unseeingly at the flower-covered casket. No one in the world seemed to exist except for himself and his dad, whom he was too late to love. Cole remembered the sheepish grin on his dad's face as he invited Cole to share pizza at the kitchen counter, the school-boy excitement in his voice when he talked about the camping adventure they would go on, how he had joked through his pain in the days that followed, and how hard he had fought to become a dad Cole could be proud of. And Cole had turned his back, ignoring him at the very moment his dad needed him most. He had chosen his homework and his internship instead of his dad. And now his teachers were urging him not to worry about school, and Orien Saint-Pierre was dead. Guilt gnawed his chest. Everything he prized was dust. He was alone.

A hand slipped into his and squeezed hard. Startled, he looked up to see Bridget beside him. She was not looking at him, but with him at his dad.

After a few seconds, she said, "You know, after my parents died, there was so much time I regretted. There was so much we never experienced together. I wanted them back more than anything in the world. The only thing that gave me comfort, that felt like a real action I did directly for them, to remember them and keep them alive, was lighting candles in their memory."

Her other hand gently opened his and placed in it a tea candle and a small box of matches. "I light candles every Sunday for them, and I can feel them praying with me."

Bridget's eyes were bright. A tear sparkled on her cheek in the setting sun.

"Where do you put it when you light it?"

"In front of an icon. Just lighting it and putting it there is a prayer. But if you want to, you can also pray that God will remember him eternally."

Cole retracted his hand in dismay. "Isn't that what Vendler wanted?"

A small smile blossomed on her mouth. "I don't think Vendler had God in mind. Remember there was no vocative —his statement was passive imperative."

Cole put the candle and matches in his pocket and took Bridget's hand again before suddenly becoming self-conscious. The motion felt like the most natural thing in the world, a simple acknowledgement of what for him had always been there, whether or not he consciously realized it, but it was different now that he had initiated it. He wondered who might be watching. But Bridget made no motion to remove her hand, and he was too happy to draw his own hand back. Even if this moment was temporary, he would enjoy it.

They stood for several minutes staring down at the coffin covered in carnations and gerbera daisies, their petals still fragrant. Finally, Bridget squeezed his hand and let it go, then walked a few paces to the waiting mound of dirt, scooped up a handful, and dropped it over the coffin. A flower shuddered as its fragile stem was pinned down, its head half buried. Bridget brushed her hands together and returned to Cole's side.

"Cole, can I ask you something?"

For one terrifying second, Cole thought she was going to ask why he had held her hand.

"Why do you want the internship?"

"Oh!"

It was the last question he expected. Had she asked it to make him feel the guilt of choosing The Lab over his dad? If so, he deserved it, but knowing Bridget, he didn't think so. He was silent for a few moments as he searched for the right answer. Why did he want the internship? His brain felt like an overcrowded storage unit as he hunted through jumbled parcels: Bridget's hand in his; the quick, comfortless hug of his mother; forkfuls of Laura Durham's food that were tasteless on his tongue; his father's bloody lip and fluttering eyelids passing like shrouded phantoms through his nightmares; the dark caverns of his own mind and Vendler's that were impossible to distinguish; and finally, the clean, triumphant smile of Orien as he sat across the desk from Cole and spoke about the future they would build together. At last, he secured the right moment in his mind.

"The thing is, I'd be an idiot not to. Orien is at the forefront of all the important developments in AI. He's leading the field, and the opportunity for a high school student to get a foot in the door is unheard of."

"I know all that, but why do you want to do the work itself?"

Cole cleared his throat and ran a hand through his hair. This was not the conversation he expected to be having at his dad's graveside. The question hung in the air as if suspended above the open grave. There were a million answers Cole could have given—that it would be exciting to be involved in creating a new technology, that his work would benefit people globally, or even simply that it was a good career decision that would open future opportunities. Instead, he left the question where it was.

Bridget cast a sidelong glance at him and said, "Just something to think about."

She patted him on his shoulder blade and was gone. Cole took one more look at the flowers and the question floating above the grave, then turned his back and threaded his way through the tombstones to the Durhams' van.

CHAPTER 38

FAMILY HISTORY

As Cole tossed a shirt onto the heap of clothes on his dad's bedroom floor, he felt nothing but disgust at the odor of stale sweat and beer that clung to it even after it had been through the wash. He had heard of survivors clinging to the clothes of their lost loved ones, inhaling scents like memories. But he had become so accustomed to avoiding his dad in life that to embrace him in death struck him as both unnatural and hypocritical. So far, making it through his first week back at school had proved harder than cleaning out his dad's belongings.

As he glanced around the empty room, he wondered if there was anything of his dad's that would make him feel more than guilt and disgust. Stripped of the beer cans and chip bags that typically littered the dresser and nightstand, the room felt oddly impersonal. The carpet was streaked with furrows from a vacuum cleaner like a field that had been harvested, leveled, and tilled, waiting for new crops to nurture. The room now smelled of quite a different type of alcohol left by sanitizing wipes. The cleaning service Mrs.

Durham hired had done their job well, scrupulously avoiding any potentially sacramental objects while whisking away the underlying detritus.

Cole had never realized before how few personal items his dad owned. There were no family photos, no books, no quirky calendars, nothing to betray personal taste except the fishing rods and camping gear, musty from disuse, that were now packed into the back seat of Cole's car. He still hadn't decided where they would go.

The only thing Cole decided to keep from his dad's room was a pair of dress shoes that fit him. It was an unexpected, sentimental impulse that had made Cole put on the dress pants he had worn to his dad's funeral when returning to clear their house, and the black leather of the shoes caught his fancy against the dark gray pinstripes of the slacks. Everything else he scooped into large trash bags to be donated or dumped. He trudged downstairs with the bags and managed to fit them into his car before returning to his dad's bedroom for one last look. Despite the carpeted floors, his footfalls echoed in the shell of the room. He stood in the doorway, wondering what he was supposed to be feeling. After a few minutes, when he didn't feel whatever it was he was waiting for, he passed down the hall to his own room, which was also empty but for some school supplies in his desk drawers and a few summer clothes.

He started with the clothes, tossing aside anything faded or small, trying to be more selective than he normally would be given the spatial constraints at the Durham home. With the inheritance from his dad, he could afford to buy any new clothes he might need. He had always dressed simply and immaculately, modeling himself after a more restrained version of Wesley Tate. Now he wondered what his wardrobe would have been like if his mother had been around to veto colors that didn't suit him or encourage an occasional whim. Smiling wryly, he thought of Bridget. In the absence of parents, she had chosen the opposite extreme, rushing wide-armed into the sale racks of second-hand stores. He wished she was with him now, giving him strength and lighting the way to a new life. The need to see her was as painful as it was sudden. He squeezed his eyes tight and refocused on the task at hand.

When he finished sorting through his closet, he glanced at his watch. It was twenty till seven, and he was hungry. He decided to tackle his desk and then grab dinner out. The first desk drawer held several gift cards won from Mr. Price's class, as well as a neat row of mechanical pencils, a large calculator, a protractor, and a compass. It had been years since he'd taken geometry, and in all likelihood, he wouldn't use the instruments again. Nevertheless, he packed them fondly into a box designated for storage. The second drawer held three blank notebooks and a binder containing the syllabi and grade reports from every class he had taken at Vendler. He kept back one notebook and put the rest in storage. The third drawer held only a lumpy, brown paper bag. Confused, Cole brought it out for closer examination.

As his skin touched the crumpled paper, a rush of memory made him stagger backward to sit on his bed. Trying to calm his suddenly rapid breathing, he opened the bag and felt inside. But the first thing he felt was not his dad's military cap. It was a crumpled piece of paper. Confused, Cole drew it out.

The envelope was addressed to Robert Erickson from Alexandria Lehmann. Cole stared at the words in shock. How had that gotten there? The letter had most certainly not been in the brown paper bag when his dad first gave it to him. In fact, they had had an argument about Alexandria immediately after his dad had given it to him. That meant his dad had, sometime in the last weeks leading up to his death, snuck into Cole's room and placed it there. But why? Why would his dad have kept anything from Alexandria, given what he had told Cole about her? And what had made him decide to pass the letter on to Cole?

Taking a deep breath, Cole drew out three sheets of fragile paper overlaid with indigo ink. There was another piece of paper too, almost as old, written in a wobbly hand. Cole took it first.

Dear Robert,

I must show you real proof: this is the note Vendler left beside my sister—your mother—after he raped her. He wrote it for you anyway, so I suppose it's right you should have it.

I hope now you will believe what I told you: what he left for you must be destroyed.

Your affectionate aunt,
Alexandria

In his haste to read Vendler's letter, Cole ripped one of its pages.

My Son,
My love to you from beyond the veil! You do not

know me now, but the time is coming, very soon, when you shall. I gave you life. I made you. Now you shall remake me. But my pen is too hasty. Let me tell you first how I discovered the secret to eternal life.

I was only a boy. My mother died young, and my father worked long hours at the mine. From the beginning I was master of my own fate, bound only to myself. I took it upon myself to discover every activity of mankind, to seek out the best way to live.

I saw men caked in soil and sweat, prying treasure from the earth. I saw men sitting at long tables dictating the course of industry. I saw men of commerce, men of law, and men of education, and none enjoyed more than fleeting triumph.

None, that is, until I crept up the rickety stairs of a dilapidated Victorian home and found its door ajar. Inside, I saw a man sitting at a stool, painting a small dog that lay asleep by the hearth. He was adding the finishing touches of textured fur, and he was so absorbed that he did not hear the creak of the door when I opened it. I stood on tiptoe to peer over his shoulder, and the force of the painting stole the wind from my chest.

Here was something alive, something immortal! The dog in the painting lay as still as its counterpart at the hearth. But some energy, invisible yet palpable, filled that painting and the whole studio with the dog's presence.

I stood as one in a trance, bound by the power of that painting and desperate to discover its invisible secret. Yet the painter uttered no words of power. He merely mixed his colors and drew his strokes with immense attention and—there is no mystery about the word to me now—with immense love.

I was obsessed. Never did I myself wish to paint, but I needed to unearth the power behind that painting. I observed artists in studios from Boston to Los Angeles and Seattle to Miami, but almost never could I recapture that first fresh flush of love I beheld in a cramped upstairs studio, the wave of immortal energy that emanated from that living portrait. I returned years later, but the man was gone, the house abandoned. Nothing remained but two tins of pears, a fur-covered blanket, the stool— and the painting. I kept that painting as a talisman of my future and swore to unlock its secret.

Later this led me to seek more exotic forms of spiritual influence that sometimes could be channeled by a human conduit and at other times engulfed me completely in its own will. Finally, through these experiments, it was revealed to me that the secret to the power I sought was bound to the very act of creation.

I made it my goal to harness that power. I

would be the greatest scientist the world had known. I would make myself immortal.

At first, I hired artists to depict me, but one by one, they failed. I bribed them, I flattered them, I threatened them, but none had the power of the man who painted the dog. Eventually I realized it was because they did not have the love for me that the artist had for his dog. I sought the most talented painters. When I found them, I discovered what they loved and tried to channel their love for that thing to me by taking it and promising to restore it after they painted my perfect likeness, or else threatening to destroy it should they fail. All to no avail.

Even love cannot give life without an unconscious outpouring of self, of sacrifice that is not only abdication but also, simultaneously, attainment. That is why, I discerned, even the small dog on the canvas I now treasured as a sacred possession could not come out of the canvas to run about. So I began to pair the paintings of myself with small sacrifices, the ritual burning of a valued possession or the life blood of an animal. The closest I got was a life-size portrait of myself painted alongside a ritual offering of a lamb. This produced a flicker of movement in the face of the painting, but it was ultimately ineffectual because it was not tied with love or with human blood.

You know where this is leading. You know

what will be asked of you, and you know the power
that will be yours in return.

Our communion feast awaits. You will find
what is needed for our ritual reunion in the underground heart of Vendler Academy, my namesake. As
the inheritor of my intelligence, I have no doubt that
you yourself will study in its prestigious halls—for
all your mother was a disposable half-wit—granting
you direct access to my legacy.

You will find my autobiography in the library.
Take it, show it to the painting above the mantle, say
my name, touch the frame—it will open to none
but you.

There in the heart of the earth you will discover
a sacred lotus. Claim it. Eat it. Lotus seed has been
known to germinate for 1,300 years and remain
viable. It will wait for you. When you have tasted
the fruit, you will know my presence. Our minds will
be open to one another, and through that knowledge
and your love my flesh will live. Together, we will
make our memories eternal. Together, we will be gods
among men.

Your father,
Vincent Vendler

CHAPTER 39

THE FINAL QUEST

Cole stared at the letter for a long time after he had finished reading it. So that explained why his father had been so reluctant to speak about his birth parents, why he had discouraged Cole from applying to Vendler Academy, why he had been so angry when Cole mentioned Alexandria, and why Vendler had been so confident that his legacy would be found. If Cole had known where this was leading from the beginning, he would never have gone near that library painting. Maybe his dad had been right.

Cole reached back into the paper bag and drew out the military cap. He could easily picture his dad's face beneath it. The leather visor was almost perfect, having no dents and few dimples, and the elegant gold leaves stretching forward from either side were still bright yellow. Above it, a blank band rimmed in gold and red eased the transition from visor to crown, slightly detracting from the proud eagle that took center stage. Cole's thumb traced the delicate insignia, and his eyes burned. He felt his mouth fall open to make breathing easier as one tear fell onto the visor. He wiped it hastily with his shirt sleeve.

A faint vibration from the phone in his back pocket startled him. He drew it out and set it on the bed beside him. It was Joanna. He took one long, steadying breath as if he meant to answer it but made no move to do so. The vibration died, then resumed almost instantly. It was Joanna again.

Clearing his throat, he slid his finger across the screen and said, "Hello?"

"Cole, thank God! Where are you? You have to get over here fast. Orien Saint-Pierre is coming to do a public search in Vendler's caves."

"Wait, what? Did you say Orien's coming to the school?"

"Yes!"

"But... I thought he was dead!"

"I know! I'm as shocked as you are, but I swear I just heard Dr. Bering say Orien's on his way. Cole, you have to hurry!"

"But Joanna, after last time..."

"Listen, Cole. Orien Saint-Pierre is going down there whether we like it or not. And whether or not you think we should have, we've already unlocked all of the passages. If Orien's found a way to get it, then whatever Vendler hid is going to be found tonight. The only question is, who do you want to be the one to find it—you, or him?"

Cole struggled to get his mind in order. Was Orien really okay? If so, why was Cole completely numb? Why didn't he feel relieved? And did he really want to go back into Vendler's cave? He regretted ever having touched that painting in the library. But Joanna was right—the fact was that they were involved whether or not they wanted to be. Vendler had said his painting would open only to his descendants, but clearly, Orien had found some way in. And if Orien was going anyway,

Cole wanted to get there first. Maybe that dream wasn't totally dead yet.

"Fine. I'm on my way. Where are you?"

"I'm already here, heading to the library right now. Get here as soon as you can—he's due to arrive any minute. I'll call Jude."

The phone went dead. Cole stared at it for one dumbfounded moment before his body kicked into action. He left the letter on the bed but replaced the service cap respectfully in its paper bag, then left the bags and boxes where they lay in transitional disarray and bounded across the hallway, down the stairs, and to his car before realizing he had left both his wallet and his keys in his bedroom. His brain wasn't working as fast as he needed it to.

Sprinting from his car back to his bedroom and down again did nothing to steady the pounding of his heart and the confusion in his mind. His fingers trembled as he turned the keys in the ignition. He had forgotten his coat inside, but he didn't have time to go back. He paused to take one deep breath, feeling like someone who was idly spectating while another man drowned, then revved his engine to life and drove. He had to keep his eyes fixed on the speedometer to make sure he wasn't taking things too fast—he couldn't risk being pulled over, but it was maddening to miss green light after green light as his car rolled sluggishly along at 35 mph.

His body forced into waiting, questions tumbled into his mind: Why would Orien betray their earlier confidence and ask for a public search? And what did "public search" really mean? Would he have Lab employees with him? School staff? He would have had to tell Dr. Bering what he was doing; did that mean he had also told him how he had discovered the secret passage? If so, what would Dr. Bering do, knowing that Cole had found an important and potentially dangerous school secret and not said anything about it? Would the administration find out that Cole and his friends had been sneaking into the school at night? Would he get expelled? Would Jude get expelled? He was reaching for his phone to call Joanna back when he saw it vibrating with her name on the screen. He answered it, and she started talking before he could.

"Don't come to the library. Park around back and meet me at the shed. Orien is already here."

Perhaps sensing his uneasiness, she kept talking, "I was staying late to clean up the ceramics studio. Mrs. Moraine had to leave early, but she said Dr. Bering and Dr. Tayne were staying late too. When I was heading out, I was surprised to see Mrs. Dixon still at the front desk, and Dr. Bering and Dr. Tayne waiting with her in the lobby. They just nodded at me as I passed—Mrs. Moraine must have told them I would be there late—but I overheard them saying Orien requested a few hours alone in the library for something that would help him at The Lab. He told them Vendler left something important that he needs."

"I can't believe he told them."

"Sounds like he didn't tell them about the caves, though. And it's interesting he wants to be alone. Maybe he didn't want to tell them how he found out about the caves."

The idea that Orien was respecting his secret, even if he wasn't reciprocating the favor by letting Cole in on his own secrets, took the edge off of Cole's panic.

Remembering that he was still on the phone, he said, "I'm almost there. See you soon."

He parked beside Joanna's car and sprinted to the shed. Its door slid open to admit him, then enclosed him in semi-darkness. Joanna flicked on her flashlight. Her face in its glow was unnaturally pale.

"I can't reach Jude or Bridget. I tried Jude five times while I was waiting for you. I left him a voicemail and sent a text, but he isn't answering. We're going to have to do this alone, just us."

The panic in her voice cleared Cole's mind. "We'll go in as we always do. Orien will probably pause to greet Dr. Bering, so we may still beat him. Come on—we've got to get going."

She nodded breathlessly. Cole led the way to the trapdoor and eased it open, then turned back to Joanna.

"You know, this time it's more dangerous than it has been. We don't know how bad the earthquake damage will be, and there's also a much higher chance we'll get caught. If we are, we'll have to explain everything. There's no need for both of us to risk that."

Joanna shoved his shoulder into the hole and said, "Get in. I'm coming with you."

Warmth rushed through Cole's body. Not having to make this final descent alone filled him with guilty gratitude. The thought of explaining himself to Dr. Bering was terrible, but it was nothing compared to the cold dread of once again facing Vendler's animated portrait, not to mention whatever else he might find in the final chamber that held Vendler's legacy. As they jogged through the underground tunnel, he wondered what Orien would have made of Vendler's ghost, and whether they would have to face it again or if its energy was spent. One thing he did know: if Vendler required more blood, Cole wasn't going to give it.

Before he knew it, they were at the ladder leading into the dressing room. The sound of wood scraping on wood as he eased it open was magnified in his ears, but it wasn't answered by investigatory footsteps. There was more light in the room than he was accustomed to seeing, but it was still dark enough to warrant Joanna's cautiously shielded flashlight. She followed him, taking long, slow gulps of air to soften the sound of her breathing. Her eyes mirrored his fear, but she nodded at him, and he crossed the stage like an actor forced into false confidence when the curtain is drawn open too soon.

On the far side of the stage, the doorknob leading into the hallway slid ineffectually under his sweaty palm. He wiped his hand on his slacks and tried again. The hall was completely silent. He took one last look at Joanna and tiptoed down the hall to the library. The door was closed. A light was already on inside.

After listening for a moment at the library door, Cole turned its knob. The room was empty. He slipped swiftly inside and closed the door again behind Joanna. As they rounded the last row of books, the LEDs illuminated Vendler's face so that for the first time, Cole saw the garish green and flushed red undertones in the cheeks that intensified the impression of a life unnaturally preserved.

Cole dragged the desk chair to the mantle, opened the passage, and crept inside. Joanna followed, drawing the painting back against the wall behind them. Dr. Bering would see the displaced chair when he came, but only Orien would know its significance, and if he really wanted this mission to be a secret, he wouldn't disclose its meaning. Perhaps Orien would assume Cole had forgotten to replace it when he had explored the caves earlier that day. He needn't know immediately that Cole and Joanna were even now a few steps ahead of him.

They were in the portrait room now, and here for the first time the ravages of the earthquake were clearly visible. The chandelier of straws straining to become stalactites had cracked and shattered on the floor. Chunks of rock lay in the basin of sand, which was miraculously still upright. Several portraits, some smashed, were sprawled on the cave floor.

In the chamber of the standing stones, the damage was even worse. One of the twelve slabs had tipped over and cracked in two on the floor, partially blocking the entrance to the chamber with Joanna's portrait. They clambered over it and into the vaulted room. Loose rock littered the floor. The light was dimmer than Cole remembered. Looking up, he saw that the window that ventilated the room was narrower than before. The shifting plates must have caused it to cave in partially. Everything else was as they had left it. The portrait was frozen and the entrance to the final chamber yawned portentously.

A crack made Cole fling his arms over his head. Joanna ran toward the exit, then swiveled back around to look at Cole: the metered thuds that followed the crack were not the onset of an earthquake—they were the deliberate footfalls of someone descending the iron ladder. It was the first time Cole really believed Orien was alive after all, and all his senses sharpened. Joanna's eyes were wide with panic.

Before Cole had time to formulate a plan, she said, "You go on. You have to be the one to present what you find. I'll stall him."

"But Joanna—"

"Go!"

CHAPTER 40

BURNT OFFERING

Ignoring the warning in his heart, Cole ran into the black mouth of the innermost chamber. The passage narrowed. He had to turn sideways to squeeze through. Jagged rock scraped his shoulders and chest. From somewhere ahead, he heard the plunk of slow-dripping water. The air was damper here, and the smell of rotting flesh intensified in the moisture. Cole was beginning to feel claustrophobic. Words whispered in his ear, inaudibly, as if born on the wind of his own breath: *The final gift I now beseech, before you reach the end of speech: a lotus grows within the mire, so taste with me our one desire.*

Panting, Cole emerged into a wide, low room. In the center of the room stood a stone slab encircled by stalagmites like candles at a funeral bier. On the stone was a lidless coffin filled with mud. Out of the mud peeked a single lotus flower in full bloom, its petals pure white. Against the blackness of the mud and cave walls, the flower seemed to glow with some otherworldly light. Apparently, Cole was supposed to eat its fruit. Not until Cole saw the flower's unblemished beauty did the idea disturb him. Was he really supposed to eat something that had been down here for decades? And what would happen if he did? Cole stepped inside the circle of stalagmites and peered into the coffin.

And then he saw it: under the mud blanket, its outline just grazing the surface, lay a completely intact human skeleton. The bones were black, even blacker than the mud, and the stench of them was unbearable. The lotus flower was growing out of the ribcage. Cole had no doubt about whose skeleton lay inside the coffin. Alexandria had said that Vendler's body had never been found, that he had wandered off one day and never returned. He must have known his end was approaching and come here to die, his body rotting in the damp ruins of the cave, awaiting resurrection. But the flesh must have long since decomposed; why then was the stench as intense as if he had just died?

With an effort, Cole swallowed his revulsion and turned his attention from the skull to the lotus flower. Cradled in the center of the petals was a fleshy, greenish yellow fruit with black seeds peeking out like frog eyeballs. There was a bite missing. Or was that just how lotus fruit looked?

Cole took a deep breath. Despite the urgency that pressed upon him, he couldn't seem to make himself move faster. He felt as if his entire life had led up to this moment. No matter what depended on it, he couldn't rush it. If what the letter stated was true, and if he took a bite of the fruit, he would know the secret to resurrecting Vincent Vendler and—the thought staggered him—why not his own father, too? All he had to do was reach out and claim the fruit that was an inch away from his trembling hand.

The first touch sent a shock of excitement through his whole body. He lifted the fruit from the flower and placed it in his palm. His head was filled with a slow thumping sound like a heartbeat. He held the fruit to his face and smelled it. It gave nothing away. His breath shuddered in and out of his chest as he tried to summon the courage to touch the fruit to his tongue. The thud of the heartbeat grew louder.

The sound of voices, Joanna's and Orien's, made him swivel to face the cave mouth. He had to decide what to do. He looked back at the fruit in his palm. In a habitual gesture of indecision, he slipped his free hand into his pocket, and his fingers brushed against something he hadn't remembered was there: the rim of a cardboard matchbox and the soft wax of a tea candle.

A collage of memories shot fast as flame through his mind: the holy scent of Bridget's sweater, inviting yet sacred, when he sat beside her on his birthday; the tinkle of her laughter, pure as a church bell above the hush of winter snow, when Joanna revealed the rescued library; the shock of her starlit eyes, pristine as mountain lakes, framing a question he didn't know how to answer when he dreamed of her; and the warmth of her fingers, delicate and strong as a pianist's, grasping his hand at his dad's graveside and infusing his whole body with courage.

His lips cracked into a smile. So she was with him after all.

A scream rent the silence. Rapid footfalls pounded the corridor behind him. He could delay no longer. The time for decision was now. He could deliver the fruit to Orien, but something like a physical force denied him that option. The decision must be his.

He drew his hand out of his pocket and looked at the matchbox and the candle in his palm. Grunts came from the passage behind him. Orien would emerge any moment. Fingers shaking, Cole scratched a match to life, lit the candle's waiting wick, and held it against the flesh of the fruit until it became a living sacrifice.

The flame caught fast. Cole had to drop the lotus back onto Vendler's chest to avoid being burned. He stood there and watched as the flame engulfed first the fruit, then the bones, then—bizarrely—the coffin. Fire shot down the stone altar to the cave floor like an electric current. A cry of reproach made him whirl around to see Orien Saint-Pierre running toward him, his silk dress shirt disarranged so that the collar hung open on one side, his eyes wide with anguished excitement. His bald head shone in the fire's gleam like a halo. Then, just as quickly as he had rushed into the room, he bolted back down the corridor, and the halo was gone.

Searing pain tore up Cole's leg. The fire was devouring the floor, running the length of the room and racing up the walls. So, the curse of consuming fire hadn't been a metaphor after all.

"Joanna," Cole whispered, and he ran as fast as he could after Orien down the narrow passage to the room with Vendler's portrait. Rock crashed and crumbled behind him. Heat scalded his back.

The light grew dimmer as he outpaced the fire. Orien must have dropped his flashlight or else outrun him, for there was no light ahead. The room with Joanna's portrait was illuminated only by the glow at his back. He called for her. The only answer was Orien's voice from somewhere very far ahead, yelling something he couldn't make out.

Then he saw her—a dark, huddled figure dimly outlined by the flame at his back. Her expression was blank, her eyes lidded. Somehow, during or after her altercation with Orien, she had lost consciousness. Cole looped her arms around his neck and dragged her out to where the standing stones glowed in the light of the approaching fire. The effort of holding her, combined with the heat of the fire, was making it hard to breathe. He crossed the room at a jog, but when he set his foot on the first rung of the ladder, his heart froze. There was no opening at the top. The basin had slid back over the entrance, no longer a guard to Vendler's secret but a barricade to his betrayer.

"No!" Cole yelled, but the protest died in a fit of coughing.

He was not going to die this way. He laid Joanna at the foot of the ladder and climbed it, pressing his fingers against the still-cool stone. He pushed with all his strength. The stone didn't budge. He took another step up, squared his shoulder under it, and tried again. The ladder rung snapped under him, and he fell onto the cave floor, blood dripping from a gash in his knee.

The flame was in the room with him now, raging through the stone circle, wreathing them in smoke, swelling without fuel. His lungs fought desperately for oxygen. With the last strength in his body, he wrenched the ladder from its base and flipped it upside down, climbing it once more and pushing desperately against the unfeeling stone. He couldn't stop coughing. The strength in his muscles was fading. His eyes grew dim.

It was then that Cole realized he would die. Vendler's cave, which had promised immortality, would become his tomb. He had pledged his loyalty where betrayal would not be forgiven, and now he would pay the ultimate price. Almost, Cole could believe he didn't care. He would be going to meet his father. But what was unforgivable was that Joanna would also die because of him. He knew now that even inaction was action. Though Joanna had led the way, he was to blame for her collapsed body and the flame that crept ever closer to devour her. That was how he had lived his whole life: refusing to take responsibility, damned by inaction. He had lived a coward.

In that moment, Cole decided he would at least not die a coward. Taking one last gulp of air, he willed himself to climb back down the ladder toward the flame. He gathered Joanna's limbs under her body and half crouched, half lay on top of her. The flame would consume them both, but it would not touch her before it destroyed him. Ultimately, the gesture meant nothing. No one would ever know he had done it, but the ability to choose to do it refreshed his heart as with dew.

The flame was on him now, burning through his clothes and forcing from his chest a cry he didn't know he had oxygen left to fuel. The air around him quivered, then concentrated into a halo of light above him. His flesh screamed. As he slipped into unconsciousness, his last thought was to wonder if he would smell like Bridget's incense.

CHAPTER 41

THE INTERNSHIP

"I've got good news and bad news."

Dr. Behrang Amini straddled the stool by the hospital bed with the easy grace of the cardiovascularly fit, wafting the scent of aftershave with him. He was a lean, good-looking man of about sixty whom his colleagues respected and whom his patients implicitly trusted despite his impossibly white teeth.

"Let's hear the good news first," Mrs. Durham said.

It had been seventeen days since Jude had found Cole and Joanna huddled in a corner of Vendler's caverns, braced against the fire. Although Cole had recovered his ability to speak and swallow without severe discomfort, Mrs. Durham was still used to being his advocate and mouthpiece. In fact, she had hardly left Cole's bedside except to cook a meal and bring it back to him, even before he could eat solid food. She said the aroma would tantalize him into recovery.

Now he sat with the back of the bed as far upright as it would go, one foot shaking with excess energy. Boredom and vigor had returned in equal measure as his body healed, even if he was still covered in one long bandage that spanned from his left hand, up his arm, around his back, and all the way across his neck and head to cover his right ear. He had seen a little of the new skin when the nurses changed his dressings, red at first like dragon breath, then shiny pink like a baby albino asp. He neither felt nor recognized the skin as his own.

"The good news," Dr. Amini said, tipping his omniscient clipboard forward, "is that you won't have to live in synthetic skin the rest of your life. The skin grafts were successful, and the donor site is healing nicely. We won't need to introduce cadaver or bioengineered skin."

Cole wondered peevishly why Dr. Amini had to impersonalize his thigh by calling it "the donor site," but he couldn't help returning the lightning flash smile.

"Of course," Dr. Amini continued, dropping the smile as soon as Cole picked it up, "there's not much we can do about the scar. Many patients ask about plastic surgery for cosmetic reasons, but I'm afraid scar tissue just doesn't have the requisite elasticity to make the operation viable."

"I don't care about that," Cole said. His voice was still weak, and the pain of speaking made his answers direct.

"Very good. Now the bad news: I'm afraid the nerves in your arm and hand were badly damaged. There's still a chance your nerve endings will recover feeling, but if that doesn't happen by the end of two years, it's unlikely it ever will. Oh, and one more thing—your hair may not want to grow over the affected area for about three months. You'll want to tell your barber to mind it on your next visit, though there again —" he winked conspiratorially "—a clever barber can work wonders. I'll let you in on a little secret. Most people don't notice since I'm so tall: I'm balding just a bit at the crown, but my barber has found a wonderful way to disguise it without recourse to surgical implants."

Cole raised his eyebrows in appreciation of the minor miracle he had assumed was Rogaine.

"So you see? There's nothing to prevent you from living quite a normal life after all this is over, despite the potential loss of feeling."

Not willing to waste his carefully metered exertion of speech on Dr. Amini's confused hierarchy of importance, Cole gave a thumbs up sign with his uninjured hand.

"I told you I had good news and bad news. Well, that's not quite true. I have good news, bad news, and excellent news. I saved the best for last." Dr. Amini paused to reestablish eye contact with Mrs. Durham before spotlighting Cole again with his lightning smile. "You get to go home today."

"Oh that's wonderful!" Mrs. Durham cried.

She jumped up and gave Cole a hug that made him glad he was still wearing bandages. His laugh became a painful cough.

"Oh Cole, you get to come home to us at last! I'd better call Jude and make sure he changed your sheets like I told him to, and of course I'll call your mom, too, unless you want to? What should we have for supper tonight? What's your favorite? Something soft and easy to chew? Soup? But nothing too hot, of course. Here, let me get your things together."

Dr. Amini smiled but raised a hand to stop her. "Hold up, not quite so fast. We need to get the discharge paperwork in order first. And Cole, I've instructed your nurse to schedule a check-up in a week. You're at an increased risk of infection right now. So far, so good, but we need to keep an eye on things.

"You'll need to keep meeting with your physical therapist to ensure you maintain mobility, but I don't want you doing anything too strenuous, okay? We'll get you back ship-shape soon, just need to give the skin a chance to bind properly. I'll also give you a referral to a therapist who can help with the

PTSD—the night nurse tells me you've been having nightmares. That's extremely common for burn victims, but there's help. Also, very important: keep the fluids going. We'll get everything ready for you to go home now. In the meantime, it looks like you have a visitor."

As Dr. Amini stood up to leave, a man walked into the room. His well-muscled form and perfectly-tailored suit exuded an aura of well-being that was a stark contrast to the sunken faces and baggy gowns Cole had grown accustomed to. Dr. Orien Saint-Pierre held his arms out to encompass both the room and Cole in his condoling smile. Orien came right up to the bed. Cole found himself holding his breath. He wasn't sure what he felt—as angry as he was that Orien had abandoned them in the caves, there was still some part of him that wanted Orien to think well of him.

"My dear Cole, how are you? Such a tragedy! I'm relieved to see you awake and mending—the last time I came, you were asleep, and the time before that, immediately after the accident, they wouldn't admit me. It's so good to see some health returning to you. And did I hear you'll be released soon? I can't tell you how glad that makes me."

"Who's this, Cole?" Mrs. Durham asked.

For a moment, Orien didn't know how to react to the unprecedented discourtesy of not being recognized. Then he walked around the hospital bed and extended his hand.

"Please forgive my incivility. I'm Dr. Orien Saint-Pierre. Cole is one of several students who applied to an internship in my organization. We became acquainted over the course of the last semester. And you are... Cole's sister?"

Mrs. Durham blushed at the obvious assumption that had been recast into a compliment.

"Oh no, just his friend's mom, Laura Durham. Might as

well be my son, though. He'll be coming home to live with us now."

Cole was touched by the pride in her voice as she said it.

"You're a lucky woman. Cole here would be an asset anywhere. Which is partly what I've come to talk about."

Cole's insides squirmed. Did that mean what he thought it meant? Orien turned to Mrs. Durham.

"Laura, would you be so good as to give us a few moments in private?"

Mrs. Durham was obviously surprised, but after a quick glance at Cole to ascertain his wishes, she gathered her scattered books, as well as a pair of Chandler's jeans she was patching, into her capacious purse and bustled out. Orien waited patiently until she was gone, then assumed a seat on the stool Dr. Amini had vacated. His nose wrinkled slightly at the bitter smell of sickness mixed with antiseptic that lay heavy about them.

"Cole, it really does pain me to see you this way. You have no idea how I've recriminated myself for that night. I thought you and Joanna were on my heels the whole way up. I had no idea you'd gotten stuck down there. As soon as I got above ground, I ran to alert Dr. Bering. By the time I went back to check on you, you had already been rescued, and all I could do was call an ambulance. I never thought your path had been obstructed; I realize now I ought to have checked immediately. Please accept my most sincere apologies."

Cole didn't know what to say, so he nodded. He had wondered often during his hospital stay why Orien had not helped them escape. What particularly troubled him was that, after Orien's altercation with Joanna, he must have known she was in no state to run when he abandoned her and Cole in the fiery underground.

"I know what you must be thinking," Orien went on, as if

reading his thoughts. "I heard later that Joanna was found unconscious. You must believe me when I say I had no idea. Joanna tried to stop me from reaching you, at first by distracting me in conversation, then later by physically blocking the way into the final room. I became frustrated, and I admit that I pushed her aside to get to you. I had no notion that the force of my action caused her to fall and hit her head on a stone, rendering her unconscious."

Cole still said nothing. Why hadn't Orien paused to check whether Joanna was okay when she fell? But then, Cole had wanted to harm Joanna in the caves, too. Maybe none of them were themselves in Vendler's underground.

"I'm glad I was able to talk to you about that. It's a weight off my mind."

Orien's posture relaxed and his smile became less weighted with sympathy.

"I read you had a stroke," Cole said. He needed at least one of his questions answered.

The flash of anger in Orien's face was as unmistakable as it was surprising, but he smoothed it with a smile that made Cole feel he was going mad. What did Orien actually feel toward him?

"How considerate of you to ask. You're right—I did suffer a minor stroke. I'm afraid one or two papers caught hold of the story before I had time to prevent it. I didn't want anyone worrying that I wouldn't hold up my promises, that Kronos would not come to be. It will come to be. The stroke delayed me. It won't happen again."

If Cole hadn't been put on guard by the changing emotions on Orien's face, he might have laughed. It sounded as though Orien was apologizing for poor behavior.

"It's *your* health I came to inquire about," Orien said, repositioning the conversation squarely where he wanted it.

"But truth be told, that's only part of what I came to talk to you about. No doubt you've heard about this, but in case you haven't..."

Reaching into his inside coat pocket, Orien retrieved and unfolded a newspaper clipping and handed it to Cole. Cole stared at the fuzzy gray and white picture of firetrucks shooting jets of water at the flaming edifice of Vendler Academy. The headline read: "Historic Vendler Academy Ravaged by Fire in Freak Accident, Hidden Scientific Research Destroyed." When he tore his gaze from the headline, he found that Orien was looking at him.

"Freak accident? Mrs. Durham told me that's what she thought it was, but I thought there must be a more official version that would come out."

A half-smile, at once understanding and comforting, tautened Orien's cheeks.

"As I gather, Joanna's presence in the building is easily explained from her work in the nearby art room, and it's quite understandable that she should have invited her friends to keep her company as she cleaned the kiln which exploded, rendering her unconscious, and that you should have heroically sacrificed your own well-being to rescue her when she got stuck under the broken equipment, and that your friend Jude, who was trapped on the other side of the room due to a collapsed beam, should have stayed behind until you were both rescued and pulled onto the lawn outside the library where the paramedics found you. That's what everyone thinks. It's what Laura probably thinks too, in case you're curious.

"At present, you see, your friends and I are the only ones who know you were under the library when the fire occurred. As for my part, I've explained to Dr. Bering, the school board, and Vendler Academy's legal representatives my exploration of an underground storage space and the highly flammable nature of its contents. I explained that even a flashlight reflecting the wrong way for too long on a glass surface such as the watch I carry could have disastrous consequences. Particularly when located so near a gas kiln like the one in the art studio.

"I've proposed to finance both a temporary facility where students and staff may complete the semester, as well as a new, multi-million dollar restoration that will leave the campus much improved. I'm happy to say that everyone was satisfied to leave the explanation of exactly what happened a mystery. After all, it results in some long-awaited improvements that, as I understand, the school was struggling to obtain full funding for. Incidentally, your own medical care and follow-up visits have already been covered as well. The media, of course, are insistent on unearthing a much more interesting and preferably pernicious explanation, but I do have my influences there as well. So all's well that ends well."

Irrelevantly, Cole thought what good fortune it was that Bridget's library lounge had been rescued before the fire destroyed it.

"Thank you," he said, thinking of his medical bills.

Indicating the newspaper again, Orien continued: "It was, after all, an accident that caused the destruction of both Vendler's secret and the school. An accident, and a misunderstanding."

The smiling lips melted into a droop of infinite sadness.

"Oh Cole, don't think I don't regret the way things played out that night. The real tragedy is, it could all have been avoided had I been more forthcoming with you."

Cole didn't know what he had expected from Orien's visit, but it wasn't this. Reproach, disappointment, and anger he was prepared to withstand, but Orien's self-recrimination almost softened Cole. Then again, Cole still remembered what had happened when he first showed Orien the secret in the library: Orien had looked, not at Cole, but at what Cole had discovered.

Orien spread his hands out in a gesture of supplication and said, "Cole, in addition to an apology, I owe you an explanation. I set you the mission of discovering Vendler's research, and I ought to have trusted you with it. But the truth is, I've never been very good at practicing restraint. If I were, I wouldn't have gotten to where I am today."

A self-deprecating smile flickered on his lips.

"When I didn't hear from you, I became impatient. I wanted to find Vendler's secret for myself, and I wanted it sooner than later. A few weeks ago, I arranged with Dr. Bering to visit the library under pretense of examining its titles. I'm sure, if you heard about my presence that day, you saw through my little charade, but no one else did. I followed what I had seen you do exactly: I presented Vendler's book, said his name, and touched the frame. But nothing happened. I wracked my mind for what I had forgotten. I tried repeatedly, but without success.

"It was then that I emailed the school for records on the entire junior class. In truth, I only wanted the names and dates of birth of you and your three friends, but I had to ask about everyone to avoid suspicion. I was convinced that there was something special about one of you. My first guess, I confess, was that it was Joanna, a theory supported by her prodigious artistic abilities. I thought that perhaps Vendler had designed his secret passage so that only an artist capable of reproducing his likeness would be able to enter, and that you were permitted reentry as an ally to whom the secret of the painting had been originally presented, whereas I had not yet been initiated by her. These laws of magic seem peculiar to us, but to Vendler they might have made perfect sense.

"After my team researched each of your talents and ancestry, however, I changed my mind. Out of the four of you, your parentage alone was obscure, and it led me to wonder whether there was a deeper magic at play.

"So I turned my attention to researching Vendler's life. It was easy to see even in his writings that he was obsessed with immortality. Less easy to discover was the fact that he had fathered a child. I wouldn't have discovered that fact at all had I not made the logical assumption that Vendler, in an attempt to secure immortality, had begotten a son he assumed would love him intrinsically and accomplish the work he had left as a series of riddles and clues. At the very least, his son would perpetuate his blood line and thereby ensure his continued presence in the world. It was only after I made that assumption that I was able to work backwards, tracing your father's appearance in an orphanage due to his only living relative—an aunt—being unfit to care for him. The orphanage had Vendler's name on record as a possible ancestor since the aunt wouldn't stop accusing him, and a little more research revealed that all the facts fit."

Cole had known all of this, but the words, spoken so blatantly, made him feel that same inevitable contamination of his existence that he had experienced after visiting Alexandria. Not for the first time, he wished he had been able to find her again. He hoped she was at peace.

"I want to make it clear that when I invited students from Vendler Academy to apply to the internship and made it a priority to conduct interviews in person, I was only hoping for an inside look at the school, possibly inside help. I had no idea that I had stumbled upon Vendler's actual progeny, not until I was unable to enter into the passage behind the painting. Your academics earned you your spot in the interview, Cole. Nothing else."

At least Cole hadn't been a puppet from the beginning. His academic achievements really had mattered—not just to Vendler's faculty, but to Orien as well. Despite the guardedness Cole now felt toward his former idol, it was still gratifying to know he had impressed Orien.

"I realized Vendler cherished very patriarchal notions of loyalty, supremacy, and lineage. It was his seed that mattered; the woman was merely an honored conduit. No doubt he counted on the natural fondness and respect of his son to desire to discover his father, find his work, and bring him back. Well, he wasn't entirely wrong, was he? That's what we all want: to know our fathers."

Orien shot Cole a sharp glance that knocked the wind out of him.

The question was rhetorical, and as soon as Orien saw its effect, he continued: "It was then that I made my first mistake. I ought to have come to you with my newfound knowledge, to have worked alongside you and ensured you had everything you needed to continue on with the mission I had given you. But I was afraid of becoming too public with a fascination that to me still seemed as fantastical as it was alluring. And, frankly, my own curiosity was growing in proportion to my frustration. I wanted the truth for myself.

"So I decided to design an experiment, to see who could get there first. It seemed to me not only an innocent diversion but also the best way to cover my bases—to allow you to feel the full weight of the responsibility even while I pursued the truth on my own. I hope you do not feel used when I tell you this, Cole. I recognize that may be what you're thinking, but I promise you, I wanted you to succeed. I wanted you to beat me. I wanted you to prove to me that the internship belonged to you, and to you only."

Orien paused, anxiously assessing Cole's expression.

Cole almost felt sorry for him. He said, "So how did you get in then?"

"It's amazing what people tell you when you listen, Cole. I've made a habit of listening throughout my life, no matter how inconsequential the source seems. And it was this that gave me my golden ticket. Your facilities custodian, Paul, happened to mention when I first visited that he had attended Vendler Academy for a few years on a scholarship set up for any blood relative of Vendler's, however distant. I knew that Vendler only had one son, your father, a fact which almost no else knew. But Paul's connection, however distant, had been public. Apparently he was the son of Vala Vendler, Vincent's older sister. Vincent would have much preferred his own child to find his research, but he wasn't above taking precautions to ensure someone found him."

Cole stared back into Orien's eyes, amazed. He had thought that his mother was his only living family. But now he was being given a new family member, one whom he already knew and liked. A small fire sprang up in his chest, and he half smiled. As soon as he was released, he would visit Paul.

Cole became aware that Orien was watching him and asked, "How did you get Paul to help without telling him about the painting? Or does he know?"

Orien shrugged. "He does, and he doesn't. When I came back to visit your library for a second time, Paul was again assigned to prepare the way, and he didn't get out of the way quickly enough for Dr. Bering's liking. It really is a shame, this urge to shuffle insignificant people out of the way. I've encountered it before, and it's never worth it in the end. These are the people who see things, who know things. I invited Paul to share a beer that evening to thank him for his help on such short notice."

Cole almost laughed. The thought of Orien in his immaculate dress clothes sipping a Blue Moon from a clouded glass at a sticky table across from Paul at the local dive bar was almost too far for his imagination to stretch.

"Paul told me all about his life, about how he hasn't gotten a raise in eight years, how students are more disrespectful of their physical surroundings than ever, and how he has his eye on a new rider mower but isn't sure the school will include it in their budget. He told me that it was a relief to his dad when Paul dropped out of school because it meant Paul could bring in supplemental income, how he sometimes wishes he could have gone on to become an engineer instead, and how he always had a natural aptitude for fixing things. He told me about the best casinos, the best fishing spots, and the best college athletes. And he also told me about his wife, Lily Ann, the love of his life. Lily Ann died in childbirth, along with their baby. He's never gotten over it, even though he was just twenty-two when it happened.

"I did then what anyone would do who had the power: I showed him a way out. I told him I had the ability to bring Lily Ann back—her and the child. I told him I needed only one small thing from him: his DNA. I explained that the genetics were a prerequisite to what I had planned. It worked like a charm. He plucked out several hairs for me then and there, which I kept safe in an envelope until needed. It was all true, just not in the way he thought, and not as soon as he expected. But he trusted me, and I wasn't going to let him down.

"With Paul's hair, I was able to reopen the passage behind the painting. And with your email informing me about the candles, I quickly made it into the room with the portraits on stones and answered the riddle—your guess was correct, by the way: the answer was about making Vendler's memory eternal; I might have inferred as much from the autobiography. I already had a pretty developed theory of how Vendler had constructed his cave system. In any case, my answer admitted me into another chamber with a blank canvas. As you know, the next test was to paint Vendler. I'm no artist. I knew my only hope of passing the test was to superimpose a digital image on the canvas, then dab on some of the original paint if necessary. I didn't want to disturb the scene in case you and your friends came down and saw the canvas missing, so I decided to leave the canvas where it was and return with a digital reproduction of Vendler that could be secured with an adhesive.

"When I returned, however, I found that you and Joanna had got there before me. I knew at once that you had gone farther into the caves than you had reported to me. I admit I became angry."

He paused abruptly.

"Why didn't you tell me, Cole?"

During Orien's narration, Cole had relaxed back into the cushions of the hospital bed and listened. Now the story required something from him.

Finally, he said: "I don't know how to answer that. Maybe because I'm not entirely sure myself why I said nothing. Partly it was because I wanted to find whatever it was Vendler hid before I bothered you again."

"And partly because you doubted me? I asked you to report to me, and you said nothing."

Cole wasn't sure how to respond, so he didn't. Instead, he asked, "You said earlier that you have a theory about how Vendler constructed the caves—what is it?"

Orien suppressed the flicker of surprise that his question

hadn't been answered. Crossing one leg deliberately over the other, he expounded his theory: "It was evident to me almost immediately that Vendler, like me, prioritized the life of the mind, and therefore that his labyrinth would contain some sort of riddles aimed at proving his successor's worthiness. After I recognized the number of compartments and the themes of the tests, I realized there's a structure behind the system: it's a brain, but upside-down."

"What?"

"Oh yes, it's quite clear. My first clue was the djed guarding the entrance: it's an ancient Egyptian symbol of immortality, and it's meant to look like a man's backbone. So the first passage you descend from the library painting is the brainstem. The room with six corridors is the cerebellum. Next, we come to the temporal lobe, or the room with the tall stones, which is responsible for memory, among other things. That's why the room's riddle corresponds to remembering Vendler.

"Next comes the occipital lobe, which is responsible for visuospatial processing. So it was fitting that the test there was to paint Vendler, which of course was also very important to his own resurrection.

"Then came the parietal lobe, which is all about sensory perception and integration, and that's where Vendler upped the stakes and got physical with his request for blood—Joanna told me when she was trying to distract me from following you. In Vendler's primitive thought patterns, life is only possible where there is sacrifice. Incidentally, that's where he and I disagree. All of my work on Kronos is built on the idea of liberating us from that perpetual cycle of death as a necessary prerequisite to life. But here again, I'm getting ahead of myself. We'll get to Kronos momentarily.

"Vendler's final room, the inner sanctum, is the frontal lobe—the seat of man's intelligence and the throne of his highest powers. Just think about it: every great thought that's ever been formed, from Aristotle to Einstein, originated in the frontal lobe. Vendler would see himself among those scientists, and it's where he would hide the secret to his own immortality. Am I right?"

Cole's mind was spinning. The theory made sense, but something about it felt superimposed. Had Vendler really meant the caves to resemble a brain? Or was it just Orien's scientific prejudice that made him see it that way?

"It's a pity we didn't solve all of this together, Cole. If we had both been more forthcoming with our information, we could have put the pieces together quite quickly and found Vendler's instructions. We could have had the final phase of Kronos well under way by now. As it is, it'll take longer than I had wished to make Kronos love."

Cole's eyes darted to Orien's. "Don't you need what Vendler left to make that happen?"

Orien laughed, a large, round laugh that was hollow at its core. "Ah Cole, that's what I thought too. I was so obsessed with finding the legacy Vendler left—the method I had selected to solve my problems—that I didn't stop to consider whether it was the only one." Casually, he added, "What did he leave, by the way? A book?"

"A fruit growing out of his skeleton. I was supposed to eat it."

It was as if a mask had fallen off Orien's face. The look of complete surprise stripped him wholly of charisma. But in an instant the skin was taut again, the poise reestablished.

"A fruit... You didn't, by chance, taste the fruit before it caught fire, did you?"

Cole noticed the careful configuration of Orien's syntax and had a sudden desire to correct it, to state that the fruit hadn't caught fire, but that he had lit it on fire. But it wouldn't help to antagonize him.

"I'm afraid not."

Orien waved a hand. "No matter. You know what I've been thinking, Cole? What difference does it make, ultimately, whether I have Vendler's legacy or not?" He paused long enough to be sure he had secured Cole's curiosity, then continued: "I know his theory, why not test it for myself? Why not proceed as if everything he said about art and love is true? Why not make Kronos on faith that it will work exactly as Vendler believed and I envision? There's nothing stopping us."

If Cole was surprised that Orien planned to continue, it was nothing to the surprise he felt now.

"Us?"

A slow, magical smile bloomed on Orien's face. "Yes, you heard me right, Cole. Together, we can take the seeds of Vendler's knowledge and actualize them on a much grander scale than he ever imagined, for the good of mankind, and without the sacrifice he imagined necessary. Together, we can reunite those separated and grant liberty to those who all their lives have been in bondage to the fear of death. Together, we can bring back your dad and give you the closure you so desperately need."

For a long moment, they stared at one another.

Finally, Cole said, "I didn't know you knew about my dad."

Orien nodded, his lips pursed in sympathy. "Cole, for me, this has always been personal. I lost my own parents, remember? Now it's personal for you too."

There was another pause in which Cole broke the intense

bond of their gaze. He had been given a room with a window, and watching the constant evolution of the clouds had become a source of solace for him. Now, without thinking, he looked to them for an answer. After a night of weeping, the winter sky was as clear as a stripped canvas.

"So what do you say, Cole? Will you join me? Cole, I'm offering you the 2025 Orien Saint-Pierre Lab Emerging Research Scientists Internship."

It was strange to Cole that the words he had hungered to hear every day since last fall when Mr. Price had first told him about the internship in his cramped, coffee-stale office should affect him the way they did now. He took his time composing his hands into a neat clasp, the uninjured cradling the injured, then looked back at Orien's eager face.

"I'm sorry. I can't."

Orien blinked. "Cole, I know you must be feeling a conflict of emotions given everything that's happened to you in the last weeks: your dad, moving homes, now this. I want to be very clear that I take the blame for what happened entirely upon myself. If I had been transparent with you from the beginning, maybe none of this would have happened. Maybe even now we would be able to use Vendler's knowledge to create Kronos, together."

"Maybe," Cole replied. "But if that's the case, I'm glad things happened the way they did. I'm sorry, Orien, but until everything happened, I didn't know what Kronos really was. I don't know how to put this, but I think we need to die."

None of Orien's muscles moved a millimeter, but the openness in his face closed as quickly as a slammed door.

When he spoke, the words were as smooth and cordial as ever: "I'm sorry you're taking it this way. I had hoped my vulnerability would help you see past our misunderstanding."

Orien stood up, extending a hand toward him. The gesture was final. Cole knew that this was his last chance to change his mind, that as soon as he grasped the outstretched hand, the opportunity would be gone forever. He reached forward and shook it.

CHAPTER 42

NEW SKIN

Cole watched Orien's retreating form until he could no longer see it from the windows that opened into the hospital hall. Then he turned back to the outside window and contemplated his future. It was a future now without the internship, without his father, and without the academic record he had fought so hard to maintain. His professors had been gracious, both after his dad's passing and during Cole's convalescence, but there was no doubt that missing five weeks of school meant he'd fallen far enough behind that he'd need to retake his harder classes. That meant graduating late with a blot on his transcripts that could only be explained after he had earned an interview, which he wasn't likely to get now at Stanford or any of the top schools he had set his sights on. He felt curiously empty and wondered whether the emptiness was disappointment or freedom.

"Where's mom?"

Jude's voice startled him from his reverie. For a moment, Cole missed the undisputed privacy of his former life, a life where his own bedroom was sacred and where meals were eaten alone in silence. He had better get used to intrusion if he was going to live with the Durhams.

"She left to give me some privacy. I just talked to Orien."

Jude let out a low whistle. There was something unusually reserved in his manner as he took the stool Orien had just vacated and began massaging his neck absent-mindedly. As Cole watched, he realized that Jude's thumb where he had cut himself and let his blood into the chalice was still bandaged.

"What's up with your thumb?"

Jude stopped massaging his neck to look at his hand, then shrugged. "Won't stop bleeding."

He wheeled the stool against the wall so he could recline with his hands folded behind his head and an ankle crossed over his knee.

"So... what happened with Saint-Pierre?"

Cole looked back out the window. "He offered me the internship. I said no."

"What?" Jude lost his balance and barely caught himself. Adjusting into a less precarious position, he said, "Why'd you say no?"

"I didn't think my dad would like it."

Jude nodded, and Cole wondered if Jude actually understood or if he was respecting Cole's need to process what had just happened.

After a few seconds, Jude said, "Look, Cole, in the caves... I should have been there."

Cole could hear the guilt behind the words, and he reacted as he used to whenever his dad blamed himself for losing Layla.

"But you were there! You came as soon as you could. You got Joanna and me out just in time."

Jude took his head in both hands. When he pulled them away again, his face looked haggard.

"You don't understand. It's because of me that you're in this state, and that Joanna is recovering from a concussion. I did see Joanna's calls come through, but I didn't answer them."

He stared unseeingly at the inane baby blue cartoons on Cole's bed sheets. Cole sensed he wanted to explain but needed help.

"Why not?"

Jude's gaze flickered to meet Cole's and then dropped back to the sheets.

"You remember my brother, Seth, who showed up at Christmas?"

After everything that had happened, it took Cole a second to register the memory, then he nodded.

"He came back. When I came home from school that day, he was already in the living room talking to my mom. You should have seen the smile on her face, like it was the best day of her life. Dad wasn't home. I came in, and Seth tried to give me a hug. I shoved him off and begged mom to see reason, but she was upset I wasn't welcoming Seth home like the prodigal in the Bible. She actually said that. I kept calling dad, but he didn't answer. Finally, it all came out: Seth was there for more money; he was going through a withdrawal and needed his next high. He was desperate. Things escalated, and he started to get violent, threatening both of us. He wasn't in much of a condition physically to take me on, but I guess the drugs or adrenaline kicked in, and before I knew it, he had me pinned against him with one arm around my neck. He told mom to get him money or he'd choke me.

"Thank God that's when dad came home. He kicked Seth out and held mom while she cried. I didn't know what to do. Then I remembered Joanna had called. I looked at her messages and got there as fast as I could, but I was too late.

"I was too late for everything. I should have pulled us out of the caves a long time ago—I knew the first time we went down there that we were dealing with a madman, but I let myself be persuaded into continuing the exploration. I thought if I just went down with you, I could protect you. I should have made us stop going down."

"But no one has that much control over someone else."

Jude blinked, and Cole barely restrained himself from smiling at Jude's surprise.

"Joanna would have kept going no matter what you said, and I probably would have too."

Jude shook his head vigorously. "But don't you see? I was the one who led us down that secret passage in the first place —that was my fault. And I should have been there for you, too, when your dad was slipping. I knew something was bothering you, and I didn't ask. I failed."

Jude passed a hand over his eyes. The defeated expression was so much the opposite of everything with which Cole associated his best friend that he didn't know how to respond.

"You didn't fail. You got to Joanna and me just in time. If you hadn't come, neither of us would be alive right now."

Jude's eyes had dropped back to Cole's sheets, and Cole couldn't tell whether his words had any effect. The only sign of change in Jude's posture was a soundless bob of his Adam's apple.

Finally, Jude said, "I can't even take credit for that. Not really. I never would have been able to get you both out of there if it hadn't been for Wes and the Dove."

"What?"

Cole was so shocked that his foot, which had still been shaking with excess energy, went completely still. Jude looked up sharply.

"I thought you knew! I thought Wes told you."

"Told me what?"

"Wes and the Dove were the ones who helped me get you and Joanna out of there. You mean he hasn't told you anything? Man, I'd better start at the beginning. Turns out the Dove did overhear one of our conversations. That first time he came to the library was pure accident, but then he heard us say we discovered something about Vendler in the library and that Saint-Pierre would want to know. He told Wes, and Wes was interested because Saint-Pierre had also asked him what he knew about Vendler. So Wes told the Dove to keep an eye on us. That's why he was always there for our study halls."

Even though none of it mattered anymore, Cole was irritated. If the Tates hadn't been so nosy, he never would have had to break into the school.

"They gave it up once you were advanced and Wes wasn't. I think Wes felt bad and told the Dove to lay off, but by that time our schedules had changed and it was too late. Anyway, I was right about one thing—the Dove did get in trouble because of us. He was in detention the evening you and Joanna got trapped in the tunnels. Wes had just come to pick him up when I was driving into the parking lot. I saw the smoke and enlisted their help. One thing I'll say for the Tates, they don't scare easily. It took guts going into that fire, but they stayed right behind me and didn't ask questions till we got you out. I took Joanna; Wes and the Dove got you. You'd have been toast if you had to wait for me to come back for you. Afterward I had to tell them everything."

Cole swallowed, and his throat burned. He had been jealous of Wes and mad at the Dove for so long, and now, apparently, he owed them his life. For a moment, he thought he might hate them even more now that he had to be grateful as well as envious, but then he laughed out loud. The laugh tore his throat, but he didn't care. Living was too beautiful a gift for any of that to matter. When he was discharged, he would find them and thank them.

A tap on the open door made them both start. It took Cole a moment to recognize the woman standing in the doorway—Joanna's long, raven hair had been cut into an asymmetrical bob, which shimmered red except for one streak that was bleached white.

"Do you like it? I call it 'She's on Fire'."

Joanna smiled ruefully and came to stand by Jude, her gait uncharacteristically tentative.

"I wanted to dye it in solidarity."

Jude laughed, then nodded at a crumpled piece of notebook paper blobbed with paint that she was holding. "What's that?"

"This? Oh, nothing. Orien gave it to me. Or rather returned it to me. It was mine. I thought it had been lost in the fire, but he must have carried it out with him."

"Saint-Pierre? When did you see him?" Jude asked, his voice antagonistic.

"Just now, in the parking lot. He stopped me on my way in."

"Why does he think he can talk to you after what happened in Vendler's caverns?"

"Jude, he explained it all. He didn't mean to shove me over, he..."

"He did *what*?"

"Oh, I thought that's what you were talking about." Joanna blushed and crossed her arms over her chest.

"I was talking about how he left you and Cole to die while he made his merry way to safety. What are *you* talking about?"

"It's like I said. I was being stupid and blocking his way so Cole could get to Vendler's secret first. Orien wanted to see the notebook paper I had in my hand—this one—and I wouldn't let him. It didn't matter a bit, really, but I was trying to buy time and distract him, so I pretended it was important. He got impatient with me and shoved me a little as he tried to grab it. That's when I hit my head, I think, but I don't remember anything after that until I woke up in the ambulance."

"That bastard!" Jude cried.

"He apologized to me," Joanna said defensively. She moved to Cole's bed and sat on the end of it. "It's over. We're good."

Jude jumped up and made for the door.

"Where are you going?" Joanna asked apprehensively.

"To give Saint-Pierre a piece of my mind."

"Jude, wait."

The voice was Cole's. He took a deep breath. His throat was getting raw from talking so much, but he pressed on.

"There's something I need to tell you. I don't know if it was fully Orien doing it. I don't think people are quite themselves in those caves. I wasn't. I tried to warn you when we all went down together, but I couldn't think how to say it. Joanna, I'm sorry, I never really told you this, but there was a time... I don't know what came over me, but I was having all these strange thoughts, thoughts I've never had before and that I know aren't me, and I... I wanted to hurt you."

Joanna shrugged and said, "You may have wanted to, but you didn't."

Whether it was Cole's admission or the fact that, by now, Orien had probably left the premises, Jude grudgingly returned to Cole's bedside. As if remembering an outlet for his anger, he snatched the paper from Joanna's hand and said, "And what's this about anyway?"

He unfolded it, staring at it and blinking several times.

Then his ears flushed red. If Cole hadn't been told to stay in bed, he'd have stood up to peer over Jude's shoulder.

"It's... me," Jude said after a minute. "When did you draw this?"

Joanna fidgeted with the hospital bed sheet before answering.

"It was when we were all outside under the maple, right before you decided we wouldn't go into the caverns again. I ended up doodling, and I guess I drew you. That's from the notebook I always keep with me. I must have torn it out later when I was testing paint colors, because I found it on the floor beside the canvas while I was waiting for Orien."

Jude let his hand drop, finally tearing his eyes from the page. "It's really good."

"That's what Orien said."

"Why did he give it back to you?"

Joanna was silent for so long that Cole wondered if she had heard the question. Then she looked Jude full in the face. "He thinks I have the kind of talent Vendler talks about in his book, the kind that can give life when combined with love."

She looked away again and bit her bottom lip severely as if she had spoken without thinking, even though she had had plenty of time to reflect before opening her mouth. Then she said to the edge of the sheet: "He offered me the internship." She cast Cole an apologetic glance. "He wanted you to have it, but he told me you said no. So I said yes."

Cole stared at her as if she were a stranger. It was true—Orien had offered it to him first, and Cole had said no. So why was the news that it had been offered to Joanna so jarring? Why did he feel so jealous and resentful?

It wasn't until he heard her voice that Cole realized Bridget had entered the room.

"I saw your nurse on my way in, Cole. She says you can

start getting your things together because she's filled out your paperwork. She'll be here to walk you out in a minute." Drawing level with the bed, she asked, "What's going on?"

Jude crossed his arms over his chest and said, "Saint-Pierre offered the internship to Cole. Cole said no, so then Saint-Pierre came and found Joanna, and Joanna said yes."

"Oh I *am* glad, Cole, but..."

A frown furrowed Bridget's face as she studied Joanna, and Cole thought how beautiful she looked even when she was troubled. Her hair, pinned above her ear by a jade pin, looked like fire in the sunlight from his window.

"But working at The Lab isn't even what you want," she said.

Joanna shrugged. "Not exactly, but I will still get to pursue art. And it will make my parents happy."

Jude muttered, "Since when has that been your top priority?"

No one said anything. Jude was busy studying his hands, one of which was balled into a tight fist, the other pressing convulsively against it. Joanna continued fingering the fringe of the sheet, her lips pursed. Cole was rapidly running through his own lines of logic for refusing the internship before drawing a blank and realizing it wasn't a logic-based decision at all.

There was a rattle at the door, and a nurse with bubblegum pink lipstick bounced into the room, a girlish smile on her face. Mrs. Durham came with her, waiting in the doorway.

"Well, I'm afraid it's good-bye to my favorite patient! Cole, you're going home!"

She handed him a sheaf of papers and talked him through what they all meant and when he was scheduled to come in for his follow-up while Jude and Bridget gathered his few belongings into a bag and moved to the door. Joanna stayed behind, ready to offer him a hand should he need it. He eased his stiff legs over the side of the bed and moved to the waiting wheelchair.

As his nurse stepped up to wheel him out, Cole turned to Joanna and said, "Jo, I'm not mad at you. I'm happy for you, if it's what you want."

He said the words before he meant them, but he knew he would regret his silence if he didn't speak now. Anxiety fell instantly from her face.

"Just do me one favor. Make sure you understand what Orien's doing. Make sure it's what you want, too."

"Deal."

She followed as Cole's nurse wheeled him out the hall and fell into step beside Jude and Bridget, their shoes squeaking on the waxed linoleum floor. Soon they were down the elevator, through the ground floor hallways, and past the receptionist's desk.

The doors opened, and they emerged into the crisp winter sunlight. Cole had forgotten air could smell so delicious. The nurse parked the wheelchair by the curb. Cole drew himself up, stretching into a fully upright position, feeling every awkward fold of his foreign skin. He couldn't believe he was really going home. As he stood beside Bridget, the shadow that had passed over him in the hospital room was as faint as a childhood nightmare. With his injured hand, the one still bandaged in gauze, the one that might never feel again, he took her hand. Despite what Dr. Amini had said, the firm squeeze she gave him tingled his skin like a miracle.

ABOUT THE AUTHOR

Photo credit Stephen Rencher

Anna Vander Wall is a poet and dark academia novelist whose work hints at the secret mysticism of places, relationships, and embodied beliefs. Her readers connect with her quirky characters while experiencing the inherent transcendence of creation through sacred objects, palpable settings, and the cycle of tragedy and rebirth.

Anna is a some-time woodworker who has a great affinity for British detective fiction, dancing, experimenting with new bakes, and hiking ad infinitum. She grew up in the foothills of the Rocky Mountains, where she resides still today with her family and her dog Goldberry.